COVENTRY LIBRARIES

This book is to be returned on or before
the last date stamped below.

Tile Hill

-3 DEC 2016

POP 3|17

2-9-22

FINHAM

(17)

1 4 APR 2023

To renew this book take it to any of
the City Libraries before
the date due for return

1 4 JUN 2016

-7 OCT 2016

Coventry City Council

HOMECOMING

Cathy Kelly

WINDSOR

PARAGON

First published 2010
by HarperCollins*Publishers*
This Large Print edition published 2011
by AudioGO Ltd
by arrangement with
HarperCollins*Publishers*

Hardcover   ISBN: 978 1 445 85559 2
Softcover   ISBN: 978 1 445 85560 8

British Library Cataloguing in Publication Data available

Printed and bound in Great Britain by
CPI Antony Rowe, Chippenham and Eastbourne

To my husband, John, and to darling Murray and Dylan, with love

1

New Year

It didn't take long for Eleanor Levine to unpack her things in the apartment in Golden Square. She'd brought just two suitcases on the flight from New York to Dublin. For a simple holiday, two suitcases would probably be too much luggage. But for the sort of trip Eleanor planned, she was travelling light.

When she'd arrived in the hotel in the centre of the city just two weeks before Christmas, the receptionist had just nodded politely when Eleanor said she might need the room for more than the three weeks she'd booked beforehand. Nothing shocked hotel receptionists, even elegant elderly ladies with limited luggage who arrived alone and appeared to have no due date to leave.

Equally, nobody looked askance at Eleanor when she gently turned down the invitation to book for the full Christmas lunch in the hotel's restaurant and instead asked for an omelette and a glass of prosecco in her room. After a lifetime spent in New York, a city where doing your own thing and not apologising for it was almost mandatory, it was comforting to find the same behaviour had travelled across the Atlantic to the country of her birth. It wasn't what she'd expected, truth to tell. But then, it was so long since she'd been home, she didn't really know what to expect.

On the plane journey, still reeling from having

1

left her warm, cosy apartment and her family behind her, Eleanor had thought about the Ireland she was about to see. She'd left over seventy years before in the steerage of a giant steamship, a serious eleven-year-old travelling to the New World with her mother and her aunt. Their belongings had fitted in a couple of cardboard suitcases, and her mother, Brigid, held the family's meagre fortune in a purse round her neck.

Now here she was, returning with several platinum credit cards, a line of letters after her name and a lifetime of experience behind her.

Apart from Eleanor herself, only one thing had made both trips: her mother's recipe book.

Now that she'd put her toiletries in the master bedroom's en suite bathroom, and had unpacked her clothes and books, she took a white shoebox out of the second suitcase.

Her wedding shoes, white satin pumps from Christian Dior, had lived in the box for many years until she'd given them to her daughter, Naomi, for her prom night.

Now her grand-daughter Gillian borrowed them from time to time, wearing them with the full-skirted vintage dresses that had been all the rage during Mr Dior's New Look in 1947. Like many modern teenagers, Gillian loved wearing vintage and often visited her grandmother proudly bearing something she'd paid fifty dollars for, and which was a replica of something Eleanor had thrown out twenty years previously. Fashion comes full circle, Eleanor thought, smiling.

Thousands of miles away from Gillian, Naomi and life in New York, Eleanor tenderly opened her box of treasures. None of them were treasures in

2

any monetary sense. But as tokens from a life lived with great happiness, they were treasures indeed. There was a dyed black ostrich-feather mask from a Hallowe'en party, the silk ribbon still tied in a knot from the last time she'd worn it, half a century before. A single pressed rose was visible through the thin layer of tissue in which it lay. Ralf had given her the rose as a corsage one night at a ritzy white-tie affair at St Regis Hotel. Under the tissue, the dried-out petals were feather-light.

There was the shell-like gold compact she'd been so proud of when she was twenty-five, the gold paint tarnished now and the pinky powder nothing but a dusty remnant on the inside rim. There was red lipstick in its black-and-gold case. *Manhattan Red*. It had been all the rage in 1944, a colour to brighten lips and hearts.

There were love letters, too, from her beloved Ralf, some with humble elastic bands around them; others, bound with ribbon. He'd loved writing letters and cards. There was permanence in the written word, he'd believed. One was the letter he'd penned when their daughter, Naomi, was born, an incredible forty-five years ago.

'I will love you and our daughter forever,' he'd concluded. She knew it by heart. Eleanor's fingers brushed the filmy folded paper but she didn't open it. She couldn't bear to see the words written in Ralf's neat, precise hand. Perhaps she'd be too sad ever to read his letters again.

There were drawings and cards from her daughter, Naomi, so infinitely precious with their big, childish writing. Though it seemed so long ago since Naomi had written them, they still made Eleanor's heart sing. Naomi had been such a

3

beautiful-hearted child and she'd grown up into an equally wonderful adult.

The third important thing in her treasure box was another collection of writings: her mother's recipe book. Originally, it had been covered with simple brown card but decades ago Eleanor had glued shiny Christmas wrapping paper on to the cover and now faded golden stars twinkled alongside burnished red and green holly sprigs.

The extra pages, added over the years, made the book bulky, and a lavender wool crocheted rope kept the whole thing tied together. It was all handwritten in her mother's sloping italics, sometimes in pencil which had faded with age, sometimes in the deep blue ink her mother had favoured.

Like Ralf's letters and Naomi's innocent little notes in their awkward writing, the recipe book was a source of huge comfort, a talisman to be held close to her chest when her heart was breaking. It had comforted Eleanor all her life and it comforted her now.

Nobody glancing at the battered recipe book would guess at the wisdom inside it. People, especially people today, thought that wisdom had to come from experts with letters after their names. Eleanor herself had plenty of those—the hoops psychoanalysts had to jump through meant half an alphabet could go after Eleanor Levine's name.

But two things had taught Eleanor that people with little academic history often knew more than the most scholarly person.

One was her mother, Brigid.

The other was her own vast experience of life.

Eleanor was now eighty-three and she'd lived those eighty-three years with gusto.

Brigid had taught her to do that. And so much more.

Eleanor had been schooled at some of the finest universities in the United States, while her mother had scraped merely a few years of education in a tiny Connemara village school where each of the children had to bring a sod of turf every day to keep the fire alight. Yet Brigid had been born with all the wisdom of the earth in her bones and a kindness in her heart that meant she saw the world with a forgiving eye.

During her years working as a psychoanalyst in New York, Eleanor had discovered that bitterness ate away at people's insides just as effectively as any disease.

People spent years in therapy simply to learn what Brigid O'Neill had known instinctively.

The recipe book was where she'd written all of this wisdom down for her daughter.

At some point, the recipes and the little notes she'd written in the margins had taken on a life of their own.

Brigid's recipe book had never really been a simple book of how to cook. It was a book on how to live life, full of the knowledge of a gentle countrywoman who'd lived off the land and had to use her commonsense and an innate Celtic intuition to survive.

Eleanor had often wondered if her mother had more spiritual awareness than normal people. Some sort of instinct that the modern world had lost and was always trying to regain. For certain, her recipe book contained a hint of magic. Perhaps

5

it was just the magic of food and life.

And really, food and life were so intertwined, Eleanor thought.

Her mother's life had been lived with the kitchen stove always nearby. Feeding people and nurturing them was a gift in itself. The old religions that made a point of the power of the feast had understood that. Food was about hope, rebirth, community, family and a nourishment that went beyond the purely physical.

Like the mashed potato with the puddle of melting butter in the middle and spring onions chopped in that you ate when you were feeling blue. Or the chicken soup made when there was nothing to eat but leftovers, but which when mixed together with skill and love and a hint of garlic became a melting broth that would warm your heart.

Or the taste of fresh berries on juice-stained lips in bed with the man you loved.

Eleanor thought of a man she'd shared a warm bed and strawberries with once upon a time.

Even sixty years later, she could still remember the sheen of his skin and the way her fingers had played upon the muscles of his shoulders as they lay together in a cocoon of love.

It wasn't something she could share with anyone now. People tended to be scandalised if an octogenarian mentioned sex. Ridiculous, really. A bit like being shocked at the notion that a vintage Ford from the 1930s had ever driven on the roads. She smiled.

She'd told Ralf about that man, her first lover, when they were first courting.

'I don't want secrets between us,' she'd said.

And Ralf had understood. Because he knew that the lovemaking he and Eleanor shared far exceeded anything she'd enjoyed with the man with the strawberries.

Ralf had loved cheese, little bits of French brie dripping off a cracker on to the plate, as they lay in their scrumpled bed and talked after making love.

She'd introduced him to Turkish apple tea, which somehow went with the cheese. He'd showed her how to make kneidlach, the little kosher dough balls he'd loved as a child. Some of their happiest moments—and there had been many, many happy moments—had been spent enjoying meals.

Food made it all better.

She'd loved it when they would wander out for dinner in one of the neighbourhood restaurants, then sit talking for hours after they'd finished eating. With a professional eye, Eleanor watched couples who were long married and had nothing to say to each other and felt sorry for them with their uncomfortably silent meals. She and Ralf never had that problem: they never stopped talking. Being interested in the person you were married to was one of life's great gifts.

Eleanor heard the clock at St Malachy's on the other side of the square ringing noon. It was a sound she'd always associate with her childhood. The family home in the tiny west coast village of Kilmoney had been two miles from the local church, and when the Angelus bell rang at midday and six in the evening, everyone stopped what they were doing to pray.

In Golden Square, only a few people would do that.

7

From her vantage point, Eleanor could see a lot of Golden Square. She hadn't chosen the apartment because of the locale, but now that she was here, she loved it. There were few of these old garden squares left in Dublin city, the letting agent had told her, and even in the property slump houses here still sold pretty quickly. The garden itself was boxed in by old iron railings with curlicued tops. At each end was a pair of black-and-gold gates with an elegant design of climbing vine leaves. Eleanor had seen something like them in the Victoria and Albert Museum in London and she was sure they were valuable. They stood sentinel over the flowers, the benches and the children's playground inside.

Despite the modern shops and businesses on one corner of the square, there was something olde worlde about the redbrick houses and the Georgian villas. Most were divided into flats now, but they still looked as though a kitchen maid in long skirts might run up the steps each morning at dawn to set the fires.

Eleanor had arrived there by accident, but she found she liked Golden Square a lot. And there were, she believed, no accidents in life. Things happened for a reason.

She'd moved in two days after Christmas, even though the young letting agent had implied that she must be mad to want to move in during the holiday.

'This is what suits me,' Eleanor had said, using the calm psychoanalyst's voice that had worked for so many years with her patients.

Suitably chastened, the letting agent had driven her to the apartment from the hotel where she'd spent Christmas. Though he was careful not to say so aloud, he wondered why anyone would want to spend Christmas or even New Year away from their families. Perhaps she didn't have a family, he decided, and at that moment, vowed to be nicer to his own mother because one day *she'd* be an old, white-haired lady—though perhaps not one as fiercely determined or as straight-backed as this one. So he went along with Mrs Levine's plans, betrayed no surprise when she explained she was Irish by birth despite her American accent, and concluded she must be a little mad, as well as being rich. She clearly had plenty of money to have stayed in a five-star hotel over Christmas, and she hadn't quibbled over the rent for the Taylors' apartment on Golden Square.

It was, she'd said, when he'd taken her to view it on Christmas Eve, exactly what she was looking for: somewhere central, without stairs in the home itself, although she was able to manage the ten steps up from the path to the front door of the gracious old villa-style house. She'd wanted somewhere elegant and well-furnished and the Taylors', with its lovely paintings and its old-fashioned furniture, was certainly that.

It was a very peaceful place to live and there was so much to see when she sat in the big bay window and looked out over the square itself.

She still liked people-watching.

'Stop already,' Ralf used to whisper when they were at cocktail parties on the Upper East Side and Eleanor's face assumed that still, thoughtful expression he knew so well. 'They'll notice.'

'They won't,' she'd whisper back.

They didn't, amazingly. Her analytical gaze was

invariably interpreted as polite attentiveness.

Golden Square, for all that she'd only been there a week, was a wonderful spot to indulge her hobby. She might not practise professionally any more, but she could enjoy observing the world.

Directly opposite Eleanor's apartment she'd noticed a striking-looking woman in her fifties with shoulder-length tawny hair come in and out of a narrow white house, sometimes accompanied by a tall, kind-looking man. On Eleanor's few trips out, she'd visited the square's tearooms, a picturesque red-curtained premises named Titania's Palace, and the woman had been there behind the counter, smiling at all, doling out teas and coffees with brisk efficiency and calling people 'love' and 'pet'.

Eleanor considered the comforting effect of being called 'pet'. It was a nice way to speak to an older lady, better than the senior citizen label 'ma'am', which always made her feel as if paramedics were shadowing her with an oxygen mask.

And the woman in the tearoom wasn't being condescending when she used 'pet'—it came naturally; she had a gentleness that reached out to people.

'Would you like me to carry your coffee over to the table for you, pet?' she'd asked Eleanor, the kind face with its fine dark eyes and dark brows beaming out over the cash register at her. She reminded Eleanor of someone, an actress, Ali MacGraw, that was it.

Yes, she was incredibly nice, Eleanor thought as she murmured, 'Yes, thank you.' She wasn't quite up to social interaction yet. She was still in that

10

place of mourning where she liked watching the world but wasn't ready to let it in.

Maybe, she thought with a rush of black despair, she'd never let it in again.

In the apartment above hers lived two sisters whom she hadn't met yet, but whose names she'd learned from the postman. The younger woman, Nicky, a petite blonde, appeared by her elegant suits to have a high-powered career, although Eleanor couldn't guess what. Connie was tall, wore sensible clothes and marched out to her car in the mornings in flat shoes and bearing piles of schoolbooks, looking every inch the capable teacher.

Watching her, Eleanor decided that Connie carried herself like someone who had no time for femininity or girlish flounces. Perhaps she'd never been told she was in any way attractive. Eleanor had certainly seen much of that in her practice. The lessons people learned in youth sank in so deep, they became almost part of a person's DNA. It could be hard to change.

Nicky was, by contrast, confident and pretty, like a flower fairy. She had a boyfriend, a tall slim lad who followed her round like a puppy, or held her hand when they walked through the square to the convenience store. The sisters fascinated Eleanor: they were each so different.

Over the way lived the chiropodist whom her doctor—well, she'd had to introduce herself to the doctor, it made sense at her age—had recommended.

'Nora Flynn, she's very good, you'll like her. No time for prattle or sweet talk, Nora. But she's excellent at what she does, runs a great practice.'

11

Eleanor liked to take care of her feet and she'd had one appointment with Nora already.

Nora was exactly what the doctor had said: good at her job and not a prattler. She didn't enquire why Eleanor had moved to Golden Square. She merely talked about bad circulation, the cold of these early January days, and how people still didn't understand the need to look after their feet. Eleanor had since seen Nora out walking her dogs in the square. The chiropodist wore very masculine clothes, yet talked to her little dogs like a mother to small children.

Eleanor hadn't made it across the square to The Nook yet, although she could see the little convenience store from her window. She didn't really need it, what with internet shopping. She ordered online and a nice young man from the supermarket delivered it and carried everything into the house for her. When he saw there was no one to help her put it away, he'd asked her where it all went and laid everything on the correct counter, so she wouldn't have to bend down to lift the bags.

That day, after he'd gone, Eleanor had nearly wept. It was the kindness that got to her. Rudeness, she could handle, but any kindness breached her defences and she felt as if she might sob on a total stranger's shoulder.

Next door to her building, she could just see the steps down to a basement flat where a big bear of a man lived with his daughter. Eleanor occasionally saw him taking the little girl—a tall, skinny child with red curly hair—to school. He seemed happy when he was with her, but when he was alone he looked different: deeply sad and unreachable.

Eleanor felt an overwhelming urge to find out what was wrong and help.

Ralf, her darling husband, used to gently chide her for trying to fix the world:

'It's not your job to make them all better.'

Eleanor remembered the early days of psychotherapy in college and the desire to improve the lives of everyone she met.

People weren't just people to her, they were potential cases of obsessive compulsive disorder, Electra complex, or separation anxiety.

Everyone in her class had thought like her.

They'd had to stop going to the main campus cafeteria for a whole month because they'd all become fixated on one of the waitresses who, in their eyes, was suffering from a psychosomatic wasting disorder and they wanted to help.

Eventually, someone confessed to Professor Wolfe, their tutor, and wondered what should they do?

Professor Wolfe hadn't taken this the way they'd hoped.

'Why do you think you can help this waitress?' he asked, head to one side, fabulously detached. 'What makes you want to help her? Has she asked to be helped?'

'I bet if you asked him the way to his office, he'd put his head on one side and say "Why do you need to know?"' grumbled one of Eleanor's classmates.

'He's right, though,' Eleanor had sighed. Psychotherapeutic help wasn't a bandage you put on a cut. It was a tool for life and it couldn't be applied unless the person wanted it applied. All the psychoanalyst could do was gently help the patient find their own particular tools; it was up to the patient to use them.

'Everyone can't be mad,' said Susannah, her roommate in college, who'd studied molecular biology and had heard many of the late-night 'who do we think suffers from X or Y?' conversations. Susannah saw life in absolutes. She was a post-doctorate student working on cancer research and there was no room for emotion. Things worked or they didn't. The mice died and you moved on.

'Mad is not an expression we tend to use in psychoanalysis,' Eleanor had said, laughing.

'You could have fooled me,' Susannah said.

There was a birthday card in Eleanor's treasure box signed *Susannah, Mrs Tab Hunter.* Susannah had been obsessed by the fifties movie star, but you couldn't call her mad.

Eleanor wondered where Susannah was now. They'd lost touch around about the time Eleanor and Ralf got married. Susannah went off to live in Switzerland to work at a university there. Eleanor pictured her: still tall, eccentric and in love with people she saw only on cinema screens.

A gust of wind made the branch of the rowan tree outside the window bang against Eleanor's window. The tiny scarlet berries on the holly bushes beneath it were all gone now. Sometimes a lone robin sat on the tree and look quizzically at Eleanor, as if asking for food.

Eleanor smiled sympathetically at him but she wasn't able any more to hang seed balls outside. That took dexterity and suppleness, things she no longer had.

There were many things she no longer had. Her beloved Ralf being the most important. No one needed her now. Her family back in New York loved her, but they had their own lives. Naomi and her devoted husband, Marcus, were busy with their furniture import business. Filan's Furniture was much in demand and, despite the credit crunch, they were expanding.

Gillian, Eleanor's adored grand-daughter, had settled into her second year at UCLA and had thrown herself madly into her new life there.

They would manage without her. She was too broken, too wild with grief to be a proper mother or grandmother any more. Worse, in her present grieving state, she might be a burden.

It was an odd feeling. All her life, Eleanor had worked and strived, both for her family and in her professional life. She solved problems, she didn't create them.

In an instant of loss, all that had changed. *She* had changed.

Which was why she'd turned her back on New York and returned to Ireland. Here she might find the answer, find out what she had to do. She hoped so with all her heart.

2

Eggs

Being able to boil an egg means you'll never go hungry. Duck eggs make the most wonderful breakfasts. When you crack open the fragile shell and peer into that golden yolk, the colour and consistency of honey, and breathe in the scent of the land, your heart sings.

The problem is the ducks. We always had a couple in the yard, Muscovy ducks, with black and white feathers and red bills, and Lord, those birds could fight. They were like a warring family. In the end, I kept them in separate pens in the coop. It was the only way.

Some people are like that too, by the way. No matter what you do, they'll fight. That's their business, love. You can't stop them fighting. Might as well let them at it, but don't get involved.

You might wonder why I'm telling you this, Eleanor, but you see, I don't want you to grow up without learning all these things, the way I did. It wasn't my mother's fault, mind. It was mine. I was a sickly child, although you wouldn't think it to look at me now. As I sit at the table with my writing paper, I'm a few months shy of my twenty-sixth birthday and I've never felt better. But as a little one, I spent a lot of time in bed with fevers and coughs. My mother dosed me with a drink made of carragheen moss and lemon juice. A weak chest, was what the doctor said, although we didn't go in much for doctoring. They were hard years, then, at the start of the century and there wasn't money for doctors for the likes of us.

My mother once took me to visit an old man who lived way over the other side of one of the islands, to a house on the edge of the cliff, because he had the cure for a bad chest. Someone said his cure was mare's milk and some herbs and a bit of the mare's tail—it had to be a white mare, mind you—but whatever, it didn't work on me.

The long and the short of it is that I didn't learn how to cook alongside my mother. Most girls learned from watching their mother at the fire. I was wrapped up in the bed in the back room with only a few books for company. Agnes brought home books from Mrs Fitzmaurice's house, and I read them all: Jane Eyre, Wuthering Heights, Tom Jones, even.

And then one day I just grew out of the bad chest. My mother wanted me to go to school because I'd been there so rarely. Again, I had my head in the books and never so much as peeled an onion. Then Mam became ill and suddenly I was the woman of the house. Agnes was gone all week and back on Sundays, the lads were out working on the land, and the only person left to cook and clean was the one person who didn't know how to do any of it.

But I learned, Eleanor, I learned. The hard way, I might add.

That's what I want to tell you. About the joy of cooking and feeding the people you love. About the skill of making dinner for ten from a few scraps. There's magic in cooking. It's like prayer, you know.

All those heads bent, hearts joined together. That's why it works. It's because of people coming together. Cooking's the same.

*   *   *

The man in seat 3C sneaked a look at the young woman sitting beside him on the Heathrow to Dublin plane. She was small, fine-boned and wearing one of those funny scarves wound around her head, the way old ladies used to wear turbans years ago. He couldn't understand it himself. Why would a pretty girl do that to herself, like she *wanted* to look ridiculous? A bit of blonde hair had escaped the scarf: it was old-style blonde, platinum, actually. Otherwise, she was very un-done-up, as his wife might say. No make-up, wearing jeans, a grey marl sweatshirt and trendy rectangular glasses. Yet despite all that, there was *something* special about her. Something he couldn't quite put his finger on.

'Are you eating with us today?' asked an airline steward. The male passenger looked up.

The steward was definitely talking to him but his eyes were on the woman in the window seat, consuming her, as if he hadn't had a good look yet and wanted his fill.

'Er, yes,' said the passenger. He liked airline food, couldn't understand why other people didn't. Food was food. 'What is it?'

'Choice of beef stew or chicken with pasta,' said the steward, deftly putting a tray down on the man's fold-out table.

19

'Beef,' said Liam, thinking he might as well eat a proper meal as it would be at least nine before he got home.

'Anything to drink?' the steward murmured as he set a small tinfoil-covered package on the tray.

'Red wine.' Liam unveiled his dinner with anticipation. It was pasta.

'Sorry,' he said to the steward, 'I wanted beef.'

But the steward had already put a small bottle of red wine on his tray and his gaze was now fixed on the girl in 3A.

'I wanted beef?' said Liam plaintively, but it was no good. The caravan had moved on.

*   *   *

Megan knew the cabin crew had worked out who she was, even though she always flew under her real name, which was Megan Flynn, and not Megan Bouchier, the name the world knew her by. Bouchier was her paternal grandmother's family name, and all those years ago at stage school she'd seen the sense of dropping the prosaic Flynn in favour of the more memorable Bouchier.

She'd hoped the Flynn would give her some protection now, along with the blue silk scarf hiding her trademark platinum curls and the little Prada glasses with clear lenses, but it hadn't worked.

When you'd spent the best part of six years appearing on television and cinema screens, and in magazines and newspapers, your face burned on to people's minds the way the FBI's Ten Most Wanted list never seemed to do. Murderers and master criminals might go unrecognised, but land a

20

starring role in a series of mediocre television shows and one stand-out British movie, and your face suddenly became as recognisable as the queen's.

The dinner trolley was locked beside her row and at least three members of the crew were looking at her while pretending not to look at her, which was a difficult trick to pull off. Airline staff were good at that: charmingly treating world-famous people with polite nonchalance.

Today's crew were reacting to her differently, though. Perhaps it was because she was no longer the adored young actress who'd been listed in *Empire* magazine as one of the 'ten most promising actors of the year' not that long ago. Instead she was the marriage-breaker pictured on the pages of every redtop in London alongside a photo of another actress, an older woman whose husband Megan was accused of stealing.

Megan had not wanted to see the papers when the story had broken. She'd tried not to look but she couldn't avoid the headline that jumped out at her from a newsstand outside a Tube station.

'Devastated!' it screamed above a picture of Katharine Hartnell, her famous, Oscar-winning face drawn, cheekbones prominent, dark circles under her eyes. Apart from her Oscar, Katharine Hartnell had been famous for being fifty but not looking it. And she was famous for being in love with her movie-star husband after twenty years of marriage—light years in movie-star terms. Megan had seen many photos in magazines of Katharine and her husband looking very much in love. In the newspaper picture, she looked more than fifty and definitely devastated.

'The other woman,' was Megan's caption, with a picture of herself she hated, showing her emerging, laughing, from a night club, her long hair askew, someone else's fur coat thrown over her shoulders and a man on each side, one waving a bottle of champagne. She was wearing a silver sequinned dress that had sunk further down her cleavage as the night had gone on and by the time the photographer—who must have made a fortune from that one picture—had snapped her, the neckline was millimetres away from her left nipple.

The small, heart-shaped face that numerous photographers had described as 'exquisite' was creased up into a huge tipsy smile and her almond-shaped eyes, the kohl smudged, glittered with the excitement of being the 'it' actress of the day. All in all, the photo was like a dictionary illustration of the word hedonism.

The story and that iconic picture meant Megan had entered the terrible world of the media's 'most hated woman on the planet'. Suddenly, people she'd never met talked about her over their skinny lattes and their newspapers, condemning her as a husband-stealer. Opinion articles were written on whether women like her put the cause of feminism back thirty years.

Megan had grown used to being loved, to having designers sending her handbags, to having magazines print admiring articles under photos of her gracing the latest premiere.

And now this. Megan the Mantrapper.

She'd fallen from grace faster than any archangel and the result was cold, hard hatred. Where once she'd been loved, now she was loathed. It was incredibly painful. Almost as painful as having her heart broken.

'Would you like dinner? A drink?' said the steward. *Somebody else's husband?* were the unspoken words Megan heard.

'No thank you,' she said with all the dignity she could muster. She'd have liked a bottle of water but couldn't face the actual transaction, having to look at the cabin crew and see what was written on their faces: pity, contempt, abject fascination. Instead, she turned to look out the window as if there was something to be seen out there instead of cloudy darkness.

Her sister Pippa had told her that escaping to Ireland was a good plan, and she trusted Pippa with her life. Once upon a time, Pippa might have run away with her but now her running-away days were over: she was the mother of two small children, with a real life in Wales and a husband. Megan would have gone to stay with them, but the press had already been sniffing around their home, making a nuisance of themselves. Besides, it wasn't Pippa's job to protect her little sister any more. That hurt too.

'Megan, love, you've got to get out of London,' Pippa had urged her. Megan's agent had been saying the same thing, but with much less kindness.

Carole Baird was not one of the 'tell them they're fabulous, no matter what' agents. Her motto was 'tell them like it is—with knobs on'. Megan's behaviour might lose her film roles and impact on her career—and therefore, on Carole's bottom line. Twenty per cent of nothing was nothing. Carole's concern wasn't moral, it was financial.

'You should go to Aunt Nora's—Kim!' Pippa

shouted. 'Put that down! Sorry, Megan, she's at the dishwasher again. We just made a cake and she wants to lick the bowl and spoon again. No, Kim. Dirty, no!'

Aunt Nora's home in Dublin was where the sisters had spent the normal part of their childhood years. As different from their mother as chalk was from cheese, Aunt Nora had toned down all Marguerite's wilder suggestions when the girls were growing up. Aunt Nora said that the French school on the Caribbean island where Marguerite was living at the time probably wasn't the best place for two kids who didn't have much education behind them, and couldn't speak French. Aunt Nora enrolled them in the Sacred Heart Convent just off Golden Square and took care of them until Marguerite's latest love affair had gone sour and she went back to London.

Aunt Nora had always been there. Solid, dependable, as unstarry a person as you could find.

Which was why Megan didn't want to have to talk to her about what had happened. Her mother hadn't judged Megan because she didn't know what judgement was. Marguerite had made too many disastrous romantic choices in her life to comment on anyone else's, but Nora—a single woman who went to weekly Mass—might.

'What about Australia?' Megan had wondered when she'd spoken to Carole. It seemed far enough away to hide from the photographers who had been camped outside her flat in London for the past ten days.

'You need family,' her agent said sagely.

I'd be out of your control in Australia, Megan thought grimly.

'Who knows what you'd get up to in Australia,' Carole said, on cue. 'Too many gorgeous men.'

Megan had to laugh, although it was one of those painful laughs. 'You don't trust me,' she said.

'Why should I?' said Carole. 'You're screwing up your career and mine too. Let's put all the cards on the table, Megan. It's not doing the agency any good being linked to someone who's wrecking her career so successfully. People are wondering why I didn't stop it. As if I damn well knew about it. You're not a pop star. People practically expect that from music industry stars, but it's not good if you're trying to make a name for yourself as a serious actress. Nobody's going to cast an actress who's just broken up what's been held up as one of the rare long-lasting Hollywood marriages. Producers and directors want a reasonably blank canvas or at least someone who can play innocent—what they don't want is a PR nightmare. All moviegoers will see now on the screen is Megan the homewrecker. This stunt has thrown away years of hard work. I'm not sure what you can do to ride out the storm, but you need to keep your head down for at least six months. And I mean down. No partying, no going to fashion shows and getting papped having fun. You need to look sorry.'

'I *am* sorry,' Megan said bitterly.

'Nobody wants to hear empty words, Megan,' Carole said. 'Only an idiot would say they *weren't* sorry. Sorry isn't the issue. People want your head on a platter. That's the downside of fame. The public get to give it and they get to take it away.'

Megan stilled. For a few moments, she'd considered telling Carole what she really felt. That

25

she'd loved Rob Hartnell. That she'd never have gone with him otherwise. Now she was glad she hadn't.

Carole had a very simple view of the whole episode: Megan had had a badly judged fling with a happily married movie star. They'd been caught and instead of the movie star standing by Megan's side, he'd run away. Three lives were wrecked, the sympathy was with Katharine, and Megan was portrayed as a femme fatale who'd chiselled Rob away from his wife.

Rob, very sensibly, had not hung about for the fall-out. He had simply disappeared, the way only the very famous or the very rich can disappear. Since that day in Prague—was it only just before Christmas?—when a photographer had caught Rob and Megan cuddling up in a tiny bar near their hotel, Rob Hartnell hadn't been seen. Megan was left to face the storm alone. 'I'm devastated, too,' she wanted to cry. But it was no use. No one, not even her agent, cared what she felt.

'The whole thing is career suicide,' Carole said, almost to herself. 'What were you *thinking*?'

Megan felt the rawness inside her and was glad she'd kept her feelings to herself. *Thinking* had had nothing do to with it, but it was better that Carole didn't know that. She would rather no one knew it. Public hatred might be painful, but it was marginally better than pity.

'Time is the only healer now, at least in the media,' Carole went on.

And what about my heart, how is that meant to heal? Megan thought, but instead she said, 'If my sister can't have me, I could go to my Aunt Nora's in Dublin.'

Nobody would expect her to go there when she had many jet-setting friends with yachts and islands and Manhattan apartments, although the friends seemed to have made themselves scarce. Katharine Hartnell was too powerful for anyone in the industry to risk offending. Only a few of the people Megan had thought of as friends were phoning up now, and more for prurience' sake than out of friendship.

Still, Ireland was the last place anybody would expect her to go.

It was also the last place she wanted to go. Aunt Nora would not throw her arms around Megan and say 'poor diddums'. She'd probably ask 'What the heck were you doing?'

But it was a home, and one the press were unlikely to know about. Her peripatetic childhood on exotic islands had been widely reported; interviewers had always been much more interested in her recollections of Martinique and Formentera than Dublin Bay.

Ireland and Aunt Nora would do, but really she wanted to hide with Pippa: lie on the bed in her big sister's attic spare room reading novels, hidden from prying telephoto lenses by rolling Welsh hills. But she couldn't compromise Pippa's family in that way.

When they'd been younger, the gorgeous Flynn sisters had set London, and occasionally LA, on fire. It seemed nothing could stop them. But that, like everything else, had changed. Now Pippa had taken herself out of the rat race and, much as she loved her sister, she had other loyalties to consider.

A couple of days earlier, on one of her sneaked

27

forays from the London flat to get groceries, Megan had treated herself to a fashion magazine—one which had featured her in their 'in the closet' series a year ago. She'd opened it to find a big article by a leading female journalist on the evils of predatory women, and there she was, Megan Bouchier, vilified as the worst offender. Horrified, she'd thrown the magazine in the bin, but it carried on taunting her, even from underneath the wet teabags.

'Who are these people who hate me so much?' Megan had sobbed on the phone to Pippa. 'It's cruel, the stuff these newspaper columnists write— the women are the worst. How can they be so vicious?'

For once, there was quiet from Pippa's end. Normally, their calls would be punctuated by an endless chorus of 'Mummy, I want . . .' or the dogs barking or someone laughing or crying—Megan had become used, although it had been hard initially, to the constant demands of her sister's life. Kim, four, and Toby, twenty months, came first now.

'I don't know,' Pippa said after a while. She sounded as if she was too tired to even answer the question at the end of a long day chasing after her small children. 'I suppose it's like the pack instinct, isn't it? Women feel threatened and blame the other woman. It's easier to see her as the snake charmer, the evil seductress, than to blame your own man for straying. You know, it's not his fault, therefore you can still trust him. It's other women you can't trust.'

It was Megan's turn to be silent. When the news had first broken, Pippa had been her greatest ally.

'He seduced you, he told you their marriage was over, it's his fault,' she'd said back then.

Even when the press had arrived at Pippa's farmhouse, scaring the chickens so much that two had run off and never returned, she'd been on Megan's side. Now suddenly she wasn't. She was fed up with it all and the effect it was having on her life. Attuned to every nuance of Pippa's voice, Megan could tell that her sister had had enough of the Rob and Megan saga.

Worse, Pippa was looking at the story from a distance, thinking about how other women would view her beloved sister, instead of standing beside her in the trenches.

It was hard to know what was the most painful: Rob vanishing, her subsequent crucifixion in the press, or the knowledge that the whole scandal had somehow severed her bond with her older sister.

How, Megan thought bleakly, could a love so glorious have brought such pain?

*   *   *

She could see the lights of the curving arms of Dublin Bay through the plane window. Her throat felt tight at the sight. Home. It was home in lots of ways. Since their father had died when Megan was ten and Pippa thirteen, they'd lived in many different houses with their free-spirited mother. Sometimes the houses of their mother's boyfriends, sometimes houses they rented. The one in Peckham was the one they'd lived in the longest, and that had been for two years, when Megan was starting out acting. She'd done her best never to say where she lived. Peckham didn't

29

sound cool enough. There had been an awful problem with damp. It was a three-bedroomed house and each bedroom reeked of damp. Pippa had had to throw out her favourite brown leather jacket because of the mould on it.

Nora's house in Golden Square was the only home which had remained constant in all that time. Not as fancy as the villa in Martinique, or as cool as the top-floor apartment in Madrid, which had only lasted six months anyhow, because Pablo had been a bit of a perv and had clearly fancied both Marguerite's daughters, so they'd left there sharpish.

Golden Square wasn't cosmopolitan, smart or trendy. It had seemed like the most boring place on the planet to fourteen-year-old Megan in the two years she'd lived there and attended the Sacred Heart Convent. The only reasonable shops in the area were the book shop and the vintage clothes shop, Mesopotamia, where Megan had once found a tattered Pucci scarf for a fiver. Granted, a lot of the clothes there were tragic, but if you rummaged, you could get bargains.

Golden Square was both homely and home. Everybody knew Aunt Nora and liked her, respected her. If Nora forgot her purse when she went to The Nook convenience store, the owner would happily wave her away and tell her to pay another time. Megan couldn't think of anywhere in the world where she knew people in the same way.

The plane banked over the city, lower all the time. Like Megan's spirits.

It was horrible, feeling that she'd entirely messed up her life almost before it had begun. She had wanted to do everything right, to be the best she could be, to be wise and kind, and yet somehow she'd ended up in a world where it was easier to go to night clubs 'til dawn, easier to hang around as part of some rock star's entourage, easier to do the wrong thing. And all the while it was as if her life was a film; she was just playing a role, just pretending she was real. It felt as though one of her choices actually meant anything because tomorrow she'd wake up and be a different character.

Except it wasn't a film and the choices she'd made had been real. So were the consequences.

Overnight her fairytale world had turned very real and very ugly.

She didn't know whether Nora or the comfort of Golden Square would solve any of that. All she knew was thatshe would give anything to be able to go back and start again.

*   *   *

Nora Flynn saw the last client off the premises and locked the practice door with relief. The heavy curtain she pulled over the door was a sign to regulars that Golden Square Chiropody Clinic was closed for the day. It had been a long one; seven clients ending with a very difficult woman at six who wanted something done about a fungal nail infection but did it mean her nail polish would have to come off?

'What?'

'I don't want my pedicure ruined, I've just had it done,' the woman said.

'You are kidding, aren't you?' said Nora.

The woman gazed at Nora, who had poker-straight undyed grey hair and not a shred of make-up on her face.

'You wouldn't understand.'

'Probably not.'

Nora could be endlessly patient. But when the woman had finally left, moaning about her messed-up pedicure, Nora had felt like shrieking, *And a plague on you too!* after her. Hell was definitely other people.

She checked her watch. Half six. Megan would be on the plane now.

'Get a taxi,' Nora had told her on the phone. 'No point me trekking through evening traffic to the airport.'

'OK,' Megan stammered, clearly taken aback but trying not to show it.

'Shall I make dinner or will you eat on the plane?' Nora went on briskly, noting Megan's surprise and moving on.

'Don't bother with dinner,' Megan said, and she sounded more like the old Megan, less like the grand movie star who'd insisted fame wouldn't change her and yet had been changed all the same.

It would do her good to be back in Golden Square, Nora thought. Nobody would be running round after her here. There was only Nora and Nora didn't do running around. Not with her knees. She was glad she didn't have to cook tonight, either. Nora knew her limits and cooking was one of them. A bit of salmon in the microwave and some plain rice would do her nicely.

The practice occupied the ground floor of the house. Normally, she'd have been sharing the space with Kevin, who was a wonderful chiropodist, but he had a week off.

'Surfing,' Kevin had said when he booked his holidays.

'Whatever floats your boat,' said Nora. 'It's supposed to be hard.'

'Not for me,' said Kevin, with the innocence of a child, and Nora thought he was probably right. For all Kev's innocence, he was very competent.

She turned off the lights and opened the door on to the stairs leading to the rest of the house. She lived on the two upper floors.

The basement was a flat let out to a pair of girls who used to work in the bank, and now worked in a bar, making far more money in tips than they'd ever made when they were changing euros into rands and yen on the foreign exchange. The agreement was one party every two months, and so far, they'd kept their side of the bargain. Nora generally got invited to the parties, went for an hour to show that she wasn't the sour-faced old bag from upstairs, and then retreated to bed with a cup of cocoa, her double-strength wax earplugs and her silk mask.

They all shared the garden at the back, although on weekend mornings, Nora wasn't bothered by the girls because, like vampires, they rarely rose before noon. Even then, they looked quite undead.

This evening, Nora thought she might sit by the window overlooking the garden and drink a glass of wine to set her up for Megan's arrival. Nora didn't like to rely on anything unnatural for relaxation but it had been a stressful day, and she wasn't entirely looking forward to her niece's arrival. Megan thought nobody in Golden Square knew what had happened, as if Ireland were some provincial backwater without newspapers or the

33

internet. Like all young people, she thought the current city she was in was the centre of the universe, and everyone who didn't live there was to be pitied.

But Nora knew it all. And if she hadn't, Prudence Maguire from the other side of the square had nearly burst a gut to tell her a few days before.

'Your Megan is in a bit of trouble, is seems. Got herself involved with a married man, broken up the marriage, or so it says in the papers. Just in case you hadn't heard,' Prudence had added, smiling like a cobra as they stood in the queue in The Nook with their groceries.

On that particular day, Nora had some soya milk, lemons for her tea and a tin of dolphin-friendly tuna in her basket. Prudence had a half-price chocolate cheese cake and a litre of lambrusco hidden under a copy of the *Irish Times*. Nora knew because she'd seen Prudence put them there.

Not that she'd say anything, any more than she'd say a reproving word to the girls in the basement flat who drank two weeks' worth of alcohol units on a Friday night. Nora didn't tell other people what to do. Didn't believe in it. Everyone had their own path to follow, was her motto. If Prudence wanted to be a bitch extraordinaire, destroy her arteries with cholesterol and turn into an old soak at home on her own, far be it from Nora to say anything.

'Thank you for telling me, Prudence,' Nora had replied calmly, adjusting her spectacles so as to get a clear view of Prudence's face with its delighted smile. 'Great day, wasn't it? Nice to have a bit of heat in your bones with the really freezing weather gone.'

Prudence's smile faltered at this. She was entirely unaccustomed to people receiving her carefully aimed gossip with politeness. Normally, the recipient would look stunned or hurt or on the verge of needing a restraining order. Nora Flynn just looked as calm as ever, round face serene. Even her smoothly tied-back long grey hair had a serenity about it. Silly cow. Probably growing magic mushrooms in her back garden, Prudence thought crossly. Stupid old bag. Nora had to be at least sixty-five, and didn't look a day over fifty. And she was still going strong. Had to be drugs, *had* to be. Those alternative health people were all growing marijuana plants in their sheds and insisting it was for their health.

It was easier to have Prudence come out and say it, Nora knew. The news would be all round the square at high speed, and this way everyone would be over the embarrassment should they bump into Megan. Even Kevin, who wasn't much of a reader, had seen it in the paper.

'Poor Megan. It's a bummer, isn't it?' he'd said.

'Yes, a bummer,' Nora agreed.

Another reason why she loved Kevin. There would be no sly glances from him, betraying the unspoken judgement that her actress niece had really screwed up this time. No, Kevin knew that things happened to people and you got on with life. *Shit happens*, he liked to say. It was a comforting philosophy, although not necessarily one you'd want embroidered on a cushion.

When she opened the door to her apartment, Leonardo and Cici, her two dogs, were waiting inside, tails wagging furiously. Leonardo, who was part-greyhound and very shivery, danced his quivering dance, while Cici, who was mainly shih tzu, all dictator, bounced up and down like a dog who hadn't been petted for at least three hours and was on the verge of phoning the animal rescue people in outrage.

'You had a walk at lunchtime,' Nora said, hugging them both. *'And* this morning. You are shameless.'

She pulled on a cardigan and her duffel coat.

Nora didn't bother much with fashion. Flat shoes, comfortable trousers and shirts worn untucked was her style. She varied the colours and the fabric, but generally, she looked the same no matter what. The hair that had gone grey in her twenties, like her mother's, was tied back or sometimes plaited. She wore suncream in summer, moisturiser in winter, and clear salve instead of lip gloss. When Megan and Pippa had stayed with her as teenagers, they'd moaned that she had no cosmetics for them to practise on.

Bien dans sa peau, as Pippa would say now. Comfortable in her skin.

Pippa understood it, but poor Megan still didn't. Megan worked in a world where the emphasis on the outside was so total and all-consuming that there wasn't any time for the inside. When Megan had first said she wanted to go to acting school, Nora had got an anxious feeling in the pit of her stomach. She didn't approve of acting or actresses. Of course, they were all 'actors' now, men and women. Another bit of tomfoolery. It wasn't a steady trade. Only a few lucky ones made a living out of it, and the rest struggled endlessly, hoping for a break. Nora had known that Megan's head would be turned by that glittery surface world, and she'd been right.

The dogs' excited barking made her hurry to open the door and as they walked out into the dark she admired, as she often did, the beauty of the lights all around the square. Golden Square's residents could be split into two groups: the people who owned whole houses, had two cars, and employed someone else to cut their grass, and those whose families had lived there for donkeys' years and who couldn't have afforded to buy one now even with the state of the market, but who were holding on for the next property boom. They cut their own grass, occasionally rented out bits of the houses to tenants, and looked enviously at their neighbours' double glazing.

Nora was one of the latter type. Her parents had inherited the house and had moved in anxiously in the 1940s, fresh from a tiny flat above a gentlemen's draper's shop in Camden Street, terrified they'd never be able to heat or redecorate this comparatively enormous residence.

They'd been so proud of their new home, but always anxious about living somewhere so grand. As if they didn't really belong.

Nobody's windows were so clean or their garden so weed-free as the Flynns'. It was as if they felt keeping the place spotless made up for the fact that they had to repaint it all themselves. It was years before they could afford to have a roofer fix the tiles. When it rained heavily, Nora's mother used to trail round the house nervously, waiting for the arrival of the next spot of damp. Unaccustomed to the whole notion of a garden, they'd kept the lawn shorn and attempted little else.

One of the biggest worries had been the behaviour of the various basement tenants over the years. Nora could remember her mother's prayers that the next lot of new people would be quiet.

'I'll say a novena to St Jude,' she'd say. Sometimes the novenas worked and sometimes they didn't. Nora's parents never wondered why, they just accepted it. God's choice was not theirs to question.

If they could see her now, Nora thought sadly. They'd have told her to keep the dogs on the lead and her father would have been following at a crouch, plastic bag in hand, waiting for the inevitable poop.

Dogs were supposed to be kept on the lead in the square, but it was easy enough to work out which animals were there and whether it was safe to let her pair off. It was safe this evening. Nora unclipped the leads and let the dogs race off under the gentle lamplight. She sat down on her favourite bench, stretched out her legs and let the strains of the day slough off her. There were only a couple of other people about. Nora liked all the doggie people in the square. Having dogs did something to people. Made them softer, gentler.

Prudence Maguire didn't have a dog; no surprise there. Rumour had it that her daughter had once had a hamster, but it had escaped, and Prudence had refused permission to have the couch ripped apart to find it. Nora imagined a ghostly hamster still rattling round inside the Maguire family couch, making little eldritch squeaks of distress that Prudence would totally ignore.

She glanced at her watch. Ten to seven. Megan would have landed. She'd be in the taxi soon, on her way. Nora closed her eyes and wished for the first time ever that her niece wasn't coming. Nora had tried hard to be a steadying influence in her nieces' lives. Her brother Fionn would have wanted his big sister to take care of his daughters when he died. But it hadn't been easy. Marguerite, their mother, was the exact opposite of Nora: a woman who lived in a state of constant, almost child-like happiness, she was prone to both wild adventures and falling passionately in love.

She was the type who clearly needed a man around and, although she'd adored Fionn, he wasn't long dead before she was anxiously looking for another strong male to take care of her.

She also had strange views on how to bring up her daughters.

When the carrots the children had planted hadn't grown in Nora's bit of garden, Marguerite stuck shop-bought ones into the earth instead and pretended to dig them up.

'That's appalling,' Nora had said, unable to stop herself. 'How can they learn about real life when you fake it for them like that?'

'They're only a few carrots,' Marguerite had laughed. 'Don't be so serious, Nora.'

And now Marguerite was sunning herself in Ibiza with her latest hunk and didn't appear to be treating Megan's situation as worrying.

'Darling, it'll all blow over,' Marguerite had reportedly said to Pippa when her elder daughter had phoned with the news.

Nora hadn't spoken to Marguerite in years. It wasn't possible to kill someone over the phone but

39

Nora didn't want to take any chances.

So Nora was left to pick up the pieces. But how could she? Megan still didn't know that huge, clean carrots didn't magically appear a couple of weeks after you planted seeds.

*   *   *

The cassette player in the taxi had been blasting out Moroccan music all the way from the airport and the driver, a very slender, dark-skinned man with long, artistic fingers that tapped the steering wheel in time to the beat, hadn't spoken at all since Megan had got into the cab.

'Very good,' was all he'd said when she gave him the address.

'This is it,' she said, sitting forward in the seat at the taxi slowed down in Golden Square.

'Very good,' he said again, applying the brakes with a firm foot.

Megan shot forward in the back seat and banged her head on the headrest of the passenger seat. The taxi driver looked around in alarm.

'It's fine,' Megan said quickly, holding a hand up in the international 'all fine' gesture.

He still looked alarmed.

'Really fine,' she said. 'I'm OK, honestly.'

She handed him the money plus a generous tip. When you didn't want to communicate, Megan had learned it was best to hand out big tips. It was like saying, 'I'm not a rude bitch because I'm famous, really, but here's a large tip, just to make sure you like me.'

'Very good,' the driver said.

It was clearly the only English he spoke. Poor

40

man. He wasn't at home here either, she thought, hauling her stuff out and shivering in the chilly night air.

*   *   *

Megan couldn't actually remember the first time she and Pippa had come to stay with Nora. Their aunt and her narrow, quirky house in Golden Square had always been a part of their lives, it seemed. Yet she knew it wasn't always so. It was only when Dad died that they'd begun to stay with their aunt for long periods of time. It was clear, though nobody had ever said as much, that Mum hadn't coped well with her husband's death, hence Nora had stepped in to take care of her little nieces.

Golden Square, with its endless cycle of interesting tenants downstairs, and various motley dogs, cats and even once, a parakeet, had filled the gap left by Megan's father. Yet everyone appeared to forget that it was Nora's brother who'd died. She had every right to be as devastated as Mum, yet she never said anything about her own grief. She'd simply moved into their lives, being there when she was needed, for summer holidays, for Christmases, her pain on hold while she did her duty.

Nora must have been watching out for Megan now because the front door opened and Nora appeared silhouetted in the hall light, trying to restrain two barking dogs.

'Hello,' called Megan, hauling her wheeled hold-all along the narrow garden path. The taxi driver had barely accelerated off with a roar of tyres, before the tears started rolling down her cheeks.

Nora gave up holding back Cici and Leonardo, opened the door wide and welcomed Megan into her arms, the dogs jumping eagerly around them.

'You're here now,' Nora said softly. 'It'll be all right, Meg, you'll see.'

Hearing the diminutive name she'd preferred when she was a kid made Megan feel even sadder. She'd had such plans for her life and what had they come to? 'Oh, Nora, everything's a disaster. I've ruined it all,' she said.

'Nonsense,' Nora replied, deciding that now wasn't the time for the lecture. She pulled the hold-all the rest of the way inside, called the dogs in and shut the front door. 'You made a mistake, people do. You feel terrible right now, but you will feel better soon.'

Despite her tears, Megan felt familiar anger prick. Nora still talked to her as though she were a child. This was the destruction of both her life and her career, not a schoolgirl escapade. She was twenty-six, not a kid.

'Come on upstairs. I've just made myself some lemon and chamomile tea, there's plenty in the pot for two. And *Bondi Vet* is on later. They're all repeats; tonight it's the one about the parrot on Prozac, you'll love it.'

Nora adored animal shows, everything from wild animals being secretly filmed in the bush to domestic cats being rescued from mad people who didn't feed them: she watched them all.

Megan thought of how she'd hoped that tonight she could talk to someone who loved her and would understand. Perhaps she could finally unburden herself and tell Nora everything. But no,

42

they were going to watch animal programmes. Still, it was better than having Nora lecture her.

'Great,' she said, with an enthusiasm she didn't feel. What she'd really like was a cool glass of white wine and a hot bath, but neither seemed to be on the menu.

The dogs split the loving between them, with Cici appointing herself carer of Megan and sitting on her lap waiting to be adored. Leonardo, shaking with the excitement of the evening, lay on the couch beside Nora, his velvety grey head on her knee.

Nobody could resist a double bill of *Bondi Vet* and with Cici there to hug, Nora could see her niece visibly relax. Megan kicked off her shoes and folded her feet up under her on the big armchair, rearranging Cici so she was snuggled close to her. Pretending to watch the television, Nora secretly watched Megan.

Her beauty had come as a surprise. Marguerite was pretty in a blonde, girlish way, and Pippa took after her. Fionn himself had been tall, attractive and had an air of great strength about him, but he was no matinee idol. And yet along had come Megan, a genuine beauty even when she was a child. There had been no teenage anxieties for her about her looks, no acne or teeth problems, nothing. She'd grown from a slight fairy of a child with cool blonde hair and enquiring dark olive green eyes into a slight fairy of a woman, with a sheen to her skin, an inner glow that marked her out. People had stared at her when Nora took the two girls out; nobody had ever assumed Nora was their mother, which might have been hurtful except that Nora had no problems with her own lack of beauty. It was like the length of your legs: there was nothing whatsoever to do about it.

It had been no surprise that film and television people had been enamoured of Megan. Even as a child playing a little gangster in a stage version of *Bugsy Malone*, she was luminous.

But not so luminous now, Nora thought. Megan was wearing what all young women seemed to wear these days: those loose, boyish jeans, flat little lace-up runners and an enormous grey sweatshirt that dwarfed her. Her skin had a greyish tinge, she looked skinny and, without any make-up, the ultra-blonde hair looked cheap and, Nora hated to even think it, tarty.

Nora had read the single interview given by someone close to Katharine Hartnell in a newspaper a client had left at the surgery. Devoid of most of the usual celebrity cover-up, it had sounded heartfelt and terribly sad. There was no blithe dismissal of a lowly actress trying to infiltrate a solid movie-star marriage. Just the assertion that this had split the Hartnells up and that her husband's betrayal had shaken Katharine to the core.

No, Nora decided. She wouldn't say anything to Megan tonight. What could she say, anyway? She wasn't equipped to counsel Megan over this. It was so far outside Nora's comfort zone that she wouldn't have known where to start.

But she felt, as her eyes stared unseeing at the Sydney vets trying to save a dog bitten by a snake, that she'd let her brother down. This wasn't what he would have wanted for one of his beloved daughters.

3

Bread

You need good-quality flour to make decent bread. Never underestimate a nice cake of soda bread with freshly churned butter for when you're tired and ready to sink down beside your own fire. Or a good wholemeal to set off a piece of cheese when you need energy.

It took me a long time to learn how to make good bread because my mother never measured a thing. She just threw handfuls in. Flour, some buttermilk left over from churning . . . I have my recipe here and I can tell you, we got more out of the flour than just bread. We got linen sheets!

I never thought we were poor, you see, Eleanor. We had exactly what everyone else in Kilmoney had, which was next to nothing. But that wasn't poor. There was this little old creature who lived in a tumbledown shack on the coast road, and we all thought she was poor. You'd see her at Mass on a

45

Sunday with her dress inside out and not much of a dress, either. She was as thin as a consumptive and hadn't a tooth in her head. Lord help us, that was our vision of poverty. We always had food to eat from our garden, the hens, the ducks and the cows, and as long as someone had the loan of a donkey to go to the bog, we'd turf for the fire. Your aunt Agnes could turn her hand to anything, and she kept us neat.

Agnes learned about nice belongings when she went into service. Captain and Mrs Fitzmaurice she worked for, and nobody could say a word against them in her hearing.

Linen sheets, she said, were the last word in luxury.

Sure we have linen sheets, my father said. And we did. The eight-stone bags that the flour came in were made of a coarse linen and when the flour was emptied into the flour barrel, Mam would unpick the bags, wash them, bleach them in the sun out in the fields, and then sew them up into sheets.

Mam had been taught to knit the thread the bags were sewn with into lace. When she got sick, I took over.

I used to think, if the likes of Mrs Fitzmaurice had to live in a small three-bedroomed cottage like us, now that would be hard for a person used to fine linen. But for us, we loved it. It was home. The Captain and Mrs Fitzmaurice never had children. She was always so interested in you, Eleanor, when you were a child, that I think she'd have liked a little one or two. So you see, I never understood us being poor. In my eyes, we had everything.

*   *   *

On a cold Wednesday evening in January, Rae Kerrigan stood on her tiny balcony overlooking Golden Square, and watched a girl with long dark hair walk along the east side of the square. The girl might have been twenty and with her hair and a long striped scarf trailing behind her, she reminded Rae of herself when she was young. The girl walked with the energy and determination of youth, long jean-clad legs striding along, carrying what looked like a huge rucksack easily. Rae had once had a similar scarf, and had been as slender, racing along with her dark hair flying.

47

Men probably loved the girl's hair. Men had certainly loved Rae's.

'You look like Ali MacGraw in *Love Story*. Never cut your hair,' one boyfriend had begged her, after a long night at a folk concert on the campus in Galway, when they were still drinking wine in her tiny bedsit at dawn. The modern Rae was able to smile ruefully at the memory. That was well over thirty-five years ago, at least, she realised.

The boyfriend would have been shocked if he saw that the long dark hair was now tawny and shoulder-length, streaked with hairdresser's clever soft browns to hide the grey that had appeared when she'd hit forty. But her winged brows were still mahogany dark, flared over the deep-set warm eyes that contributed to Rae's thoughtful, penetrating gaze.

Still, that boyfriend would have changed too over the years; he probably bore as much resemblance to the earnest young philosophy student with floppy brown curls as she did to the girl she'd once been. She'd be fifty-eight on her next birthday and her life had taken paths she could never have imagined back then.

Along the way, she'd got married, had her beloved son Anton, and she'd traded her career in human resources for something a little different. Despite what she'd thought all those years ago, everything had worked out. Well, nearly everything.

She'd once read a spiritual saying that encapsulated her early life: for your heart to open, it first has to break. Rae's heart had certainly been broken, but she'd recovered, more or less.

The girl who'd prompted the memories reached the corner and was gone from sight. Rae hoped, for the girl's sake, that she'd had an easier life than Rae had by the same age. She wouldn't wish that on anyone.

She took a sip of her steaming tea. The sun was low in the sky and the light shone through the two sycamore trees outside the balcony, creating a soft acid green light on the front of her house. She loved to get a little fresh air in the evening. Just for a moment in the cooler weather, and longer in summer. Her favourite place was sitting on the tiny first-storey balcony on her narrow white house, with Golden Square spread beneath her, music coming from the open French doors behind her and a cup of tea in her hand.

The balcony was too small for any actual furniture. In fact, it wasn't really a balcony, just a ledge off the master bedroom. But it was a glorious place to lean against the iron railings and think about the day.

Evening was muted. As if people's voices were less harsh, cars moved more slowly along the streets and even the dogs barked in a more lazy manner. The closing down of the day, time to relax. Certain times of day should be bottled, she decided. A late afternoon like this one would be very therapeutic: in times of stress, take two sips of Quiet January Twilight, a drop of New Year's Eve Excitement, and a large spoonful of Winter Dawn.

Pity it wasn't that easy.

They were lucky, living in Golden Square. The houses surrounding the gardens were mainly beautiful old redbricks, with narrow three-storeys like Will and Rae's, a couple of cottages and a line of 1930s villas thrown in, with one apartment block.

On one side of the square there was a swathe of local shops including a proper butcher's and The Nook, which sold everything from aspirin to apples. There was a dry cleaner's, a small restaurant that changed hands every year like clockwork, and the Old Claddagh Bar, the local pub, which still did a roaring trade in processed cheese sandwiches on factory sliced white bread.

Every year, the latest owners of the restaurant walked into the Old Claddagh, sniffed at the sight of the sandwiches and the tomato-shaped plastic ketchup container, and walked out happily, convinced that the local pub wasn't much competition. They'd bring ciabatta and miso soup to the area, they thought, and nobody would go near the pub for lunch ever again. By the end of the year they'd be leaving with their tails between their legs as it transpired the locals liked processed cheese sandwiches with their pints at lunchtime and found ciabatta bread very hard and dry.

Nestled between The Nook convenience store and the Old Claddagh Bar was the only other eatery to have survived the restaurant curse of Golden Square: Titania's Palace Tearooms, which Rae had managed for the past fifteen years. She could see it from her little balcony: a double-windowed shop painted a rich olive green with the name in cursive lettering in gold over the shop, and an old-fashioned cast-iron sign sticking out over the door: Titania's Palace Tearooms.

The tearooms were still going strong, as Rae and Timothy, the owner, had long ago realised that keeping it simple and cosy worked. People could go into Titania's Palace and sit quietly reading the day's newspapers with nobody talking to them, if

50

they wished, or they could enjoy warm company. They could eat cupcakes smothered in pink icing or low-cal bran muffins. Rae's management theory was that once a customer experienced the welcome of Titania's Palace they wouldn't be able to resist coming again.

Rae loved the tearooms.

'It's peaceful,' she told Will.

'It's noisy as hell when I go in there,' he teased her gently.

'But it's nice noise, enjoyable noise,' she pointed out.

And it was. The noise was of people enjoying themselves, talking, chattering, laughing, waving hello to so and so, all in the comforting atmosphere of the place. Her son Anton liked to say there was an invisible forcefield around the place, and once you entered, you were stuck in Kindland.

'You have got to stop watching so much *Star Trek*,' his father joked. 'You'll be learning Klingon next.'

On the drive of the house beside Rae's, she could see her neighbour, Claire, coming in with a bag of shopping. Claire was wearing her pink velvet coat with the fluffy fake fur collar. She'd been wearing that coat for twenty years now. Rae could remember when Claire had acquired it. The coat had created quite a scandal among some members of the residents' association, especially Prudence Maguire, who was hideously jealous of Claire's bleached-blonde glamour and ease with her own sexuality.

Ironically, it was Prudence—who'd loudly prophesied juvenile delinquency and immoral

51

lapses in everyone else—who was practically estranged from her family. Claire and Evan's kids had grown into kind, caring people who appeared to have achieved happy lives. When Claire's daughter, Rachel, turned up in the square with her family, car windows open and music blaring, the children piled out, laughing and giggling, dying to see their grandparents.

Rae's eyrie and the sanctuary of the tearoom window meant she could see Prudence's house a lot of the time. No laughing carloads of grandchildren ever pulled up there. Rae pitied her neighbour, even if she didn't like her very much.

Prudence reminded Rae a little of her own mother-in-law, Geraldine Kerrigan. They were both judgemental and determined to see the negative side in any situation. The only difference was that Rae didn't have to spend time with Prudence but Geraldine was coming for lunch on Sunday. Rae normally loved the slowness of Sunday, but not when Geraldine was coming, an event which happened with increasing regularity as Geraldine grew older.

And nothing, nothing would be done the way Geraldine liked it. The table would be too fussily decorated or else Geraldine might remark that Rae must have been too busy to set things properly. The roast would be overdone or too bloody in the centre. The vegetables would be wrong for a person with such a sensitive stomach, or else carrot puree was suitable only for people with no teeth, surely?

Still, Geraldine had done one wonderful thing in her life, which was giving birth to Rae's husband Will. Meeting Will had been one of the blessings of

52

Rae's life: her son, Anton, had been the other one. He was grown up now, in London working full time for the political magazine he'd gone to on a placement during his politics degree. Sometimes the old white house seemed empty without him, with no head stuck in the fridge roaring, 'What can I eat, Mum?' and no noisy footsteps running up and down the stairs at odd hours, yelling, 'I'll call when I want to be collected.'

His absence had partly been filled by Rae doing more volunteer work for Community Cares, a local charity that some people described as the second social welfare system. They helped people when there was nobody else, offering financial aid and friendship.

Her tea was nearly cold now. She'd spent too long standing on the balcony thinking. Rae finished it off, went inside her bedroom and closed the balcony doors tightly. She loved their bedroom. It was like a warm cocoon, with wallpaper the colour of honey, a quilted yellow silk eiderdown and old gold picture frames on the walls with black-and-white photos of their family over the years. On Rae's side of the bed were piles of books waiting to be read: on Will's side was a photo of Rae and his single book—he didn't read in the same crazy, haphazard way she did, with three books on the go at all times.

Each time she looked at this lovely warm room, Rae thought how lucky she was. Unlike most people, she got to see just how lucky she was every single day.

When people asked her why she worked as a volunteer for Community Cares along with running the tearooms, she rarely replied truthfully.

Rae knew that the people who asked in such astonishment wouldn't have understood the true answer.

'But why? Why would you want to go into horrible council flats like Delaney and see all those drug addicts?'

'It's rewarding,' she would say simply and change the conversation. She'd long ago learned that it was impossible to change people's firmly set views on poverty and deprivation. Geraldine, her mother-in-law, was one such person. In all the time Rae had been working for Community Cares, Geraldine had never once said a nice thing about either the work or the people being helped.

'I suppose somebody has to do it,' was as much as she could bring herself to say.

Geraldine prided herself on her family's standing in society. Being involved with the dregs of society didn't make the slightest sense to her. Surely people would want to distance themselves from poverty?

To the other sort of people who asked Rae why she worked with the charity—the ones who seemed to understand and who recognised that it could be hard to be exposed to other people's pain every day—Rae told half the truth:

'Helping people gives me peace.'

She didn't say that she'd had first-hand experience of the strife that came from poverty and deprivation. Though Rae had been married to Will Kerrigan for twenty-five years and had lived in the comfort of Golden Square all that time, in her mind's eye, she was only a few steps away from the Hennessey girl who had grown up in a run-down bungalow on the outskirts of Limerick city.

Ironically, she didn't remember Community Cares coming to her household to help, but then, her parents would probably have yelled at the volunteers and called them 'do-gooders!' They were touchy about anyone they thought might be looking down on them.

Set up in the 1930s to help the poor, over the decades Community Cares had grown to a country-wide organisation with branches in every town. It wasn't religious, just humanist. Nobody was ever turned away.

Rae and her CC partner, Dulcie, normally made calls on Tuesday evenings and Wednesday afternoons, like today. Theirs was a perfect working relationship as Dulcie was different from Rae in every way that mattered. Dulcie was seventy and had worked with the charity for over twenty years. Small, grey-haired, with bright, inquisitive eyes and an addiction to nail art, she had seen everything life could throw at a person. She was also great fun.

Today, they'd made two calls in the Delaney flats. Over the ten years she'd been a volunteer, Rae had spent hours in the Delaney flat complex behind Golden Square. A trio of down-at-heel redbrick council blocks, Delaney One, Two and Three housed many fatherless families and elderly people who relied on state cheques and money from CC.

Rae had never felt afraid there. CC was viewed as a part of the fabric of the place and respected by the residents like no other organisation, because they actually helped. Besides, Rae could always see beyond the sullen gazes of the kids who loitered by the landings to the lonely desperation behind. The way they looked at the world was a mask, as much to keep the pain in as to keep the rest of the world out.

'I hope the rest of January is as good as today,' Dulcie had muttered as they hurried from her van to the graffiti-scrawled entrance of Delaney One. 'Not a bit of rain, and it's really quite mild.'

'We wish,' said Rae, smiling. She'd loved the day of sun too.

'If you can do rain dances, why can't you do sun dances?' Dulcie wondered.

'Howareyase girls,' yelled a voice.

It was Mickey the Madser, a name he'd given himself, waving a brown paper bag with a bottle inside as they walked up the grim concrete stairs. The lifts in Delaney were always broken.

'Have youse got a few bob to spare?' he roared. His hearing had been damaged many years ago and he always shouted.

CC had paid Mickey's gas bill several times and often gave him food shopping vouchers—ones that couldn't be exchanged for alcohol.

'Not for Buckfast, I'm afraid,' Rae said.

'It was worth a try,' said Mickey, unabashed.

Janet, who lived on the third floor with her three children, had the door open and the kettle boiling by the time they got to her. 'I heard you talking to Mickey,' she said. 'Who needs an alarm, right?'

An alarm would have been useless in Delaney. The network of kids would spread the news of any visitor's arrival at high speed and if someone was determined to break into one of the flats, they would, alarm or no alarm. Janet's ex, who was constantly trying to fight his addiction to heroin, had broken in several times looking for money.

Janet was twenty-seven, looked closer to thirty-seven and kept the small flat as neat as a pin. The three children were industriously doing their homework at the kitchen table while Rae, Dulcie and Janet shared a pot of tea and talked. CC had helped pay for Janet's accountancy night courses. But it was still proving hard for her to get work.

'It's the address,' Janet said, without a shred of self-pity. 'If I apply anywhere local, they take one look at the address and say, "Forget it, love." Nobody wants to hire anyone from Delaney. They think we'll rob them blind.'

She wasn't bitter, just resigned. That was why her three children were made to sit down and diligently do their homework every night. Janet was determined that education would get them out of the trap that was Delaney One.

After Janet's, Rae and Dulcie headed across to Delaney Three where Mrs Mills, an eighty-five-year-old, lived with her mentally disabled son, Terence. Hugging was theoretically forbidden on the job for a variety of reasons but Mrs Mills always hugged the CC volunteers. She hugged Terence too, and her ginger tom, Liberace. Both Terence and Liberace got the best of everything and Mrs Mills herself wore clothes she'd owned for fifty years, clothes that were now too large for her shrinking frame.

She was looking for some money to take Terence to the Marian shrine at Lourdes, where she'd taken him every year since he was a small boy.

'He gets some comfort from it, I know he does,' Mrs Mills said, petting Terence's huge knee with love. Terence was a gentle man but big. Rae wondered how his fragile and ageing mother dressed him every day, carefully putting on the adult diapers he needed. A public service nurse came in three times a week, but she was retiring soon and wouldn't be replaced.

What would Mrs Mills do then? But she never complained, not about anything to do with her son.

'I've got nearly all the money saved,' Mrs Mills added proudly. 'Just another seventy is all we need.'

'We'll talk about it at the committee next week,' Rae promised.

She was afraid that there wasn't enough money this year to help send Terence to Lourdes. The CC's list of clients had grown exponentially in the past couple of years. People who'd once donated money at the charity's church collections were now asking for money themselves.

'I understand.' Mrs Mills put a tiny, pale hand on Rae's. 'Lourdes is low down the list, Rae, I understand.'

She didn't look sad or upset, Rae realised with surprise.

'What happens will happen.' Mrs Mills finally let go of Rae's hands. 'I've got some chutney for you,' she added. 'A friend of mine gave me a couple of pots at Christmas.'

She bustled off into her kitchen and left them sitting alone with Terence. He didn't smile or say anything. Terence lived in his own world. Lack of oxygen at birth, Mrs Mills explained sadly. He might have been handsome in another world, Rae reflected with pity. A strong, handsome man who could look after his elderly mother in her later years. Except Terence would always remain a child, the cared-for instead of the carer. 'It's lovely chutney.' Mrs Mills appeared carrying two jars with fabric-covered lids.

Rae and Dulcie had been given many things over the years. Rhubarb from someone's back garden, many hand-made cards from children, sometimes a few roses wrapped in tinfoil. It was always the people who had the least who wanted to give the most.

Rae put her jar into the small rucksack she used for CC visits, then she and Dulcie took their leave.

'Isn't she sweet?' Dulcie said as they trooped down the concrete stairs, trying not to smell the ever-present scent of urine.

'Yes, she's wonderful,' agreed Rae. 'I don't know how she copes, to be honest. Perhaps it's easier to let your mind float off; easier than dealing with the daily reality, that's for sure.'

Rae was still sitting on the bed, thinking about Mrs Mills when Will's voice broke into her daydream. 'Hi, love, I'm home.'

'Coming,' Rae replied.

She'd give Will some of the chutney to try. He loved cheese after dinner. When they were first married, Rae had teased him that cheese and crackers were the 'posh person's dessert'.

'Oh yes, I suppose you had trifle in tin bowls?' Will would joke.

'Trifle? We couldn't afford trifle!' she'd say.

They'd never had dessert in the Hennessey household. A lot of the time, they didn't even have dinner. Few days passed when Rae didn't close her eyes and say thanks for the life she lived now. She was so grateful for all she had, but that gratefulness was tinged with sorrow over the past. And the past never left her.

4

Vegetables

When my mam was dying, she only had one worry. That I'd look after my sister, Agnes. She never married and Mam knew that was hard on her, for all that Agnes used to say she had no use for men at all.

Except your father, Joe—she was fond of him. He was like a brother to her. But apart from Joe, Agnes liked to pretend she couldn't care less what any man might think of her.

She had courted in her youth but the man she loved, Mikeen Clancy, had been killed in the War of Independence. He was twenty-five, as gentle a man as ever came out of County Galway, but gentleness doesn't stop bullets. The light went out of Agnes after that. His mother and his family got to grieve, but there was no ring between Agnes and Mikeen. Only an understanding in their hearts. If you married a man, you were entitled to grieve when he died.

Being hopeful of marriage didn't count.

Agnes cried on her own at night. When they got Mikeen's body back, nobody gave her a lock of his hair to keep.

It wasn't easy, being a spinster in our parish. Years later, when we'd upped sticks and moved to America, it was all different. On the streets of Brooklyn, there were plenty of women without chick or child or man, and nobody pitied them. But in Kilmoney, a woman without a husband was in a different class altogether. A husband gave a woman standing in the community. With no husband, you might as well be a child.

In truth, there were few men as capable as my sister around. Nobody would run a house like Agnes, and she was so good to you, Eleanor, like a second mother. But I think she lost hope when Mikeen died, and no other man looked at her the same way when they saw her sadness.

She put a lot of her love into the garden. If she was down, she went out into the garden and pulled up a few weeds. When it came to vegetables, parsnips were her favourite. She liked to cook what we used to call green, white and gold—mashed parsnips and carrots with parsley on top. But her favourite dish was pan-roasted parsnips. A good housekeeper should always have a little bit of duck fat in her pantry and use that to coat the parsnips. Roast them until they're crisp on the outside, speckled with black pepper.

'Bia don lá dubh,' as Agnes used to say. Food for a black day.

*   *   *

Connie O'Callaghan wasn't sure at what point she'd become a professional single woman. But she was reasonably sure of precisely when other people had accepted her as such. It was around the time of her thirty-ninth birthday, nearly a year ago, when people had stopped telling her about this or that man they knew who was 'gorgeous, just right for you' and started inviting her to events without a *plus one.*

When she was in her early thirties, after she'd split up from her fiancé Keith, people did their best to fix her up with every single man within a fifty-mile radius.

She'd gone on dates with a few guys from the bank where her cousin worked, but nothing had come of it, apart from a greater understanding of what actuaries really did, courtesy of one man who had no other conversation.

There had been several dinner parties where she'd arrived and surveyed the men, wondering which one was the 'fabulous man, simply fabulous', and every time her guess had been wrong.

He had never been the one she liked the look of. Invariably he turned out to be the one she'd assumed lived with his mother, had a stamp collection and had never been on a date before.

Men were produced for her like rabbits out of a magician's hat. But it hadn't been love at first sight on either side.

Connie hadn't just relied on blind dates in those early, post-Keith years. There was no staying at home with a DVD box set and a tub of ice cream, either. No, she'd been out there looking for love.

There had been scuba-diving weekends. Connie wondered whether she'd made a mistake, learning to dive in rugged Donegal where the icy grip of the Atlantic meant that, once you got out of the water, you put on your heaviest jumper, something thermal and very possibly a woollen hat to get the heat back into your body. Nobody had ever fallen in love with a woman across a crowded pub when that woman had cheeks puce from exposure and dressed like she'd just come in from a polar expedition.

Connie was too sturdy to look good in polar outfits. She was at her best in nicely slimming dark denim jeans with a silky top in indigo or sea blue to bring out the pale blue of her eyes, and with her cloudy dark hair loose around her face.

The art class she'd tried hadn't been successful either. There were far more women at it than men, and at least three-quarters of the men were there because their heart attack rehab therapists had suggested watercolour painting as an ideal way to enjoy a less stressful existence.

Against her better judgement, she'd gone on a yoga weekend. The men there were amazing: so flexible they could tuck their feet behind their ears, should the occasion demand it. But it seemed as if worshipping at the altar of Hatha-toned bodies turned them off anyone with a slight overspill on the waistband of their jeans.

'I don't think I'm too fat,' Connie had grumbled to her oldest friend, Gaynor, on the phone once she got back from Hatha Heaven. 'But I felt it there. At least when I'm doing the stand-like-a-tree pose, my upper thighs are nice and chunky, so my other foot has something to wedge itself into. Skinny people can't do that, can they?'

Gaynor was her sensible married friend. Gaynor never talked on the phone after seven at night, which was when Connie liked to phone people, as Gaynor was doing the endless things related to getting the children to bed. Sometimes, Connie felt tired just talking to Gaynor about the whole nighttime routine.

'When I've got Niamh in bed, she keeps getting out and wanting a drink or a wee, and even though Charlie's allowed to go later, it takes so long for him to brush his teeth, and by then, Josie wants to talk to me. She likes talking just before she goes to sleep, and now she's in secondary, she needs to talk. Well, they do, don't they?'

Connie sometimes found it hard to sort herself out in the evening. How on earth did Gaynor manage? It was like running a huge corporation and making sure everyone in it had clean teeth, clean pyjamas, the correct teddies and all their emotional needs sorted.

'I don't know how you do it,' she said.

'Nonsense,' said Gaynor briskly. 'You'd be able to, if you had to.'

'No, I wouldn't.'

It was easier to say that. Easier than picturing herself with a child of her own. *Her own child to hold and love forever.* No, it was too painful to imagine that, because she wasn't going to get it. So she cut off all thoughts of children.

She worked with kids every day, but they were teenagers and if anything was destined to put a person off the concept of motherhood, it was facing thirty bored teenage girls five times a day in St Matilda's.

Gaynor had never tried to set Connie up with men.

'She's got too much sense,' said Nicky, Connie's younger sister. 'Blind dates are so insulting. It's like saying you can't find a man on your own and a third party has to step in to fix you up.'

Connie was nine years older than Nicky, and occasionally it seemed that those nine years were an enormous chasm.

She had never felt insulted by people trying to find a Mr Right for her. When the man in question was a bit odd, she did wonder if her friends knew her at all, but she appreciated that they were doing their best.

What she'd found mildly insulting was when they

stopped trying to set her up. When the blind dates dried up; when she was asked only to girls' nights out because the husbands and boyfriends were at football matches: *that* was upsetting.

Am I now officially too old to date? she wondered. But she couldn't share this with Nicky.

Even though the sisters had the same parents, shared an apartment in Golden Square, and spent a lot of time together, Connie had come to realise that they were from different generations. Nicky glowed with confidence, enthusiasm and a firm belief that, if she wanted something badly enough, she'd get it. Connie, teetering at the sharp end of her thirties, knew from painful experience that wanting something wasn't enough. Life didn't give you what you wanted all the time.

When she'd been Nicky's age, she'd been engaged to Keith, sure that life would bring her marriage, children and happiness. And then Keith had told that he loved her 'but not like that. Not *in love* love, if you know what I mean . . .'

Connie hadn't, but Keith wasn't asking her opinion. He was telling her.

'We're like brother and sister now,' he'd gone on. 'You're so funny, Connie, and we have great fun, but that's not enough.'

He'd gone off, dated many women, and was now, apparently—Connie still had a few spies in the Keith camp—seeing a twenty-four-year-old Texan philosophy student and telling people he wanted to marry her.

It was simple. There weren't enough men to go around, and the ones that were around could afford to be choosy and wait till they were forty-five, then marry child brides.

66

Connie had somehow missed her chance.

She wasn't thinking of missed chances this icy Thursday morning in January as she stood under the shower in Apartment 2B in 14 Golden Square, fiddling with the shower controls. She was cross that the shower had broken again and wondering where she had put the attachment for the bath taps, because she couldn't go to work without a shower, and she wouldn't have time for a bath. Baths were a nighttime activity, when there was time to luxuriate and when Nicky was out with Freddie, her boyfriend. Freddie was in the apartment so often, he almost lived there and Connie had too often wandered out of the bathroom with a towel half round her, only to find Freddie had miraculously appeared and was sprawled all over the couch watching Sky Sports.

Not that Freddie was the lascivious sort. On the contrary, he treated Connie like a sweet elderly lady and would have had to be given CPR if anyone had suggested otherwise, towel or no towel.

'Nicky!' she yelled now, giving up and stepping out of the bath. She wrenched open the cupboard under the hand basin and an avalanche of shampoo, fake tan and body lotion bottles fell across her feet. 'Have you seen the hose attachment for the taps? The shower's broken again.'

'What? No,' yelled Nicky from her bedroom.

Nicky had been out at a book launch the night before and was going into work late. There were times when Connie envied her sister her fabulous job and this was one of them. In St Matilda's, even if you'd been in the school till midnight every night for a whole week during the end-of-term run of a play—*Lady Windermere's Fan* last year—there was no option for arriving later in the morning to make up for it. Classes started at ten to nine and both pupils and teaching staff were in trouble if they were late. Whereas at Peony Publishing, where Nicky was an assistant editor, when there was a book launch the night before, some laxity was given with regards to office hours the following morning.

Connie pulled her fleecy pyjamas back on and marched into the kitchen to begin rummaging through the big cupboard where the vacuum cleaner, the ironing board and the mop lived. It was crammed with junk and many weekends started with Connie deciding that this was the one where she'd tidy it out. Sadly, this never happened. The lure of buying the Saturday papers and enjoying them in Titania's Palace with a latte and a couple of cupcakes always won out.

'Damn, blast and double blast!' Connie gave up. It was nearly eight and she had to be out the door by twenty past. In the bathroom, she performed an imperfect toilette with an inch of lukewarm bath water, then ran through her normal high-speed make-up application. There was no point doing too much, as working in a girls' school had taught her that it was impossible to compete with the professional level of make-up application the girls managed. Any dodgy eyeliner work would be noticed and, if it was the fifth years, commented upon.

'Miss O'Callaghan, what happened to your eyes?'

Connie would not be able to resist a joke under the circumstances, which the fifth years loved, and

68

which the principal, Mrs Caldwell, hated.

'You're too familiar with the girls, Ms O'Callaghan,' she'd sniff.

Connie no longer cared about the principal's dressing downs. She liked being able to have fun with her pupils and the day she could no longer crack a joke, she'd give up teaching.

Now, she dressed in navy, with black tights, her voluminous grey coat and flat black shoes. Unlike her sister, who was of fairy proportions, Connie had taken after her father's side of the family and was five nine in her socks. Another reason it was hard finding a man. The world was full of small men who took it as a personal insult to their masculinity if a woman was taller than them. Comments about Napoleon only enraged them further.

'Did you find it?' Nicky hung on the door jamb, half asleep, wearing bed socks and a stripey nightie. Her highlighted hair was sticking out at all angles, yesterday's mascara was creased round her brown eyes, but she was still pretty. Connie never thought for a moment about whether it was difficult having a sibling so gorgeous. In her eyes, Nicky was just Nicky, the baby sister Connie had longed for and had mothered ever since she was born.

'No, I didn't. Start running a bath now if you want to wash without developing hypothermia.'

'Crap,' muttered Nicky. 'I need to wash my hair.'

'What time are you due in work?' Connie asked. 'Patsy will fit you in for a quick wash and blow-dry, I'm sure.'

Both sisters loved the old-fashioned hair salon round the corner.

Nicky rubbed her eyes. 'Yeah, I suppose.'

Connie whisked a brush through her hair, it was her crowning glory, their mother liked to say. Her hair was shoulder length, the rich brown of a cinnamon stick and glossier than any L'Oreal commercial. Her eyes were large like her sister's but they were a plain old brown and didn't flash with amber fire the way Nicky's did. Compared to Nicky, Connie knew she was ordinary and she didn't mind, because Nicky deserved all that was good and wonderful. But sometimes, just sometimes, Connie wished she was beautiful too.

*   *   *

Unlike the rest of the planet, where being paired-up was practically compulsory for everyone from humans to swans, it was easy to be single in St Matilda's. Many of the teachers had been there donkey's years and the place was split fifty-fifty between married and single. The scattering of nuns from the convent helped. Old Sister Benedict, who'd been in the order since the Pope was in short pants, froze in horror if she so much as heard anyone discussing boyfriends. The equally old but entirely adorable Sister Laurence looked fondly on any talk of the opposite sex, but believed—as she often told wide-eyed girls in her religious education classes—that men were innocent folk and intelligent women knew better than to rely on them for anything.

'A career, girls, a career is the answer!' was her mantra.

Nobody in the staffroom set up dates and nobody in the school looked down on anyone for being single, apart, perhaps from Sylvie Legrand, who had wanted to get married since she knew such a thing existed.

Today was Sylvie's last day at St Matilda's before her wedding. Sylvie taught French, chemistry and, unofficially, how to wear a scarf like a good Parisian. Chic was a hopelessly inadequate word to describe her. Connie felt another word needed to be invented, something with greater scope to encompass how utterly glamorous Sylvie managed to be for all that she wasn't particularly good looking.

It was a talent, Connie decided.

'You look tired,' were Sylvie's welcoming words to her in the staffroom.

Tactless was another inadequate word to describe Sylvie—or perhaps the tactlessness was just an absence of Irish flummery. *Plámás*, as it was named in the Irish language. Plaw-maws. Even if a person were half dead and in urgent need of medical assistance, in the Irish rulebook it was customary to say, 'You're looking *great!*'

Connie liked the Irish kindness better, but then which one of them was getting married in a few days and which one was pathetically single? Maybe men liked straight-talking women and didn't rate ones who were trained to say the right thing instead of the honest thing.

She might have saved herself years of boredom if she'd said, 'I don't fancy you,' within minutes of each new date instead of spending weeks working up to saying something kinder that approximated to the same thing.

'I stayed up late watching the *Mad Men* box set,' Connie admitted to Sylvie now. There was no

71

point lying to her French colleague, she'd get it out of Connie, one way or the other.

'Why always the box sets?' demanded Sylvie, who tended to get more exotically French, losing all sense of grammar, when she was irritated. 'Why not the wine bar or the salsa classes, huh?'

Sylvie had dragged Connie to a tango class once. It had not been a success. As with life in general, there hadn't been enough men to go round and few of them were tall enough to partner Connie.

'I like box sets,' Connie pointed out. 'And I've given up wine bars and salsa classes for good. Anyway, you can make me look less tired later, for tonight. I'll need a lot of that under-eye-bag-banisher thing you use.'

It was Sylvie's hen night that evening and the teachers who were invited were all going to Sylvie's house first to get ready. Connie suspected it was so that all of them would be turned out to her French friend's high standards and not let her down in the restaurant.

It would not be a wild, crazy night, partly because it was a week night and partly because Sylvie didn't like wild nights. It was to be a dinner in an elegant French restaurant in the city. No mad drinking in a crazy bar, and definitely no wearing of L-plates and fake wedding veils for Sylvie.

In a few days, Sylvie would fly home to Paris for her wedding to the gorgeous Isaac, a tall, dark Belfast man with saturnine good looks and a low, deep voice. She'd met him at a rugby match in Dublin and he'd swept her off her feet. Only a few of the staff, Connie included, would be attending the wedding. The principal had been very annoyed that it was taking place in the middle of term, but

72

Sylvie had somehow talked her round. Isaac's brother would be home from Australia, Sylvie's sister would be back from Argentina: with family dotted around the globe, the time suited perfectly. Sylvie didn't want a little thing like work to get in the way.

Tonight, Sylvie would look stunning, no matter what she wore. Connie herself planned to dress in a pair of black jeans with a loose chiffon blouse, which hid a multitude. Thirty-nine was definitely a watershed in terms of figure. Connie couldn't seem to shift that extra bit of fat around her middle.

Luckily, Connie never felt any hint of envy towards her friend. Sylvie was just Sylvie, you couldn't change her.

Connie's mother didn't see it the same way and was forever anxiously telling her daughter that there was no point hanging around with a glamorous woman like Sylvie, because all the men went mad for her, and no wonder Connie was still on her own.

'With friends like that, how do you expect to find a man? The coal won't shine beside the diamond, will it?'

There wasn't really an answer to that. Her mother didn't mean it to be cruel: just honest in a worried way.

Perhaps once Sylvie was married, her mother would look round and find something else to blame for Connie's inability to get a man. Connie sighed at the thought.

'I won't have time to make you all up,' Sylvie was protesting. 'There are eight of us. I am not Wonderwoman.'

'You are to us,' laughed Connie. 'All right, I'll plaster a bit more make-up on later. We won't let you down.'

'Tell me again: what do you mean, you are giving up wine bars?' Sylvie demanded. She was like a dog with a bone when it came to Connie's single status. 'You will be alone forever if you do not try. Do you think men lurk on the streets waiting for us to find them? *Non!* We have to look for them!'

'I have looked,' protested Connie. 'I'm exhausted looking. I want him to start looking for me.'

'How will he find you, if you are at home watching television?'

'He'll have a ladder and he'll see me in my window,' sighed Connie. 'I don't know. I give up, Sylvie. I'm taking this month off.'

'You need a facial,' said Sylvie, peering at Connie's face with a beady eye. 'You are all congested. Too many pastries. Look at your pores!'

'You can make me look fabulous tonight and hide my big pores,' said Connie, and hurried off to her class.

The day flew.

Her congested pores notwithstanding, Connie had a quick sandwich and a cup of tea at lunch in the staffroom where a cake was cut for all those people who wouldn't be coming to the hen night. Then she headed to the library because it was the only quiet place to do some marking.

After lunchbreak, she had the first years, followed by double history with the fifth years, which she wasn't looking forward to because she was too tired for their antics. You had to be in the whole of your health for a giddy bunch of sixteen-year-olds.

Today, there was wild excitement because they'd got something planned as a send-off for Miss Legrand, who was their class teacher.

After history class, there was to be a small party for her departure. Needless to say, not a shred of work was being done and as Connie watched her students pretend to read about Charles Stewart Parnell, she knew they were all communicating with each other about the party. Notes, sign language, whispered sentences—if only they were as good at history as they were at plotting.

There was absolutely no point in trying to counter this behaviour. A wise older teacher had once told Connie that a class is like a tidal wave and once it turns, it turns. 'Save the lesson for another day, or you'll go insane with impotent rage.'

She'd also told Connie that deafness was a useful aid for teachers too.

So Connie admired the girls' party hairstyles and thought about how it felt like the end of an era. When this school year was over, Sylvie would be leaving St Matilda's for good. It seemed like only yesterday that the two women had started out as new teachers in the school together. Now Sylvie would be gone to start married life with her husband in his home city, Belfast, and Connie would stay on at St Matilda's, growing old with the nuns.

The school bell rang lustily, taking Connie by surprise. She liked to give pupils a five-minute warning near the end. But today, it didn't look as if the fifth years cared. They leapt to their feet and swept the books off their desks at high speed.

'Bye, Miss O'Callaghan,' they murmured as they raced out, dropping their textbooks on her desk.

So many of them were impossibly glamorous, Connie thought. Their long shaggy hair was exquisitely styled each morning. Outwardly, they looked like confident young Valkyries. It was only through teaching the girls that a teacher would learn how young and worried they sometimes were.

It seemed as if half the school was crammed into the fifth years' classroom by the time Connie made her way there. Sylvie was sitting on the desk surrounded by cards and with a giant sparkling gift bag on her lap.

'Please tell me this is a present and not something to do with a tampon and red ink from the art room?' Sylvie said loudly.

The assembled girls roared with laughter.

'You laugh, huh? But poor Mr Shaw, he did not laugh, *non?*'

Only Sylvie could get away with a joke about the trick played on the quiet maths and physics teacher.

'*Non, mademoiselle!*' the girls roared back.

Finally, Sylvie unwrapped the package inside the gift bag. It contained two Irish crystal champagne glasses with a bottle of champagne.

'There is writing,' Sylvie exclaimed. '*For Mademoiselle Legrand, for the most romantic day of your life, Year Five.* I love it, girls!' she cried.

Connie, who'd been expecting a jokey present or even a red satin negligee with white marabou—it was from the fifth years, after all—choked back a tear. Why this touched her after a whole day thinking about Sylvie's hen night, she had no idea.

But suddenly, she realised that Sylvie was going to have the most romantic night of her life next month when she got married, while she, Connie, had no hope of ever sharing something so special with a loved one. Sylvie would now have what Connie wanted so much: her own family. Sylvie and her husband had bought a pretty three-bedroomed house in Belfast. Everyone had seen the photographs.

The second bedroom was to be a spare bedroom and Sylvie was going to keep her clothes in it like a proper dressing room, she'd informed Connie. The third bedroom was to be the nursery.

'I will paint it yellow. Yellow is good whether it is a boy or a girl,' Sylvie pointed out.

Connie had said nothing but thought again of how wonderful it must be to be able to plan your life with such confidence. Sylvie was getting married and she was sure that a baby would follow. She'd probably got her eye on a diamond band in Tiffany's to mark the birth of said baby.

Connie had nothing planned for the rest of her life.

She'd never cried watching *Gone with the Wind* or even *Sleepless in Seattle*, but now, standing at the back of the fifth-year classroom, she wanted to burst into tears.

*   *   *

Nicky O'Callaghan beamed as she skipped down the steps of the house and hopped into the driver's seat of her car. She almost waved at the silver-haired, older lady who lived in the apartment below hers, and who was sitting in her bay window,

77

looking out on to the square. Such was her happiness, that Nicky wanted to smile and wave at everyone. But the woman wasn't really staring at Nicky in her car: she was gazing into the middle distance, there but somehow not there.

She did, however, send a bright glinting smile at the man at the roadworks where she got held up for ten minutes. Nicky's smile was infectious.

The man at the roadworks looked back suspiciously. It was unheard of for gorgeous blonde women with glossy red lips to grin at him with delight when he was on kango-hammer detail for roadworks that brought the traffic down Amiens Street to a standstill.

He chanced a wink at her as the lights finally turned green and she managed to edge her Mini Cooper forward and off down the bare expanse of road ahead.

And she winked back! He decided he'd chance the lottery at lunchtime. It was definitely his lucky day.

Nicky wanted to wink and smile at everyone today. Not that she didn't smile a lot anyway: she had a lot to smile about, she knew. But today was special.

Today was her first day as an engaged woman. Last night, after the book launch, Freddie had taken her out to a late dinner.

There was rarely much in the way of food at book launches, just nibbles and wine, so if you stayed too long, you ate nothing, drank too much and made a holy show of yourself in front of your colleagues, your boss, and if you were spectacularly unlucky, press photographers too. Nicky was far too clever to fall into that trap, so she drank water at launches and ate afterwards.

She'd been telling Freddie all about the author's speech, and how gratifying it was to have been thanked by the author.

'Scarlett's the first author I've edited from the start of her career. I feel like I've been a part of everything that's happened, I can't tell you, Freddie, how amazing that feels . . .'

When she'd started in Peony as an editorial assistant five years ago, she'd had to prove herself by spending a lot of time doing the vital but painstaking copy-editing work that took place after the author and their main editor had agreed on a final manuscript. Scarlett Ryan was the first author she'd been let loose on, so to speak, and when Scarlett's debut novel had been a success, she'd insisted that Nicky was part of that success.

'Dominic, the managing director, was there and Scarlett kept saying how much she owed me and what a fabulous editor I was! She said I'd *showed her how to find her true voice*. It was wonderful.' She stopped long enough to take a sip of wine.

'This is delicious,' she remarked appreciatively. 'Expensive, I bet. I thought you were broke, Freddie. Are we celebrating something?'

And that's when it had happened. Freddie, wunderkind of Mesmer Marketing, boyishly handsome with his floppy dark fringe, hopeless at laundry but sterling when it came to doing dishes, had slipped off his chair in the fashionable Le Pinot Noir bistro, got to his knees and whipped a small box from his inside breast pocket.

Normally, nothing surprised Nicky. She was legendary for it. She noticed everything, from how low they were on milk in the office fridge, to how up-to-date the department was with getting through the slush pile of manuscripts. But in the excitement over Scarlett, she hadn't registered Freddie's air of excitement. She noticed it now, along with the glint of something that sparkled.

'It's a diamond,' she said in shock, fingers brushing Freddie's as she held the small blue box.

'Do you like it?'

The ring was clearly new but made to look old, with a small round diamond surrounded by teenier specks of diamonds in a platinum band. For all her fondness for labels and fashionable clothes, Nicky was a romantic at heart. Huge diamonds meant *nothing*. This tiny but beautiful ring was proof of Freddie's love for her. He'd gone and chosen it himself, which was quite something because Nicky had strong opinions on such things.

'Here,' she said, holding out her hand. 'Put it on.'

With shaky fingers, he took the ring from the velvet surround and slid it on to Nicky's delicate finger.

'Oh.' They both sighed as they admired it.

Nicky was so petite that on her finger, the tiny ring looked totally at home.

'I was thinking,' said Freddie, 'let's get married soon. We don't have the money for a big bash, so we could have a small wedding. Nobody will mind, everyone's broke, things are different now.' He rushed on. 'That way, we can save money for somewhere to live. What do you think?'

She touched her newly beringed hand to his cheek.

'I think that's a great idea. I was never a fan of those big, expensive weddings,' she said gently, she, who had once upon a time dreamed of two hundred guests, a live band, wall-to-wall cream roses and a marquee decorated in floaty white muslin. Now that the time was here, all that seemed quite immaterial. They would be married and that was all that mattered.

People in the restaurant clapped as they watched Nicky gently kiss her fiancé.

Neither of the pair took a blind bit of notice of the rest of their meal. They talked about limited guest lists and how they'd present the plan to their respective parents to ensure there was no griping over endless second cousins once removed who now wouldn't be invited.

In the taxi on the way home, they sat in joyous silence and held each other. Nicky honestly had never felt such peace.

Now all that remained was to tell her sister. Nicky knew that Connie would never begrudge her happiness. On the contrary, Connie had always wanted everything for her little sister. But this was different. This was telling the person she loved second best in the world that she was getting married—something Connie had always longed to do but had the opportunity snatched away from her by that waster Keith.

Connie had always done everything first: moved away from the family home in Wexford, gone to college, got a job, bought her own place. Now, for once, Nicky would be breaking new ground first and for Connie that was bound to be hard.

She'd be abandoning Connie too. The apartment in Golden Square belonged to Connie, although Nicky paid rent, but they'd lived there together since Connie had bought it ten years before.

For the first time in years, Connie would be

totally on her own. Would she be all right? Nicky wondered.

*   *   *

When she got home after the hen night, Connie went into Nicky's bedroom where her sister was half-watching an old film, and lay down on the bed next to her. Severalunaccustomed glasses of wine sloshed around inside her, along with dessert wine—Sylvie had insisted, although it was sickly sweet—and what with the wine and the melancholy, she began to cry.

'I'm so happy for her about the wedding and everything,' Connie sobbed. 'I love Sylvie and she deserves to be happy, but Nicky, don't I deserve it too?'

Nicky had looked so stricken that Connie sobered up at high speed, and apologised.

'I'm fine, honestly. Everyone was getting maudlin by the end of the night, and I kept thinking about Keith—not that I'd want him back, or anything, but you know, it was my chance to settle down and . . .' She stopped talking. She couldn't, wouldn't, say anything about her diminishing chance to have a baby. It was too painful to speak out loud, even to Nicky. Better to keep it hidden in her heart.

'Oh, Connie, I'm so sorry.' Nicky still looked stricken.

Connie clambered up the bed to hug her sister. 'Don't mind me, I'm a mad old lady, I'll turn into one of those ferocious spinsters of the parish and you can get married and have eleven children, and I'll drive them all insane. We can take over the whole of this house and all the kids in Golden Square will be afraid of me. Mad Miss O'Callaghan who lives with her sister and the eleven children. What do you think?' she grinned at Nicky, who gave her a very half-hearted grin back.

Eventually, Connie got off the bed.

'I'll have a terrible headache in the morning,' she said. 'Please, I beg you, get me out of bed at seven thirty. Mrs Caldwell will be like a weasel if the hen-night people are late in.' The Principal considered good time-keeping to be on a par with saving the world from destruction.

'I'll wake you,' Nicky said, in such a voice of gloom that Connie spent the next hour in bed berating herself for worrying her sister. Some people got what they wanted in life and some didn't. it was futile to cry over being a have-not rather than a have. Life *wasn't* fair. She knew that.

And finally, exhaustion got the better of her and she dozed off.

5

Potatoes

The famine road isn't far from our house. It's a stony route to nowhere, built to give men a few coppers when the countryside was riddled with potato blight. Perhaps your generation won't hear much about the famine—it's true, we've grieved enough about it, but it would be a pity if people forgot the past.

Ireland isn't the only country to have suffered starvation. Agnes said she heard them talk at the Fitzmaurices about the people out in Africa who have nothing. There are little babies with bellies big from hunger. It must break a mother's heart to watch a little one starve and not be able to find a crumb to feed it. It would break mine. A bit like the people eating grass here when there was nothing else.

Every time I pass that famine road, I thank the Good Lord for what we've got. Thanks for you, Eleanor, thanks for my beloved Joe, thanks for Agnes, the best sister ever. I get on my knees to say thanks for all the gifts I've been given. To some people, I haven't got much, but I know I've had the best of life.

Sister Benedict in the convent says not to feel guilty over our luck in life. We all have our crosses to bear, she says, even though not everyone can see them. All lives have some pain.

This isn't the story the canon says, mind you. Pain is what you get for sinning, according to him.

The canon has lived a sheltered life and sees every sin as worse than the cities of Sodom and Gomorrah put together. You should hear him at funerals. Most poor corpses are two inches from hellfire, to hear the canon speak. I don't think he's in his right mind. There's no joy in the man. God is kind, my mam used to say. I like to pray to that God and not the canon's one.

It's strange that the potato blight killed so many and still we live off the potato. Your father never thinks it's a proper dinner unless there are potatoes in it. Agnes is the same, for all the fine meals she's had at the big house.

My mam's Cally is the best dish you'll ever have with potatoes. There's many names for it, Colcannon is one, but in this part of the West of Ireland, we call it Cally. Take some nice floury potatoes and boil them in their skins. When they're falling apart, *tear the skins off, mash them, make a round shape on the plate and then pour the sauce into the middle—melted butter, with a little hot milk and some chopped spring onions. Then eat. When life is falling apart all around you, this is as good a comfort as any, I promise you.*

*　　　*　　　*

Every morning since she'd arrived in Golden Square a week ago, Megan had woken to the noise of building work coming from across the street. The sounds of drills, diggers and builders laughing were comforting, familiar. There was always somebody building or extending something on her street in London: she was used to it as the background of birdsong and bleating horns from the street below.

So every morning, waking to the building hum, she enjoyed a sliver of time thinking that life was still glorious. She'd stretch, revelling in the feel of her body between the sheets, the body that Rob loved. For one misguided second it seemed that the day lay ahead of her with dazzling brightness: Rob's smile as he saw her, the director's smile as he told her that her performance was breathtaking . . .

Then she'd wake up properly and real life shoved out her fantasy dreamworld. Everyone hated her, her career was over and her heart was broken.

The next step in the morning routine would be awareness of something furry shifting on top of the duvet and then a rough tongue would lick whatever part of Megan was out of the covers.

'Cici?' she said the first morning and the shape had wriggled with delight.

Leonardo liked to lie on the floor on the other side of the bed and Megan's sleepy voice was all he needed to start his welcoming proceedings.

Both dogs would clamber on top of her, licking and wagging their tails eagerly.

After a week, they had the routine down to a fine art. With enough licking and snuffling, they could force Megan out of bed and into the kitchen to give them dog biscuits, and then, once she'd had her morning coffee and cigarette, she might take them for a walk. Nora, of course, would have gone to work.

It was her own fault, she knew, for setting a precedent that first day. But today she had a mission to accomplish on the walk. She'd decided she needed a disguise.

It took ages to clip the leads on because the dogs were dancing about so much, but she wanted to take them with her because she figured she'd looked less strange wearing glasses she didn't need and a dark bandana to cover her hair if she was hauling two dogs along. Mad people often had dogs. Once out of the door, the dogs pulled towards the garden in the square but Megan dragged them in the other direction.

There was a highly glamorous hairdresser's about half a mile away, all smoky glass and exquisite hairstylists. She wouldn't go there. They'd take one look at her and know exactly who she was, and in the fashionable clubs of the city—which they would frequent—the news of both her arrival and her new hair colour would be that night's gossip. On the west side of the square, however, tucked in front of the Delaney council flats, was Patsy's Salon, a place that had probably looked old and faded twenty years ago but which she'd noticed the night she'd arrived. She'd found the number in the phone book yesterday but it just rang out. So today she took a chance and went to make an appointment. If Patsy's was closed, she'd just buy a home dye kit.

Patsy's was remarkably busy for a place that clearly hadn't been redecorated for many years. There were three baby-blue basins, all being used, and two women under dryers, talking loudly to each other over the noise.

One girl was delicately putting Velcro rollers into a very elderly lady's silvery purple hair.

Megan stood for a moment watching.

'Can I help you?' said a woman with curled hair an unnatural red, who emerged from the back of the shop.

She had to be fifty, and boasted an hourglass figure all poured into very tight Capri jeans and a red gingham blouse fastened by buttons which looked to be under considerable strain. Megan would not have been surprised if the woman had launched into the chorus of 'D.I.V.O.R.C.E.' right there and then.

'I'm Patsy,' the woman added. 'What can we do for you?'

'I need a haircut and a change of colour.' The words came rushing out. 'I want to look different,' Megan said. 'Totally different.'

Patsy didn't blink. Women had come into her shop before looking forlorn and needing a new look. You never knew what life would throw at you. Patsy's response was to help any woman when she could and not ask questions.

'Take a pew. I'll be with you in five minutes.'

'N-now?'

'No appointment necessary,' said Patsy, pointing to a sign that said just that on the salon's pink brocade-papered wall.

'That's unusual,' said Megan, still a little startled by the speed of it all.

'I never know what's coming up next,' Patsy replied, in a voice that said she'd seen quite enough, thank you very much, and would it all stop coming, please. 'Sit down right here.'

'Oh no, I can't stay,' Megan said, recovering herself. 'I brought my aunt's dogs. I was simply trying to make an appointment.'

Patsy looked outside where Cici and Leonardo were tied to a lamp post and looking in with abject misery. 'They're not used to being left, are they?'

'No. I'd better go.' Megan felt inexplicably as if she might cry. Nothing worked; she was a stupid screw-up. She couldn't even think properly.

Patsy surprised her with a soft hand on Megan's elbow.

Which was when Megan really started to cry.

'A man! It has to be about a man,' nodded the little old lady with the silver blue hair. 'They're all bollixes, except when they're small.'

'Stick to cats,' said one of the ladies under the dryer.

'No—dogs,' interrupted the other one. 'Cats are like men: stay when they feel like it and off out the

89

door when they don't.'

Patsy ignored the philosophical chatter, went outside, untied the dogs and brought them inside the salon.

'Sit,' she commanded. And they sat.

She then calmly fed the two dogs a couple of plain biscuits, put a cup of unasked-for sweet tea in front of Megan and gently began unwinding her bandana.

'Right,' she said, looking at the platinum curls that brought movie-star glamour into the salon. 'I see what you mean.'

She grabbed a towel, looped it expertly around Megan's head, and busied herself mixing up colour. In ten minutes, Megan was unrecognisable in that her head was covered in gunk and she was perched under a dryer with a very well-thumbed copy of a craft magazine. The dogs, somehow soothed by the hum of Patsy's salon and stuffed full of biscuits, lay at her feet and slept. There were other magazines around. Gossipy ones with glamorous pictures, but Patsy knew precisely who Megan was. Which was why she'd given her a magazine with knitting patterns and advice on how to turn a tea towel into a cushion.

'Will I take much off?' she asked when Megan was back at the mirror with wet, dark hair.

'What would make me look different?' Megan asked.

'I'd go short, if I were you,' said Patsy. 'Very short. You've got the face for it. And believe me, you'll look different.' She began to cut.

Megan thought of Freemont Jackson, the Covent Garden artiste who'd been doing her hair for four years now, and how removing so much as a centimetre was a matter for an hour-long consultation. When she'd gone from being long-haired to having shoulder-length hair, he'd nearly had to be medicated. Well, *more* medicated.

'Those luscious curls, they're so *you!*' he'd said wistfully.

And now here was Patsy, cutting away calmly, taking large chunks from Megan's wet hair, and there wasn't a dramatic hairdressing flounce in sight.

Megan felt unmoved as her shorn hair fell on to the salon's black nylon gown. It was cathartic having this done, almost like wearing a hair shirt. She was punishing herself, doing away with the sexy, girlish creature who'd got into so much trouble.

As Patsy cut, Megan closed her eyes and tried not to think about Rob Hartnell's hands as he ran them through her hair.

'You're so beautiful,' he'd said. 'My fairy princess.'

In the luxury of their hotel in Prague, he'd held her constantly, his hands on her face, around her waist, stroking her hair. She'd felt like a fairy princess in this magical city, with the sugared almond cupolas outside their windows, and the dark, romantic beauty of the Hotel Sebastien inside.

'Let's run away together,' he'd said. But he was the one who'd run, alone.

Two hours after she'd entered Patsy's, Megan looked at her new self in the mirror. For a woman whose own hair owed little to subtlety, Patsy was very good at hair colour. Megan had never had dark hair in her life. Even in films, the closest she'd come to dark was a mousy blonde. But now, with the inky black crop that clung to her small head, she looked like another person. She'd relied on her hair, she realised: relied on sexily flicking back blonde tendrils. It had *defined* her in some way. Blonde, pretty, child-woman.

With her skin a little tanned, she looked as if she could be from a different race. An exotic Arab woman with strange olive green eyes, dark eyelashes and a wary expression, no longer the kittenish golden girl but a watchful, grown-up woman who had seen something of life. Now, her straight nose made her look exotic instead of ethereal. The fairy princess was gone for good. It was very odd to see this stranger in the mirror. Odd, and a huge relief. Nobody would recognise her now. Megan wasn't sure she recognised herself. 'Thank you.'

'It suits you,' Patsy said.

Megan wasn't a hugger, but she felt like hugging Patsy now.

'Come back when the roots grow out,' Patsy said. 'If you're around, that is.'

As Megan paid about a tenth of what she'd have paid Freemont for the same work, she replied: 'I'll be around.'

*   *   *

A part of Megan's new routine was dropping into the chiropody practice downstairs at lunchtime to say hello to Nora. She'd gone in impromptu on the first day and encountered the receptionist, a bird-like woman with wildly fluffed-up grey curls and lots of purple mascara, who cheerfully told her that Nora was with a client.

'You must be Nora's niece,' the bird-like lady had said with delight. 'I'm Angeline, well, people call me Birdie.' She held out a tiny hand and Megan shook it.

'Yes, I'm Megan,' Megan said, waiting for the inevitable moment of '—oh' as recognition hit.

It never came.

'Nora says you're here on a break,' Angeline had gone on happily. 'I must say, a holiday sounds gorgeous right now. I could do with one myself. I normally go to the Canaries in the winter, but you know how it is: money's tight!'

She even sounded like a bird, Megan decided, with that chirruping voice. No wonder she got called Birdie.

'Have you ever been to the Canaries?' Angeline went on. 'Well.' She didn't wait for an answer. 'Gorgeous, that's what they are, gorgeous. Even if I say so myself. Spain is great, altogether. I have a friend, and she goes to Alicante for the whole of the winter with her husband, and it's cheaper than being here. Miles cheaper, she says.'

Megan nodded. Nothing else was required.

'You were walking the dogs, I saw you,' Angeline continued. 'I like dogs, but cats are very good company. Sir Rollo, he's my cat, a Persian blue. Picky eater, I can tell you, but he's so gentle. Never killed a mouse in his life!'

'Do you prefer being called Angeline or Birdie?' asked Megan.

'Birdie!'

Megan sat down in one of the waiting-room chairs. There was something peaceful in listening to Birdie's chatter.

'Do you live around here?'

'No,' shrieked Birdie. 'I wish I did. I love Golden Square. I'm on the avenue, it's not as pretty but we have a cycle path!'

Having got used to Birdie's chatter, Megan now dropped in every day. Birdie enjoyed discussing the soaps from the night before and, on occasion, the weather.

'Cooler today but the real-feel is not too polar,' Birdie might say.

On cold days, she wore two sets of thermals.

'See! Anthracite with pink ribbons!' She pulled a shred of thermal fabric up from her flat bosom for inspection. 'Nice thermals are so hard to come by. I don't like those white ones that go grey in the wash.'

'Where did you get those?' asked Megan.

'The Internet. Fabulous bits and bobs online.'

Between clients, Nora came out and chatted too, but they talked more generally of the next client, how the dogs had behaved on their walk and if Megan would organise dinner.

It was clear to Megan that her aunt and Birdie didn't talk about soaps or frillies on the internet.

She said as much to Birdie.

'Nora's a woman for science,' Birdie explained. 'She's not like you and me. We're girlie girls. Even though your hair is not girlie. Patsy did it for you?'

Megan reached up to touch the shorn dark locks. It was still strange to feel the nakedness of her jawline and neck.

'I wanted something different.'

'Very Ingrid Bergman,' pronounced Birdie. 'I'd try it myself, but I like the bouffant look.'

After dropping into the clinic, Megan was in the habit of walking through the pretty little square en route to Titania's Palace. The eccentrically decorated tearooms looked like something you'd expect to find in an Austrian ski resort, complete with pine furniture, red sprigged curtains and Tiffany lamps casting an amber glow over the place. Even the pastries and buns were unusual, with lots of flaky pastry things dusted with icing sugar and the Greek honey-and-nuts dessert baklava instead of the usual scones. Everything about the place was comforting, from the comfort food inside the polished glass case to the friendly chatter going on all around.

Megan, who was used to a life of not eating, felt a pang of hunger as she looked at the cakes, but passed them by and asked for an Americano with an extra shot of espresso.

'Of course, my dear. Anything else?' said the woman behind the counter. She had very dark eyes and slanted eyebrows to match, almost like a person with Native American blood, Megan thought. Her face was alight with motherly warmth.

Please don't be nice to me, Megan thought, or I'll cry.

'No,' she mumbled. Then added: 'Thanks.'

She took her coffee and sat at a window table where she could look out. It wasn't that she wanted to see anything outside. These days, she couldn't focus on anything for long because all she could see was the past. But at least when she was staring out, people were less likely to recognise her. After years of trying to be noticed, Megan Flynn wanted to disappear.

*   *   *

Megan loved members' clubs. The ones where you had to have money and powerful friends to get in. Money wasn't quite enough, you had to *be* somebody.

She loved being somebody. Even the tiring bits— 'It's Megan Bouchier! Can I have your autograph, I love all your films' when she was coming out of the changing rooms in the Oxford Street Top Shop—were wonderful.

Other stars in her firmament complained about it loudly, but Megan never did.

According to Carole, her agent, it was due to lack of attention as a child. 'All the big ones are like that, sweetie. Nobody loved them enough when they were little and, by God, they're determined to make up for it now.'

Megan had laughed when Carole said that. 'Not all of them, surely?'

'Yes, all of them. And stop calling me Shirley. Oh, the old jokes are the best.'

They'd been in the Victory House Club at the time, drinking dirty mojitos—Carole's own concoction, which used two types of rum—to celebrate Megan getting the part in *The Warrior Queen*. Carole's business partner, Zara Scott, had joined them. Both in their mid-forties, tough and energetic, the two founders of Scott-Baird International worked hard to make sure their agency ranked as one of the most powerful in the business. It had been Zara who convinced the director of *Warrior Queen* to consider Megan for the part of the Roman princess. He hadn't wanted her to start with, he was looking for an unknown, not the girl who'd blown the screen away in a Cockney gangster movie where she'd had to wield a sawn-off shotgun. But Zara had persevered until he gave in and screen-tested Megan, and suddenly she was cast: a part many actresses would have killed for, playing opposite the craggy heart-throb Rob Hartnell in a historical epic.

On their third mojito, they'd moved on from sheer joy to discussing the ins and outs of Rob's marriage to the Tony and BAFTA-award winning actress, Katharine Hartnell.

'Everybody says Katharine and Rob have one of the strongest marriages in the business,' said Carole. 'I never really trust that type of schtick. Sounds like something made up for the papers.'

'No, it's supposed to be true,' said Zara. 'I have it on very good authority. Apparently Rob and Katharine are still crazy about each other. Hard to believe, isn't it?'

'Well, you wouldn't kick him out of bed for getting crumbs in it, would you?' Carole said. 'He's like a brunette Robert Redford, only sexier, if such a thing were possible. Lucky Katharine, that's all I can say.'

'She's pretty stunning too,' said Zara. 'For her age,' she added.

'Yes, for her age,' Carole agreed. 'Why do we say that about women? Nobody ever says a man is good for his age.'

Zara erupted into laughter. 'If you're going to go all soft on me, Carole, then get out of the business, will you?'

97

Carole finished her drink and looked around for the bar staff. 'Sorry, I slipped into nirvana there. Forgot that male actors are "distinguished" when they reach fifty, and female actors are finished, unless they want to play wise old grannies.'

'Or do lots of theatre,' Megan added.

'Katharine Hartnell has done a lot of theatre,' Carole went on. 'I've seen her in *Hedda Gabler*. She was mesmerising, and very beautiful.'

'Yes, she is beautiful,' said Megan.

'She's so creamily pale with those Spanish infanta eyes,' Zara observed. 'She must have had some work done.'

They all considered this.

'But not much, just mild tweaks. Not the full facelift, eyebrows-on-your-hairline job,' Zara finished.

'Less is more,' Carole said.

'Should I get botox?' asked Megan, examining her face in the mirrored surface of the table in front of her.

'It's too soon for you,' Carole advised. 'Later, maybe. The problem is doing too much of it, mind you. You've no idea how many people get hooked on it. Let's be honest, decent directors want some movement in the face. That porcelain doll look is on the way out. You can't act if you can't actually move any of the muscles in your face.'

'As long as you can move your lips to ask "What's my motivation in this scene?" when you have to snog Rob Hartnell!' teased Zara.

'Stop!' said Megan. 'I'm bloody terrified. He's an icon.'

'A very hot icon, and you have a huge love scene with him,' Carole said.

'That's making it worse, not better,' Megan laughed, although she was excited at the thought. This wasn't happening to anyone else, it was happening to her. She'd somehow got this magical part where she would be acting opposite a man she'd watched, rapt, like everyone else, on the Odeon screen when she'd been younger. She'd be up there on the screen with Rob. It was heady stuff.

'Don't worry.' Zara patted her hand. 'Carole or I will stand in for you on the day. You only have to ask. I can bear to snog Rob Hartnell if it's for a greater purpose.'

*   *   *

In Titania's Palace, Megan Flynn sat with her empty cup and looked at all the people around her. Once, she wouldn't have envied them anything. They had dull lives, she'd have told herself: the women with the grocery bags pooled around their feet, the young mothers with small children wriggling red-faced in high chairs, the men poring over crosswords or chatting just as avidly as the groups of women.

As she'd danced the night away in clubs and at wrap parties, posing for photographs and plotting with her agent about what she'd do next, Megan had thought these people were buried alive.

How could they not want to do what she did? How could they be happy in their humdrum lives?

But now she looked at them and she could see the lure of the simple life. They might have no excitement, but they were secure and happy in this cosy world of Golden Square.

None of them would be filled with anxiety at the prospect of the rest of their lives. None of them were waiting for someone to find them hiding out in Dublin. None of them had had their hearts broken. Or so she thought, in her self-centred way.

Was a boring life a good trade-off for that?

6

Mushrooms

Never underestimate the power of a simple mushroom. When I was young, Agnes and my mother would head off at dawn on summer's mornings to search for mushrooms. Nobody thought of growing them in the vegetable garden along with the potatoes and cabbage. Mushrooms were the fairies' gift to us, my mother would say: like soft pincushions scattered on the grass as the sun rose.

You had to be quick, mind, or else the cattle would trample them and they'd be gone.

Home with their pot of mushrooms, we'd put the fattest on top of the range and sprinkle a little salt on them. Roasted like that, with the heat rising up into the mushrooms and the pink pleated underbelly turning brown, they were the most delicious thing you'd ever eat.

They made a great feast with a bit of scrambled egg: a plate of earth brown mushrooms with the juices running out of them and the eggs like yellow clouds beside them.

Even now—and it's a long time since I walked a green field to pick a wild mushroom—I can still taste the freshness of one roasted on my mam's range.

It was the simplicity we loved. Agnes had told us of the grand feasts in the big house, with sauces you had to stir for hours.

Hollandaise for asparagus was the fashion at the time in the grand houses. I've since tried asparagus and all I can say is, give me a roasted mushroom any day.

But the humble mushroom is proof that sometimes the best things in life are found growing wild and free right under your nose. Don't rush so fast, Eleanor, that you can't see the wild mushrooms around you.

Two weeks into January and the rains came. Rae wasn't sure which was the lesser of two evils: the fact that the rain raised the temperature from an icy minus three in the early morning or the fact that at least when it was freezing, it didn't rain.

Will was awake and reading when Rae woke up one mid-January morning with the sound of torrential rain bouncing off the windows. She peered at him sleepily, then looked at the clock. Only six thirty, still dark.

She wriggled over in the bed and snuggled up against him, loving the solid heat of his body beside hers. He was always warm. She wore bedsocks and fleecy pyjamas, which she'd learned to like when she was menopausal and prone to night sweats.

She'd hated the sweats. Waking up to a cool film of perspiration and with her hair stuck to her head as if she'd been swimming.

But she'd found the loss of fertility even harder. Menopause was one of those words she winced at. The end of fertility. There was something horribly final about it.

Even if she was too old to have a child now, the *ability* to have one was something precious.

And yet the ability to have children had brought her pain along with joy. Rae could never look at a baby in a pram without feeling a surge of an old pain rise up in her.

'Hello, love,' said Will.

'You're awake early,' she murmured.

'Couldn't sleep. Did you sleep well?'

102

'Really well. Sorry you didn't.'

Rae lay for a moment more, doing what she'd done for so many years: gently nudging the past back into its box in her mind.

That done, she stretched luxuriously. She didn't have to get up for another hour. Bliss.

She loved lying in, half-sleep. When Anton had been little, this had been the thing she'd missed the most: the dreaming time at weekends before she got up to face the day. Anton had been a particularly early riser. He was born when she was twenty-nine. He was now the same age she was when she'd given birth to him. She tried to imagine her beloved son as a parent—not that there was any sign of him settling down yet.

He'd be a gentle and thoughtful dad, she thought. He'd been the tallest of his class for years, built like a rugby player but totally lacking the rugby player's ferocious sporting instinct. She'd always thought he'd work with animals in some way. She remembered the gentleness of him when he was sitting in the dog's basket, stroking her silky ears. Instead, he'd turned that sensitive, thoughtful side into political analysis.

And he was happy. That was all she wanted, really.

She was lucky, despite everything that had happened. She *must* remember that.

Rae's mind roved about, flitting into Titania's and the morning ahead. Patsy from the hair salon wanted a table for ten at lunchtime and a cake for a birthday.

'Candles?' Rae had asked on the phone.

'Definitely no candles,' Patsy had answered in her raspy, smoker's voice. 'She's gone beyond candles. But something with shoes would be nice. She loves shoes. They love you back, too.'

Rae laughed. She liked Patsy and her sharp, dry humour. Patsy was another person who hadn't been brought up in happy-familyville, Rae was sure of it. There was a sense of kinship between them, even though neither had ever said a word about their past to the other. But sometimes, you *knew.*

Patsy never looked at Rae as if she were a comfortable married woman who helped out with Community Cares to fill her spare time. She understood that Rae was helping herself by helping other people, in the same way that Patsy helped the women who turned up at Patsy's Salon sporting red eyes, black eyes and faces full of pain. Patsy welcomed them in, put the kettle on and made them beautiful. Beauty, like cups of tea in Titania's, was sometimes more than skin deep.

'I was thinking . . .' Will put down his book.

Rae struggled out of her half-dream and sat up against the pillows. 'You don't want to hurt yourself, love,' she teased.

In retaliation, Will stretched his long fingers under her armpit and found the tickliest place.

'You win,' she said, laughing.

'I was going to suggest a fabulous holiday to cheer us up after the winter,' Will said, 'but seeing as you think I'm Mr Thicko . . .'

Rae leaned up and nibbled his ear. 'Go on, Mr Thicko,' she said, 'you know I love you.'

'Well, I was thinking—before I was rudely interrupted, that we haven't had a holiday for two years. What about a cruise?'

Rae gave a little gasp of shock. She'd always

wanted to go on a cruise, but cruising holidays always seemed too expensive whenever she'd idled away time looking at the prices on the internet.

'Do you think we could afford it?' she said. Inside, she was thinking that they must be able to afford it. Will was the finance person in their marriage. Even though she managed Titania's, the café belonged to Timothy. He gave her budgets and sorted out cashflow. Rae herself had never been that comfortable about money.

Left to her, she and Will would never spend anything in case some catastrophe occurred and they ended up penniless. Her parents had been permanently broke. Her work with Community Cares showed her nothing but people who lived on the edge of the abyss.

'I was looking at the bank statements on the internet last night,' Will said. 'We could do it this year, for sure.'

'Yes, but would it be wise?' she asked. 'Who knows how long the economic downturn's going to last. You're not that busy, Timothy might turn round and close Titania's . . .' Rae felt the familiar twinge of money worries overcoming all thoughts of the holiday she'd always wanted.

'Listen, we are doing fine financially, love,' Will said. 'We don't spend money, Rae, we're so careful. The downturn is here and, yes, I'm doing half the work I was a year ago.' Will worked as an architectural technician for a local business and, as building work was at a standstill, he was working only on the company's projects in the Far East. 'But we're fine. We have no mortgage, we could survive on half the money we're earning now.'

Rae thanked God silently for the bequest from

Will's father that had allowed them to pay off their mortgage fifteen years previously. They'd bought the house long before the property boom, so they'd paid buttons for it compared to what it was now worth.

'Rae, how long have we been talking about a cruise?'

She allowed herself to relax. 'Since Anton was small and we knew there was no way in heck that he'd cope with being closeted on a boat,' she said fondly. 'Think of all those seaside holidays.'

'Crazy golf,' Will said.

They both groaned.

Anton had taken a mad passion for crazy golf when he was ten and no holiday was complete without a trip to a course. Will and Rae had spent many hours trying to whack golf balls into clown's mouths and windmills.

'Disney in Florida?' It had taken them three years to save up for that holiday.

'That was amazing,' Will said with a sigh. 'I don't think I could do any of those rollercoaster things again.'

'You were brilliant for going on them all,' Rae said. She was terrified of heights and just looking at some of Orlando's rides was enough to make her central nervous system go into shock.

'I'd love a cruise,' Rae said, and suddenly she wanted it so much she felt as if she might burst out crying with the sheer joy of it all. She *was* so lucky. She had her wonderful son, her wonderful husband, and now this unexpected treat. When she thought of how sad her life had looked all those years ago, she'd never dreamed she could have this happiness.

'I love you, Will,' she said, winding her arms round him.

'Mr Thicko loves you back,' he replied, kissing her. 'That's a very sexy outfit you're wearing,' he murmured, moving the neckline of her definitely unsexy fleecy pyjamas so he could nuzzle her neck.

'It's designed to drive men wild with lust,' Rae agreed. 'If it's disturbing you, I could take it off.'

'There's a thought,' he murmured, and then they didn't talk for a while.

*   *   *

Forty minutes later, they were up, dressed and getting breakfast. They moved easily around each other in the kitchen. Rae turned the coffee machine on, Will laid out cups and plates. She toasted some wholegrain bread; he found the marmalade she liked and put out plum jelly just in case they were in the mood for that.

It was the precise opposite to the way Rae had grown up; mornings then had been taut as a violin string, the air trembling with arguments that might erupt at any moment. One wrong word was all it took for Glory Hennessey to start throwing plates and insults at Paudge, with him throwing them right back. Rae had hated it, and had learned how to blend into the furniture so she didn't get involved.

As a child, she perfected the adult ability to take the emotional temperature of a room within two minutes of entering. If the room was happy, she'd do happy, but she wouldn't really *be* happy. Her happiness was surface only. Play along with them, but don't really relax because in two minutes

107

happy could be over and major screaming fit could be the order of the day.

When she was at school, the teachers thought her a strangely silent child. It was habit. Talking turned into saying the wrong thing so easily at home. Silence was the wisest option.

Even now, Rae could still feel her stomach clench when she heard people rowing.

It was no accident that she'd married a man who was gentle, thoughtful and rarely spoke without first considering the likely effect of his words on the other person.

By eight twenty it had stopped raining. Rae kissed Will on the cheek and they both headed off to work: she to Titania's down the street, and he to his office in the long back garden of their house.

She took the long route to Titania's, walking all around the garden itself, where the heady earthy smell of wet soil obliterated all other smells. Despite the wet, a couple of dogs were rolling in the grass, seemingly trying to wriggle themselves into the ground in pure pleasure.

Rae recognised Nora Flynn's little greyhound and her fluffy pompom of a dog that loved to bounce along self-importantly. But Nora wasn't with them. Instead, a slender dark-haired girl with an elfin face and big haunted eyes sat on the bench watching. She'd been in Titania's a few days before and Rae had recognised her as Nora's niece, the actress. Rae hadn't been able to recall her name, but was sure that when she'd last seen the girl, she'd been a pretty blonde slip of a thing, not a dark, sad waif.

Rae was aware that there had been some scandal. Someone at the counter in Titania's had talked about it recently, but she'd listened with only half an ear. Rae was wary of gossip. Often, she found it to be wildly inaccurate and she hated the casual cruelty of the celebrity magazines.

She'd wanted to welcome the girl—Megan, that was her name—to Golden Square the other day in the tearooms but she'd looked on the verge of tears, so Rae had decided to say nothing. There were times, she knew, when kindness tipped you over the edge.

Today, Megan looked less sad.

'Hello,' Rae said. 'I'm Rae Kerrigan, from the tearooms. You're Nora's niece, aren't you? Welcome back.' She inhaled the earthy scent of the park. Lots of people didn't appreciate nature in winter: she loved it, the sense of hibernation before the earth slowly unfurled herself into beauty again. 'It's beautiful here, isn't it? You could be in the middle of the countryside.'

The girl said nothing, just watched from under lowered lashes.

She was wary, Rae realised instantly. Speaking non-judgementally and idly was required.

'Aren't dogs funny? I love the way they enjoy the simple things.' On the grass in front of her, the fluffy dog was wriggling in an orgy of pleasure, making little contented snorts.

Rae bent to rub the dog's pink belly, murmuring 'Hello, pooch,' and she could sense the girl softening beside her. Animals were the true arbitrators of decency: it was hard to be the sort of person who'd convincingly stroke a dog and then lash out at the human being beside them.

'She loves that,' the girl said in a slightly husky voice.

109

'They all do,' Rae said, getting back to her feet. 'My son loves animals and when he was a kid, he was always coming home with things he'd rescued. Apparently, when a dog lets you pet its belly, it's at peace.'

'In Cici's case, she's at peace and she also thinks she's an Egyptian princess lying there waiting for the grapes to be peeled for her,' the girl said drily.

Rae laughed.

Sensing she was being talked about, Cici sat up, shook herself to get rid of all the debris from the grass, and went to have a proper sniff of Rae.

'She's adorable,' Rae said, reaching down for one more pet. 'See you around,' she added, with a smile at the girl.

'Yeah, sure.'

For the first time, the girl looked at Rae straight on and Rae caught her breath. She hadn't really seen her face in Titania's, not properly, because she'd kept her head down. But now, Rae could see she was lovely, like a silent movie star in an old photograph, with more angles and high points than a normal person's face.

And yet there was huge sadness there. Rae wished she'd paid more attention to whatever Megan's story was. Not for gossip's sake, but so she could understand. The gist, according to the people at the counter, was that she'd romanced a very married movie star. But this wary girl didn't look like a femme fatale to Rae. No, there was something more to it than that.

She left the square by the vine-covered black-and-gold iron gate opposite Titania's and said thanks for the blessings in her life.

It was one of her tenets: saying thanks every

110

single day. Some people wrote gratitude journals, and Rae liked the idea, but she preferred a more living gratitude method. Every day, she said thanks for what had happened.

Thank you for Will, thank you for allowing us to have a good life and be able to plan a holiday when so many other people are barely surviving. Thank you that my life is calm, not like that poor girl in the square.

And always she added, *Let Jasmine be happy too, please. Wherever she is, let her be happy.*

*   *   *

When the older woman from Titania's Palace had said hello to her, Megan had frozen. Not another fake friendly person. Some awful cow with sly eyes had sidled up to her in The Nook the previous day, and said: 'You look different with that hair, missy. Not so starry now.'

Megan had put down her basket and fled the shop.

But this woman—Rae, did she say her name was?—had been different. Nice. Welcoming.

Over the past two weeks, the routine of Golden Square had settled around Megan like a soft blanket. Each morning, after Nora had gone downstairs to the clinic, the dogs would gradually wake Megan. Animals were so much more comforting than people. There was never any censure in their eyes, except when they felt walking duties were being neglected.

Then Megan would make coffee for herself and stand outside the back door, often shivering in her dressing gown against the coolness, while she smoked a cigarette. It had been a long time since she'd lived in a house with a garden. It felt both strange and familiar. Nora wasn't much of a woman for gardening, so the long hundred-foot garden was a tangle of briars and old trees. Although Megan didn't know much about nature, she knew the biggest tree in the middle was a horse chestnut, but only because she could remember finding conkers under it when she was a kid.

Leonardo and Cici would head off into the undergrowth, noses glued to the ground as they followed scents. Then they'd return, wet from the morning dew and covered with bits of twig and grass, to sit beside her.

'I shouldn't be smoking beside you,' she found herself saying on many occasions. Which was strange, as she'd never worried about anyone else being affected by passive smoking before. Smoking had been part of who she was, like wearing mini dresses and little pixie boots. But here in Nora's house in Golden Square, smoking, a bit like her normal clothes, didn't quite work. It was, Megan felt, as if she'd sloughed off the old skin of Megan Bouchier and was returning to Megan Flynn.

A few weeks was all it had taken. Carole had phoned her mobile a few times with updates on the disaster area that was her career.

An earthquake in the Far East and another wave of terrorist threats, coupled with a pop star's illness and a reality TV star's live breast-reduction operation had now claimed the headlines from Megan the Mantrapper.

'You're so lucky,' Carole said. 'That earthquake's taken the heat off you. And thank God for

112

Destiny's boob op.'

Megan had actually watched a few minutes of the breast-reduction programme, until Nora had come into the sitting room and caught her at it.

'Merciful hour, they're like space hoppers under her chest. How did any surgeon do that to the poor woman?' Nora stared at the television in horror.

'He's taking them out now,' Megan said, searching for the remote control.

'Not a moment too soon. They look like they might burst. I'd say she hasn't seen her toes for a few years. Imagine the state of *her* feet.'

A rare bubble of real giggles erupted inside Megan.

'The press haven't given up, you know. Don't get complacent,' Carole warned.

'I'm not,' said Megan testily. 'I'm just fed up. I want to go back to work.'

At least if she was working, she wouldn't have time to think about what had happened with Rob.

'Until you get offered a few decent roles again— and not slasher movies from people who know you'll do anything now in desperation—you have to stay low. All decent offers have dried up. You hadn't signed the contract for the costume drama, so they don't want you any more. Thank fuck they'd finished with you in Romania. You'll have to fly over to London for post-production work, but that's not for another couple of months. You should do something charitable. Raise your profile in a more positive way. Do you want us to sort something out for you?'

'No,' said Megan, filled with misery at the cynicism of it all. Find a charity and pretend to care about something: that was the best advice

113

from her old world.

There was no news of Rob Hartnell, other than the usual media speculation about his whereabouts. He was on a billionaire's yacht in the Pacific or on a private island in the Caribbean or the Indian Ocean, depending which magazine you read.

'He was supposed to be shooting a movie in Stockholm now. One of those crime thrillers,' said Carole. 'It's been postponed, which means the production company is mad, which means the studio is mad, which means they all hate you. Rob Hartnell is box office magic, so there's no way anyone's going to hate him. One of the Hollywood gossip blogs says that you dreamed this up to garner publicity.'

Megan felt nauseated. 'Aren't you going to refute that?'

There was a pause. 'Let's just see how it plays out, right?' said Carole.

Just thinking about it made Megan depressed.

Sitting on the bench in Golden Square, watching Rae walk away, she lit another cigarette. She wasn't surprised the woman didn't seem to recognise her: nobody would these days—which was one plus. The last thing she needed was for the media to find her here.

She lived in jeans and cardigans, didn't wear make-up or even bother to brush her hair: it was so short, it didn't need brushing. She ran her fingers through it and it settled. She was still astonished every time she looked in the mirror to find this dark-haired, wary stranger looking back at her. But the glory of her new look was that it gave her some privacy.

114

In London, she was used to paparazzi following her every move at film premieres and parties. After her hit Britflick, they'd trailed her for a few weeks, selling their pictures of her to the celebrity-watching magazines. She'd made an effort to dress up, had even enjoyed it.

'You mean they papped you buying coffee in the local shop?' Pippa had said the first time this strange phenomenon had occurred and Megan phoned immediately phoned her to report.

'Yes,' said Megan proudly. 'I mean, I know it's intrusive, but wow!'

'What were you wearing? Not your pyjamas, please.'

'No,' said Megan, laughing. 'I'm wearing my skinny jeans, a cream T-shirt with chiffon sleeves, that Vuitton scarf everyone wants—they sent it to me!—and a beret with a flower brooch on it.'

'All that to go round the shop to get a latte?'

'I made an effort, Pippa,' Megan said, suddenly irritated. 'That's why they papped me. I'm not Julia Roberts, you know. I'm only good if I look good. I dressed up on purpose.'

'Oh.'

Megan remembered that conversation now and felt a small dart of unease. She'd been angry at her sister for not understanding her world. A world where getting papped mattered; it meant you were somebody. Now she saw the downside of that world. She missed what she had once had. Here, apart from Nora, nobody thought Megan was anybody. That was hard.

Instead of her old glamorous life, her days involved coffee, smoking, walking the dogs, more coffee in Titania's Palace if she could face being out in public, and then staying home watching daytime TV. Hiding. It was soul destroying.

'Come on, walkies over,' she shouted crossly at the dogs.

From the distance, they quivered at this new, tough Megan, and stayed away.

Oh, let them run on for a minute longer, she decided.

If anyone had changed it wasn't her, it was Pippa. She'd once understood Megan's life. She'd gone to the movie parties, she'd hung round with Megan's friends. And where was she now? Not holed up with Megan, sympathising about what had happened. No, she was at home with her kids, slowly sliding on to the side of the moral police.

She'd only rung twice since Megan had come to Golden Square. That said something, didn't it?

Nothing had happened in the few weeks since she'd come to Golden Square. Nothing had changed in her life, except that the trees in the small square were showing new growth, and early daffodils were starting to come out. She was just waiting in limbo. It was horrible.

A small, fat brown dog of indeterminate parentage lollopped along to greet Cici and Leonardo. Fed up, and just to do something, anything, Megan got off the bench and walked through the square to the play area, which was cordoned off from doggy poo by a low fence. Two young women with toddlers in pushchairs had just arrived and were starting the complicated business of unhooking the children. It seemed to take ages, this clip and that clip. Megan had watched Pippa do it with Kim when she'd been younger, but she'd always found it too hard. She'd put Kim into the pushchair, but someone else had to fasten the harness.

'She'll fall out if I do it,' Megan said.

'Just do it,' Pippa had said once, then sighed furiously and rushed over to do it herself. Megan had been upset. Pippa never used to speak to her like that, but instead of saying sorry, her sister concentrated on her daughter. Like it was some strange motherly ritual, this pushchair thing. Settle Kim's solid little body in properly, manoeuvre her arms through the straps, click them up, all the time talking in a soft, soothing voice.

Megan hadn't wanted to speak, she was too hurt, but all the same she found herself mumbling, 'I'm sorry, I'm just no good at that sort of thing.'

Pippa hadn't even turned round. 'You'd be good at that sort of thing if you wanted to be,' she'd said shortly.

Megan had gone home soon afterwards. She couldn't bear cross words or confrontation. Better to leave. She'd hopped in her sporty little MX5 and driven off, music blaring.

She'd never tried to do anything much with Kim after that, or with Toby when he came along. Megan was no good with children: she was like her mother. Ready to please men, not so good with kids.

One of the children in the playground reminded her of Kim as a squirming toddler. Same dark hair, same solid little body. Kim had grown taller now, and was all legs and skinny arms, but once she'd been a sturdy little person like this child.

The woman extracted her daughter from the pushchair, gave her a kiss, then set her down to toddle off to the sandpit.

Megan burst into tears. She'd never felt more lonely in her whole life.

*   *   *

At the end of January, St Matilda's third and sixth-year students sat mock exams in preparation for the real state exams in June. In a cruel twist of fate, the mock exams coincided with a two-day rock festival and a severe strain of flu.

'I'd edit ten books before I'd do exams again,' said Nicky with feeling. 'Those poor girls. And they're missing the festival. If I was doing my exams, I think I'd bunk off to go to the festival. You need time out, right?'

'Just as well you're not a teacher,' said Connie, shocked. 'Nothing should make you miss your mocks.'

But the flu had other plans for her. On the morning the exams were due to start, Connie couldn't go in to the school to cheer on her girls as she was stuck in bed feeling violently ill. Her whole head ached, her eyes couldn't bear any light at all and the very notion of food made her want to retch.

For three days, she had to lie in bed motionless.

'Apparently, it's only flu if it's raining fifty euro notes down outside and you're too sick to run out and pick them up,' Nicky said to her sister, from the sanctity of the doorway, on Connie's fourth day off work.

'It's flu,' moaned Connie, who couldn't have moved even if entire gold ingots were raining down outside. Was that in the Bible? A plague of gold ingots? Or was she delirious and bewildered after spending too much time in a Catholic girls' school?

Sister Lavinia had lots of mad Bible stories, one for every occasion, and Connie often got them mixed up. There was one about foolish virgins and lamps, and she still couldn't recall the moral of the story.

'Do you want me to get you anything before I go to work?' Nicky said.

Connie shook her head.

'OK, see you later. And phone if you feel really bad or something. I could come home, you know . . .'

Connie shook her head again. She was incapable of speech.

She rolled over in the bed, pulled the duvet up to cover her head and went back to sleep.

Miraculously, she woke at noon feeling strangely recovered. Still weak, after three and a half days in bed and no food apart from flat lemonade and toast, but better.

Cautiously, she sat up. Still better.

And suddenly, she was ravenously hungry. She was shaky on her feet when she made it into the kitchen to ransack the fridge. Without her to fill it, the fridge was a wasteland of old yogurts, a few slices of ham, and some milk. There was only one slice of bread left, no cheese, and worse, no chocolate.

She quarter-filled a bowl with the remains of a box of cereal and ate in front of the telly. She was still hungry but there was literally nothing else to eat, except things like cans of beans or soup. Connie longed for a toasted cheese sandwich followed by something sweet.

Titania's Palace, she decided; she'd go there.

She brushed her teeth and her hair, pulled on her red fleece and a coat, and stepped out into the bitter January air to cross the square. She looked like hell on earth, but who'd be looking at her?

*　　　*　　　*

Megan liked the fact that the staff in Titania's Palace were all friendly but not nosy. Nobody tried to engage her in conversation. They were welcoming, but perfectly happy to let her sit at a window table with her Americano with its extra shot of espresso. She could pretend to look out the window and stare off into the middle distance, lost in her own world.

They played cool music too, generally female torch singers from the 1930s and 40s. If Titania's Palace was a person, she'd be a throaty, comforting lady with sex appeal, a huge-hearted person who was utterly comfortable in her own skin.

Megan wondered if there was an actual Titania? The motherly woman who ran the place was called Rae, so perhaps she'd just liked the name.

Megan had watched Rae a few times when she'd been there and it was obvious why the place was such a success with her running it. She appeared to know everyone, and had a smile and a word for them all. It wasn't like a coffee shop: it was like being welcomed into someone's house.

Megan had seen Patsy from the hair salon in there too. Patsy's hair was a darker, more vibrant red this week. She had a way of nodding hello that said she'd totally understand if you wanted to be alone, but she was there, if you felt like talking.

120

Rae and Patsy weren't there today, but the place was jammed with the lunchtime crowd. Megan kept her baseball hat low on her head, and snagged a two-seater window table when a couple of people got up to leave.

She put their dishes on one side of the small table, and settled herself on the other side.

Conversations flowed all around her.

'. . . She's useless around the office. Can't type for peanuts because she has gel nails. The filing system's shot to hell, and when the boss comes back from his holidays, who's going to be to blame? Not her, oh no. She'll say it's all my fault . . .'

'. . . three stone. Imagine losing that much weight! They deliver food to your door and you can only eat that. It's expensive, she told me, but it's worth it . . .'

'. . . I don't know what to buy him. Would cufflinks be special enough? I want it to be special . . .'

The gentle ebb and flow of conversation was interrupted by a woman's voice: 'Do you mind if I sit here? There's nowhere else.'

A tall woman with a cloud of beautiful dark brown hair stood at the other seat. She was muffled up in a big coat and held a tray bearing a toasted sandwich, a frothy coffee and one of Titania's enormous lemon-and-poppyseed muffins.

In London, Megan would have said no. Here, things were different.

'Of course,' she said, and began to move the previous occupants' dishes into the middle of the table.

'Normally, I wouldn't interrupt, but I can't stand

121

at the counter. I need to sit. I've just had flu,' the woman explained. 'It's OK,' she added quickly, 'I'm not toxic any more. I met the doctor at the counter and he said not to cough my guts up on to anyone, but I should be fine. I love GPs, don't you? They're so laid back. Unless your leg is hanging off, they tell you to take an aspirin and call in the morning. Wouldn't you love to be that relaxed?'

'Er . . . yeah,' said Megan.

She'd thought she was giving a seat to another solitary diner. It appeared she'd said yes to a companion.

The woman wriggled out of her ginormous coat. She was late thirties, Megan reckoned, and from her clothes to her unpainted nails, was clearly the very opposite of high maintenance. Even though her round face was shiny and make-up free, there was a wonderful vitality to her. And she had such smiling brown eyes.

Megan used to be impressed by high-achieving thinness and Botox undetectable to all but the most knowing eye. Nowadays, she found she liked people who smiled at her without recognition.

'You're probably relaxed anyhow,' the woman went on, unloading her tray. 'Young people are. My sister's always telling me that my generation are going to drop dead with clogged arteries by the time we're fifty. It's all the worry, all the stress.'

She sliced open her sandwich and gazed at it happily.

'Buddhism's very good for stress, they say. I've always liked the sound of Buddhism,' Connie went on. 'But there's a lot of work to it. If only you could get it inserted or something. A painless operation and you'd wake up with inner peace and the ability to remember a mantra.'

Megan laughed.

Connie bit into her sandwich and moaned in pleasure. 'Bliss, I love these.'

She was glad she'd chosen to sit here. She'd seen the pretty dark-haired girl walking those dogs and the poor thing always looked so lonely. Besides, Connie hadn't felt up to talking for three days, and now she wanted human company.

There was silence as Connie ate and Megan decided it would seem rude if she now stared out the window again. The conversational tennis ball was in her court. She'd almost forgotten how to do idle chitchat.

'Do you live around here?' she asked finally.

'Across the square,' Connie said. 'With my sister, in the first-floor flat of that pale green house.'

Megan peered through the trees. 'Pretty,' she said. 'I live over there with my aunt. The redbrick one on the end. I'm staying with her for a while,' she added.

'The chiropodist,' exclaimed Connie delightedly. 'I'd love to see her professionally, but my feet are terrible. You'd need an industrial sander to get close to them and I'd be so embarrassed. It's like pedicures. I've never had one.'

'Yeah,' nodded Megan, who'd had pedicures in some of the world's most glamorous spas and had never worried for so much as a second as to the state of her toes.

'You're not a chiropodist too, are you? I didn't mean that you'd use industrial sanders, it's just that, for hard skin . . .'

Megan shook her head. 'Lord, no. I'm not a

123

chiropodist. Can't stand feet.'

'I had someone massage my feet a few times,' Connie said thoughtfully. Her eyes glazed over and Megan could swear she saw tears appearing.

Thinking of Keith massaging her feet always made Connie think of pregnant women. *'Put your feet up, love,'* the prospective daddy would say, gently massaging his pregnant partner's feet. The idea always made her cry. She even hated looking at foot spas.

'Goodness, that old flu makes you weepy at the oddest things,' Connie said brightly.

But Megan, who never normally noticed other people's pain, had the strangest sense of seeing through the fake chirpiness. Suddenly, she felt a sense of kinship with this woman. She'd been hurt too. The man who'd massaged her feet was in the past, there was no doubt about it. Megan wasn't foolish to have had her heart broken: it happened to other women too.

In her old life, Megan would have ignored the glint of tears on another woman. In her experience, other women generally ignored her tears. But that was the old life. The old Megan.

Impulsively, she reached out a hand. 'I'm Megan Flynn,' she said.

'Connie O'Callaghan,' said the woman. 'I don't know what came over me. Must be the flu,' she said, dabbing her eyes with her napkin. 'It was years ago. The feet-massaging thing.'

'I'm not sure that time matters much when your heart is broken,' Megan reflected.

'Yes!' said Connie. 'You're right. Nobody else agrees with me. They all think there's a statute of limitations on love, but there isn't.'

'How long ago was it?' Megan asked cautiously, still not confident in her role as female friend.

'A long time ago,' Connie said. 'Longer than I care to think about. He's with someone else now. We share a couple of friends, so I get to hear all about him. I'm beginning to think that's a mistake,' she added thoughtfully. 'How about your guy? Do you still know what he's up to?'

Connie had no idea who she was, Megan thought happily. What a relief. 'He's gone off someplace,' she said. 'I'm not really sure where.'

Megan thought of the newspaper articles which would doubtless tell her where Rob was supposed to be hiding out. Being a superstar meant people offered you remote holiday islands when you needed to get away and the photographers had to hire boats and use telephoto lenses to get any shots at all.

'We worked together,' she added, 'and he was married.'

She waited for Connie to recoil.

But Connie merely gave her a rueful smile.

'Don't tell me: he was your boss, his wife didn't understand him and if only he could start again with beautiful you, life would be fabulous?'

'Something like that.'

Although there had been nothing remotely funny about any of it, suddenly Megan saw the humorous side. She'd thought it was so different with her and Rob, except it wasn't different at all. Connie had summed it up perfectly.

*   *   *

Megan had felt the familiar pre-film anxiety as

she'd packed her suitcases in her small Notting Hill flat to head off to location. She'd just bought the flat. Carole had told her it was a good investment, even though it had taken all her money, a fact which scared her. Small UK movies didn't pay very well and despite Carole's assurances that she'd start making decent money once *Warrior Queen* came out, Megan still wasn't entirely convinced. They'd been broke her whole childhood, it would take time to get over that.

She loved the flat, though. It was in an old house, a two-bedroomed flat with high ceilings and a tiny south-facing balcony off the kitchen, where Megan liked to sit outside with coffee. She hadn't much furniture yet, but she'd had great fun choosing a complicated coffee machine that sat gleaming in her kitchen.

The one thing she did have lots of were clothes, and packing was difficult. Even though Megan knew she'd need warm clothing to layer over her medieval costumes between takes, she still couldn't resist putting in some pretty dresses and her current favourite outfit, a pair of pale skinny jeans and a long cashmere cardigan that she wore over a pale pink sequined camisole that made her look about nineteen instead of twenty-six.

In the peculiar world of filmmaking, the first scenes were on-location ones in a windswept Romanian castle, scenes from the middle of the movie where the princess, Megan, fell in love with her new father-in-law, Rob. The director, Sven, clearly wanted to mix things up by throwing his cast into the hardest scenes first. It was a neat trick to give the film momentum, another plus when location shooting was so expensive and time was money.

'From nought to sixty in a few minutes,' Megan said on the phone to Pippa. She was standing outside her trailer, huddled up in a down jacket and smoking a last cigarette. Her hair was tied up painfully and she wore a plaited wig as part of her Roman princess garb. It all felt uncomfortable.

'Think of paying off the flat,' Pippa said comfortingly.

'Yes,' said Megan, looking down at her hand and realising that it was shaking. She'd had too many cigarettes and too many coffees. No wonder she was shaking. Inside her trailer, Megan gargled with mouthwash to get the nicotine off her breath. Rob didn't appear to smoke and she was going to have to kiss him, after all. This was a crazy job. Where else did you have to lie on top of and snog the face off a national icon when you'd only met them three days before?

Rob had been very nice, albeit a bit distant, and polite. So far on set, he'd barely had anything to do: a scene in the castle's draughty hall that shook when fierce winds rippled down the Carpathian mountains. There had been none of the charisma of the true movie star who could switch on the charm and light up everything. Megan knew he could do it, she'd seen his King Lear at the National Theatre. She wondered if he was here to pay a tax bill, 'phoning in' the performance, as some critics described actors who took roles they didn't care about and might as well not have been there for all the effort they put into it.

A knock on her trailer told her it was time. Megan breathed deeply.

She was scared. Her previous acting work had

been with people her own age, and her own experience. It had been a giant lark. This was different.

Perhaps some actors got paid vast sums of money because it was one of the few jobs where you had to be willing to relinquish self totally and do whatever the director demanded. It was like being taken over by aliens: becoming something or someone entirely different. After ten years in the business, since the age of sixteen, she understood totally why so many performers ended up in rehab. Opening up your soul to vitalise a performance was agonising work. When the show was over, and the gaping hole was still open, it was all too tempting to numb it with alcohol, drugs or sex.

'Hi,' said the national treasure when they met on set.

'Hi,' said Megan nervously. Use the nerves, her acting coach would have said. Today, the nerves refused to be used and danced merrily inside her, making her feel nauseous. It was hard to look luminous and beautiful when you thought you might throw up at any moment. She'd gone over this scene with the director, talking about what he wanted. She'd have loved to have been able to do the same with Rob, but icons did not show up for read-throughs and didn't give out their phone numbers for long talks. Not like the cast on her last film. They'd all become pals. Rob Hartnell was not.

Unlike an astonishing number of big stars who were a disappointment in the flesh, he was tall, rangy, still clearly very fit and still unreasonably gorgeous for a man thirty years her senior. In heavy velvets and brocades, he was regal and golden, his famous hair still rich brown despite sprinklings of grey, his blue eyes undimmed, and his face—untouched by surgeon's scalpel—though craggy with age, was still redolent of his youthful beauty. He didn't speak as they waited through the interminable last-minute lighting and camera adjustments. A method man? she wondered. But no, if he was method, he'd have been storming around, eyes blazing because his character was a fierce monarch who specialised in wars. He was not the sort of king who would die peacefully in his bed but one who would perish on the battlefield, fighting to the last.

As yet another angle was worked out and the long wait continued, Megan sat on her chair and wished she'd learned to knit like so many actresses did. Perhaps she should have tried embroidery; that would have helped her stay in character, perhaps. Did Roman princesses do needlework? She focused her mind. She was a feisty woman meeting the first man she couldn't control . . . It didn't work. She still felt like a very young actress about to play the most important role of her career with an experienced actor, someone who'd been in the theatre, someone who probably hated working with naïve youngsters.

'We're ready,' said a voice.

Sven the director nodded at her.

Megan stood on her mark, trying to think herself into being a feisty foreign princess alone for the first time with the man who'd had her kidnapped in the hope that by marrying her off to his middle son he could forge an alliance between the two kingdoms.

She knew her character, had familiarised herself

with the look and feel of her, and yet here, on the set, the character had fled. Rob still didn't even look at her. This was going to be hell, she thought.

And then, in a flash, Rob was gone and in his place was King Varl, all-powerful, controlling, looking at her with hungry interest. Megan had no idea how he'd done it, but he was someone else, he *was* the king. Something in her responded but it wasn't an actor's response. She felt her legs tremble under the scratchy heavy gown. She stammered out her lines, feeling herself actually blushing as he stared at her. Some purely intellectual part of her brain knew this was all good, powerful stuff. The camera would love it, Sven would wet himself with delight. And the instinctive part of her didn't really care how good her performance was, all she cared about was having this man's eyes on her, caressing her, telling her with his eyes what he was going to do with his hands later.

He had to reach out and touch her cheek, half paternal, half something else entirely. Megan leaned into his wrist, closed her eyes, although that wasn't how she'd planned to do it. His palm was cool and she wanted nothing more than to have it slip down and nestle against her breast.

Afterwards, they walked off set together in the direction of their trailers. People handed them anoraks and Megan reached into her pocket for her cigarettes. She lit up as she walked, utterly conscious of Rob nearby, walking with his people who were all chattering to him about phone calls and how brilliant he'd been in the scene.

'Can I have one?' he said, and Megan turned around, wondering if he was talking to her.

Someone in his entourage offered a pack of cigarettes, but Rob ignored it, looking pointedly at Megan.

'Sure,' she said, passing over her packet.

They stopped outside his trailer and she watched him pull the cigarette out, then she tried to hold her hand steady as she flicked on her little silver lighter. It shook and the flame went out.

Rob covered her hand with his and flicked the lighter into life. Megan inhaled swiftly at his touch.

Just as quickly, he removed his hand and took a long draw on the cigarette.

'The scene went well,' he said, in a very normal voice. 'We should talk about it, how we go forward. Sven would love us to get this right.'

He waved his entourage away with a hand. 'I'll smoke this outside,' he said. 'Don't want to stink up the trailer. Else you'll all want to smoke inside.'

They laughed politely.

'Mike, can you come back in fifteen and we can go through the messages?' This to his assistant, a short guy in glasses.

Everyone wandered off.

Megan could barely smoke, she was shaking so much.

'What just happened back there?' she said suddenly. Had she imagined it?

Rob looked down at his cigarette, nearly half-smoked, then threw it on the ground impatiently. 'I haven't smoked for fifteen years,' he said. 'Fifteen years. Katharine would kill me if she saw it.'

Megan nodded calmly but inside, she was falling apart. She'd made a mistake. A huge one. He'd been acting, not feeling. It hadn't been real. When

131

he mentioned his wife, that was the hint. What an idiot she'd been to mistake acting for reality.

'You want to come in?' He held open the door of his trailer.

'Sure.' She stepped inside, feeling embarrassed, waiting for him to let her down gently and explain that this often happened. Perhaps tell her exactly how often it had happened, offer a litany of other young actresses who'd fallen for him and had mistaken acting for real life. How to apologise for that?

'I just want to say, Rob—' she said, as he shut the door.

She got no further.

He pulled her close, as close as they'd been earlier that day. Megan felt the exact same shiver.

'What do you think happened? Why do you think I'm smoking? So I have something to do with my hands to stop myself grabbing you.'

'Oh.' Megan stared up at him.

'We can't do this now, not now and not here. I have never cheated on my wife,' he said, seeming almost bewildered.

And then he kissed her again, like on set earlier, only this time there was nobody to yell 'Cut!' when his hand grazed her nipple. Megan leaned into his body, her hands clinging to him, her mouth open under his, eager, frantic.

She knew there would be a bed in his trailer; there was in hers, though hers was much smaller. She wanted him to throw her on it and to rip off her clothes. She wanted his body on hers, in hers. She wanted him now.

'Fuck,' he said, leaning back. 'Not here. Please.'

She nodded shakily. Not here. Right.

132

'Where?'

'Prague, the last night, we can do it.'

Sven was passing when she came out of the trailer five minutes later, her head still reeling, her mouth raw from Rob's kisses.

The actress in Megan rescued her. 'I feel so guilty,' she told Sven. 'Rob says Katharine is going to kill him because he's smoking again. I know it's my fault—I've always got cigarettes.' She waved her pack as proof.

Sven laughed. 'If Katharine comes after you for that, she'll kill you! It took her years to wean him off them. But it's hard not to when you're on location. The rules change, right?' His look was penetrating.

Megan nodded gravely, as if to say it was all about the film. But it wasn't. Her life had just changed for ever.

*   *   *

Connie said she was going to order another coffee.

'Are you sure you don't want something to eat?' she asked, looking at her own empty plates.

'No,' said Megan. She was slim by nature, but nature had been helped by the actress's code of not eating. It was the only way. She was so used to it that eating something in Titania's would be a traumatic event. Coffee and fags for breakfast, fruit and rice cakes for lunch, fish and vegetables for dinner. Wine, champagne and vodka didn't count.

'You're too thin, if you don't mind me saying so,' Connie said in her teacher's tones.

Megan laughed at the notion. 'In my job, you

133

can't be too thin.'

Connie looked horrified. 'What do you do?'

'I'm an actress.'

'I thought you were go ing to say you were a model,' Connie replied. 'Those poor girls, it's not natural to make them that skinny. Are you . . .' she paused, trying to say the right, non-hurtful thing '. . . working right now?'

Megan was touched. In many of the circles she moved in, other people were pleased to learn an actor was out of work. *More chance for me*, they thought. Which was a first cousin of: *I knew it was fluke when she got those roles, I could have done it better and now the casting directors agree!*

'No,' she replied. 'I was, but it's over now and I've nothing lined up.' Understatement of the year.

'Never mind, something will come up, you wait and see.' Connie reached out and patted Megan's hand. 'Golden Square is a great place for a break. You must come to dinner with my sister and me. You'd love Nicky, she's nearer your age and works in publishing. You'd meet Freddie too, he's her boyfriend and they're joined at the hip. He's a sweetheart.'

'Are you seeing anyone right now?' Megan asked carefully.

Connie laughed. 'Oh sure, who'd have me?'

Megan frowned and opened her mouth to say something, but seeing Connie's closed expression, decided not to.

*　　　*　　　*

After the coffee, Connie stopped off at The Nook to stock up the fridge and buy some magazines to read in bed, then went home. Megan was sweet, she thought. Nicky would like her too. They'd have her to dinner some night. It had to be hard, being a young actress these days. Broke, always trying to get a commercial here or a small acting part there.

When Nicky got home from work, Connie had recovered enough to be sitting on the couch in her pyjamas, with a china pot of tea in front of her, the magazines read and the evening news on.

Once they'd chatted about Nicky's day, Connie told her about meeting Megan in Titania's.

'She had a fling with a married man, God love her,' said Connie. 'She reminds me of someone, you know—'

'She reminds you of that girl in the papers who had a thing with Rob Hartnell,' said Nicky, 'because that's who she is.'

'Oh.' Realisation flooded through Connie. There had been a paragraph about Rob in one of the magazines. No one knew where he was.

'Kevin, who works with Nora, told me,' said Nicky. 'He says nobody's supposed to know or else the place will be over-run with gossip columnists. Is she nice?'

'Megan?' Connie didn't have to think about it. 'She's lovely. Sort of shy, if that's not a strange thing to say about an actress. But she is.'

Snippets of newspaper articles about Megan filtered through Connie's head. There was no way the wary, dark-haired girl she'd met in Titania's was the supposed brazen creature who'd snared a married man. No way at all.

Connie remembered who it was Megan had actually reminded her of: a girl she'd taught years ago. The girl had been pretty and outwardly confident, but secretly very vulnerable. Connie had felt protective of the girl and she felt the same now about Megan.

It looked as if Megan had it all—certainly all the things people valued: beauty, talent and fame. What she'd managed to hide was that she was deeply hurt underneath that glamorous exterior. Everyone hid things, Connie knew. She certainly did. She hid her sadness so well that nobody would suspect it. Which meant that she and Megan had a lot more in common than Nicky would ever know.

7

Imbolg, festival of light

Eleanor had moved the walnut writing desk into the large bay window. When she sat at the desk to write, she was facing the trees of the square, their dark branches reaching up bleakly into the grey of the late January sky.

A brass lamp with a creamy silk shade cast a mellow light around her, and in the fireplace behind, a gas fire burned merrily.

Eleanor liked to write in longhand on yellowing legal paper. This was the way she'd taken all her notes during her years practising, until Gillian her grand-daughter had taught her how to use a computer several years before.

'Do you think I'm too old to learn all this stuff?' Eleanor had asked Gillian. They'd been in Eleanor and Ralf's apartment on West 73rd Street. The teenage Gillian had dropped in to see her grandparents and had found Eleanor getting frustrated trying to set up an email account on her newly purchased laptop.

'Nonsense, Grandma, you're never too old. You'll pick it up pretty quickly. You're good at surfing the web, aren't you? This is just an added bonus. You'll love email.'

Gillian had turned back to the laptop and Eleanor had smiled affectionately at her beloved grand-daughter. In skinny jeans, Converse trainers and a little knitted camisole, Gillian Filan was the very picture of a cool New York teenager. She had a mane of dark, shiny hair, perfect skin from years of Dermalogica products and a hint of silver eyeliner on those big chestnut-hued eyes, but in every other way, she was an O'Neill woman from the small Connemara village of Kilmoney. Strong, kind and gifted.

'Gran, do you know how to set up documents and stuff like that? 'Cause I can key in whatever you want,' Gillian offered.

Eleanor thought of all the things she wanted to write.

'No, my dearest, I'll type it in myself. You're never too old, right?'

At the window of the cosy apartment in Golden Square, Eleanor thought back to that day. What age had Gillian been? Fifteen, sixteen?

She was such a loving girl. Never talking back or sassy to her parents. Not a saint, either. But a smiling person who walked into a room and made it a happier place.

When you were fifteen, your grandmother seemed ancient. Older than time itself. But Eleanor hadn't felt old then, for all that she had to

137

have been knocking eighty.

Age was a state of mind, she liked to say then. She and Ralf enjoyed doing crosswords and sudoku. They adored quiz shows, and many a holiday had been spent playing Trivial Pursuit.

Granted, Ralf took a handful of pills in the morning and his knees were so arthritic, he creaked when he got out of bed.

Eleanor herself suffered from high blood pressure.

'It's familial,' said her doctor when she calmly pointed out that she was the least stressed person she knew. 'Take the drugs, Eleanor. It's not a comment on your mental state.'

Despite all of that, she hadn't felt old. Until now.

She'd gone to the doctor in Golden Square to have her blood pressure checked yesterday, and had sat in the waiting room with the only person she'd seen around who was of her vintage. Eleanor was not used to chatting with strangers in the doctor's waiting room, but nobody had told Pearl Mills that. A small, white-haired lady, Mrs Mills was accompanied by her son, a giant of a man who was clearly mentally disabled. Pearl had smiled broadly at Eleanor when she arrived.

'Hello,' she said. 'I'm Pearl. This is Terence. You must be the lady who has taken Carolyn Taylor's flat.'

Within five minutes of talking to Pearl, Eleanor was overcome with enormous sympathy for Pearl's bravery.

'Terence and I will be going to Lourdes later this year,' Pearl confided as they waited in the simple room decorated with calming pictures of landscapes.

Eleanor didn't know much about the Marian shrine, so Pearl told her all about it and the comfort she got from it.

'The people helping the invalids are wonderfully kind,' Pearl said. 'It's like my burden is shared when I'm there. Not,' she added quickly, putting a hand on Terence as if he might be offended, 'that it's a burden, really, but you know, taking care of him can be hard.'

Eleanor wanted to cry at the bravery of this frail woman with her huge burden and her even bigger heart.

Terence was calm enough sitting there, although Eleanor wondered was he always so placid and how tiny Pearl might manage such times. He was deaf, Pearl explained, and his limited speech was very hard to understand, but Pearl understood and talked to him gently.

'Is it expensive to go to Lourdes?' Eleanor asked, then regretted it.

Pearl's tiny wrinkled face had fallen. 'Very,' she said. 'We haven't much money, you know, and it's hard to stretch what little we have to fill all the gaps. But we'll manage. I have to give him all I can. While I'm still here.'

There was silence, the sort of silence Eleanor was well used to. In therapy, huge things could be said and then a silence was required as the speaker considered the enormity of what they'd just uttered out loud.

'That must be a big worry for you,' Eleanor said neutrally.

'Oh yes.' Pearl patted Terence again. Her eyes shone brightly with unshed tears. 'Who will look after him when I'm gone? They have good homes for people like Terence, you know, but I couldn't send him there. He'd be lost without me. I've always taken care of him.'

At that moment, Eleanor thought despairingly of her mother's book. There was much in it about death, although Eleanor had avoided those parts when she'd been flicking through it. She knew her mother's words would help. They were written from the heart, all her lessons on life, pain, happiness and food. But right now, Eleanor couldn't bear to read the lessons. She was grieving too much.

Then the doctor had poked her head round the waiting-room door and Pearl had gone in with Terence, leaving Eleanor on her own, thinking.

Eleanor realised now she was staring out into Golden Square again instead of working on her diary for Gillian.

She'd never kept a diary, not the way her mother had, and it was harder than she'd thought, this writing down of truths, even for a woman who'd studied human truths and how to impart them.

But there was so much she wanted to tell Gillian, so many lessons. She needed to do it before it was too late. All the things Eleanor had learned would be lost and Gillian would have to live her life without knowing.

That you could always change your mind.

That people were fundamentally good.

That guilt and self-doubt never helped anyone.

That you needed to love and respect yourself before turning your attention to anyone else.

Gillian had grown up being loved, and she seemed to know a lot of this, but Eleanor wanted to make sure. She wanted to pass her wisdom on, the way her own mother had done.

Since she'd come to Golden Square, Brigid's voice was often in her head in a way it hadn't been for years.

Even important dates reminded her of her mother.

It was coming close to Imbolg, the Celtic festival of light. Rebirth after the darkness of the winter.

It fell on the first full moon in February, signalling the end of the ice of winter.

Brigid had been very keen on the old Irish legends and stories, and Eleanor had grown up knowing them as well as she knew the stories of the saints they taught in school.

In Kilmoney at Imbolg it would still be cold with an icy wind racing in from the sea. Despite that, Mam, Granny and Aunt Agnes would decorate the house with the first wild flowers and would cook up a special feast that was for the women only. The men would go off down the road to play cards in Grimes' bar while their womenfolk sat and talked up a storm, drinking strong tea and eating the leftover Christmas cake specially kept for the night.

It was the start of lambing and she could remember her father, Joe, being out in the freezing night helping with the early lambing. Sometimes, a sheep would reject her lamb and Eleanor's father would carry the squirming soft bundle home, where it would be raised in the kitchen for a few weeks, bottle fed with an old bottle and a baby's teat. Lambs looked so delicate but they were strong in reality, pushing at the bottle with those fiercely strong faces, urging for more and more milk.

Had life been more simple then? When it was harder merely to survive, did people get on with it and not tangle themselves in knots over who they were and why life had shaped them a certain way?

Eleanor no longer knew.

After a lifetime of thinking she understood life, she now felt as if she'd been nothing but a voyeur all along. As a therapist, she'd seen client after client and listened to their stories, yet she'd never really been part of their world. What had she done to help them? She didn't know. She couldn't even help herself now.

She must have been crazy to come on this trip to Ireland. She'd thought it would give her peace, but it hadn't, not yet. Where would it all lead?

8

Soup

Your aunt Agnes got the most wonderful cookbook from Mrs Fitzmaurice.

Some foreign lady had left it behind in the big house, although Agnes and myself laughed at the notion of a real lady knowing the slightest thing about cooking. Not that I knew many ladies, but being in service in the big house, Agnes met them all. None of them knew

142

how to cook, although they probably thought they did on account of all the time they spent discussing menus with their housekeepers. There could be seven courses easily at a meal, Agnes told us, with soups, salads, terrines, fowl, meat, syllabubs, ices.

The cookbook was French, written by a Madame St Martin, and we pored over it. There were sauces for everything and Madame St Martin insisted that copper-bottomed pans were an absolute necessity. We ignored that bit on account of not having copper anything. My best cooking pot had a heavy iron bottom that the gypsy metal man had put on for me. You could put a hard bit of lamb shoulder in there for hours without it ever getting overcooked, and at the end it would simply melt off the bone.

Madame St Martin's chicken soup had loads of garlic in it and it was a miracle.

That winter, there was a lot of snow and Joe spent most of his time out in the byre with cows that were calving. He'd come in perished with the cold, and I got into the habit *of having a pot of chicken soup on the range.*

Up to then, I'd only known how to make a bit of gruel, so the chicken soup was a godsend.

Your aunt Agnes said we should write to Madame St Martin and tell her how well it had all gone, and I said that was a great idea. We never got round to writing that letter, but I like to think that every time we cooked her chicken soup, I said thanks in my heart.

*   *   *

Connie hated February for two reasons: the winter gloom and Valentine's Day. She did her best to ignore them both. During February, she never bought magazines because they were full of recipes for romantic dinners for two. Instead, she went to the local library every week and immersed herself in crime novels. Crime scenes, bodies, cops arguing with the Feds and a nice detective with personal problems and a case to solve. Perfect.

She also worked on her list. Her fantasy ideal man list.

Long legs. Definitely.

Had to be taller than she was.

No children, ex-wives or former girlfriends he was still in love with.

Great sense of humour a must.

Fit, but not obsessed with the gym. Not a yoga

person.

No insane mother in the background who didn't like him dating people. Connie had never personally gone out with such a man, but a colleague had, and Connie had told her right off that any man who'd cancel a night out because *'Mummy isn't in the mood to be left all on her own',* was not a serious proposition for happiness.

All his own hair, obviously. None of that comb-over or pernickety fluffed-up hair that couldn't be touched. Connie had once, briefly, dated a man who was going bald and it was as if his entire life's work was hiding this fact. Connie's affectionate nature had been rebuffed because head-stroking wasn't allowed in case it ruined the careful arrangement of the front of his hair. Tom was the man's name and the romance hadn't lasted. He spent much more time looking in mirrors than Connie ever did. He used a lot of hairspray on the fluffy bit of hair he had left at the front, and God forbid that the wind should blow it back to expose his forehead. Connie felt sorry for him, but not sorry enough to keep seeing him. She liked people who were realistic. If you were going bald, it made sense to have one of those short haircuts and be done with it. Connie was realistic about herself: after all, *she* didn't think she was Angelina Jolie, now, did she?

She liked working on her list. It was fun, a bit like having double chocolate chip cookies in bed with hot milk watching a soppy film. A guilty secret. Even talking about the list would be like admitting that she had given up on finding a real man and was now entering the realms of fantasy man.

145

It would be like saying 'I love romance novels and costume dramas with Mr Darcy-ish men,' and she could never own up to that because people would laugh at her.

Strangely, she'd wanted to tell Megan that first day in Titania's Palace. She'd had the weirdest feeling that Megan would understand that it was easier to imagine a fantasy man than place any trust in the world of real men. And then she'd come to her senses. Saying she was pretty much done with love herself might have sounded defeatist.

Megan might have been bruised by love but she had time on her side. Time to find endless men and reject them.

Connie had no time left.

Without Mr Perfect, there would be no baby nuzzling into her breast, looking up at her adoringly. She never made a list about babies, their names, whether she wanted a girl or a boy: that would have hurt too much and too deeply. No, a fantasy list about a perfect man was a nice way to wile the hours away.

When Megan had come to Connie and Nicky's for dinner shortly after they'd first met up, Freddie had been banished so the three women could have a female-only night.

'I'd like to meet her,' grumbled Freddie.

'You will,' said Nicky, 'but she's coming for a nice comforting girlie dinner because Connie says that's what she needs, not to be looked at by someone who has seen her first film four times and used the freeze frame till he almost wore the DVD out.'

Connie had smiled at Nicky's wonderful confidence: she trusted Freddie's love for her and she trusted in her own sense of self. Nicky didn't imagine that Freddie would be blinded by Megan's looks or status.

Megan had been visibly anxious when she'd arrived, bearing a pot of white hyacinths as a gift.

But Connie's huge welcome and Nicky's impressed, 'Oh, you are so tiny, even smaller than you look on the television!' had instantly broken the ice.

'You're the teeny, tiny generation,' Connie laughed. 'I'm part of the Amazonian goddess generation and you pair are the small pixie generation. I hope you brought your appetite,' she added to Megan, enveloping her in a big hug. 'I've ordered deluxe pizza, garlic dough balls and coleslaw.'

'Connie's a slave to coleslaw,' Nicky revealed.

'And Diet Coke,' Connie added, 'as a sop to our figures. Well, *my* figure.'

It had been an enjoyable evening. Nicky and Megan got on like a house on fire, and only the fact that both Connie and Nicky had work the following morning broke it up before midnight.

'I wish I was going to work,' Megan sighed. 'I'm going slightly mad right now. Nora says Birdie is going away to Spain later this month and I could stand in for her.'

'I wish we had something you could do,' said Nicky thoughtfully. 'You could read for me, perhaps?'

'You could take the fifth years for history when I'm at Sylvie's wedding in Paris,' Connie added.

'You never know, there might be a fabulous man there for you,' said Nicky hopefully.

'Yes,' said Connie. Nicky was right, you never

147

knew. She mustn't be defeatist.

* * *

The right man hadn't been at Sylvie's wedding in Paris, although Connie, thanks to Nicky's prodding, had gone over there with high hopes.

The wedding had been great fun and had started off fabulously.

Connie was travelling with four other teachers from the school—all single—and they were, they all agreed, as mad as any tour of schoolgirls.

'If the principal could see us now,' Grace, who taught geography, laughed as they raced round Dublin Airport duty-free, spraying themselves with expensive scents none of them could afford.

'There's still time for her to come,' said Connie mischievously. 'I could phone and say, "Mrs Caldwell, you'd love it, we're going night clubbing every night, and you know how much you like to dance . . ."'

'Perish the thought,' shuddered Vivienne, who taught art and whose creative style of dress and behaviour made it unlikely she would ever feature on Mrs Caldwell's Teacher of the Month board.

The hotel Sylvie's mother had recommended turned out to be tiny, very chic and close enough to the Seine that they could see it from the small balcony in Grace and Connie's room.

They'd doubled up to save money, but Grace pointed out that if she got lucky with a delectable French man, she'd go back to his place, so Connie could sleep alone in peace. 'Makes sense,' she'd said to Connie.

The unspoken message was that Connie would

hardly be bringing a handsome Frenchman back to the room.

'Absolutely,' said Connie, who felt her own confidence breaking into smithereens. Grace was only thirty-two and very attractive. Of course the delectable Frenchmen would fall for her, while Connie didn't have a hope with any of them. What had she been thinking? She should have stuck with her idea that her dating days were over.

Gorgeous French guys would fancy younger women who would consider passion on a first date, not a sailing-towards-forty schoolteacher who hadn't had sex in so long, she'd pass out with shock if a man suggested it without six months of courtship. French men would also know that a woman of her age was listening to the ticking of her biological clock. They might see the desperation in her eyes that few other people seemed to be aware of.

Grace was the belle of the Irish contingent. The grey silk dress that Connie had privately thought was far too understated that morning in their hotel room, turned out to be the perfect thing to wear to an elegant Parisian wedding. It was Connie's cerulean blue chiffon skirt and matching blouse with a grosgrain belt which looked overdone and fussy among all the crisp, eau de nil shift dresses, real pearls and two-tone Chanel pumps.

Nicky had prophesied that there would be no table for singles at a French wedding.

'They're too cool for that in France,' she'd told Connie. 'Bet they'll mix everyone together, English- and French-speaking, married and non-married. Here, we stick all the poor single people together at hopeless tables full of the mad single

149

cousins and strange uncles, so they feel like losers as soon as they get there. They won't do that in Paris.'

Connie had wondered when Nicky had become so wise on the subject of matrimonial customs, but it turned out, she'd been right. Connie and Grace had been seated at a table with some of Sylvie's old schoolfriends. There was no sense that anyone was looking to set them up with single French men. There didn't appear to be any single French men. Besides, Connie quickly learned that Sylvie hadn't described her as a woman on the lookout for love. No, Connie discovered that her reputation was as Sylvie's fun Irish friend, the jolly one whom everybody loved, who had a great sense of humour. She wasn't the girlfriend type or the wife type. None of Sylvie's friends looked speculatively at Connie as though she was a threat. No, they beamed at her and cheerfully told their husbands to dance with her.

Grace was a different matter. None of the husbands were told to dance with her.

Connie ate two chocolate puddings—much to the shocked amusement of the slim women on her table, who hadn't even eaten all their actual main courses, never mind pudding—and danced with everyone with such gaiety that nobody could have known that she was crying inside. If she was destined to be the mad, fun auntie at the party, she'd play the part.

*   *   *

The day after the wedding, Grace had been determined to stay in bed late. There was no sign

150

of the others at breakfast, so Connie assumed they'd all partied till the small hours. She'd been in bed at a very respectable twelve thirty. There had to be some compensations for being the cheerful, funny one. Sylvie's friends had insisted on driving her back to the hotel and one of the husbands had been ordered to escort her to the hotel door.

In bed, wild-eyed with the pain of discovering her status as funny, non-marrying woman, she'd stayed awake till three: long enough to hear Grace creep in.

''S me, Connie, sorry to wake you. Oops. Sorry about the noise. Oops.'

Grace knocked over everything in the bathroom when she stumbled in there but finally made it to bed and, eventually, Connie drifted off to dreams of herself as the bride with no groom in sight.

'I think I'll go to the Louvre and meander around,' she told the Grace-shaped lump in the other single bed after breakfast.

'Whatever,' mumbled Grace.

Paris wasn't any more romantic a city than any other, Connie decided as she walked along the streets. It was more its reputation than anything else. A fabulous marketing ploy. *Come here if you're in love and, if you're not, you will feel incomplete and like a total loser, so you have to come back as soon as you do fall in love with someone.*

It was a win-win situation for Paris all round. She and Keith had never been a city-break couple. They'd liked activity holidays like skiing and that sailing course they'd taken off the coast of Turkey.

He'd worked in a bank but the perks had included decent holidays, so they'd gone away on

151

amazing vacations. In the seven years they'd been together, they'd gone skiing every winter and had toured South America as well as the Far East.

They'd been engaged a month and had been tentatively discussing a honeymoon trip to Australia when Keith had dropped the bombshell.

'You know the way we say honesty is the best policy . . .' he'd said, and Connie had been about to tease him over sounding like an insurance commercial, when he went on: 'I have to be honest with you, Connie: it's over. Us. For me, anyhow. I know you must feel it too. I love you, but I'm not *in love* with you, and I should be, shouldn't I?'

'Shouldn't you what?' Connie had heard exactly what he'd said. It was simply that she couldn't believe he'd said it. This was Keith, the man who'd lain his head on her belly in front of the fire the weekend before, and said he was perfectly happy. Admittedly, they'd been out with friends and some wine had been consumed, but still. How could you be perfectly happy one week, and not the next? How could he have asked her to marry him and then break it off a month later? Shouldn't there have been some signs of him not loving her any more, and if there had been, why hadn't she noticed?

'I'd like us to be friends,' Keith went on, ever hopeful. 'We've been together for so long.'

'I don't want us to be friends,' Connie said, sobbing now. 'I want us to be together, that's all.'

'It's over, Connie,' he said. 'You need to face facts. We should never have got engaged. The past month has shown me that. I don't want to get married. At least we hadn't got as far as putting a deposit on a house. Now that would be a nightmare to sort out.'

And telling everyone that the engagement was off—a month after it had been announced—*would not* be a nightmare? Connie stared at him, shocked and hurt. But it had been no good. He was strangely unmoved by her pain.

'You must have known,' he kept saying, as if she was only denying it to annoy him.

A day later, he'd moved his stuff out of the pretty flat they shared. Connie had been numb.

'Phone me, won't you, and tell me how you're doing?' Keith said.

Connie seized upon these words as proof that Keith did love her and was merely going through a crisis brought on by friends phoning up delightedly asking them about wedding plans now that they were engaged.

'Please, Connie, don't kid yourself,' said Gaynor angrily when she heard this new theory. 'He's simply hoping you won't throw yourself down the stairs and blame him in your suicide note. That's all the asshole cares about.'

Instead of making peace with the fact that Keith had inexplicably changed his mind, Connie tormented herself over not having noticed how he'd felt. This not noticing was her fault. If she had noticed, she could have changed herself, changed *something*. When he started going out with other women, she tortured herself wondering where she'd gone wrong.

Should there have been more romance in their relationship? Connie had never been a woman for sexy knickers and bedroom stripteases—was this a mistake? She cast her mind back to their engagement. Keith had definitely asked her to

153

marry him, but they'd been at a friend's wedding at the time. He'd been hit by wedding-envy, the thought that this gorgeous party with friends could be theirs. *That* was what had gone wrong.

His proposal hadn't been heartfelt and yet she'd been carried away, convinced it was, because marrying Keith was what she wanted.

*   *   *

Connie joined the queue at the Louvre and decided she would set her mind to art and culture for the rest of the day. There was something infinitely soothing in great museums: if love had deserted you, at least you could lose yourself in the brilliance of long-dead civilisations.

Besides, how many artists had painted their greatest works when they were dying inside of love? Exactly. She'd be among friends in the Louvre.

*   *   *

Home from Paris after Sylvie's wedding, Connie told no one how it had been. Even Nicky. Freddie was in the apartment even more than usual and it seemed as if there wasn't any time alone with Nicky to confide in her.

Besides, it would have sounded so sad and hopeless. As if she wanted Nicky to sort it out, and that wasn't Nicky's job. *She* had to look after Nicky, not the other way round.

No, Connie decided resolutely, she would keep her misery to herself. She needed to get a life and stop obsessing about her lack of love and the decreasing chances of her ever becoming a mother.

She would not spend weekends in the homestore buying more rubbish to prettify her bedroom—she had three sets of twinkling fairy lights over her mirrored dressing table already. Any more and the room would be a fire hazard.

Connie wasn't a pink person in any other area of her life except her bedroom. The apartment had wooden floors, pale walls and pretty Scandinavian-style furniture in shades of white. Inspired by a magazine photospread of a Swedish designer's house, Connie had gone for neutral soft furnishings accented with pale blue curtains and cushions. It was all calm, simple and pretty.

Except in her bedroom, where she'd lost the run of herself. The walls were covered in a sprigged pink wallpaper, the bed had a draped pink muslin canopy and there were so many fluffy and frilled throw pillows on the rose-coloured satin bedspread that it took five minutes to throw them off when it was time for bed.

The single woman's bedroom was her castle, Connie liked to joke to her sister.

But it had gone too far. Its romanticism now mocked her. Especially in February, season of red envelopes and roses. No, she was going to find something to make herself useful.

For a start, the postman had left them a letter addressed to 'Mrs E. Levine' that should obviously have gone to the elderly lady downstairs. Rather than just put it in the correct slot, Connie decided to use it as an excuse to visit their new neighbour. Maybe she could offer to go to the shop for her, or fetch some books from the library. Grabbing a box of luxury chocolate cookies that she happened to have in the cupboard, she walked downstairs and rang the bell of the ground-floor apartment. After a moment the intercom crackled into action.

'Hello, Mrs Levine, it's Connie O'Callaghan from upstairs,' she called.

'Hello, Connie,' a soft American voice replied.

Once the door opened, Connie forgot all thoughts of the library. The woman standing before her was not her vision of a little old lady who needed friendship, large-print romantic novels from the library or soft mints she could eat in spite of her dentures.

'How very nice to meet you,' Mrs Levine said.

She was still tall and straight despite her age, and although age had probably dimmed their colour, her eyes were the shining blue of sapphires. Her hair was a cloud of soft white curls around an oval smiling face that, though lined like a piece of exquisite old vellum, glowed with inner light. Mannish tweed trousers and a cream silk shirt worn with a long woollen cardigan gave her the air of Lauren Bacall in an old movie, and around her neck were tortoiseshell glasses on a neat gold chain. Although she could be anywhere from seventy to eighty years old, Connie realised that there was absolutely nothing little-old-ladyish about Eleanor Levine.

Connie found her voice, said, 'Hello, Mrs Levine,' and held out her hand, which was grasped in a surprisingly firm and warm grip.

'Please come in. And you must call me Eleanor.'

Connie had never been in the apartment below hers, even when the Taylors lived there. She saw now that it was the same layout but entirely different, thanks to its period furniture and gold-framed paintings on the wall.

The windows were larger though, and Connie saw that her neighbour had been sitting at a chair beside the vast bay window, a cup of tea and an upturned book on a small table beside the chair.

'The square keeps distracting me,' Eleanor Levine said. 'I read a bit, then find myself staring out at the garden or watching the playground.'

'Me too,' said Connie. 'It's addictive, looking on to the square. Whole scenes unfold in front of your eyes like a movie.'

'Exactly,' said Eleanor, looking impressed. 'I can see you're a kindred spirit. I spend altogether too much time watching my neighbours. I've never done it before, but here, I seem to look out every five minutes. I expect the cops to turn up any day to arrest me for stalking.'

Connie laughed. 'Golden Square lends itself to people-watching. I didn't look out the front window once when I lived at home, and I come from a small town where it's almost an Olympic sport. But that's more ...' she searched for the right the word '... *nosey* looking out. What we do here is watching with interest.'

'That's good,' Eleanor agreed. '*Watching with interest*. Shall I make coffee and you can tell me what you watch with interest?'

'I can make the coffee for you?' offered Connie, suddenly realising she'd come to help her elderly neighbour and she wouldn't be much help if she sat down and let the old lady do everything.

'I'm fine on my feet today,' Eleanor said with a wry smile. 'I have, as you might have noticed, bad days when I use the stick, but today my aches and

157

pains are manageable. Thank you for my letter and the cookies.'

'Ah.' Connie waved her hand. 'They're only a token to welcome you.'

'It's very neighbourly of you to visit with me, Connie. I haven't had many visitors so far.'

Eleanor led her into the kitchen and Connie sat on a stool at the counter and watched as she ground coffee beans and put them in the coffeemaker.

'Tell me about yourself,' Eleanor went on. 'I've seen from your piles of books that you're a teacher. What do you teach?'

'History.'

'That must be exciting.'

'It is, I love it. Although, it's not without its hard days. Teaching, that is. There are days when nobody wants to learn and you don't really want to teach any more. Then sometimes you get the kid who wants to learn.'

'I know, the ones with the spark in them,' breathed Eleanor, her blue eyes so very bright.

They were, Connie decided, a young woman's eyes, full of vitality, staring out of this lovely old face.

'Did you teach?' she asked, because Eleanor clearly knew what she was talking about.

'For a time. I'm a psychoanalyst and I did a little teaching here and there.'

'Wow.' It was Connie's turn to be impressed. She sat up straighter on her stool.

'You're doing it,' Eleanor said, and turned back to the coffee. 'When people hear what I do, they sit up straight. Some people think I'm going to start analysing them on the basis of how they hold their wine glass. Others jump right in and tell me how they've been feeling down since their pet died and they divorced their husband, and do I think therapy would help, because they're on medication and it's not really working.'

Connie laughed. 'I suppose it's like meeting someone who is a hairdresser and your hand instantly reaches up to your hair and you start making excuses. "I meant to wash it today but I didn't have time, and it looks better than this normally, honestly!"'

'That's it,' Eleanor replied.

'I guess the psychoanalyst version of that is "I've been meaning to do some work on my ego, but my subconscious won't let me."' Connie suddenly wondered if that made sense. Were the ego and the subconscious the same thing? She'd never got the hang of psychology. 'Are you working while you're here?' she asked, changing the subject rapidly.

'I've retired.' Eleanor said it with a finality that put an end to that conversation as she placed cups on the counter and poured the coffee. 'Sugar or cream?'

'Both,' said Connie.

They talked about the people Eleanor saw from her window.

She was fascinated by the tawny-haired woman who lived with her husband in the tall white house opposite and called her 'pet' in the tearooms.

'That's Rae Kerrigan and her husband's Will. She runs the tearooms and works for Community Cares. She's fantastic. I don't know her that well, but she has a kind word for everybody. Goodness shines out of her.' Connie stopped. 'I know that sounds strange, but it does. When I meet her in the tearooms, I feel warm and healed, somehow. Too much caffeine, probably!'

Uses humour as armour, Eleanor noticed. A powerful protection, and one that was just as hard to break through as people who used bitterness as a shield.

Eleanor stifled the urge to ask what Connie's feelings of warmth felt like and what sadness the warmth was healing? This was a new neighbour, not a patient.

'What is Community Cares?' she asked instead.

'It's a charity that takes care of people in need: underprivileged families, people who've lost their jobs. Most of the people who work at local level are volunteers.'

'I see,' said Eleanor. 'Can't be easy work.'

'I doubt it,' Connie replied and sighed. 'I've often thought I should do something like that, but I've never actually got round to doing it.'

She didn't say that she'd put off talking to Rae about Community Cares because somehow working for the charity seemed to symbolise putting aside her own hopes and dreams.

In her hometown on the east coast, women got involved in charity work after they'd reared their children. You gave back to society when your little ones had grown up. It would seem too much like giving up on the idea of Connie having her own family if she started doing that now.

'Two doors down from Rae is Prudence,' she said, moving on, 'and trust me, she does not make you feel warm when you see her. She's got short dark hair, is very keen on a pale blue anorak that she wears no matter what the season and has a

160

scowl that would turn the milk sour, as my granny, Enid, would say.'

'I love those old sayings,' Eleanor said. 'My mother had a store of them and I can't quite recall them all. I've seen Prudence.' Short, thin and walked in a furtive manner, Eleanor thought. Like someone who was always running fearfully.

'She's a total cow. Was very rude to Megan, who's staying with her aunt, Nora Flynn, at the end of this row. Megan's an actress and she was in the papers over something.' Loyalty forbade Connie to say more about Megan than this.

Connie had felt stupid for not knowing who Megan was, but proud of how kindly Nicky had handled the matter that evening at dinner in their house.

'We'll find a nice Irish guy for you,' Nicky told Megan firmly. 'Someone with no strings attached who will worship you like the goddess you are.'

Megan had half-laughed and half-cried.

'And who is this Megan?' Eleanor asked.

Connie considered how to answer this. Megan wasn't the sort of person who could be confined to a one-line answer. Connie could see precisely how outsiders might see Megan merely as a starlet who'd snared a famous movie star, but she reckoned that the situation was more complicated than this. Even though she assumed that horrific publicity and having to hide would undoubtedly have affected even the hardest person, Connie instinctively felt there was a deeper vulnerability to Megan.

'Megan Bouchier. I don't know if you've heard of her. She's mid-twenties, very beautiful—almost unreal looking, actually, like that Afghan girl who

161

was on the cover of *National Geographic* all those years ago: haunted green eyes and a gorgeous face. She used to be blonde but now her hair is short, very dark. You might have seen her walking her aunt's dogs, a greyhound and a fluffy little white dog.'

'Yes,' said Eleanor. 'I've seen her. I'd like to meet her, and your sister.'

Talking to Connie, it came to Eleanor that perhaps meeting people was the answer. She'd spent far too long here in the apartment, alone with her thoughts.

'We'll fix it up,' said Connie, pleased.

Eleanor poured more coffee.

'Who's the nice-looking man who lives next door in the basement apartment?'

Connie looked confused. 'Which man?'

Eleanor smiled inwardly. She was pretty sure Connie was unattached, unlike her sister who was obviously dating that sweet young man. And yet Connie hadn't even noticed the not unattractive guy next door. Tallish, well-built and with close-shorn reddish gold hair. Although he rarely smiled when he was alone, when he was with his daughter, a skinny little girl with the same colour hair, his smile would break any woman's heart. 'Red hair and he's got a daughter.' She couldn't say definitely that he was single, but the only women she'd noticed seemed to be other parents ferrying the girl home.

'Oh yes, I've seen them,' Connie remembered without much interest. He always looked a bit distracted and hadn't noticed Connie. 'I don't think they can have lived there long. A year or two maybe.'

Eleanor couldn't help herself: she had to dig deeper.

'Nicky's dating someone, isn't she? How about you?'

'Nicky's seeing Freddie and I'm available,' said Connie lightly.

'OK.' Eleanor paused. Years of practice had made her an expert at emotional archaeology: the trick was the correct question and a neutral tone of voice. 'Were you married before?'

'No, nearly married.' Connie fiddled with her coffee cup restlessly. 'We split up. Probably just as well,' she said, without conviction. 'I'm better off without him.'

Again said without conviction, Eleanor thought. It was as if Connie was repeating what everyone else had said to her but she didn't really believe it.

'This way, I can look for the perfect man,' Connie added lightly.

Definitely said without conviction, Eleanor thought.

'Love is never where you think it is,' she agreed. 'Research suggests that lots of people meet their partner at work.'

Connie grinned. 'Not an option for me, unless they sack most of the teachers and hire new ones. Besides, there's more to life than a man.'

Ah, thought Eleanor. She loved it when her instincts were right.

'Of course,' she said neutrally. 'Family, career—'

Connie's sweet open face fell and Eleanor felt a moment's doubt. What was she *doing*? She wasn't here to analyse people who dropped her mail off for her. But she was so sad and lonely, and this was the only thing she knew. It was a little exploration, that's all . . .

'You must love your job.'

'I do,' Connie said slowly. 'I didn't make a choice, if that's what you're thinking. The fabulous career as a trade-off for no personal life. It just happened.'

'Most people don't make that choice, per se,' Eleanor said. She would never have said such a thing in an actual session, but then this wasn't an actual session. 'We find ourselves doing things because of old scripts we've never let go of.' How to summarise all this easily? 'The man you think you're better off without, he's had an effect on you and your choices.'

'You mean him leaving me affected me more than I think?'

Eleanor nodded. She drank some of her coffee, let the caffeine flow into her. She loved coffee but it no longer loved her. More than two cups a day and her sleeping patterns went awry, and she ended up awake in the middle of the night. The philosopher Sartre had hated three o'clock in the morning. She hated it too. In the middle of the night, failure and sadness came to roost in her mind.

'I have a list,' Connie said suddenly. 'It's a bit silly. Actually, it's totally silly. I do it for fun because I'm not going to ever meet a man like the one on the list. It's a list of criteria for the perfect man. First requirement is, he has to be tall.'

'Why is that so important?'

'Because men don't like women who are taller than them.'

'Don't they?' Eleanor had a way of asking questions that bounced the need to reply right

164

back at a person, a bit like playing tennis. 'Why do you think that?'

'They don't, though, do they?' Connie said weakly. 'I've never met a man who was with a woman taller than he was. Well,' she considered, 'Keith, my ex-fiancé, he was just the same height as me and I could never wear heels with him. Not that I'm a great one for high shoes—they hurt, don't they?—but he didn't like me being taller, you see . . .'

Eleanor let the silence lie there comfortably for a while.

'Maybe not all men are like Keith?' Connie said finally.

'Probably not,' agreed Eleanor.

'Maybe I've made the list too precise so that nobody can ever live up to it?' Connie didn't know why she was telling Eleanor all this, but she was, and Eleanor seemed to understand what she was talking about without being emotionally involved. It wasn't like discussing it with Nicky (too young and happy) or Sylvie (too in love) or even Gaynor, her married friend (too exhausted from endless cooking and childcare). Eleanor seemed to like talking about deep things and she had such an interesting overview. Like she was devil's advocate or something.

Eleanor nodded. 'Lists can . . .'

She was considering her words carefully, Connie could see, giving the conversation such concentration.

'. . . be self-defeating,' Eleanor went on. 'Lists can become a way to lessen the importance of something. It's too enormous to cope with, so we break it down into a list and then it has less power over us. And that's shutting the door on what we have to deal with. Do you think?'

This was clearly Connie's cue to reply. She nodded. She'd never thought of it that way before. Was writing a list of all the things she wanted in a man really just an avoidance tactic or a way of lessening the power of it in her head? *Here's my funny list and, no, I don't want a man anyway, it's just a laugh, I'm happy the way I am.*

'But it can be useful too,' she protested. 'I like making lists, it clarifies ideas in my mind.'

'Perhaps when it's "things to do", that sort of list,' Eleanor said. 'But for the person you want to spend the rest of your life with, can that be broken down into component parts? Also, is this list an avoidance tactic so you don't have to face something you'd rather not?'

Connie's mouth fell open but she shut it sharply.

'Right,' said Eleanor calmly. 'Once you get it all firmly in your head what you *really* want from a relationship instead of the ideas left over from Keith, then you can start again.' She decided to go off-piste, so to speak, and deliver one of the truths she'd forgotten until recently. 'Life is about getting by, Connie. Surviving. It's never perfect and we self-sabotage for any number of reasons, but if you try to understand all that about yourself, you can be happy.'

*   *   *

At home afterwards, Connie realised she had asked almost nothing about Eleanor herself. For sure, Eleanor hadn't volunteered anything, but Connie still should have asked.

She was becoming self-obsessed. So she didn't have everything she wanted in life, but so what? And yet Eleanor hadn't said that it was OK to accept not having it. In fact, she implied that it wasn't foolish to look for more.

You can start again, Eleanor had said.

Had Keith taken all the fight out of her? She'd been youthful and full of energy with him. When he left, she'd become old overnight.

On a whim, she sat down at the small laptop computer she and Nicky shared, and Googled Keith.

It took a while to find him and when she did it was on a social networking site.

Because she wasn't a member of the site, his photo only came out as a hazy silhouette, but it was him, she was sure of it. She'd recognise the shape of his head anywhere.

His relationship status said: *engaged*. Connie stared at the screen without moving.

Engaged.

His 'favourite things' were condensed into five words: *Michaela, love of my life.*

A twinge of pain hit her.

Then Connie peered more closely at the listing. That couldn't be right. Keith was the same age as she was. Forty in August. And yet, according to this, he was only thirty-six. His birthday fell on the correct day, just the wrong year.

He was pretending he was younger!

Quite why this cheered her up, she didn't know, but there was something infinitely amusing to think of Keith claiming to be in his mid-thirties because he had a much-younger girlfriend.

She closed the site and turned off the laptop. No

more mindless surfing over Keith. Pretending-he-was-younger-Keith.

No more self-sabotaging.

She felt better already.

*   *   *

'You still haven't told her?' Freddie couldn't believe it.

It had been three weeks since he'd proposed and Nicky still kept the ring on a long golden chain around her neck, because she couldn't wear it on her finger until she'd told Connie.

'Why not? And put it on your finger. She won't notice,' he said.

Nicky looked at him grimly. 'Just because you wouldn't notice it, doesn't mean Connie wouldn't. Of course she'd spot an engagement ring on my finger. Women notice things like that. Just like you noticed that woman in the pub last night who wasn't wearing a bra, and had the fakest tits I've ever seen in my life.'

Freddie objected. 'I only glanced at them. At her,' he amended.

'I'm just saying: men notice fake tits and women notice engagement rings.'

'I can't tell my parents until you tell yours and Connie,' he said. 'I know we're only going to have a small wedding, Nicky, but we have to get going with it or there won't be one at all.'

'I'll tell her soon, I promise.'

'When?'

'Tonight, OK?'

*   *   *

168

Connie looked at all the short men in the supermarket that afternoon. Normally, she only noticed tall men and petite women. Petite women reminded her of Nicky, and tall men made her run through her mental checklist.

But not today. No, this was a new start to her life. Talking to Eleanor had given her new hope. So what if Keith had liked her to wear flat shoes and had been threatened by her height? Not all men would be. She'd put the Keith baggage in the mental dustbin and was moving on.

The supermarket was jammed with Saturday afternoon shoppers but Connie was serene as she wheeled her mini trolley up and down the aisles. Nicky had said Freddie was at a football match and, for once, he wouldn't be around that evening, so the sisters had arranged to have dinner together.

'We could order in an Indian takeaway, and I'll get wine and dessert,' Connie said happily, looking forward to it.

She spent so many Saturday evenings at home alone. Of course, Freddie and Nicky went to the cinema with her and took her to concerts and parties, but she often felt like a third wheel. Not any more. Look out short men!

As she was parking the car, she spotted the man from the next-door apartment out of the corner of her eye. Eleanor had mentioned him, so Connie tried to look closer without it being obvious.

He was hefting groceries out of his truck and the little girl was helping by picking things she liked the look of out of the bags and just carrying those in. Her russet hair was in a long, neat plait down

169

her back and Connie had a moment of wondering if the little girl's father had plaited it. He must have. Her mum was never around, he was clearly a single father. There was something both touching and sad about the idea of him patiently plaiting his daughter's hair.

Something made him look over at Connie, who went red because he might guess she'd been staring, and then gave a little wave hello. He smiled politely and turned away. Feeling unaccountably disappointed, she dragged her own shopping from the car and lugged it up the steps.

* * *

'I've something to tell you,' Connie said, when she and Nicky sat down at the table that evening. She'd lit candles, had taken the good glasses out for their wine and water, and the takeaway had all been decanted into Connie's best dark-red tableware. The curtains were closed, Michael Bublé was crooning quietly on the stereo, and everything was cosy.

'You do? Me too,' said Nicky, her mouth full of naan bread.

'Oh, you first!' said Connie cheerfully. Nothing could dim her enthusiasm.

Talking to Eleanor had been like a tonic: she felt so energised, so ready to take on the world.

'Well, I wasn't sure how to tell you. We've talked about it . . .' Nicky hesitated. There was no point in beating around the bush, she had to just do it. 'Freddie and I are getting married. In April, hopefully. We want to do it quickly. I mean, why hang around when you've made up your mind? I want you to be bridesmaid, of course.' The words came out in a rush.

She looked at Connie's kind, round face with its warm eyes and gentle, usually smiling mouth. Connie blinked quickly, as if she had an eyelash in her eye.

Magnificently, she rose to the occasion. 'Nicky! I'm so thrilled for you!'

And she was utterly thrilled that her darling, precious little sister had found absolute happiness. Connie shoved her plate aside, pushed her chair back, and was beside Nicky, hugging her.

'I was so worried!' Nicky was saying. 'I know how hard it must be for you because of Keith. He's a waster, a total louser. He wasted years of your life, and Freddie wanted me to tell you straight away—'

'You should have, but I'm happy you're telling me now,' Connie exclaimed. 'It's wonderful. When did he ask, have you made any plans?'

'None yet. We wanted you to know first. Oh, Con, I love you. I wanted to tell you straight off because it's so exciting.' Nicky drew a gold chain out from under her sweater. On the end of it dangled a delicate engagement ring, which Connie grasped and pronounced 'beautiful!'.

At Connie's urging Nicky slipped the ring on her finger and they both admired it, then Connie had to turn on the main light so they could see the jewels more clearly.

'But Freddie should be here if I'm the first person you're telling,' Connie said. Inspiration struck. 'He's not really at a football match, is he?'

No,' admitted Nicky. 'Freddie isn't out at all. I just wanted some peace so I could tell you in private.'

171

'Get him round!' said Connie. 'Phone him! I'll order some more takeaway from Khans; I can rush round to pick it up and get some champagne. We must celebrate.'

With one last hug for her sister, she left the table to get her coat and her purse.

'What was your news?' asked Nicky, reaching for her mobile phone to ring Freddie.

'Oh nothing, compared to yours, just that I met our new neighbour today. You'll like her, she's great.'

*   *   *

Connie got another helping of tandoori chicken, more naan bread and another order of dhal. She picked up a bottle of champagne in the off-licence, and then took a trip into The Nook to buy chocolate for later, when she was in bed. Chocolate nearly always helped. She lingered near the circular book rack where paperbacks were squashed into the top and Mills & Boon novels were lined in the bottom. Tonight, the chocolate might not be enough. *The Bride's Ransom* shone up at her, with the kind of picture that had been her fantasy for as long as she could remember: a bronzed man with a hawkish, proud face, holding a fragile but beautiful woman tightly to him. In the middle of the day, Connie could walk past the rack without blinking. But come nighttime, when she was lonely and sad, she wanted to be the one of the women in the Mills and Boon pictures, being held and protected.

Freddie was at the apartment when she got back.

'Brother-in-law-to-be!' she greeted him with a

172

hug.

'I knew you'd be happy when you heard,' he said innocently. 'Your sister's an awful worrier.'

'I know,' Connie said cheerfully.

She reheated the original meal and served it all up, whereupon they ate happily and toasted Freddie and Nicky's engagement, and talked about the plans.

The engaged couple had drawn up a shortlist of guests already, and had discussed venues. Connie and Nicky's parents' house in Wexford was small and they had a tiny garden, so there was no room for the party there. Freddie's parents had lost a lot of money in bank stocks, and had downsized to an elegant but modest two-bedroom apartment on the outskirts of Cork.

'That's another reason we want to keep the wedding small,' Nicky said.

'I know, but even though they'll understand, they'll still be upset that all the mad aunties and uncles can't come,' Connie warned. 'People can get very emotional about weddings,' she added, privately thinking that this sentence must surely qualify for understatement of the year.

'You'll help us explain it to them, won't you, Connie?' begged Nicky, and Connie managed to keep the smile on her face.

'Of course,' she said. 'Now, when are you planning the big day?'

'April,' said Nicky. 'Rochelle in work is taking half of May off, and we can't really go on holidays at the same time as she handles my authors when I'm away. So we can get married in April and have our honeymoon with a clear conscience.'

'Great,' said Connie calmly. 'And, er, where are

173

you planning to live?'

It was a hard question to ask—she loved having Nicky living with her, and could quite happily put up with Freddie moving in too, if it meant she could keep Nicky with her.

'That's one of the really exciting bits!' Nicky said, beaming at Freddie. 'The top-floor apartment in Freddie's house is going to be free at the start of April. It needs a bit of work, but we've talked to the landlord and he'd love us to have it. Steady tenants, he called us.'

Freddie grinned at this.

'It's got two bedrooms and an amazing view of the harbour. Much better than Freddie's.'

'That's wonderful,' Connie said, the smile still fixed on her face. 'Wonderful.'

At eleven, pleading tiredness, she went to bed.

From the living room. Connie could hear laughter and happiness. She was so pleased for Nicky and Freddie, but they must never know how achingly lonely she felt in her pink boudoir. Connie pulled the frilled covers up around her, broke off a couple of squares of chocolate, and began to read *The Bride's Ransom*.

9

Roasts

You're too young to remember the big storms in the 1920s, Eleanor. There were bad winters with fierce winds that felt as if they'd take the

174

thatch off the house. One March, when you were just three years old, we had the worst storm of all. Several trees went down in the garden. The biggest, an ash, hit the side of the house and knocked in part of the gable wall. My mother and Agnes shared that bedroom, and what a night we had. We got the bedding out of the room, but my mother's pretty cabinet with her little bits of glass and china was badly smashed.

Your father said he'd fix it up as good as new, and he did.

He also mended the wall. It took him a month, but when Joe said he'd do something, he did it right.

The night he finished, we had roast dinner to celebrate. There was no butcher in Kilmoney, so we had to go to Clifden, the nearest big town, if we wanted to buy meat. Kilmoney was tiny then, you see. Like everyone else, we kept a pig and always butchered our own bacon and salted it in a big oak barrel for winter. We'd kill a chicken, if we had one, on a Saturday for Sunday's dinner. For anything special, like a piece of beef to roast, we'd go to Clifden. Even today, I still get a warm feeling inside me when I smell a roast. The trick is to have the oven as hot as you can bear it and then sear the sides of the meat, and that makes it tender on the inside.

We couldn't always afford a roast for Sunday dinner, so if the funds were low and the tallyman was at the door, you couldn't beat some boiled bacon and cabbage. The loin is the best cut, with a decent bit of fat on it. Boil the bacon for an hour, changing the water a few times and skimming the froth off the top, then twenty-minutes from the end, add the cabbage into the pot. By the time it's all cooked, the bacon will melt off the fork. I like a little mustard with it. I had a flowery egg cup I used to make the mustard powder up in. It broke when we moved from Kilmoney and even now I think no mustard ever tasted as good as it used to in that egg cup. It wasn't the mustard, it was the place, you see. The egg cup reminded me of home. Nothing's sweeter than home, Eleanor.

Rae liked walking into the tearooms and seeing it the way the customers saw it. The scent hit people first: there was always cinnamon because of the apple-and-cinnamon muffins; a hint of vanilla from the lemon-and-vanilla poppyseed cake; and then there was the subtle spice of coffee. Rae liked to offer interesting coffees and this month her special was Rwandan.

This particular morning, Rae had had two cups of coffee already and it was only half nine. Timothy, who owned the tearooms, had been in and they'd gone over the books. Business was flourishing.

'People like their small treats,' said Timothy with relief. He owned a building company as well and that was in dire straits.

Rae felt sorry for Timothy. A gentle, balding, middle-aged man who lived in one of the biggest houses in Golden Square, he'd had a hard life despite the material things he owned, like a top-of-the-range Mercedes and a holiday home in Florida. The source of the difficulties were definitely his wife, Sheree, who never appeared to be happy with anything. She didn't approve of Titania's, although Timothy had bought it with a view to her running it.

Thankfully, Sheree's desire not to sully her hands with work had turned out to be to Rae's benefit.

'You do a great job, Rae,' Timothy went on. 'With you here, this place just runs itself.'

Rae nodded, although it wasn't quite that easy. She ran the place with a team of loyal women workers, nearly all of whom had children and looked out for each other.

When Anton had been small, Rae had organised rotas to ensure that everyone was accommodated.

If Livvy's little girl was running a temperature, Rae got someone else in early to do the baking, and when Sonja had needed extra time off because her newborn baby had been diagnosed with reflux, Rae had kept the job open and given part-time work to her next-door neighbour Claire's eldest daughter, who was going to college and wanted a few hours' work every week.

Today, there was a rota of ten local women working in Titania's, with one man, Pavel, a patisserie chef who'd once worked in the finest restaurant in Warsaw and who now made magical cakes for the inhabitants of Golden Square. Rae could quite happily go away for a week knowing that Titania's was in the best of hands.

Friendliness, cleanliness, beautiful food and a great welcome were the watchwords of Titania's.

This morning, Patsy from the hairdressing salon was in deep conference with a thin woman who was crying and kept taking paper napkins from the table dispenser and wiping her face with them.

Rae knew better than to interrupt her.

'Mary,' she whispered to the youngest waitress in the house, 'go over and fill up the coffee cups at that table. Don't listen and do your best to look as if your mind is somewhere else, OK?'

'Sure,' said Mary, whose aunt Livvy had worked in Titania's for donkey's years and who knew better than to question any of the mad requests made of her. Rae knew her stuff and if Rae felt that looking mindless was required for this table,

178

then that's what they'd get.

'Vivienne, put on something lively on the CD player,' Rae added to the small woman at the till. Ella Fitzgerald was singing mournfully about lost love.

'Gotcha,' said Vivienne, spotting Patsy and her guest. She rifled through the CDs. 'Aretha Franklin demanding respect?'

'Perfect.'

Rae went into the kitchen and talked to Pavel, who was just leaving for his shift in a big hotel on the other side of the city. He was a fabulous worker but Rae worried Titania's would lose him. He was working too hard, surely something had to give?

There was no time to ask him, he was rushing.

Denise, who took over when Pavel was off, admired the mille-feuilles he'd made earlier.

'He's an artist,' she said.

'An artist with pastry,' agreed Rae.

She talked to the staff, did a stock check, and then came out front to work the till.

The elderly American lady who was living on the other side of the square was waiting for a latte, her smiling face gentle in repose.

'Hello, pet,' said Rae.

The woman's mouth curled up slightly into what might or might not have been a wry smile and Rae instantly regretted using the term of affection. She must have offended this lady.

'Forgive me,' said Rae, 'I don't know your name and I don't mean to offend you.'

'It's Eleanor,' said the woman.

'I'm Rae. Welcome, Eleanor,' said Rae, instantly liking the lack of formality. If Will's mother was

179

there instead of Eleanor, she'd have insisted on *Mrs Kerrigan*, because 'manners matter, Rae!' While this elegant white-haired woman who walked stiffly, though with grace, was simply Eleanor.

She was older than Will's mother, but she didn't wear her age like armour, distancing herself from other people. Instead, she wore it lightly, a veil of wisdom and warmth.

'Being called "pet" is very comforting, actually. That's why I smile,' Eleanor went on. 'Not in disapproving amusement, I can tell you.'

Rae relaxed. 'Thank you. I don't always know everyone's name and I like to, so when I don't, I say "pet" and "love". Some people don't like it.'

'Only the churlish, surely?'

Rae grinned. 'Yes, but I can't say that when I'm behind the till.'

'Rae is a pretty name. Is it short for something?' Eleanor asked.

'I was called Rachel as a child,' Rae admitted. She didn't want to say that, one day, she'd been called Rae in school and it had stuck, more because she liked it than for any other reason. Rachel was her parents' name for her, which was why she'd been happy to leave it behind, like so much of her past.

'Somebody told me Rachel is Hebrew. Will I take the tray for you?'

'Thank you.' Eleanor stepped back politely and waited for Rae to go first. She thought of mentioning that her husband had been Jewish and their daughter was called Naomi, another beautiful Hebrew name.

A table by the window was free and Rae carried

180

the tray to it.

'Thank you,' said Eleanor graciously, and sat down gingerly.

She was in pain, Rae could see, but for all Eleanor's friendliness, Rae sensed that she was a person who liked to keep her life private.

At the table nearby, Patsy had succeeded in comforting her friend. The woman's face was no longer tear-stained and she was finishing off one of the apple-and-cinnamon muffins.

As Rae passed, Patsy shot her a grin that said *thank you.*

At three, Dulcie arrived to pick Rae up for a couple of Community Cares visits. They went to Delaney again, then across Kilmartin Avenue where a young couple with a small baby had both lost their jobs and needed to move out of their flat into a cheaper one. Unfortunately, the landlord was refusing to give them their deposit back, and due to the enormous grey areas in the housing law, they didn't know what to do.

Dulcie recommended them asking a housing charity for advice. Sometimes, a phone call from somewhere official-sounding brought unscrupulous landlords to their senses. But only sometimes.

'Poor things,' she said as they left. 'I'd love to tell them to talk to the community housing officer, but he'd make it worse.'

The local housing officer was a man who felt that anyone asking for his help needed to be humiliated first for the crime of being poor and disadvantaged. He only wanted to help people who crawled in on their hands and knees, and his favourite trick was to reduce clients, particularly the female ones, to tears.

The two women were silent as they headed for their last visit. Rae tried to calm herself. She was no use to anyone when impotent rage was fuelling her. But it was hard to be calm when you witnessed decent people being treated badly because they were poor and without power.

The last house on the list was round the corner from Golden Square but on the other side to Delaney. The more expensive side.

Wellington Gardens was a cul-de-sac where six huge new houses sat in a spacious semi-circle. When they had been built five years ago, the property pages had been full of superlatives about this new, American-style road.

'Wisteria Lane comes to Dublin,' the papers had said.

Rae and Dulcie had been to a coffee morning in one of the houses once, where a charitable-minded woman had invited her wealthy friends in to raise funds for CC. They'd admired the tiled hallway, shiny woodwork and a kitchen that came straight from an interiors magazine—and Rae had thought ruefully of her own kitchen, with its admittedly big but very unglossy old gas cooker, and cupboards which hadn't changed a lot since the previous owner had been in situ in the 1980s.

She'd taken the generous cheque and by the time she got home, her sense of self had reasserted itself. She liked her kitchen, even if the units didn't all match.

Dulcie reminded her of this coffee morning as they drove into the road. 'The *style*. Jim still laughs at me about it. I went home and gave out stink about the state of our house, and why we'd need a skip to take out all the old furniture before we

182

could even *get* people into the house to have a coffee morning.'

Rae laughed. Dulcie had hit the nail on the head, as usual.

'I was the same,' she said ruefully.

'Well, you do compare, don't you?' Dulcie continued. 'I suppose comparing makes you appreciate what you've got when we're going into poor Mrs Mill's house. She doesn't have a giant cooker and a huge dishwasher or any of that stuff.'

There was silence as Dulcie negotiated the way past a fleet of shiny SUVs parked outside one house.

They pulled into the drive of the fifth house on the estate. The Lodge was surrounded by a thick four-foot hedge that was wonderful from a privacy point of view and even more wonderful if you were a burglar.

Dulcie rang the door bell and within seconds a dark-haired woman in a purple tracksuit opened the front door a crack. Her face was pale and her long hair lank.

'Yes?' she said, eyeing them both with a combination of anxiety and suspicion.

'Community Cares,' said Dulcie. 'We talked on the phone?'

The woman they were to see was named Shona, but they didn't use names on the doorsteps in case they were at the wrong house, in which case they'd apologise and retreat. Respect people's privacy at all times, was part of the charity's rules.

Shona nodded, opened the door and said nothing until they were inside.

'The neighbours—' was all she said then.

Rae and Dulcie understood. In some

neighbourhoods, CC were like part of the family and welcomed as such. Here, in the land of new wealth, having to call on a charity for financial aid was comparable with being found shooting up heroin in an alley.

They followed Shona's slight figure through to a large living room. In so many ways, the house was a match for the elegant house where the coffee morning had been held. The Lodge was a riot of subtle floral prints, all gorgeous stuff like in magazines Rae flicked through in the doctor's waiting room. A Chinese silk rug spanned the huge living room with its large designer sofas, real oil paintings hung under golden picture lights: it all spoke of money.

According to Dulcie, who'd got the details from head office, the woman had no food in her huge American fridge to feed her two children. Her husband had lost his job, the money was gone, the house was worth less than the mortgage and there was simply nothing left to sell. The bottom had entirely fallen out of the art market. Nobody wanted to buy her oil paintings. There was no gas for the glossy four-wheel-drive jeep on the forecourt, on which they were unable to keep up the payments.

Without waiting for them to talk, Shona began an her litany of woe.

'We've tried to sell everything,' she said. 'The car, the paintings, my jewellery. Diamonds make almost nothing, did you know that? Why did our mothers tell us to get diamonds?' She held out bony hands that Rae guessed had once been manicured every week. Rae never got manicures, but then her mother had never told her to get diamonds, either.

'Diamonds are useless. And shoes.' Shona's voice rose dangerously. 'Second-hand shoes have no value at all. People admire them. "I love your shoes," they say, but they won't buy them off you. And the children—how do I tell them . . .'

This was the point at which people often broke down. Rae and Dulcie had been in many expensive houses this past year, and it happened every time. No matter how stoic the person was, the thought of their children's disappointment brought them to their knees. Losing money in a giant economic meltdown could happen to anyone and was survivable. But no longer being able to give their children everything when they'd been brought up to expect it, that was the worst failure of all.

Rae could understand these feelings. Children were the repositories of so many hopes and desires. She'd never wanted her son to suffer any of the hurts she'd suffered.

'Lyra's in an exam year, her Junior Cert,' Shona went on. 'She keeps having nightmares. And Katya was supposed to be going on the school skiing holiday next year, but I've had to tell her there's no way we can afford it. They're only still in the school because we paid in full last September. She'll have to leave and she was so looking forward to the skiing . . .'

Rae saw Dulcie's mouth set in a firm line. Dulcie disapproved of such carry on as people sending teenagers off on skiing holidays with their private school.

Rae looked around the room as Dulcie talked through the normal CC issues like finding out what Shona and her husband were doing legally, checking to make sure they weren't in danger of being thrown on to the street with the children, which would be another issue to solve.

'No, it's not that bad—yet,' Shona said.

That's when she began to cry. Not pretty crying, but silent ugly tears that made her face turn blotchy.

Rae could sense that Dulcie didn't like Shona. When you'd worked with someone for as long as they'd been together, you could tell. Dulcie had very specific views on people for whom she had sympathy. Anyone who was doing their best to get out of the poverty trap and who wasn't taking drugs, drinking like a fish or spending every spare cent of the children's allowance on cigarettes was fine. In Dulcie's book, someone like Shona— who'd once had everything, hadn't appreciated it and had now spent it—didn't fit the sympathy category.

'Come on, now,' Dulcie said firmly when five minutes of crying was up.

'You don't understand,' Shona said, still sobbing. 'It's awful, I don't know how to cope.'

'We'll help,' Dulcie went on.

'If only Conor could find another job. Look at us. We can't pay the credit-card bills. We have nothing, nothing.'

Rae felt sympathy overwhelm her. She understood the horrible fear of having nothing and not knowing where to turn. 'I know that it doesn't look like it now, but it's going to be all right,' she began. She was a very calming person, everyone said. It was partly what made her so brilliant as a volunteer with the charity. She instinctively knew what to say to people in despair.

Dulcie flicked a glance at Rae.

She was made of tougher stuff than Rae and her gaze said: This woman still hasn't a clue.

But Rae understood that the woman's life had changed more than she could cope with. The drop from luxury to poverty was a steep one: the shock took longer to wear off.

'You will be all right,' Rae said again. 'You won't starve.'

She ticked off points on her fingers. 'You have two healthy children, the bank are not going to repossess your house, there is hope that in time that you will be able to sell this house and have enough to buy a smaller home. Your husband might find a job—or you might!'

Rae could sense rather than see Dulcie's eyebrows raising. Rae knew she was verging ever so slightly into 'with my crystal ball . . .' territory and that nobody knew any of this for sure, but she felt that hope was part of the prescription for a woman in Shona's situation. It wasn't enough to help her with food for the kids; she needed to be told that one day her life might improve. That would be worth more to her than a fifty-euro shopping voucher for a supermarket chain she wouldn't have dreamed of going into before.

'You think so?' Shona said bitterly. 'It doesn't feel like that to me, I can tell you. I'm broken, my husband is broken, and that's all our daughters see. I can't imagine us ever getting out of this.'

'None of us can see the future,' said Dulcie crisply. She began to write in her notebook. 'Let's make a list of out-goings.'

Afterwards, Rae got silently into Dulcie's car and felt about a million years old. She wanted to go home, find Will and give him a huge hug. At least they'd never had to go through this with Anton. Imagine the pain of it –

Dulcie interrupted her thoughts.

'You're brilliant, Rae, but you're too soft,' Dulcie said firmly. 'There, I've said it and I don't want to be a horrible old bat, but you can't fix her. She seems a touch unrealistic, but things will improve and she'll come out of it all right. She could go back to work herself.'

'I know, Dulcie, but think of the pain she's going through now. Mrs Mills isn't in pain for all that Terence makes her life so difficult. They may be broke but they're coping. Shona isn't coping and I hate seeing that.'

It hurt her to see another person's naked pain. Like those young people today with the baby, no jobs and a nasty landlord. She wanted to help but there seemed so little she could do, even working with Community Cares.

'She'll have to cope,' Dulcie declared. 'Everyone has to. You cope and I cope. We've gone through hard times.'

'True.' Rae nodded. It was good to remember that.

Dulcie was right: try as she might, Rae couldn't fix the world.

*　　　*　　　*

Denise greeted her in the café with the news that Pavel had phoned to say he wouldn't be in for his shift at Titania's the next morning.

'If he wants to leave, I'd prefer if he just told us,' Denise said huffily. She'd taken the call and was

188

insisting that Pavel wasn't ill and that this was a scam because Pavel was going to better-paying job interviews.

'Pavel's a very honourable person,' Rae said. 'He must be sick. He wouldn't let us down for another job without telling us.'

'Hmmph,' was all Denise would say. But Rae knew she was right. It was a nuisance, that was all. She locked up and left for home.

The heavens opened as she was running across the square and even though it was a short trip, she got soaked.

Will had lit the fire in the living room: Rae felt its warmth as soon as she stepped into the hall. 'Hello, love, I'm home,' she shouted.

Will didn't shout back. He must have gone back to the garden office. He did that sometimes: came in to heat up whatever dinner she'd prepared earlier, then went back to finish up his work.

Rae didn't bother with her evening cup of tea. She wanted to change out of her wet clothes as soon as possible. The last thing she needed was to catch cold.

Upstairs, she had a speedy shower, then stood at the window brushing her hair and looking on to the square. It was dark now, but under one of the street lamps she could make out the cluster of purple-hued early irises she'd admired that morning. Each one an Old Master all by itself, delicate purple-edged petals drooping like a child's bottom lip. In the heavy rain, the irises were hanging their heads under the weight of water.

Her mind kept drifting back to the woman from the big house that she'd met earlier. She had more than a touch of affinity for poor Shona today. Rae

189

could understand what it felt like, not wanting people to find out the truth. It wasn't that she was ashamed of her past, but it was easier to forget it. When you left it behind, you could start again any way you wanted.

When she said she came from the West of Ireland, people so often assumed she came from a scenic spot. If you came from the town, you just said the name of the town, so the vastness of saying 'the West' implied a remote cottage in the shadow of some beautiful mountain, with stonewalls, elemental views and the roar of the ocean just a mile away.

Rae wasn't the sort of person who lied, but she was always deliberately vague about her home. Let people picture the scenic spot and the odd cow peacefully outside.

It was better than telling them about the ugly concrete bungalow outside Limerick city with the broken-down cars on the drive. Easier to vaguely say *yes*, she loved the wildness of nature in the West, than to mention that their garden back home had almost no plants left alive in it when she last saw it. The back garden was filled with sparse, heavily mossed grass and the front was concreted over. Rae was so competent and so kind that she knew her friends in Community Cares assumed she'd come from a home where kindness was the currency. But it hadn't been. Chaos had been the currency. Chaos, poverty and the high-octane rows that came from two people who should never have married being stuck together in a tiny house with a child they didn't want.

She went downstairs. In the kitchen, Will had laid the table and put her favourite cherry-red napkins out. There was still no sign of him.

A casserole she'd made and frozen at the weekend was heating in the oven and there was rice measured out by a saucepan, ready to cook.

Rae busied herself checking the casserole and boiling the water. When the rice was simmering, she went back up to the hall where the morning's post lay on the hall table. Will would have taken any business letters down to his office. All that would be left were probably bills and she'd better open them now.

Taking the post back to the kitchen, she peered at the rice to see how it was doing.

There were two bills addressed to both of them, and an official-looking letter addressed only to her.

She ripped it open, scanned the first typed line and froze.

Dear Rae,

I am writing to you in connection with a birth which occurred in the Blessed Helena Nursing Home in Limerick on 27 August 1969.

We are trying to track relatives of that baby and thought you might be able to help us with further research.

It that's not the case, I am sorry for bothering you by mistake. If you can help, can you phone me on the number given at the bottom.
Yours sincerely,

Moira Van Leyden

Underneath the line explaining that Moira was a

191

social worker was a mobile phone number.

Rae stared at the letter blankly. She had never fainted in her life. She didn't believe in it. Fainting was for truly ill people or the elderly, not for healthy people. But now Rae could feel the blood leaving her head and knew that, if she didn't sit down, she would fall to the floor.

She sank on to a kitchen chair and read the letter again.

She'd been waiting for this all her life with both great hope and great fear.

The hope was that one day she'd meet the daughter she'd thought about every day since she'd last held her in her arms. People sometimes said that about things—that they thought about something or someone every day, and it sounded ludicrous. But Rae knew it was entirely possible to do this. She'd done it. Not one single day had gone by that she hadn't wondered about her baby. Jasmine.

The fear was what this revelation would do to Will and Anton.

Rae had never kept secrets from Will. Except for this one.

How could she tell him now that she'd lied by omission all their married lives together? How could she tell her husband and son that, at the age of sixteen, she'd had a baby girl and given her up for adoption?

*   *   *

She could still recall exactly when she'd discovered she was pregnant. It was a freezing January day in 1969, and it was on the verge of snowing. Rae's

192

class in school were due outside for games and they all gathered gloomily in the cloakroom where they changed into their sports skirts and gym shoes and muttered about how it was too cold, and Miss Ní Dhomhnaill was a sadist for making them go out on a day like this.

Rae didn't want to play camoige on a freezing pitch, she didn't want to go anywhere at all. She wanted to curl up in a ball and beg God to let her period come. She was five days late. They'd been five days of worrying.

She sat down on the cloakroom window ledge and rested her body wearily against the glass. Around her, her classmates talked and changed. She heard someone whispering and saw another girl reach into her school bag and take out a packet. Rae recognised the white and blue packaging of a sanitary towel. Something, if she was right, that she herself wouldn't need for a long time. In that moment, Rae knew instinctively that she was pregnant.

Years later, she wondered how she knew for sure. What instinct had told her? She hadn't felt it with Anton, had barely dreamed it was real—her punishment for what happened when she was sixteen.

With Jasmine, she'd known for sure.

She'd got to her feet, grabbed her coat and school bag, and pushed her way blindly past everyone, not wanting people to see the tears.

'You're bunking off games?' said Shelley, who was one of the few friends she had in the class. Shelley's parents had a farm six miles from Rae's shabby bungalow. They'd been friends since they were little. Shelley's parents were kind to Rae and never let their disapproval of her parents interfere with their daughter's friendship with her. Other people weren't so kind. It didn't matter how nice she tried to be: other people judged her by her parents.

People admired Rae for her work ethic and for arriving spotlessly clean every day from the unpainted, shabby bungalow. Nobody had ever seen the inside. The Hennesseys didn't do entertaining.

But Rae's hard work wasn't enough. People didn't want their daughters hanging around with the Hennessey girl, no matter that she seemed like a decent creature. Look at the parents. Who'd want their child going into that house? No, it was easier to keep the Hennesseys at a distance.

'I feel sick,' Rae told Shelley now.

'You've got a hangover, haven't you?' Shelley said with a hint of admiration. 'I'm warning you, Rae, that Davie is a real boyo. Don't trust him, right?'

'No,' said Rae faintly.

It was all gone way beyond that. There was no one to blame but herself. She'd been the one who'd had a fight with her parents, she'd been the one who'd gone to the disco in anger because there was no money in the Hennessey house for the extra lessons that would help Rae in her state exams in June. Maths wasn't her strong point, but with a little extra work, the principal had told her, she'd get there.

But Paudge and Glory Hennessey made it clear they had no intention of paying for extra lessons.

'Get away out of that,' Paudge had roared at her when she'd raised the subject. 'Far from bleeding grinds you were raised. You go to the convent and that's good enough for you. It was good enough for your mother.'

Rae had felt the anger rise in her. Normally she said nothing: it was easier. But today, something burst inside her.

She'd turned on them, on her unshaven father sitting in the threadbare chair with a bottle of beer in his hand, and her mother, sitting beside him calmly rolling a cigarette, her long dark hair greasy. The house was filthy despite Rae's efforts. There was nothing on for dinner—there rarely was—and it was cold because the Hennesseys hadn't bought coal for months. Paudge's unemployment cheque got cashed in the pub. Coal for the fire was a long way down the list of his priorities.

'Good enough for her, was it?' Rae shrieked. 'I'm sure the nuns hold her up as the example of excellence. "Look at Glory Hennessey, hasn't she done well? Thank goodness she never did any extra lessons or bothered with exams, because she's turned out so well without all of that."'

'You little bitch.'

Rae felt the flat of her mother's hand sting her cheek.

'After all we do for you!'

Rae sat there, immobile. There would be a mark on her face, she thought blankly. Her mother hadn't hit her for a long time, but she was very strong and a flat-handed slap left marks. Rae didn't care about the mark. She wouldn't bother covering it up with make-up like she once might have. Everybody knew what her parents were like: why bother to pretend otherwise?

Davie and his bottle of whiskey in the youth club disco had seemed like a life raft. He'd been after Rae for a long time.

'You're beautiful, you know that?' he'd say.

Rae could see that there was some sort of symmetry in her face and she knew other girls admired her dark eyes, slanted eyebrows and the cheekbones that made them call her 'Cheyenne'. But she didn't see it as beauty.

True beauty was cherished and loved, wasn't it? Like people in films who were loved. How could beauty come out of her life?

Tonight, she didn't pass Davie by. He was one of the Sullivans; they were all pale-faced with midnight hair and heavy five o'clock shadows. Menace surrounded them, but Davie was all right. Eager.

Unable to believe his luck when Rae smiled at him and let him lead her on to the crowded dance floor, he murmured that he had a bottle of whiskey hidden in the cloakroom. Rae wasn't normally one of the teenagers who drank. Tonight was different. Tonight, she'd be everything everyone thought she must be: a member of the crazy, reckless Hennessey family.

'Get it,' she said to Davie. 'I need a drink.'

They stood at the back of the hall and, hidden behind the people who lined the edge of the dance floor, they shared the bottle. Davie drank it from the bottle but Rae couldn't.

'Get me something to mix with it,' she gasped after the first sharp bite of whiskey.

Davie came back with red lemonade in a glass. He poured a little in. Rae took the bottle and filled the tumbler to the brim.

'You're going wild tonight, girl!' he said, pleased.

Kissing him wasn't so bad after all the whiskey. They danced the slow dances, Davie holding her tighter than anyone had ever held Rae before. Bobby Goldsboro was singing 'Honey' and it felt nice to be held, nice to be dancing with this warmth inside her.

She giggled as they made their way down Main Street. Davie was intent on taking her somewhere. In the back of his uncle's butcher's shop, he said. He worked there at weekends, he had a key.

'Oh yeah,' she said sleepily. Now all she wanted to do was lie down and sleep.

'Come on,' Davie said, hauling her along. 'You were the one who wanted to go wild.'

He had keys to the back of the shop and they crept in. Inside, it was freezing. Rae began to wake up and shivered.

'Cold rooms for the meat,' said Davie.

'Is there music?' she asked.

There was a small transistor radio in the shop itself. Davie brought it into the back office and its crackling filled the air.

He searched the drawers of a filing cabinet and came up with another bottle, this time of clear liquid. Rae had never drunk the clear, illegal whiskey. Some kids were given spoonfuls of poteen mixed with cloves, hot water and sugar when they were sick. But not Rae. Paudge Hennessey liked poteen and would never have wasted it on his daughter.

This time, there was no red lemonade to mix with it.

Rae drank. She didn't like the taste, but she wasn't being herself tonight. She was being the

197

other Rae, the true Hennessey.

When Davie began to kiss her and his hands fumbled with her top, pulling it up to reveal her white bra, she didn't stop him.

'You're a beauty, Rae,' he mumbled heavily, kissing her.

Even Davie, with his clumsy caresses, was kinder than her parents.

When it was all over, Davie leaned against the wall and smiled. 'That was amazing,' he said, breathing heavily. 'Did you enjoy it?'

Rae patted his cheek fondly. Had she been supposed to enjoy it? At least Davie cared about her. Nobody else seemed to.

There was a small toilet at the back of the storeroom and Rae went inside and threw up, the whiskey burning as much on the way up as it had on the way down. Then she sat weakly on the toilet itself and wiped away the stickiness of Davie, and her own blood.

She wondered why people got so excited about sex. She'd read bits of dirty books that Coral, her cousin, had lent her, and in books, sex was exciting. In books, women screamed loudly and panted, and men told them they adored them and would kill to possess them. In real life, Davie had done the panting, not Rae, and it had been quick, so quick. It had hurt too, the feeling of something alien in her body, in *there*.

There hadn't been pleasure, just nothingness, the same nothingness she'd felt since that afternoon at home.

She flushed the toilet and sat down on the lid. The tiredness was gone. In its place was an ancient weariness.

Lies came back to haunt you, Rae realised. Lies were like cracks in a foundation wall. If they were there, they would make themselves seen eventually. No matter how well the wall was plastered or painted or whether expensive wallpapers were hung, one day, the crack would work its way out to the surface. And then, the only question would be why you hadn't dealt with the crack in the first place, why you'd hidden it.

She heard the back door open slowly. Will called her name.

'Rae, hello love, sorry I was so long. I was on the phone.'

Rae quickly folded up the official letter until it was a small square, then she stuffed it with the envelope into her pocket.

'The rice is nearly ready, I think,' she said, and somehow, her voice was steady.

There had been times early on when Rae could have told Will. But she'd never found the courage. Then it was too late. She met his family and after that she feared to lose him.

'I had lunch with my mother today,' Will said, sitting down at the table with a sigh.

'Really?' said Rae, trying to calm herself down.

Will met his mother twice a month for lunch alone; it was easier that way. For years, Rae had gone along too and she'd felt an enormous relief when she convinced Will that his mother liked to have him to herself.

Geraldine Kerrigan adored her son and there was no room for a third party in the relationship.

Rae had long since decided that it was easier to get out of her mother-in-law's way.

'The good news,' Will went on, 'is that she met the surgeon this week and he's going to replace her hip. He's got a cancellation on Monday and he's going to do it then.'

Rae kept spooning out the casserole. She'd seen many people confined to barracks due to hip replacements or hip breakages. Anything to do with hips meant a lot of inactivity, pain and other people looking after you.

'When?'

The week after next. The thing is, Rae—'

'—she'll need looking after,' Rae said, interrupting. 'Is she going to a nursing home? To Leonora's house?' Leonora was Will's older sister, an identikit version of her mother. Similar in so many ways, the two women had a testy relationship at best.

'She *can't* go to Leonora's,' Will said.

Why can't she? Rae wanted to ask. It's not my fault your mother and your sister are at each other's throats.

'I know she can't go to Leonora's,' was what she actually said. Despite being in a state of shock about the letter, she knew what had to be done. Geraldine would come to them. Rae would have to continue to pretend everything was all right and that her long-lost baby hadn't reached out a hand from the past.

The only plus of the letter about Jasmine was that it had blunted the effect of Will's news. Normally, Rae would have felt dizzy at the idea of Geraldine coming to stay. She tried to engage with practicalities.

'When is she coming? Where is she going to sleep?'

Geraldine would have to be on the ground floor, but where? How would they manage?

'I was thinking that perhaps we could set up a bedroom in the living room,' Will said. 'That way, she can use the little bathroom in the hall.'

Many years before, they'd installed a shower and loo under the stairs in the hall.

It was small and not what Geraldine was used to.

The idea of Geraldine living in their home for three, perhaps four weeks, suddenly made Rae quail.

But not for one second could she let dear Will know this.

'That's a great idea about the living room,' Rae said evenly. 'We ought to start sorting it all out tonight.'

'Thank you, love,' said Will, and it was almost worth it for the smile on his face as he looked at her. Almost.

10

Feasts

Use your best china for a feast— that's my advice. You want to welcome guests into your home and what could make them feel more welcome than the sight of a beautifully laid table with flowers, candles and the nicest china? Your best doesn't have to be fancy, either. The first time I had Christmas dinner in my home, we were poorer than church mice and, out of ten plates, only two matched. We hadn't a penny. Eleanor, your cradle was the bottom drawer of the chest, although it was prettier than any shop-bought cradle once I'd lined it with a hand-sewn quilt and your woollen blankets edged with satin ribbon. But nobody thought we were poor once they saw the table. I'd worked all winter on that tablecloth with scraps of embroidery silks. I had a lot of reds, so there were poppies on it— not like any poppies Joe said he'd ever seen, but I laughed at that, gave him a swift slap with my dishcloth, and said they were my version of poppies. Joe's mama had crocheted lace for the edging of the tablecloth with the fine white thread that came from the linen bags of flour.

Joe had won me two big tumblers of carnival glass at the fair in Galway, so I picked a big handful of ivy and made up the tumblers with the ivy trailing down the sides. I love carnival glass, the swirly orange colour lit up the table with the ivory candles perched in the middle. I stuck a bit of rowan in the sides too, in honour of the fairy folk. My mam went to Mass every morning but she was raised knowing about the fairies.

Our china was a mish-mash, but there was a sprig of holly berries on each plate, and when the goose was laid in the middle, Joe said the Grace, and we all said Amen. I looked down that table, at all of them, the family we'd started collecting, and I knew there was no better way to celebrate than to cook good food for them. The food is only a bit of it, you see. It's the heart of the person who's doing the cooking. The intention. That's what makes it a real feast.

Sometimes you have to conjure a feast out of thin air. I remember when Joe's uncle died and there was nobody left in his homeplace to have the wake. I got a big piece of bacon. You can't beat a good piece of bacon when you have to come up with a feast in a hurry . . .

Megan watched the man in the airport with the camera around his neck. He wasn't a tourist, not with that sleek, black Canon and state-of-the-art telephoto lens. If the Hubble Telescope went offline, the man's lens could probably stand in and magnify Mars.

Paparazzi, definitely. Probably there to photograph some celebrity that his news desk knew was flying in, but any photographer worth his salt would realise that photos of someone like Megan would make a fortune, so if he spotted her, she'd be in trouble.

Megan pulled her grey bobble hat down around her ears and felt glad for the safety of baggy boyfriend jeans and a hooded sweatshirt that was three sizes too big. She'dbeen in Ireland for six weeks and, so far, nobody had spotted her.

She found a seat in Arrivals as far away from the photographer as possible and sank down into the collar of her sweatshirt, trying to look like a bored teenager. It was entirely possible to disappear in public, despite what many famous people claimed. Megan and Rob had managed to hide very well in Prague at first.

*　　　*　　　*

'Are we crazy?' she'd asked Rob, as they took the lift up to their suite in the Hotel Sebastien, both of them in dark glasses and baseball hats, trying to look like tourists. It was a flip question, but Megan was serious.

This was their last chance to step back from the brink, and even though she wanted to be in bed with Rob Hartnell more than she wanted anything in the world, an inner voice was urging caution.

'Why are you asking that?' Rob said, linking his fingers with hers.

Megan shrugged. 'I don't know. Anxiety, I guess. Something's making me nervous.'

'Don't be.'

The lift shuddered to a halt and the doors slid open.

'We're meant to be together,' he whispered, as he ushered her into his rooms.

In the huge suite with its over-sized furniture and formal sitting room, Megan felt a strange combination of anxiety and excitement overwhelm her. This was even more stunning than she'd imagined. The hotel's dark beauty was like a backdrop for a play. Through open double doors, she could see a big bed with a carved headboard and filigree gold-painted lamps hanging on the walls at each side.

Rob wandered into the bedroom while Megan stood in the middle of the sitting room and imagined a steely matriarch onstage, sitting on one of the velvety couches, delivering her lines. She shook her head to get rid of the image. This wasn't a play, it was her life.

Rob returned and took her hand. He was smiling. 'Never mind all this,' he said. 'Come with me.'

His big hand was warm and gave her comfort. 'Now,' he said, with satisfaction. 'I'd heard about these baths . . .'

The bathroom was perfect in its 1900s glory. The

old gold-hued silk wallpaper was torn in places, and the giant marble sinks were worn, but a claw-footed bath big enough for four people sat in state in the centre of a sea of Siena marble. A big old-fashioned jar of pale blue bath salts with a navy satin ribbon stood on a pile of snowy white towels.

'I think we need a bath after our trip,' he said huskily, his mouth close to her ear.

In that instant, it didn't matter that Megan was anxious. Rob reached over and unbuttoned her coat. He pulled her baseball hat off and released her hair from its ponytail. She didn't move, merely leaned her back against him, eyes closed, and let him touch her.

Then he turned her round and bent down to kiss her, his mouth fierce on hers. She sank into him, letting his body support hers as they melded together.

Every day on set, Megan had watched this man surreptitiously. Many other people had too. People couldn't help staring at Rob Hartnell. It wasn't the fame. Her co-star, Seth, was also world famous and sexy, not to mention much younger, yet he didn't have the magnetism of Rob.

Once Rob was on set, people's eyes were drawn to him. If he laughed, they laughed too. When he gave them *that* smile, they were like besotted parents staring at their first born, smitten.

'Star quality,' was what Megan's agent, Carole, called it. 'It's utterly inexplicable, you can't explain it to anybody, but it's real. Only a few people have it and boy, is it a powerful force.'

After weeks of dreaming about Rob, and of snatching kisses and caresses in hidden moments, Megan was finally with him properly.

She reached up to run her fingers over the breadth of his shoulders, feeling his muscles flex as he held her. His face was moving down her neck now, his hands exploring, sliding her coat from her body, his fingers slipping inside her shirt to trace the lines of her collarbone. He'd done this on the set with the entire crew watching. Now, he did it for real and she could allow herself to moan softly in response. His lips cruised the bones of her chest and moved to nuzzle the swell of her breast.

'Perhaps we'll leave the bath for later,' he murmured. They were moving back towards the bedroom, and on to the bed. In a tangle of arms, clothes came off. They were naked together, heated skin on skin. Rob was a big man and lying with him in the huge bed, she felt fragile and protected.

This was what she'd been waiting for.

*　　*　　*

At the airport, Megan forced herself to stop thinking about it. The memories were too raw, too painful. An image of Katharine Hartnell's face in the newspaper came to mind. Finely arched eyebrows over eyes that glowed with pain, the high cheekbones stark and too big for her face. That pain was all Megan's fault.

NO. Stop thinking about it. Stop.

She hastily wiped her eyes with the long sleeve of her sweatshirt, then texted Pippa quickly.

Photographer in arrivals hall. Meet you beside taxi rank. Sorry.

She was always saying sorry, now. With her head down, she made it outside and fumbled for her cigarettes. She hadn't meant to smoke before hugging the kids. It wasn't good, funny how she'd never thought that before. But being with the dogs had made her aware of it.

She had to wait half an hour before her sister appeared. Pippa looked tired and older than her thirty years as she tried to push a trolley with one hand, and manhandle Toby's pushchair with the other. Kim was perched a tad precariously on top of the suitcases, and she beamed out at her aunt with delight.

'Look at me, Meggie, look at me!'

'Be careful!' said Pippa in the faintly hysterical tone that Megan had noticed her sister using since she'd become a mother.

'She's fine,' Megan said, and reached up to hug her niece.

'She's not fine,' said Pippa tightly. 'It's a nightmare, travelling alone with them.'

'I had to come out here to hide,' Megan began.

'Yes, sorry,' Pippa said, and let go of her trolley to embrace Megan.

Megan sighed as she buried her face in her sister's shoulder, smelling the rose perfume that Pippa always wore.

For a moment, it was like having her sister back again, the other part of herself. But then Toby began to cry, and Pippa bent to talk to him, and Megan stood watching, feeling left out again.

She shoved the bags into the back of Nora's old Ford Fiesta, and let Pippa strap the children into the car seats Nora had borrowed from one of her neighbours. Kim and Toby were like child models from a clothes catalogue. Toby had Pippa's mop of fair hair and his father's brown eyes and warm

208

smile, while Kim was fair with bluey-green eyes like her mother and an adorably naughty expression on her face. Once, Pippa had looked like a model too, but now she was exhausted looking and had definitely put on weight. She hadn't mentioned that on the phone. A few years ago, it would have been the first thing she'd have talked about. Not any more. Her priorities had changed.

When Pippa, Kim and Toby were all installed in Nora's house in Golden Square, it was very cramped. Cici kept getting stood on and then howled in outrage. Leonardo was doing a funny backwards dance as Toby rushed at him, arms out for a hug.

'Leonardo can be an anxious animal,' Nora said, deftly steering Toby in a different direction.

'Would he bite?' asked Pippa worriedly.

'No,' said Nora, but Megan could see that Pippa didn't believe her. How odd. Once, Nora was the person in the sisters' lives who knew everything and who could be relied upon. How to get tar stains out of Megan's beloved jeans, how to put together a geography project on oxbow lakes ... She was the opposite of Marguerite—'*don't call me "Mum", it makes me feel ancient*'—who prided herself on not knowing anything that might be considered mundane.

Oh, she knew how to make men fall in lust with her, all right. Or how to coax someone into letting them borrow a beach buggy for a whizz around the dunes. Or even how to mix a cocktail using a coconut as a glass. But she knew nothing that was any real use.

It had been Nora they had turned to for all that.

And now, Pippa didn't trust her. Another change brought about by marriage and babies.

Megan felt that strange prickling sensation in the base of her neck again. Everything was changing and she hated it. But it was ludicrous to feel jealous of her little niece and nephew. They were her family, she should adore them as part of Pippa. Why then did she feel so separate and left out?

Dinner that evening was loud and slow. Nora had bought ready-made chicken Kievs and, in a supreme and unusual effort of cooking, was going to do a complicated thing with potatoes, cheese and cream.

'The recipe says it's actually quite simple,' Nora murmured, reading the cookbook thoughtfully.

Pippa shook her head.

'No, sorry, Nora, they won't touch that.'

'But you will, won't you?' asked Nora.

'Me? Yes, but not the kids.'

Pippa wrenched open the fridge and stared into it, forehead furrowed. 'Any peanut butter?'

'No, sorry,' said Nora. 'I wasn't thinking, Pippa. I should have known better. What do we need?'

Pippa ticked it all off. 'Peanut butter, white bread—I know, they should be eating brown, but if they eat anything, I'm delighted. Proper butter, soft white cheese for sauces, full fat milk. Fromage frais, bananas, grapes, plain chicken breasts.'

Toby came to investigate the fridge too, and thought he might climb into it.

'No, love, you can't do that.' Pippa picked him up expertly and held him to her. He snuggled in like a baby chimp clinging to its mother.

Megan watched.

'I'll get the shopping,' she said quickly.

The Nook only had crunchy peanut butter, and no fromage frais. Megan spent ages comparing other pots of small yogurts. If they didn't say 'suitable for children', did that mean they were or they weren't? She ended up getting yogurt drinks with drawings of cartoon animals on the pack.

Nobody said hello to her or commented on her unusually full basket. Normally, she bought cigarettes, newspapers and an occasional baguette for Nora. Some of the people in the square talked to her in The Nook these days; kind, well-meaning chat. As if once you visited the shop regularly, you were a local and therefore entitled to be part of the daily conversations of Golden Square. Today, there was no one Megan recognised in the shop.

It took her ages to find it all and her basket weighed a ton.

A man at the top of the queue was giving out because the credit-card machine wasn't working and he had no actual cash.

'What sort of a shop is this?' he was demanding crossly, as he went laboriously through his pocket looking for bits of change. 'You're going to have to wait while I find some money—oh, that's ten cents, right, here's twenty cents . . .'

The young guy behind the counter shrugged as if to say, 'Don't ask me, I just work here.'

Megan tapped her toe, turned around and idly looked into the basket on the floor behind her. A bottle of wine, a couple of glossy magazines and a packet of just-add-water risotto lay there, along with a jumbo bar of chocolate. It was the sort of haul Megan herself used to buy when she lived in London. The woman's shoes were fabulous. Silky leather platform heels with delicate cut-outs.

211

Probably horrendous to walk in, but so cool.

She looked up at the person it belonged to, a slim, fashionably dressed woman around her own age with short streaky blonde hair. Once-a-month visits to the hairdressers, Megan theorised, and she should know. At least there was damn all maintenance in her midnight-dark crop.

She felt no kinship with this woman, no sense that they belonged to the same tribe any more. But then, Megan wondered, what tribe did she belong to now?

*   *   *

Kim and Toby wouldn't touch the yogurt drinks but ate some cereal with milk.

'Major food group,' said Pippa wearily as she swept cereal off the floor.

'Shouldn't they have something more substantial?' Nora asked worriedly.

'Yes,' said Pippa, 'but it will take an hour to coax them to eat two bites and I haven't the energy for that.'

It was half past ten by the time Pippa got the children to sleep.

Megan and Nora were watching television when Pippa came into the room.

'Sorry, I have to go to bed,' she said, standing at the door. 'I'm shattered.'

Megan knew that if she wanted to talk to her sister at all, she'd have to follow her, so she went into Pippa's room, the bedroom they'd shared as children. It hadn't changed much: it still had the red-and-green flowery curtains, giant amaryllis set amid huge fat leaves, with tiny poppies dotted here

212

and there at random. Instead of two single beds with white-and-red check bedcovers, there was now one double bed with a pure white duvet and a woollen blanket folded across the bottom. The children slept on two fold-up camp beds placed either side of Pippa's bed.

Pippa took off her shoes and lay down with a sigh of sheer exhaustion.

'Why are beds so comfortable when you're tired?' she asked in a whisper.

Megan lay down next to her. They both stared for a moment at the wallpaper with its honeycomb colour. That too was unchanged since their childhood.

'You do look wrecked,' Megan said.

Pippa snorted. 'No, sis, tell me what you *really* think!'

'I didn't mean it like that. You simply look worn out.'

Pippa adjusted her pillows. 'That's what small children do, they suck the lifeblood out of you.'

Megan turned to face her, astonished.

'And you love them for it,' Pippa went on.

Megan lay quietly for a few minutes. She had so much to say to Pippa but she wanted to let them settle back into being together first.

'Pips, it's been terrible.'

There was silence from the other side of the bed.

Megan turned to see that Pippa had fallen asleep. She gently pulled her sister's jeans off, but left her blouse on, and pulled the duvet up over her. The big talk would have to wait.

*　　　*　　　*

Megan woke to great roaring cries from a small child. Toby.

'What –?' She pulled a pillow over her head to block the noise out but it went on. 'Stop, please,' Megan moaned and then it did.

Thank God –

'Meggie!' The door of her bedroom slammed open and Kim's voice punctured the silence. 'Mummy's sick. She won't get out of bed and I need to do a wee-wee.'

Megan managed to crack her eyelids open enough to look at her watch. Half six.

By the time Megan had dragged herself out of bed, Kim was stamping her feet with irritation.

'It's OK,' Megan said. 'I'm sure Mummy's not sick—'

'She IS!'

Kim stood in front of the toilet, waiting.

Megan sat on the edge of the bath, also waiting.

'Help me. Pull my jammies down!' ordered Kim.

Megan pulled. 'Will I help you get up on to the toilet?' she began. She'd never done this before.

'No!' shouted Kim in outrage. 'I do it myself.'

'Fine.'

Megan sat on the bath again. She was still sleepy and all this was exhausting.

It took five minutes to finish the process, by which time Megan was wondering if she could go back to bed again.

But Kim had other ideas. Taking her aunt's hand, she led her into the spare bedroom. Toby was still fast asleep in his bed, despite all the earlier shrieking, and Pippa lay in the big bed, looking green.

'I'm sorry,' she said weakly, not moving. 'It must

214

be flu. I threw up several times in the night and now I just feel exhausted. All my joints ache. You'll have to mind the children, Megan. I just can't.'

'Me?'

'I can't, Megan, I'm dying.'

'But I don't know how to . . .' started Megan, wondering if Nora could take the day off work because *she* hadn't a clue how to take care of two small children. Not for a whole day, anyway.

' 'Course you do, it's not hard. Please, Megan.'

'What will I do?'

'Get them up, give them breakfast.'

'What will I give them?'

'Anything. Ask them.' Pippa groaned and rolled over in the bed. 'I feel like throwing up again.'

Kim watched from the end of the bed with interest.

It was, Megan realised, up to her.

'I'll get you a basin,' she said.

Once Pippa had the basin, Toby woke up.

He sat up, saw his mother was lying in bed and not paying attention to him, and began to cry again.

'Don't be a baby,' scolded Kim, with the authority of a four-year-old. 'Meggie's looking after us.'

'I love you, Kim,' said Pippa weakly. 'Toby, love, Meggie's going to mind you because Mummy's sick.'

Toby wailed louder.

Megan stood like a statue, wondering what she should do. She'd never done anything with Toby before. She'd fed Kim a few times when she'd been a baby, but first babies were like royalty: their mothers didn't want to let them out of their hands.

Megan had never had Kim for long before Pippa whisked her away. By the time Toby came along, Megan had given up offering. It saved Pippa having to come up with reasons why she needn't bother.

Pippa covered her head with the pillow. She must be really ill, Megan decided, going over to Toby's bed and scooping his protesting little body up.

He roared with greater volume.

'You'll have no trouble in the theatre, young man,' Megan joked, trying to keep it all cheery. 'They'll hear you in the cheap seats.'

Toby wasn't amused by the banter.

From under the pillow, Pippa mumbled: 'Bring his teddies to the kitchen or he'll cry.'

'Which are your teddies?' Megan asked over Toby's cries. Then inspiration struck. 'Can you help, Kim?'

Kim walked to her baby brother's bed and picked up a blue-and-white striped cat.

'Cat,' she said flatly. 'I have a fairy. Do you want to see it?'

'I'd love to,' Megan said. Toby's wailing was beginning to get to her. 'Let's all leave Mummy to sleep, shall we?'

'OK,' said Kim, placing a plastic silver tiara on her head, before collecting a fairy in a lurid pink-and-purple outfit. 'This is Fairy Princess. She's fableeous.'

'Oh yes, fableeous,' Megan agreed.

In the kitchen, Toby was so delighted to see Leonardo and Cici that he stopped crying. Megan took advantage of the fact to pop him in his high chair and put dog biscuits on the floor around it, so the dogs clustered around him and he began to giggle.

'Let's get you breakfast,' she said.

Kim looked at her gravely. 'Toby's nappy is smelly,' she said.

For a second, Megan felt like saying: What do you want me to do about it? But then she realised that she was in charge. She'd never changed a dirty nappy before. Wet ones, yes. Dirty ones, no.

'Right,' she said brightly. 'Where's the nappy bag?'

*   *   *

Nora came upstairs at lunchtime and smiled at the trio in the small sitting room. Toby was watching a kids' TV show, and was covered in the chocolate hazelnut sauce that Megan had found he liked eating with plain biscuits. She was sure that eating quite so much of it was bad for him, but it kept him quiet and that was all that mattered. Kim was in the centre of a giant pile of what looked like Nora's good printer paper, with a solitary squiggle in crayon on each page. The dogs had been banished to the kitchen, and Megan sat on the ground between the two children, with chocolate sauce on her face, and what looked like dried cereal on her sweatshirt.

There was something so normal about this scene of domesticity, that Nora beamed at them all.

'You look like you're having fun,' she said.

'Auntie Nora, look, I did you a picture!' Kim leapt up and brandished one of the sheets of paper.

'I love it,' Nora said, turning it around as she

217

tried to work out which way was up.

Megan, who'd just spent one of the most exhausting mornings of her life—children *never* stopped, how did Pippa manage?—got off the floor and threw herself on to the couch.

'Fun is tiring,' she said in the children-are-present voice she'd got into the habit of using during the morning. It was a tone of voice that worked.

'Let's all try to be as quiet as little mice as crying might wake poor Mummy,' sounded better in this voice than *'Be quiet!'* shouted at high decibels.

'I knew you'd be able to do it,' Nora said to her niece. 'You were always good with smaller children when we were in the square when you were young.'

Megan felt absurdly pleased.

'How's Pippa?' Nora added.

'I haven't been up all morning,' Megan said. 'If you watch the children, I'll sneak up now.'

Pippa was awake, said she was no longer throwing up, but still had a slightly green tinge to her.

'Thank you, Megan,' she croaked. 'I couldn't have got up and taken care of them.'

'You look a bit better,' Megan said, then realised she wasn't actually telling the truth. Pippa looked worse than Megan had seen her for years, and it wasn't anything to do with her green pallor. Her face was puffy and tired.

Carb face, that's what it was, Megan realised. She knew about it from a Los Angeles nutritionist who insisted that all Europeans turned up in LA with the bloated faces of carbohydrate eaters. Carbs were evil.

'You're all right. You don't do carbs, do you?' the

218

nutritionist had said, shooting an all-encompassing gaze over Megan's face and body.

Megan shook her head. At the time, she was doing pretty appalling nutrition all round. Lots of late nights, cigarettes and bottles of white wine in clubs all over London. It was only some genetic fluke that allowed her to do all that and still look glowing.

'Watch the alcohol, though,' the nutritionist had added. There wasn't much she missed, Megan realised. 'Sugar piles on the wrinkles.'

'Are you looking after yourself?' Megan asked her sister now. 'You look tired.'

'Thank you for that vote of confidence,' said Pippa sardonically.

'Sorry,' said Megan. 'I didn't mean it that way.'

'No, I know I look dreadful. It's been tough since all of this came out.'

Megan bit her lip. 'I'm sorry,' she said again. All she was doing these days was apologising. 'I hoped it hadn't upset you too much.'

'It's not so much me, really. It's Colin's parents. They hate all that stuff in the press and we're dragged into it. They're very normal people. Sorry.' It was Pippa's turn to apologise.

Megan was stunned. 'They hate me that much! But they know different, you've told them, right? They've met me, they like me.'

'They do,' protested Pippa. 'But they don't see you. I don't see you. You never come to see the children and, to grandparents, that's a sign that you're not interested.'

'I looked after Kim and Toby all day today!'

Pippa spoke very gently. 'That's the first time you've ever babysat them, do you realise that? It's been hard for me, Megan, too. I miss you, but your career has changed you into someone I don't know, someone I don't see. I miss the old you.'

Megan felt as if she'd been punched in the stomach. She and Pippa had fought before, but never like this. Yes, they'd had late-night, post-party rows, but this was different.

Pippa was warming to her theme.

'I live in a small town now and we're trying to put down roots, have a real family, like *we* never had. Remember what it was like? How we never fit in anywhere? How we used to wish Mum was more like an ordinary mother, then we wouldn't have had to leave her to be with Nora.'

'We loved living with Nora—' Megan protested.

'Yes, we loved Nora, I *do* love her, but she wasn't our mother. Mum was hardly an ordinary parent. I want something different for Kim and Toby,' Pippa said, 'and it's like you've chosen Mum's sort of world, that crazy racketing-round-the-world-after-a-man existence.'

Megan could take it no longer.

'Fine, I get it,' she snapped. 'You're perfect and I'm the awful homewrecker.'

'I didn't say *that.*'

'No, but you meant it.' Megan didn't know if she could cope with being so hurt. This was worse than what had happened with Rob Hartnell, worse almost than being on every newspaper as the harlot who'd ruined a good marriage. This was being rejected by the person who'd been there for her all her life.

'I don't see you as a homewrecker,' Pippa insisted. 'It's just that you don't stop to consider other people. Mum's attitude to life is never to worry about what people think, and it's not very good training for the real world. In the real world, sometimes you *do* have to care about what people think.' Pippa paused as if to breathe. 'That never mattered to her because, if things got too hairy, she just moved on, we all just moved on. Imagine if I did that with Kim and Toby? Imagine, if every time I ruined a relationship, I just picked them up and moved on?' Pippa shuddered. 'I could never put them through that.

'That life affected both of us in different ways, Megan. I decided that I didn't want that sort of life. And you . . .' she paused. 'You decided that you wanted one thing out of that sort of life: you wanted the protector, the guy Mum was always looking for. The one who was going to look after her and us. Except, he never did look after us, did he?'

'I'm not looking for a protector,' said Megan furiously. 'I'm perfectly able to look after myself.'

'Yes, you are,' said Pippa, 'and you're very good at it. But the first chance you get with an older man who looked like he could take care of you, you went for him.'

'It wasn't like that,' said Megan, 'I told you.'

'Actually,' said Pippa, 'you haven't told me. I worked it out. You've spent your whole life being the little girl. Even the way you dress: it's all cute little girl-child. It's time to move on.'

'You mean it's time to move on because it's upsetting your husband's family,' said Megan shakily.

'No,' said Pippa. 'I'd love you to move on, because having a husband and children is the most wonderful thing you can do. But you're too like Mum, you'll never be able to do that, not if you stay the way you are now. And because of that you'll miss out on true happiness. That's what I'd like for you: true happiness. Please, listen to me, Megan.'

Megan had had enough. She hated confrontation of any sort and she needed to get away from all the painful things Pippa was saying.

'I never meant to hurt you, Pippa. And I'm sorry you miss me. I never meant that to happen.' She whirled out of the room and ran to the hall, pulled on her trusty skiing hat and her jacket and left the house.

*   *   *

Eleanor took her walking stick to the gardens, just in case. She hated using the stick but sometimes when she sat down it was hard to get back to her feet. She didn't want to be stuck on a park bench waiting to be rescued.

It felt wonderful to be outside with the sun on her face. Too much time sitting in the apartment was bad for her. At home in New York, she'd had quite a busy social life and had walked everywhere. Before . . . Before Ralf had died. Here, she spent a lot of time alone: reading, writing and looking out her window.

Being outside was like entering a painting you'd spent ages staring at. She was transported *inside* the world of the painting instead of staring at it from her window.

In the acid-yellow sycamores, she spotted two goldfinches, red-streaked heads and golden wings making them stand out from the blue tits and sparrows. Pigeons ambled around the grass,

222

pecking things in an exploratory manner. Eleanor watched out for squirrels: she'd seen them in the trees, the grey ones instead of the gentler red ones she remembered from her childhood.

At home in Kilmoney, there had been a sweet old sheepdog named Patch and he'd adored chasing squirrels. Once, he'd found a dead one and had dragged it around joyfully like a child with a teddy bear until Eleanor's mother had realised what it was and yelled: 'Drop!'

Thinking of home made her smile. It always did. Eleanor knew she didn't smile as much these days.

After a lifetime of helping people read the map to survive their lives, she wondered whether she had lost the ability to survive it herself.

The park was empty apart from the bench in the furthest corner, where a dark-haired girl in jeans and a puffa jacket sat scrunched up, her head on her knees, clearly in distress.

The old instinct to reach out to people in need rose up in Eleanor like a wave. There were plenty of other places to sit but she found herself walking towards the girl.

Perhaps it was her slow, silent walk, but she had reached the seat before the girl looked up, a pale beautiful face streaked with tears.

Go away, her face said.

But Eleanor was made of sterner stuff. She sat down stiffly and was conscious of the girl moving so that she was facing the other way.

No matter. Eleanor could wait. Time was the one thing she had in abundance.

She watched two mothers walking into the playground with three small children in tow. Happy shrieks filled the air as the children launched themselves at the seesaw and the sand pit. A man in a suit with a takeaway coffee and a briefcase marched from one side of the park to the other, talking volubly on his mobile phone. A bus lumbered up the street beside Titania's Palace, swaying like a grand old dowager. Golden Square went about its business and here, on a bench, Eleanor waited to see if the girl wanted to talk.

Although Eleanor was looking ahead, in her peripheral vision she was aware of the girl straightening up. She folded slender legs underneath her, yoga-style, sighed heavily and leaned back against the seat.

'Beautiful day, isn't it?' Eleanor said.

'Yeah.'

Eleanor let the silence fall again.

'Would you like to talk about it?' she asked.

The girl shook her head but she kept her body turned towards Eleanor.

'I'm not the neighbourhood busybody,' Eleanor went on. 'Or maybe I am.' She laughed out loud. 'I used to practice as a psychoanalyst, so maybe I am secretly becoming the neighbourhood therapist.'

A crazy giggle escaped from the girl's mouth. 'Sorry,' she said, putting a hand to her lips. 'I didn't mean to laugh. It's weird, though. You're kidding me, right?'

'I'm not kidding at all. I'm a psychoanalyst.'

For the first time, the girl sat up straight and appeared to scrutinise Eleanor.

She unfolded her legs and held her hand out formally.

'I'm Megan. I've just had a row with my sister.'

The words were out before she could stop herself. Why did she say that? It was so unlike her to discuss personal stuff with a stranger. But this stranger was a psychoanalyst and therefore was probably bound by one of those doctor/client confidentiality clauses. Or would that work on a park bench with a stranger?

'Eleanor Levine, pleased to meet you.'

Mrs Levine's hand was firm and warm. In fact, she wasn't so little-old-ladyish at all, Megan decided, looking at her properly. She was glamorous in spite of her age. She looked like one of those elegant East Coast actresses who adored Ibsen, were friends with wildly intellectual playwrights, and had studied with Stanislavski.

'I've met a friend of yours—Connie O'Callaghan.' Mrs Levine went on. 'She lives in the apartment above mine.'

'Yes!' said Megan, and her smile lit up her face. Eleanor sighed with pleasure. She loved beauty, could spend hours in the Met or the Guggenheim, and here was more true beauty. Megan's face was a perfect oval with the finely carved bones of an alabaster Greek statue, and those hypnotic eyes.

'You're an actress, Connie told me,' Eleanor said. 'I am afraid I haven't seen any of your work.'

Megan gave a wry little smile. 'It might be better that way,' she said.

'Not because you're a bad actress, I think,' Eleanor said, feeling her way.

'No, because I'm the cautionary tale of what not to do when you're an actress.'

Again, Eleanor waited. It was amazing how human beings were hardwired to talk when they instinctively knew they were in the presence of someone who wanted to listen.

'How does therapy work?' Megan asked

tentatively.

'Well, first of all, if you're a patient, we have a contract. We agree a time every week, you turn up and I listen. That's our contract—that I will always be there. Your part of the contract is that you must turn up too. If you don't, you still have to pay me. It's making it formal, so you don't decide to self-sabotage. If you commit to it, you commit.'

Silence again. Another bus trundled down the road past Titania's. Two in a short period of time, Eleanor thought. Incredible.

'And if I don't want to talk?'

'Eventually, you will. I can think of very few people who haven't talked.'

'It works, right? It fixes people?'

Eleanor shook her head. 'It's not about fixing. It's about making you able to live your life to the best of your ability. You need to understand yourself so you can survive. My job is to provide the insights from the information you give me. I am not your friend, I am your therapist.'

Eleanor felt herself grow weary. That was part of her problem now. After a lifetime of being on the sidelines of her patients' lives, she was tired of that.

So long as Ralf was alive, it had been fine. It had never mattered that she'd been on the periphery of her patients' lives—she could come home to him and he made her feel whole again.

Now he was gone and there was nothing to connect her with the world any more.

'You are working over here?' Megan asked.

'I've retired,' Eleanor said, aware that she sounded tired now. 'Not that someone like me ever retires. It gets into your soul—probably it's the same in your work?'

Megan shrugged as if she didn't care.

'You mentioned being the cautionary tale for actresses. What did you mean?'

Eleanor was close enough to see Megan's beautiful eyes fill with tears.

'I'm sorry I was rude earlier,' Megan said hoarsely. 'I'm upset. I'd love to talk to you sometime, but not now, OK?'

She got up, smiled briefly, and almost ran out of the park.

Eleanor stayed a moment longer. She hadn't been kidding when she'd told Megan that what she did was an intrinsic part of her. Talking to patients had always fascinated her: the piecing together of their stories was enthralling. She felt a spark of energy inside. It would be good for both of them if Megan came to see her properly.

11

Fish

Living beside the sea means there's always food. We were lucky in Kilmoney because we had the ocean on our doorstep.

You'd laugh at it now to think of people saying sorry for dishing up scallops and butter for dinner when there was no money for meat. Here in New York, people in fine restaurants pay good money for shellfish, and we had as much of it as we wanted.

Your grandmother's family used to collect winkles from the shore. Hard work it was, I can tell you. Those were the days before the waterproof boots and they'd spend the day knee-high in water on the rocks, filling a basket—creel we used to call it—with periwinkles. Many's a poor family lived on winkles and cockles, cooked in milk for the children. When I was young, my mother made me eat shellfish three times a day in March to keep the cold out. I can still taste the salt tang of the sea when I see cockles today.

We ate salmon if we were lucky enough to catch one, but the best salmon rivers were owned by the folk in the big houses, so we hadn't the rights to fish those rivers. But your aunt Agnes had a friend out Bohola way who'd sneak out at night and fish in one of the rivers. I was never sure if we should eat salmon caught that way or not. Agnes used to say that the rivers belonged to no one, and we had as much right to them as anybody else.

My favourite fish is fresh mackerel, bought on the quay from the man who hauled it out of the ocean, and cooked that day in a little flour and butter.

We were lucky that none of the family were fishermen. I never looked at the sea with the wild white foam from the waves without saying a prayer. So many families lost men to that sea. Every family who fished had a different stitch in their woollen jumpers, so their bodies could be identified if they drowned.

The tradition in the area was to put a live periwinkle in the corner of the house on St Brigid's Day to protect the fishermen. The young priest, the man who was full of fire and brimstone, did his best to stop the women doing it. But they didn't heed him. They did what made them feel better. That's a good plan.

*   *   *

Searching for a wedding dress was like going on an expedition to the Arctic, Connie decided. You knew you might be gone some time, but you had a hope of it working out all right in the end.

Nicky had made a mood board compiled with ripped-out bits of various bridal magazines.

'I like structural shapes, but these fluid lines are great too,' she might say thoughtfully to Connie, who had no idea what she was talking about but was ready to be enthusiastic nonetheless.

Weddings were a whole other world, Connie had discovered: there were entire magazines on wedding flowers, and fat books on etiquette, speeches and what a bride might need on her wedding day. Had all this been around when she was engaged? She had no idea. Her bridal dreams had been mistier things based on her walking up the aisle with Keith waiting for her.

Nicky's other constant topic was plastic surgery. She was editing an Irish guide to cosmetic procedures and, in Connie's opinion, it had made her obsessed.

It was a cool morning, and they were out on their first foray into actual dress hunting.

'The book's called *Plastic Fantastic*,' Nicky explained. 'The surgeon who's written it is fabulous, but the best bit is the section on when it goes wrong. Not his work, obviously. You really wouldn't believe what people will have done.'

'Really?' said Connie, who was still exhausted and had found it hard to get out of her cosy bed at eight. She didn't think she'd ever been in the shops that early at the weekend.

'You have to watch out for the shiny foreheads,' Nicky went on. 'The thing I can't understand is why anyone would do it in the first place.'

Nicky didn't really want to know the answer

because she thought she already knew it, Connie realised.

Nicky thought it was stupidity. Connie knew it was fear: fear of ageing.

'Why would you bother?' Nicky said dismissively. 'All that nipping and tucking and injecting. It's kind of sad. There's this woman who works in the shop two floors below us, she must be sixty but she dresses from Top Shop. Honestly, she had her first face lift at forty, the other girls in the shop say. And her eyes—they're like cat's eyes now, she's had so much done. Why?'

Connie knew why. The days when she could get away with a swish of foundation across her cheeks were gone. Somehow, in the last year, her face had changed. In the mornings, her eyes were puffy and her cheeks retained the creases from the pillow for an hour. She looked tired even when she'd had nine hours' sleep.

She could totally understand why a sixty-year-old woman would want to look younger when she had to work in the expensive clothes shop below Peony's offices. It was probably on a par with going to work in a school populated with gorgeous teenagers. On a good day, a person could cope with it. On a bad day, it was all she could do not to put a paper bag over her head.

Ahead of them was their destination: Bridal Heaven, a one-stop bridal shop.

'And she does that thing with her lipliner—you know, drawing the line bigger than her lips really are. It's awful,' Nicky was saying.

With a giant push, she opened the heavy door into the store, a grey-carpeted haven with walls lined with every shade of white, from dazzling

231

snow to lush cream. Scented candles wafted rose and grapefruit into the air and the music was muted Tchaikovsky.

'This is nice,' Nicky said appreciatively.

'Yes,' agreed Connie, but her mind was on the woman with the lipliner trick. Who wasn't guilty of that sin sometimes? Just a smidgen of lipliner to fake bigger lips. Connie didn't consider herself vain, but there were times when it was hard to face the ageing person in the mirror. And she wasn't even forty. What would it be like when she was fifty?

Nicky was too young to understand, but she would, one day. They were part of the modern generation of women who weren't supposed to age. They were supposed to look like blemish-free, unwrinkled girls in skinny jeans and heels forever. Their mother hadn't had these worries. She'd cut her hair short once she hit thirty, and had taken to wearing comfortable long skirts and flat, lace-up shoes with sheepskin lining.

Connie could remember her mother preparing for a Christmas party and debating whether to wear her old blue two-piece (tie-front blouse and gathered, long skirt) or her black velvet dress (long sleeves with a lace frill on the hem). There had been no panic about getting her hair done, applying the latest make-up, or trying to look as good as women ten years younger.

It was different now. Ageing was taboo.

A sales assistant, a bright youngster who introduced herself as Jen, settled them into a changing room, and then the sisters began to roam the dresses.

'You tell me what you like and I'll get sizes,' Jen

232

said cheerfully.

'Something unconventional,' said Nicky confidently. 'I don't want to look old-fashioned, I want to look chic. Do you know what I mean?'

She tried on a rash of slinky silk satin dresses that followed the contours of her body like a second skin.

'Too clingy,' she decided critically. 'Getting the right underwear would be a nightmare.'

'Some people wear two pairs of control pants on the day,' Jen volunteered.

'I'd rather have lumps and bumps,' said Connie, horrified. She could never understand control underwear. It hurt. Besides, all the fat went somewhere. If it wasn't allowed stay on your waist, it squelched out above and below the control bit.

Next, Nicky went for column dresses with sleeves, without sleeves, with one sleeve, with a bit of lace on one shoulder.

She hated them all.

'We're never going to find the dress,' she said miserably.

'Nonsense,' said Connie, who'd thought Nicky looked beautiful in all of them. She was used to her sister's perfectionism. Jen brought a tray of tea and some biscuits.

'I can see why people spend all day doing this,' Connie said wearily, taking a biscuit for energy.

'Some people spend several days,' Jen, said.

Connie quailed.

'Not me,' said Nicky confidently.

'I'll bring some more gowns for when you've finished.' Jen left them alone to have their tea.

Another hour passed, and Connie was beginning to think they would never get out of Bridal

Heaven, when Jen arrived with an armful of lace and tulle.

'I know this isn't what you want,' she said to Nicky, who was perched on a grey velvet pouffe eyeing the frou-frou dress sceptically, 'but I've found that sometimes, what you want and what works can be two different things.'

Nicky shrugged. I'll humour you, her expression said.

Connie went back out to look again while Jen helped Nicky into the dress. They were so beautiful, she thought, fingers touching laces and satins. The tangible expression of hope and joy.

She hadn't bought a dress for her wedding to Keith all those years ago.

'Thank goodness you hadn't got that far,' her father had said. 'If you had the dress and then he left you, well, that's breach of contract.' Poor Dad. He was such an innocent. In his mind, being dumped once you'd bought the dress would be a sign that you should head to the courts to sort it out. There had been no talk of how Connie's heart had been breached by Keith. Her family had declared Keith a waster and decided that it was just as well Connie wasn't marrying him.

She'd bought bridal magazines though, and had wondered what she'd wear when the time came. But the time had never come.

Nicky gasped so loudly that Connie rushed back into the changing room, half-expecting some disaster: a bit of sleeve ripped, a zip come apart. But there was no disaster.

Her sister stood with both hands covering her mouth, stunned into silence by the sight of herself in Barbie's dream wedding-gown.

'I love it,' she said, shocked.

Connie took in how the cream chiffon with a sweetheart neckline clung to Nicky's small waist, then foamed out into blossoming whirls. 'It's gorgeous.'

Jen looked suitably smug. 'I told you both,' she said.

'But I don't want a traditional dress,' Nicky insisted.

She did a twirl, then another one, because the skirt flowed out like a ballerina's when she turned.

'I want something simple and chic.'

She piled her hair on top of her head with one hand, then held out her skirts with the other and tried a few more twirling movements.

Jen stepped forward with a couple of giant hairclips. 'Let me,' she said.

With professional ease, she clasped Nicky's blonde silky hair on top of her head, then raced out of the changing room for a moment, returning with a twinkling silver tiara and an old-fashioned veil of heavy lace.

She arranged both on Nicky's head quickly, then stood back. 'Now.'

Connie couldn't speak. At last, Nicky looked like a fairytale bride.

'I love it,' Nicky sobbed.

Connie beat Jen to it. She ripped a couple of tissues from the box on the small coffee table.

'I really do love it,' Nicky said tearfully.

Connie held her sister tightly and smiled at Jen over Nicky's shoulder. 'I do too,' she said.

That night, Connie went to dinner at Gaynor's.

Gaynor had gone from head of human resources for a major computer conglomerate to running a house, the parents association at her children's school, as well as working one day a week in the HR department of a chain of clothes shops.

If they hadn't known each other since their schooldays, Connie thought she might have been totally overwhelmed by Gaynor.

'Gaynor's watchword is capable. It's the only one that will do for her,' Connie used to say to Nicky. 'She could run the whole country in her sleep. No, she could run *the health service*—that's what she could do. She is *that* good.'

'I don't think anyone could do that,' Nicky said, shaking her head.

'Gaynor could. I was talking to her on the phone the other day, and she'd already given the dogs a bath because they'd rolled in cat shit, had made four casseroles to freeze for the week's dinners, organised a play date for little Niamh, sewed on labels for the other kids' uniforms, written a stack of emails about the parents committee meeting— and that was by eleven in the morning. That afternoon, she was going to do two hours in the charity shop, pick up the kids, take Josie to ballet and Charlie to football, pick them up again, take them home, make sure all the homework was done, and be at the school for a meeting with the teachers at eight. The health service would be a doddle for her. Oh, I forgot. She was going for a run at lunchtime because she's not getting enough exercise. If I was her, I'd be lying down watching *Oprah* with a cool cloth on my head.'

'You've never lain down with a cool cloth on your head in your life,' Nicky said crossly. 'You work really hard.'

'Yes, but when I'm finished work, it's finished.

For Gaynor, it never finishes.'

Connie was thinking of this as she sat in Gaynor's kitchen with a glass of wine and watched her friend supervise the kids doing their homework at the table in the dining room, shoo the dogs out from underfoot, and cook osso bucco at the same time.

Connie loved going to Gaynor's. It meant being in the bosom of a family without having to actually do anything. Everything happened around her.

'Did you learn that poem? You know you've got drama tomorrow,' Gaynor said, stepping over a dog to stir the selection of saucepans on the stove.

Connie, who never used more than one saucepan at a time at home, watched with fascination.

'Yes,' moaned Josie, Gaynor's eldest, who was thirteen and had transformed overnight from an awkward child into a lanky fair-haired goddess with long slender legs and doe eyes. How did that happen, Connie wanted to know. It had never happened to her. She'd gone from being a plump, too-tall child to being a plump, too-tall teenager without any of the transformational beauty along the way.

Was there a new breed of humans on the planet? It was on the tip of her tongue to ask Gaynor if her daughter was some beautiful alien, but instead she drank more of her wine, ate some crisps and told Gaynor about Nicky's wedding dress.

'It sounds nice,' Gaynor said absently, still multi-tasking. 'I didn't think she'd get married so early, though. They don't these days, do they?'

Connie didn't want to talk about social mores in the younger generation. She wanted to confide in Gaynor, one of the few people she felt she could bare her soul to, about how Nicky's forthcoming wedding was making her feel.

'I'm thrilled for her, but it does make me think about Keith,' said Connie quietly. She didn't want Josie to hear. In her experience, teenagers were deaf at all moments apart from when some highly sensitive information was being imparted, whereupon their listening abilities cranked up to CIA standards.

'Keith?'

Connie tried and failed to stifle her annoyance. 'Yes, Keith—the man I was going to marry, remember?'

She needed to discuss this, to get it out of her system with someone who'd known Keith and what he meant to her. Perhaps then she could move fully on, the way she and Eleanor had discussed.

'Oh God, yes, Keith.' Gaynor didn't stop what she was doing. In one swoop, she drained the whole pan of pasta.

'You haven't forgotten about him?' Connie said, aware of a certain shrillness in her tone.

'Of course not,' Gaynor said. 'But, Connie, that was a long time ago, you've moved on. I don't know why you're still even talking about him. You should have wiped that moron from your mind years ago.'

'Yeah, kick him to the kerb,' remarked Josie from the homework corner. 'Like, old boyfriends are losers. Forget him and move on.' She waved one hand in a complicated, MTV-inspired move that said: *It's OVER, girlfriend!*

'I was going to marry him,' hissed Connie, purposely ignoring Josie.

'Years ago,' said Gaynor, leaving the sink to

throw the pasta into another saucepan.

'Well, yes—well, no, actually. Only eight years ago.' Connie did the mental arithmetic. She was thirty-nine now, she'd been thirty. 'Nine years, OK, nine years but—'

'—but,' interrupted Gaynor, 'you should have moved on.'

She stopped cooking, came to stand in front of Connie, and for the first time since her friend's arrival, picked up her own wine glass and took a huge gulp. 'Connie, I am bone tired of this conversation. Speaking as one of your oldest friends, I want to tell you that. Keith is long gone and you are still on your own because you haven't moved on. You think you have, but you haven't. You are stuck in the past and you have no interest in new men because nobody will ever match up to your mythical list of perfection. I don't know how you came up with that list in the first place, because it's not as if Keith was perfect, but you've set the bar so high, no man can ever match up to it.'

Connie forced herself to breathe. 'Gaynor, that's an awful thing to say. Of course I've moved on.'

'You haven't.' Gaynor took another swig of her wine. 'Kids,' she roared, 'do your homework in your bedrooms. I want to talk to Connie alone.'

'New hair, Connie,' advised Josie as she gathered up her books. 'The long bob is so over.'

'Her hair is fine,' snarled Gaynor.

'Mom, if she only got a proper cut, it would be fierce, but there's no shape, no product . . .' Josie finished with a shrug, as if to say *no hope*.

'Go, kids.'

They all shuffled off, leaving Connie and Gaynor

behind.

'I am your oldest friend,' Gaynor said in a softer voice. 'As soon as you told me that Nicky was getting married, I knew what it would do to you . . .'

'It's not doing anything to me,' squeaked Connie. 'That's not what I wanted to talk about—'

'It is, love.' Gaynor put her hand on Connie's, which somehow seemed even more ominous. 'I told Pete you'd be in bits—'

'You told Pete!?'

Pete was Gaynor's husband. Connie had been with Gaynor the day she'd first met him, she'd been Gaynor's bridesmaid, she'd taken Gaynor on her first post-baby weekend and left Pete taking care of six-month-old Josie. She adored Pete, but it was part of the fabric of their friendship that she and Gaynor could discuss him. She suddenly felt ridiculous to realise that, of course, it worked both ways. Gaynor would discuss Connie with Pete. They would talk about how poor, sad Connie would be miserable when her little sister got married and moved out. *Poor lonely Connie with three sets of twinkly lights over her dressing table—* Gaynor had seen them and said they were lovely, but *she* didn't have twinkly fairy lights. She had photos of her children and a studio shot of her and Pete on their tenth anniversary.

Self-awareness flooded through Connie.

'I don't want you to be sorry for me,' she said hoarsely.

'I'm not.'

'You are! You, with your fabulous family and your saucepans and—' Connie waved an encompassing hand around the cosy kitchen with all its happy-family paraphernalia: kids' drawings on the walls, school notes Blu-tacked on to the fridge, photos of the whole family on their summer holiday in Greece. 'You have all this and I have twinkly lights over my dressing table. I'm a cliché, right? All I need now is to start adopting stray cats and I'll be the perfect, mad unmarried woman. If I can get the cats to pee all over the house, so the whole place stinks of it, so much the better. The best bet would be if someone did a television show on people being mean to cats, and they ended up at my house with the seventy-six cats I can no longer afford to feed so people could look at me and say "Didn't she used to be normal?"'

'I'm sorry,' Gaynor said, horrified. 'I didn't mean to upset you. I'm so blunt, too blunt—I'm sorry, Connie.'

'You're right,' Connie said bleakly. She got to her feet. 'I hate to turn my back on your cooking, Gaynor, but I can't stay. I'd be no company.'

'Please don't leave,' Gaynor begged. 'I put my foot in it, both my feet. Pete says I don't know what I'm saying half the time, I just let my mouth run on—'

But Connie had her coat on. She didn't want a goodbye hug, so she hurried to the door and waved. 'I'll phone,' she said, and she made it out on to the footpath without breaking down.

Gaynor's street was quiet now. It was after six in the evening and cars lined the street. Lights burned in all the houses and as she walked to her car, Connie could see family life going on in the homes she passed. There were kids watching cartoons, women walking in upstairs rooms with babies cradled to them, teenagers grumbling as

241

they took the family dog out for a walk, doing their after-school duty. It all came down to this, didn't it? Family. Marriage. A significant other. Without that, you were nothing.

There would have been no point explaining to Gaynor that Keith had blocked her from moving forward, that she had sabotaged herself because she'd been hurt by him, and now she planned to change. No point explaining all that.

Gaynor was married with kids and she thought anyone who wasn't, knew absolutely nothing. Connie's inner journey would sound daft to Gaynor.

Connie slammed the door on her car and managed to extricate it from the tiny parking space without banging into any other cars. Gaynor's words rattled round inside her head.

She would never be so hurtfully blunt. Why did Gaynor think she could speak like that to Connie? Had singledom become such a recognisable social handicap that people felt obliged or justified in commenting upon it? Couples always wanted to know when singles were going to meet a man, settle down and have babies—or had they decided she hadn't a maternal bone in their body?

'Yes,' Connie wanted to say. 'I hate sex, I loathe men and, as for children, I couldn't eat a whole one!'

As she drove on to Golden Square, she started to cry. A grey pick-up truck was in the place where she usually parked outside her house. Connie glared at it, tempted to drive into it with rage. It would be easy. Just lean on the accelerator, push . . .

A man came out of a garden gate nearby, one of the big old houses that were mostly apartments.

He moved towards the truck and Connie gave him her death stare. Stupid man!

It was the man with the red hair and the young daughter.

He turned and looked at her, as if he'd felt her piercing gaze, and then he ambled over to her car, making a motion with his hand to say *roll down your window.*

Normally, Connie followed strict 'all strangers are axe murderers' rules but tonight, something devil-may-care took over. It would be a foolish axe murderer who'd attempt to get the better of her tonight. He'd get a few whacks with his own axe.

'Yes?' she barked.

To his credit, he didn't blink but said: 'I know you usually park here. When I got here and your car wasn't parked, I thought you might be out. I'll move to the back lane.' There was resident's parking on the lane behind the houses but it meant a longer walk to your front door, and most people tried to find a spot outside their door.

Under normal circumstances, Connie would have said no, don't move, it's fine. It was hardly her space, after all. Just that she liked to park there and was usually home in time to do so.

But tonight, reason had deserted her.

'Good!' she snapped and rolled up her window.

When he moved the truck, she parked and then stomped inside with her head held high.

What was the point of trying to change your life? Nobody noticed. Even Gaynor thought she was a hopeless case with twinkly lights over her dressing table. She might as well sink into that hopelessness, forget about men and a future, and just buy the seventeen cats.

12

Other feasts

Olivia, who came to Kilmoney as a lady's maid with one of the ladies in the big house, taught Agnes how to make rugelach and matzo balls. Joe's mama loved them both, and Joe was astonished because he said she never used to like anything foreign—by which he meant anything that came from outside of Connemara- but I reckon that might have been his father's influence. I never met his father, but he sounds like a man who wanted everything his own way.

Joe's mama was such a gentle soul, she wouldn't have stood a chance. Most likely it was Joe's father didn't like anything foreign and she just went along with that.

Olivia was a sweet girl, but sad. There had been a man she'd loved but he'd gone away, and she'd ended up working as a maid. She and Agnes were great friends, and many times, when Olivia's mistress was in the big house for August,

Olivia came to us for dinner.

Olivia cried when she saw the feast the first time she came. Myself and Agnes had done it all quietly and Agnes had spent ages making a little candle holder with the seven candles like Olivia had told her about. The chicken soup was simple enough, a lot like my own mam's broth but with more garlic and without the barley. There was no way I could get my hands on pomegranates. I did my best, but all Mikey Jr from the shop could come up with was oranges, and I made the cake with them instead. There wasn't much call for pomegranates in our part of the world, and Mikey Jr was still talking about them the day we left for America. He did his best for Olivia, though. 'She's a fine-looking woman, for all that she's not a Catholic,' he said to me.

Which was almost a declaration of love for a man like Mikey Jr, married as he was to morning Mass, confession every Saturday and the life of the Little Flower of Lisieux.

'Unleavened bread,' said Olivia,

walking round the table and touching it all reverently. Cooking is food for the soul, we agreed.

*　　　*　　　*

In Geraldine Kerrigan's world, everything had a place. Once a thing slotted into that place, they were there forever. Like the car keys in the slightly cracked Belleek china bowl on the table in the hall.

Woe betide Juanita, Geraldine's twice-weekly cleaning lady, if she moved them.

'Juanita,' Geraldine would say loudly. Juanita didn't speak English too well and Geraldine liked to think that volume would improve matters. 'Juanita, no keys on kitchen table. In the bowl! Bowl!!'

Sometimes, Geraldine spoke longingly of Red Oaks, her childhood home, where there had been several maids, not just one person coming twice a week to carelessly spray far too much furniture polish on the piano. Then she'd grow annoyed with herself for getting all misty about the past. Her mother would have risen above it all, and so must she. That was true nobility: the ability to rise above all life's trials. Her mother had been one of the Fitzgeralds of Lismore and dealing with tragedy and joy with the same stoicism was what the Fitzgeralds were known for.

But still, her mother had never had to deal with a series of foreign girls who only stayed for six months before moving on. Geraldine knew she was hard on the girls, which was why they left her employ so quickly, but really, how else did they expect to learn?

246

If they'd seen the amount of work a maid had to do in Red Oaks, they'd have been happy to tidy up Geraldine's neat two-bedroomed townhouse in Howth.

In much the same way as the keys lived in the Belleek bowl, people had a place too. In Red Oaks, Mummy had entertained a lot and was very firm on the importance of protocol. Geraldine had grown up with a strong sense of social hierarchy.

Carmel De Vere, her friend from the bridge club, agreed with her.

Carmel had problems with the help too.

'Veronika completely destroyed my cashmere twin set,' she wailed.

The two women were sitting in Geraldine's private room in the hospital the day before Geraldine was due to be discharged to stay with Rae and Will.

They'd already discussed Geraldine's hip and how marvellous the surgeon had been, and how miraculously well it was healing four days after the surgery. Much consideration had been given to how much the hospitals had deteriorated since the demise of the matrons, and now they were on the familiar territory of domestic matters.

'Nobody knows how to clean cashmere any more,' Geraldine said mournfully. 'Such a pity.'

'I remember years ago buying Dawn one of those pretty Marks & Spencer's cashmere cardigans for Christmas,' Carmel said. 'She washed it at forty degrees. Silly woman.'

Dawn was Carmel's daughter-in-law, and the two women had spent many hours discussing her failings. Being hopeless at cooking and wildly amused at herself whenever she cremated a meal had topped the list of faults, until Dawn decided that forty-five was just the age to have a tummy tuck and breast implants. Privately, Geraldine thought Carmel would never recover from the shock.

'You're so lucky with Rae,' Carmel went on, and Geraldine felt a twinge of guilt.

Carmel had met Rae many times and thought she was marvellous. Which she was, certainly in comparison with Dawn. But there was no easiness between Geraldine and Rae.

Geraldine knew in her heart that Rae would not relish having her mother-in-law for a three-week convalescence. But Geraldine was willing to put up with it if it meant she would be with her darling Will.

Besides, it was Rae and Will's house or a nursing home. She'd never even contemplated staying with her daughter, Leonora. Heavens, no.

It would all be fine, though. Rae would do her best. She wasn't exactly out of the top drawer of society, but she was kind. Heaven only knew how she'd turned out so well, given her background. Not that Geraldine liked to cast aspersions, but really, the Hennesseys were shocking. It appeared that Rae didn't have much to do with her family, which was good, Geraldine felt.

As Carmel's conversation followed a well-worn path about Dawn's shortcomings, Geraldine put thoughts of Rae out of her mind and focused on Will. Mothers weren't supposed to have favourites, but they did, didn't they? Leonora had been too argumentative, too fond of her own way to be an easy child. As an adult, nothing had changed.

But her beloved Will made up for it. He was so

248

like his father, the same kindness and gentleness.

'I'm sure Will and Rae will spoil you,' Carmel was saying, 'and that's what you need.'

'Yes,' said Geraldine contentedly, 'that's just what I need.'

The following day, Geraldine sat in the passenger seat of her son's car and looked at 33 Golden Square without any fondness. She'd never liked the tall, white house. It was shabby somehow, and Rae should have cut down the wisteria years ago before it had taken hold of the porch. But no, Rae wouldn't listen to reason.

'Wisteria's so pretty, it would be a shame to cut it back, like taking it out of its home,' she'd said, or some such nonsense.

Ludicrous, Geraldine thought. Plants didn't have homes, they went where they were told.

'Did you tell the spiders you wouldn't put them out of their homes too?' Geraldine had said in response.

When Will and Rae had bought the house, it was a total wreck. Geraldine had advised them not to buy it. The place was infested with cobwebs, and the windows were black with dirt. Only the besotted would buy it.

Twenty-five years later, they were still here and the house had improved—well, it couldn't have got any worse. The wisteria was still there, sprawling bigger than ever, with woody branches looped around the whole porch. Half the front of the house would have to be cut off if a person were to remove the wisteria now.

Rae did have a good touch with the garden, Geraldine conceded, but it was probably because she was from the country. Geraldine had never been to Rae's part of the world, but she was sure it was one of those ugly little small-holdings with potatoes growing everywhere and nothing nice in the way of dahlias. Geraldine liked dahlias. They were so reliable.

'I thought we could have Leonora round tonight for dinner,' Will said as he helped his mother out of the car.

'I don't want any fuss tonight,' Geraldine said. 'I want to settle in, get my things around me. It's hard leaving hospital and not going back to your own home, you know. If you could have moved in with me, I wouldn't have to do this—'

'Mum, this is the best way,' Will said quickly. 'Rae and I both want to look after you. I'll phone Leo and tell her you're too tired.'

'Yes, do that.'

Geraldine allowed her son to steer her up the garden path as if she were already an invalid. It was soothing, being helped along like this. Will was such a dear boy.

Rae had obviously been waiting because she opened the door before Will could get his key in the lock.

'Welcome!' she said, and the scent of cooking wafted out of the open door behind her.

'Rae, hello.' Geraldine proffered one cheek for a kiss. 'Is something burning . . . ?'

Rae laughed easily. 'Goodness no, not yet, anyway, Geraldine.' She opened the door to the living room, which she and Will had spent the past three nights organising. It had been transformed into a bedroom, complete with Anton's bed—the transportation of which downstairs had nearly killed them both. There was a pretty little bedside locker from the spare bedroom, a vase of flowers on the mantelpiece, and a small fern beside the bed. The television was set at the correct angle so Geraldine could sit in bed and watch TV, and Rae had brought the kitchen radio in case her mother-in-law wanted radio too. There was a water jug, a glass, tissues and a box of biscuits on a low table, and extra rugs at the end of the bed in case Geraldine got cold. There had been something soothing about working so hard to get everything ready: it meant there had been no time to think about the letter or Jasmine.

Geraldine took one look at it all and sniffed. 'It's hard to be away from your own place,' she said mournfully.

Rae patted her arm, managed a smile at Will and said blithely: 'I'll go and check on dinner.'

'Mum doesn't want Leo to come,' Will said quickly. 'She's too tired, I'll phone her and tell her now.'

Downstairs in the kitchen, Rae stirred a saucepan on the stove and put the kettle on to boil. Normally, Geraldine's remarks would have made her furious, but not tonight. There were some plusses to being distracted. Compared to the turmoil that was going on in Rae's mind, her mother-in-law's mindless nitpicking didn't register.

Besides, Rae knew in her heart that Geraldine wasn't a malicious woman. Her problem was a tact bypass and the belief that saying what she thought was always the wisest option.

Since Rae's plan to have Leonora over so that the Kerrigan family would have each other to talk to had backfired, Rae decided that music would help. In the great living-room revamp, the stereo had been moved into the kitchen, so when she served dinner a couple of hours after Geraldine arrived, Rae put a Vivaldi CD on at a level that was just above background music.

'Isn't it relaxing having classical music on during dinner,' she said loudly, as Geraldine sat down.

There was no way Geraldine would criticise Vivaldi, Rae had decided. Classical music was always acceptable in her mother-in-law's mind because it was a sign of culture, therefore Geraldine wouldn't dream of saying to turn it down.

Rae closed her eyes as the joyous violins of 'Spring' rippled through the room. What was it about some pieces of music that just ripped into your soul?

But tonight the pure joy of Vivaldi merely highlighted the pain Rae was feeling inside. She hadn't had a moment's peace since she'd received the letter about Jasmine. It was like opening up an old wound to find it hadn't healed at all, was still as raw and agonising as ever.

She'd loved Jasmine with all her heart and giving her up for adoption had been the most devastating moment of Rae's life. It was a devastation she'd carried alone, and now she simply didn't know how she was going to tell Will or Anton about it.

*   *   *

Being tall made it easier to hide the baby bump. Rae often wondered, if she'd been short, how it would all have turned out. People would have known earlier, she might not have entertained the fantasy of keeping her baby, a fantasy that broke

252

her heart.

As it was, she went to the charity box of school uniforms and got the biggest, baggiest navy sweater she could find.

The spring of 1969 wasn't a time for baggy clothes for teenagers. All the other girls in Rathangan wanted to wear fitted, bum-skimming dresses and they adapted the uniform to make it fit this fashion.

There was war every day as girls arriving in school with heavily kohled eyes and skirts turned up to mid-thigh got sent to the headmistress for a lecture, from which they emerged sulkily unpinning their skirts. Rae had been one of them. But not any more. With her voluminous jumper over the long school skirt—carefully held up with safety pins and, later, by a belt—Rae Hennessey looked the image of a diligent pupil.

She worked harder than ever.

'You don't come out with us any more,' Shelley complained to her. 'You've gone all quiet.'

'Studying,' Rae said blankly. 'I need to do well in my exams.'

There was a germ of an idea in her head: if only she could get top marks in her state exams, then she'd get a decent job when she left school and be able to take care of the baby. She would not live at home with her parents with her child, never. She needed a ticket out of there and education was the key.

The baby would be born in September or October, she reckoned inexpertly. She'd leave school after the exams, get a job to earn money, and maybe, maybe it would all work out.

She was weeks away from the big exams in June

when her mother confronted her.

*   *   *

Rae was just home from school, exhausted after hauling her heavy bags of school books around. There was no point leaving things in her locker when she was trying to revise at night.

Her father wasn't home. Instead, her mother was in Paudge's seat in front of the television, but she got to her feet when Rae came in.

'You're up the pole, aren't you?' Glory Hennessey folded her arms across her chest and her eyes raked her daughter's body.

Rae said nothing. What a horrible expression to describe pregnancy.

'Whose is it? Tell me, whose is it? The little fecker. Your father will kill him.'

'Why?' asked Rae.

'Why do you think? For pawing his daughter, that's why. For bringing another brat into the world.'

'As if he cares,' Rae said.

She rarely said anything caustic to either of her parents, and since the last time when her mother had hit her, Rae had said even less. Now, with her baby inside her, she felt a surge of maternal courage.

'Don't talk back, you little slut,' growled her mother. 'You should be ashamed of yourself.'

Glory moved forwards with her hand raised to hit out, but anger flared in Rae.

'If you lay a finger on me, you bitch, I'll call the guards and press charges,' she roared, making her mother stop in her tracks. 'You might think you're

254

tough, but wait till you go to jail for assaulting your pregnant daughter.' Rae wished her baby didn't have to feel her rage but she had to protect them both. 'They'll love you in any prison you go to: usually it's men who hit pregnant women. Think of what they'll do to you inside.'

It was the first time Rae had ever known her mother speechless. The first and the last time, Rae decided.

It didn't take her long to pack. There wasn't much to take with her. She'd have liked to have taken the small cream dressing table she'd painted herself, but who knew where she was going to end up? Instead, she filled some plastic bags with her possessions—they had no suitcase in the house: when had any of them ever been on a holiday?— then stuffed her make-up and few pieces of cheap jewellery into her schoolbag.

There was no sign of her mother when she went downstairs to phone a taxi. Probably gone to the pub to drown her sorrows in Smirnoff.

While she waited for the taxi, Rae searched all her father's hiding places for his emergency stashes of cash. Paudge was infamous for hiding money when he was drunk or stoned, and then not being able to find it later. Rae had a pretty good idea of all of his hiding places. She found a few pounds stuffed under the seat cushion on his armchair, a few more in an old tea box at the back of the larder, and finally, a twenty-pound note in an empty box of Major cigarettes under his side of the bed.

It wasn't a fortune, but it was better than nothing. When the taxi arrived, Rae piled her stuff in slowly and climbed in beside it. The driver

255

hadn't moved to help. This wasn't the sort of area where taxi men got out to help punters with their luggage: someone might whip the hubcaps off the car while you were out of it.

'Where to?' he demanded when a panting Rae had shut the car door.

Rae knew what she must look like: a pale, shapeless girl leaving her decrepit house with a few paltry plastic sacks as luggage. She lifted her chin proudly. She was not going to be ashamed ever again.

'The unmarried mother's hostel in Cappagh Street in Limerick,' she said.

The man looked at her as if sizing her up.

'That'll cost you,' he said. 'It's going to take at least forty minutes.'

'I can pay,' said Rae, waving the twenty at him.

The cab, an old Escort smelling so strongly of car freshener that it made Rae nauseous, set off down the street. Rae didn't look back. There was no looking back any more.

*   *   *

When dinner was over, Rae shooed Will off to take care of his mother.

'I'll tidy up,' she said.

'You're so good.' He dropped a kiss on to her forehead.

No, thought Rae, I'm not good at all. I've kept a huge secret from you for years.

Upstairs, the letter lay hidden in an envelope in her bedside drawer. Though she'd taken it out from time to time to touch it, she hadn't phoned the number. She wasn't sure she was able to do that yet.

She'd waited so many years for news of Jasmine, and now the news was here, she was frightened. What if her daughter hated her? What if Will and Anton would hate her for keeping this secret from them? Rae couldn't bear to think of them all hating her for her actions all those years ago.

13

Spring Equinox

Golden Square resembled an Impressionist painting now spring was thoroughly underway. When Eleanor looked out of her window, she gazed on to an explosion of colour as the trees thrust new buds up to the sun, and flowers burst into bloom. The song had been wrong, she decided: there were more than forty shades of green; there were hundreds, from the acid yellows illuminated by sunlight, to rich viridians and glossy olives as tiny leaves shot out and buds unfurled on sprawling branches.

The growth of trees hid some of the square from her view and it wasn't as easy to see the houses on the opposite side. The plus side of this was that the warmer weather and the beauty of the garden square meant that people walked there in the evening, whereas in the colder months, only the dog walkers and people with small children ventured in.

This evening, Rae from Titania's Palace was out walking with her husband. Eleanor had been

257

watching Rae with interest. She'd seen her often in the café and once, when she'd bumped into Pearl Mills and her son in the square, Pearl had spotted Rae rushing down the street and had waved at her.

Rae worked for a local charity, Pearl explained, and Eleanor remembered that Connie had told her that.

'She's so very kind and she's never in too much of a rush to listen to you. Lots of people don't bother with you when you've got troubles,' Pearl added darkly. 'But Rae does.'

Eleanor watched Rae rush across the square morning and evening, dark hair flying, full of energy for both her jobs. Not many people worked full time and volunteered so many of their precious leisure hours with a charity. Eleanor wondered what was behind Rae's commitment to Community Cares: a sense of social duty or something darker, something painful from her past? She decided that Rae was simply one of those wonderful people who had a social conscience.

Connie was easier to read. For a start, Eleanor saw her regularly and they had become tentative friends.

Not because of Eleanor's overtures, she admitted to herself. It was Connie who seemed determined to befriend her.

Since that first meeting, Eleanor had had dinner and afternoon tea in Connie and Nicky's apartment.

'It's so pretty,' she'd said that first time she'd come to tea—less of a commitment than dinner. Eleanor still felt too raw to let people into her world too quickly.

'You've got a flair for decorating, Connie.'

'I've told her that,' Nicky said, 'but does she believe me? No.'

Eleanor had liked Nicky, although she'd expected not to. Nicky appeared so glowingly confident that Eleanor thought she'd be a bit insufferable. Eleanor liked people with a bit of doubt inside them: pain rubbed off the hard edges somewhat.

But for all her confidence, Nicky wasn't a bit hard-edged. Instead, she was that rare creature: happy within herself and genuinely kind.

And very funny.

She kept both Connie and Eleanor amused with stories from the world of publishing.

The managing director's nephew had written a book and it had arrived in Peony Publishing like an unexploded bomb.

The short straw had gone to Nicky, who'd had to read the novel and report back.

'Which would have been fine, if it had been anyone but Dominic's nephew,' Nicky explained.

It had taken Nicky precisely fifteen minutes to decide she hated it. The nephew was a stranger to grammar, clearly felt that spell checking was for the little people and hated full stops. If he could make a sentence run on for an entire paragraph without a full stop, he was happy. Arrogance bounced off the page. It was not an enjoyable reading experience.

Normally, such a book would merit a standard 'thank you so much for submitting your novel but we feel it isn't right for us and we wish you the best of luck with it elsewhere' letter. How to handle the rejection when the author was a close relative of

259

the publisher and his mother was going to France with Dominic in a month's time was another matter entirely.

'What did you do?' asked Eleanor, fascinated by this moral dilemma.

'I told the truth,' said Nicky, surprised. 'What else would I do? I said it wasn't for me but perhaps another editor might like it, and that either way, it would need serious work.'

'And Dominic wasn't angry with you?' Connie fretted.

'No,' said Nicky. 'He's good that way. More tea, Eleanor?'

Connie mothered her sister, Eleanor could see. This mothering had given her focus when she'd been abandoned by her feckless fiancé, but now that Nicky was going to be married herself, Connie was in limbo.

Eleanor felt the urge to help her, to guide. But that would mean taking down the walls Eleanor had put up to cope with her own pain. Was that wise?

She felt the same about Megan. They'd bumped into each other in Titania's a couple of times, and Megan had taken her black Americano to sit with Eleanor and her crossword and green tea.

'I hate that stuff,' Megan had said, looking into Eleanor's cup and wincing.

'I prefer coffee too,' Eleanor pointed out, 'but I like to sleep.'

'Good point,' Megan agreed. 'I'm sleeping better since I've started working at Nora's. Birdie's off in Spain and it's fun, actually. Kevin, the other chiropodist, is a laugh. He keeps trying to get me out with his girlfriend for nights out.'

'Work is good for the soul,' Eleanor said calmly.

'I thought that was inner peace?'

Eleanor laughed. 'Inner peace is hard to come by, but work helps.'

'You don't work any more,' Megan said thoughtfully.

Excellent point, Eleanor thought. 'I'm too old to work,' she said blithely.

'You're not too old to do anything.'

Eleanor smiled. 'Thank you for the compliment.'

Then, to change the subject, because Eleanor didn't like to discuss her inner thoughts with anyone, she took her travel brochures out of her handbag.

She was waiting till the weather got better to go on her trip West. Through the internet, she'd found a company that organised guided tours of the Western seaboard and they'd sent her their brochures.

We promise you the real experience of Ireland, not a fake, leprechaun-filled idyll, but a place where you'll see everything from the moonscape of the Burren to the small, wind-swept islands off Connemara. Our tour guides know the area like the back of their hands and whether you're interested in Ireland in general, or searching for the land of your ancestors, we'll help you.

Eleanor loved the sound of it. Ralf would have loved it too, she thought wistfully. How often had they talked about this trip? Now she was doing it when he was gone. It didn't seem right. They should have taken more holidays, should have worked less.

Somehow, fifty years had flown by and they'd never gone to find the small house where she'd

261

grown up.

'Are you going on a trip?' said Megan, picking up one of the brochures, as Eleanor had hoped she'd do.

'I'm thinking about it,' was all she said.

Back home, she sat at her window seat overlooking the square and let the memories flood in. The brochure showed lots of pretty houses in the West, including a couple of painted-up thatched ones that didn't spark any memories of her own home. She didn't remember much about the house in Kilmoney. She could recall the size and warmth of the kitchen, the great heat given off by the fire and, later, by the black stove that cost so much and had revolutionised their lives. Many pots could sit on the top and boil, if the fire was strong enough, and there was a small oven for baking in. From out of its black maw would come fresh, steaming soda bread, which they'd cover with butter made by Mam's own hands and finish off with a slick of blackberry jam from their own hedgerows.

She could still see the gleaming painted brown of the bench seats and could remember her mother down on her hands and knees polishing them. It was a small farm kitchen and yet it *shone*, no matter how often the sheepdog slunk in to lie under the table or how many muddy boots tramped in and out.

As a child, Eleanor used to sit on a stool with her feet resting on the iron ledge of the stove—the only part of it she was allowed to touch. To one side was the tall cupboard where the family bible lay, and where Mam kept her sewing things on hand for repairs or turning an old dress inside out when the outside became faded and worn.

On the other side of the stove was the shrine to the Sacred Heart, a dark print of a bearded, kind Jesus with one upraised palm facing out and with an opening in his chest where a burning flame blazed. Underneath was kept an actual burning flame in a tiny oil lamp with a crimson glass cover, its light flickering day and night in the kitchen.

This benevolent Jesus seemed at odds with the lessons she'd learned in school. Fire and brimstone and the terrifying world that was purgatory. Eleanor imagined it as an endless red place, where people crawled up through the fire, their only aid the prayers of the living—although quite what the practical help of these prayers might be, she didn't know.

It would have been truly terrifying if her mother had backed up the fire and brimstone message. But Brigid didn't. She was never in thrall to the power of the church. Eleanor could recall a visiting missionary priest coming to the house and being sent packing by her mother—an unheard-of event in the 1930s.

'Stop with your talk of the devil!' her mother had declared. 'You'll frighten the child. There's enough pain on the earth without calling for more in the afterlife.'

The priest had stalked off, shocked.

Eleanor could still see his outraged face. Her mother had been courageous at a time when not many people argued with the clergy. But Brigid's religion was a kinder, gentler one based around love, and she had a healthy respect for all faiths.

Along with tales of angels and saints, there were stories of the Celtic gods and goddesses, tales of the fairy people and their other world. Mam and Granny knew that, while man might build stone churches on the land, the very land itself was a source of huge power and possibility that no man-built creation could emulate.

The coming weekend would be the Spring Equinox, a time of awakening and fertility in the landscape. Once, people had celebrated the goddess Eostre, the earth goddess, by using eggs as a symbol of new life and rebirth. Some cultures, Eleanor recalled, had made dragons to carry for their celebrations.

She wondered what the Spring Equinox meant in Kilmoney now.

Ralf had been interested in the idea of dragons as processionary aids. He'd been interested in everything.

It was one of the many things she'd loved about him. He was never finished learning, whether it was a new word or a new idea in *Time* magazine.

'Listen to this!' was his mantra, followed by him reading something to her from the newspaper. He loved environmental articles, anything to do with space, and new scientific data.

He bypassed things on relationships. 'You tell me everything I need to know, honey,' he'd say to Eleanor, but if there was anything about new research on the brain, he'd read it with fascination.

'Human beings are incredible machines,' was one of his favourite sayings.

It was horribly ironic then that the first stroke had affected his brain so badly.

Eleanor hadn't been with him that time, a fact for which she had never quite forgiven herself. She'd been getting her nails done, a vanity she rarely had time for, but they were due at a big party that weekend and she was making an extra effort. When she'd come home with a bag of fresh bagels from the man on the corner, she'd known instantly there was something wrong because there was no music in the apartment. Ralf lived his life with music in both back and foreground.

Chet Baker might be playing in the morning, and then Lena Horne would sound out in the afternoon. Bernstein and Sedaka would compete in any one day with Mozart. That day, Ralf was supposed to still be there when Eleanor got home, but there was no music.

'Ralf!' She ran through the apartment, fingers held aloft the way the manicurist told her to, and came upon him in their bathroom, lying on the floor.

'My love, what is it?' she cried, crumpling on to the floor beside him. When he tried to speak with a distorted mouth, she knew what it was.

'It wasn't your fault, Mum. It would have happened if you'd been here or not,' Naomi said as they waited in the hospital.

Naomi looked so like Ralf: tall and with his brown eyes, warm olive skin and the Levine nose, narrow and aristocratic. When she cried, her dark lashes looked so long and spiky, it appeared as if she was wearing false ones. Recalling how Ralf used to call her Bambi when she was little, Eleanor began to cry.

Afterwards, the rehabilitation centre were so very kind to both Ralf and Eleanor.

The speech therapist warned Eleanor that Ralf might never recover his speech totally.

'That's fine,' Eleanor said loyally. 'As long as I

have him with me.'

But it wasn't so straightforward. Eleanor would have taken Ralf and loved him no matter what the stroke did to him. For him, it was different. The doctors had told them both about speech and language difficulties, about memory loss and difficulty learning new things. They'd spoken to both Ralf and Eleanor about this: there was no sense of telling her alone because the man beside her was no longer able to comprehend. There was no doubt that Ralf understood. His eyes followed her about the room when he sat in the wheelchair in the apartment. Tried to speak to her but the words came out jumbled up.

No matter how many times a day Eleanor stroked his face and said: 'I love you, I know you're still here with me,' she could feel his anguished eyes telling her this was destroying him.

The man who'd loved to learn about brains and who'd rejoiced in the genius of human beings was at the mercy of his own failing brain and his wife could do nothing about it.

Eleanor got out of her chair at the window in Golden Square and switched on the television. She couldn't think about this, not now. Her darling Ralf. How she missed him.

She didn't look at the brochures again for several days. She hadn't the heart to.

14

Irish Moss

In Brooklyn, nobody would believe how much we used carragheen moss in cooking.

'Seaweed?' they'd all say. 'You're joking.'

It's no joke. When I was a child, I used to take carragheen moss boiled up in milk for my bad chest. I hated it, in much the same way I hated the ginger and pepper my mother would sprinkle on hot milk for me when I was sickly. But seaweed was our medicine for many years. It would build you up if you'd been ill and people with bad coughs swore by it.

My mother and sometimes Agnes collected the carragheen from the rocks at low tide in the spring and summer. Dark red and purple, it looks like mermaid's lace until it dries, when it's hard and you can chew it, the same way cowboys in the films chew on dried beef.

Many a poor family round our way got their vitamins from

carragheen when they hadn't enough to put anything but potatoes on the table. Peasant's jelly was a jelly made from boiling moss in water and leaving it to set.

My grandmother used to soak the dried moss in cold water, then boil it up in three cups of milk until the herb had dissolved. She'd add burdock root and broom top and boil it up to make cough syrup. Or else she'd use the plain moss in milk for everything from an inflamed chest to the rheumatic pain her husband used to suffer from.

Carragheen blancmange was a favourite dessert in the house, and you could use it to thicken all manner of sweet puddings, but you had to be careful not to use too much or the taste of the Atlantic would overpower the dish.

To make blancmange, add soaked carragheen to milk, lemon rind and a bit of vanilla essence, if you have it. Beat up an egg yolk and sugar, pour in the milk mixture, then whip up the egg white and fold it in slowly. Leave it to set overnight and it's the *sweetest, most delicate pudding you'll ever eat.*

It was an unexpected gift, my mother said: the sea's unexpected gift to us all. You never know when the unexpected gift is going to come out of nowhere and cheer you up.

*   *   *

Megan loved working in the chiropody clinic. You never knew who was going to turn up and, best of all, at the end of the day, you just put the answering machine on and left. The work didn't follow you home and make you endlessly anxious.

Being out of her normal life like this was fun, like researching for a part, which was always exciting because you got to slip into someone else's world, but you didn't have to stay. Just long enough to get the flavour of how it felt.

For the gangster movie, she'd spent a day with some of the other cast members in a flat with a few professional criminals. The director, Jonnie, had set it up.

'These are hard men,' he'd said, barely able to contain his excitement. Despite affecting a Sarf London accent, Jonnie was truly Home Counties, having grown up in an old rectory complete with a tennis court and gone to Eton. But he loved the underworld and talking to the hard men and pretending to be a hard man himself was his dream.

Megan was mildly amused by his adoration of

269

East End gangsters, including the accent and the lingo.

Over the years, she'd carefully cultivated a neutral accent and preferred not to link herself with any class or place. It was easier if you were chameleon.

She'd liked one of the guys Jonnie had found. He'd been in prison for armed robbery, but he seemed sorry now, not just sorry he was caught and had done ten years inside.

The other man, Roofie, frightened her. There was a wildness about him, nothing sexy or attractive, but a sense that he truly didn't care about society's rules. His own rules mattered most to him. Fifteen years, on and off, in a maximum-security prison, hadn't changed that.

Megan had shimmied into playing the admiring girl.

'Roofie, you must have seen it all,' she'd said, wide-eyed to make him like her.

Roofie had looked at her as if he could see right through her act, which made her more scared.

'Is Roofie his real name?' she asked the other guy, later.

'No. His trick is throwing people off roofs. Roofs, Roofie, get it?'

The Golden Square Chiropody Clinic was blissfully safe in comparison.

The only threat, Nora had implied when Megan first took over from Birdie, were the man-mad women who needed to be kept away from Kevin, the other chiropodist.

'Women are strange creatures,' Nora said. 'Kevin does something to them. Or at least they hope he will. They look at that innocent, kind face and they see salvation. I have no idea why. He tells them he's got a girlfriend, but it doesn't stop them.'

Megan had enough experience of looking at men and seeing salvation to decide that even if Kev threw himself at her, she was not interested in him, especially since he was attached. It was, therefore, a relief early on to find that Kev was attractive but entirely not her type.

'It's good to meet you,' she said determinedly, shaking his hand hard. 'I can't believe we haven't met till now.'

'Yeah,' said Kev happily. 'Good to meet you too. Hope things are OK, you know. All that press stuff . . . bummer. Nobody cares about that stuff round here. Hey, do you cycle?'

Nora looked on fondly as Megan replied that, sadly, she hadn't cycled since she was about ten, and had never been that keen on it then. 'I liked rollerskating more,' she said.

'I do that. It's rollerblading now,' Kev said.

'Right,' said Megan gravely. 'I'm not sure I'd be any good at that.'

'Myself and my girlfriend are going at the weekend,' Kev said.

'I'll get back to you,' Megan said, nodding. Her social life was looking up. She was having a pizza with Nicky and Connie O'Callaghan tonight, and there was the possibility of rollerblading with sweet Kev at the weekend. It was a far cry from her old life, but it was strangely comforting.

These people were becoming her friends. They knew who she was and what had happened, and they still liked her.

* * *

Connie went to Patsy's salon to have her hair cut.

'Just a trim, Patsy,' Connie said, sitting in front of the mirror and noticing all the flaws in her face. Where had all those lines come from? 'I don't know what Nicky wants for the wedding, so I'd better keep it long.'

'Wear it the way you want for the wedding,' Patsy advised. 'I've no time for that bride madness where they want to rule the world for one day.'

'You know that Nicky's not a bit like that,' Connie said. 'She only wants me to be happy.'

'She's a rarity,' Patsy agreed. 'I've seen plenty of brides who want the bridesmaids done up like Hallowe'en horrors just so they don't outshine them on the big day.'

'I'm hardly likely to outshine Nicky, now, am I?' Connie said cheerfully.

Patsy glared at her. 'With that attitude, I don't know why you bother coming in here at all.'

'Oh God, just cut it, will you?' Connie groaned. 'I don't want a life-coaching session, just a haircut.'

The girl sweeping the floor let out a snigger. Patsy sent a death glare in her direction.

'I've a good mind to dye it orange,' Patsy said, when she'd stopped glowering and had started trimming. 'How are the wedding plans coming along, then?'

'Fine. We're having a hen night with her friends from school and the people from work the week before.'

Patsy kept trimming. 'We could have a bit of a Golden Square hen party,' she said. 'There's plenty of us here who'd like to give her a decent send-off, but we'd be out of place with Nicky's

272

work crew.'

'Of course you wouldn't,' protested Connie loyally, consumed with embarrassment at the realisation that she, as bridesmaid, had forgotten their neighbours in all the party plans.

'Rae and Dulcie mightn't, but I wouldn't be on for a night in a posh club or anything like that.'

Nicky's workmates had indeed suggested organising a cocktail party at a glamorous city-centre club.

'What could we organise then?' Connie asked.

'We could have it here,' Patsy said. 'No, what am I talking about—we'll have it in Titania's Palace. Isn't that a great idea?'

*   *   *

Nicky admired the cupcakes Connie had organised for her. There were pink swirly ones, white chocolate ones with dark chocolate stars on them, tiny carrot cakes with little orange marzipan carrots on top.

'I love it all!' she said delightedly.

Livvy from the tearooms had put the wedding march on the stereo, and Nicky laughed as she paraded through the premises, smiling at everyone, hugging her friends and displaying her engagement ring.

Soon, everyone was enjoying tea, coffee and the bellinis Connie had brought in a couple of big flasks.

The only person there who didn't look happy was Rae.

In spite of the general air of enjoyment, Connie noticed that Rae's beautiful face was strained and tired. She was doing her best to smile, but it was clear that her heart wasn't in it.

'What's wrong with her?' whispered Connie to Patsy.

Patsy shrugged in reply. 'She's been like that for weeks. The mother-in-law is staying with her. She had a hip done and I think she pushed herself in the door there, and I know she drives Rae mad. Not that she'd tell you anything, but you can tell, can't you? She's a right old rip. Thinks she pees eau de cologne, that one.'

Connie giggled.

'Is that it, then? The mother-in-law's not staying for good?'

'You'd want to have been very bad in a past life for that to happen,' Patsy said darkly.

'You know what you're talking about with the mother-in-law thing,' Connie said suddenly.

Patsy's laugh was dry. 'My first husband was a pet of a man and his mother was a cast-iron bitch.'

'Your *first* husband—' repeated Connie. Wow. First implied that there had been a second. And she personally had never even got one.

'How many husbands have you had?'

Patsy laughed properly this time. 'My own or other people's?' she said. 'I heard someone say that once. It's brilliant, isn't it? Ah no, I only had two. That's enough for any woman.'

'There's no Mr Patsy now, is there?' Connie asked. She was on a roll. She and Nicky had often wondered about Patsy, but she'd never been that forthcoming when she was in the salon. Here, though, it was different.

'No Mr Patsy. A few wannabes, though. And you?' Patsy's eyes were shrewd. 'No man on the scene?'

'I haven't even made it to the altar once and you've had two husbands,' Connie sighed.

*   *   *

Megan went over to sit beside Eleanor, who was sipping herbal tea.

'Had your two coffees?' she asked.

'Yes,' said Eleanor, smiling.

'You know, Nora drinks buckets of the stuff,' Megan said.

'Nora is twenty-five years younger than I am,' Eleanor pointed out.

Megan couldn't hide her surprise. Eleanor didn't look that old.

'It must be hard not to drink coffee in New York,' she said now. 'There are so many gorgeous little cafés there.'

She was fascinated by Eleanor's life in New York. Megan had visited the city, and once spent three weeks there living with one of her friends, a girl who had a trust fund and a growing coke habit. It had been fun, but sort of nocturnal. Megan still didn't know where anything was during the day: they only went out at night, and then, it was in cabs or limos to parties. At the time, she'd thought it was fabulous fun. Now, she reflected, it had been a bit one-dimensional. Party to party with the same people, all desperate to have fun, all desperate to be famous.

'New York is great for coffee lovers, but we do good herbal tea too.'

'I'd love to live there,' Megan said mistily. 'Properly live there, not just stay with someone for a week or two. Does it stop being exciting when you live there?'

'No,' said Eleanor. 'It's a fascinating place. I'd say that New York has a heart. Everyone there is an immigrant, there are very few people who start off in New York, so we're all blow-ins, and you can become a part of it very quickly. Everyone's in the same boat, from the movie star to the kid serving coffee in a diner.'

'Did you know any movie stars?'

'A few. But in New York, nobody treats them any differently to anyone else. They have to go to LA for adulation.'

Megan laughed at that.

'Did you have any movie stars as patients?' she asked.

'I can't tell you that,' Eleanor said. 'But people are people, Megan. Whether they're famous or not. We all have the same doubts and fears.'

'So, no dirt then?' Megan said.

Eleanor grinned at her. It was the first time Megan had attempted to make any sort of joke with her. Up till then, Megan had behaved as if Eleanor was about to launch into a therapy session there and then, analysing her from her conversation.

'No dirt.'

Megan made her think of Gillian for some reason, even though there was a good seven years between Megan and her grand-daughter. For all her experience, Megan had a sliver of the childlike innocence of a younger person. It was the strange world of celebrity: she'd grown up with sophistication all around her and no chance to grow as a person.

Eleanor thought again of her proposed trip to her hometown and she knew how hard it would be to go on her own. Darling Gillian or Naomi would have been the perfect travelling companion in one sense, but Eleanor couldn't do that. She'd never be able to go through with what she had to do then. She sighed and changed the subject.

'Are you working full time with Nora?'

'For the moment, but Birdie's back in two weeks. I've been thinking I should move on,' Megan added. 'I've been here since New Year, long enough for everyone to have forgotten about me, so I was thinking of going back into the world. Not London.' She shuddered. She couldn't bear to think of her old flat where she'd hidden out when the story had broken. 'Los Angeles, perhaps.' Other actors said it was a hard place to make a home, but she couldn't settle in Golden Square forever. 'What about you?'

'Oh, I still want to take a trip back to my home in Connemara,' Eleanor said. 'When the weather's better.'

They were both waiting, she and Megan. Waiting for life to begin again. Megan's would, but Eleanor wondered if it was all too late for her.

*   *   *

Eleanor got into bed that night and watched a little television on the small portable set. She had never been much of a fan of television. It tortured people with its vision of happiness. How many clients had come into her rooms worrying that their lives weren't like that of the people on the small screen? Through her practice, she knew

277

enough television writers to know that the happy lives that played out on TV sets around the world were indicative of what people fantasised about rather than any reality.

Eventually, she switched off the box and her bedside light, and lay in the darkness, hoping that sleep would come.

The nights were the worst. By day, she could feel as if she were still part of the human race, but at night, the loneliness came and overpowered her.

'Night night, Ralf,' she whispered.

15

Holy Days

Holy days and fast days were hard going, especially for anyone working the land. On holy days like Ash Wednesday, you had to be up early to walk to morning Mass and get the ashes on your forehead. The ashes were from the burned palms from Palm Sunday, and they'd be mixed with oil and the priest would anoint people's foreheads with this mixture in the sign of the cross.

I can still smell that oil. Catechism oil, we used to call it. It was like the smell of the tabernacle at a funeral, when the canon waved incense over the coffin.

Agnes was once given a tiny vial of perfume that smelled of the Far East, with incense and amber in it. I couldn't bear the smell of it: it reminded me of being a child in the church, and the thought of the cold, hard corpse in the coffin beside us. We were all used to death, you know, Eleanor. Not like people today. We all went to the funerals, and as a small child I'd kissed the marble-cold forehead of many a corpse. In a way it was good: death held no fear for us.

Ash Wednesday was the start of Lent and it was a day of fasting. You could eat no meat, only one decent meal and two small collations—which were tiny meals.

My mother always cooked us cod on Ash Wednesday with a little butter and a few small boiled potatoes. There were no second helpings and no pudding. Just a small meal and a decade of the rosary afterwards.

We all ate fish on Fridays.

Pin-bone your fillet of cod—my

mother used her fingers and so do I—and then poach it in a little milk with a pinch of pepper on top and a bit of dill, if you have it.

*　　　*　　　*

The local shop was not the place to go on the eve of a wedding in the village. Not when you were the older, unmarried sister of the bride-to-be. It was an act of recklessness on a par with arriving at the gates of hell with an ice cream. Everyone would want to discuss marriage, engagements and 'When's *your* big day going to be, love?'

So when Connie pushed open the door of Flanagan's for Everything! she took a deep breath. She loved Flanagan's with its bizarre combination of things for sale—*Buy bleach and get a packet of boiled sweets free!* Mr Flanagan had been running it for donkey's years and, while the lure of the big supermarket had certainly dented his business, there was always steady custom for Flanagans. After all, where else could you buy the makings of an apple pie along with something to trap those pesky mice?

Connie's grandmother, Enid, liked to reminisce about the good old days when Mr Flanagan Senior used to stand behind the counter and get things for the customer.

'You had a list and you gave it to him, and while you had a sit down—there was always a comfortable seat at the counter—he got it all.'

'Yes, but it took him hours,' Connie's mother,

Barbara, would point out. 'Someone else would come in and he'd talk to them about the price of a tin of custard powder, then he'd be off to answer the phone, and you'd be waiting.'

'But you knew all that was happening in the parish by the time you left,' protested Enid. 'I liked that.'

'You should get email, Nan,' advised Connie. 'You could stay in touch with the Courtown Bay mafia that way.'

Flanagans had moved on in the sense that customers could choose their own groceries, but they still had to run the gamut of Mr Flanagan Junior, who was every bit as interested in gossip as his father had been.

'Connie, as I live and breathe!' he declared, while the over-the-door bell was in the death throes of its welcoming jingle. 'Weren't we just talking about you!'

'Hello, Mr Flanagan,' said Connie, abandoning all hope of a drive-by shopping spree. At the counter was Mr Flanagan and the Courtown equivalent of Wikipedia, Mrs Hilary Leonard, who knew everyone and everything that went on in the locale.

'Connie!'

Mrs Leonard was very short and when she threw her arms around Connie, she got a good hold of Connie's middle, and squeezed tightly.

'Your mother said you'd be in.'

Since the need for extra milk and some brown sugar for coffee had only just transpired, Connie wondered how her movements were already accounted for. But that was Courtown Bay for you: other people knew what you were going to do even before you knew it yourself.

'I suppose they're all at fever pitch down in the house?' Mr Flanagan said, eager to talk.

'Enid's rheumatism is at her again,' Mrs Leonard leapt in. 'But she has some of those tablets left, doesn't she, Connie?'

Again, Connie had to bow to Mrs Leonard's superior knowledge. Either she had the O'Callaghan family phones bugged or she had psychic abilities.

'Gran's rheumatism is bad again,' she agreed, 'but she's determined to be well enough for tomorrow.'

'It'll be a great day for your family,' Mr Flanagan said. 'I won't make the church, now, because of the shop.' He said 'shop' with the sort of reverence a US president might reserve for 'the Oval Office'. 'But I'll be up for the meal. I wouldn't miss seeing your sister married. She's a lovely girl, Nicky.'

'Oh, gorgeous, and she'll make such a beautiful bride—' began Mrs Leonard.

Connie could sense she was about to start describing the dress, which nobody apart from Connie, her mother and Nicky had seen so far. But she wouldn't put it beyond Mrs Leonard's powers to know what it looked like.

'I'll have to get a move on,' Connie said cheerfully. 'They're expecting me back with the milk.'

'You're a good girl.' Mrs Leonard patted her arm affectionately. 'Always thinking of others. You were like that even when you were little. Well, younger. You were never little. But it must be handy being so big when you're a teacher. None of the little monkeys would dare to cross you!'

282

Connie decided against explaining that whacking the students was no longer part of a teacher's role.

'I supposed it'll be you next?' Mr Flanagan said archly.

Mrs Leonard's eyes were big as she waited for Connie's response.

Connie winked. 'That would be telling...' she said.

She bought milk, sugar and a big bar of chocolate, said her goodbyes and headed for the door.

'I hope it'll be you next, Connie!' roared Mr Flanagan. 'Getting wed, I mean.'

'Thanks.' Connie managed a smile and let the door swing shut behind her.

Leaving home might allow a person to reinvent themselves. But five minutes back in her hometown, and it was as if she'd never left.

She was no longer Connie O'Callaghan, career woman with her own flat, nice holidays, a pension plan.

She was Big Connie, the tall one of the O'Callaghan girls, as opposed to Nicky, who was the dainty one. Careers cut no ice here, unless you ran a giant corporation and were on the business pages looking grave.

In fact, Connie thought grimly, reversing out of her parking space, even if she *were* running a corporation, someone would be bound to wonder was there any sign of her getting married yet.

It wouldn't be enough to run a company, fly in a private Lear jet and holiday in fully staffed villas in Gstaad. No, a husband would have to be part of the package.

It was the same everywhere. The whole planet

283

was obsessed with why single women were alone. Why? If a woman so happened to have got that far in life without a significant other, so what?

The fastest-growing demographic in the world was single women. Or so she'd read. Maybe it was like that so-called 'fact' about how women over thirty-five were more likely to be killed by terrorists than to get married, which had turned out to be totally made up. But still, if there were loads of single women out there, why couldn't they start a union? The Stop Bugging Us About Why We're Not With A Nice Man Union. Or the Don't Ask Us About Our Sex Lives, And We Won't Ask About Yours Union.

Even Eleanor, who had been the epitome of the career woman in many respects, seemed to want Connie to find a man. She'd even flagged up the single father next door. For sure, he looked nice enough, though he hadn't shown her much interest. And she'd been quite short with him that time he'd parked in her space, so he probably had her marked down as a bit of a mad old bag.

She sighed. Once you'd passed your man-magnet sell-by date, it was better to accept it. If only everyone else would.

'You got chocolate. Great,' said Nicky when she got home.

'Next time there's a grocery crisis, *you* have to go to Flanagan's,' Connie muttered and ripped a couple of squares out of their packaging.

'You got the third degree?'

'Judge Judy couldn't have done it better.'

*   *   *

284

The following morning, Nicky's wedding day, Connie woke up with the sense that it was going to be a fabulous day. The sky was cloudless, the clock radio in her old bedroom in her parents' house had woken her by playing one of her absolute favourite songs ever—'Walking On Sunshine'. And yesterday's utter conviction that she was going to wake up with an outbreak of hormonal spots had turned out to be totally wrong.

'Blemish free,' she said delightedly to her reflection once she'd rubbed the toothpaste off. To be on the safe side, she'd used this old wives' remedy to dry up any possible outbreaks. The only problem was the scrubbing required to get dry toothpaste off her face.

'You smell very minty,' said Nicky, when they met up in the kitchen, both in pyjamas and looking for coffee.

'My teeth and my face are going to be dentist-white today,' Connie said, giving Nicky a hug. 'This is your day, darling girl. It's going to be wonderful.'

'I hope so,' Nicky said. 'I feel a bit Bridezilla-ish today.'

'Is that like Godzilla? Are you going to stamp out a city?' Nothing could dampen Connie's mood.

'No, just worried and possibly obsessed. All this work has been leading up to one day: today. What if it all goes wrong?'

'Do you trust Freddie to be there waiting for you?' asked Connie, who had utmost faith in this fact herself.

'Of course.' Nicky smiled.

'That's all that matters,' Connie pointed out. 'You have a dress, he has the ring, you've got the money for the party. Anything else going wrong is mere caprice.'

*　　*　　*

Nicky was a beautiful bride. And Freddie's face never lost its smile all day as he stared at his new wife with an expression of delight and disbelief.

'They're like a couple of kids, aren't they?' Connie's dad, Arthur, said to her fondly as the newly married couple arrived at the reception to a round of applause.

Connie nodded. 'Yes, Dad,' she said, and had to search her small handbag for another tissue. She'd cried all her mascara off already.

The day raced on in an atmosphere of happiness, and soon the hotel staff were clearing away tables to make room for dancing, and a buffet table was set up with sandwiches and cake stands filled with tiny cupcakes, which had been Nicky's idea.

Connie hadn't thought anyone would have any room for more food after the meal, but her mother said they'd have to try some of the cupcakes, 'just to see'.

'I'll get some,' Connie suggested. Barbara O'Callaghan looked tired now. The length of the day showed on her face, so like Nicky's. 'You sit here and I'll come back with a plateful, so we can choose.'

The DJ was setting up his equipment, and the room was still in the mid-way state between formal dinner and party. Connie idled beside the pastel-coloured little cakes. They were like mouse's cakes, she decided, so pretty and dainty.

The plate full, she turned back and could see her mother had been joined by the gossip-loving

Mrs Leonard. She was always marvellous entertainment, and would, doubtless already have gathered a vast amount of information about the day: who was ignoring who and who'd nearly worn the same dress as someone else but had a change of mind at the last minute, thankfully.

Connie was three steps behind her mother when Mrs Leonard's voice reached her.

'She's a great girl, your Connie. Is there still no sign of her getting married?'

Connie stood frozen. The two women were facing the other way, heads together. They didn't see her.

'I've sort of given up hope,' Barbara said apologetically. 'After a certain point in your life, you're too set in your ways to get married. Lord knows, I'd have never stuck with Arthur if the two of us didn't practically grow up together.'

'That is one way of looking at it,' Mrs Leonard agreed. 'I say the same thing to my husband, you know. Don't think he understands it. They all think they're a catch, don't they?'

'True. The likes of Connie, they have it all. Why would you give that up to have someone ask you to wash their dirty socks? It's having it all, you see. We didn't have that in our day.'

Mrs Leonard nodded in agreement. 'Having it all! In our dreams,' she said. 'They were different times, though, Barbara. There was no pill, no condoms.' She lowered her voice. 'No vibrators.'

'You're right there, Hilary,' Connie's mother said gravely.

Connie had to cover her mouth with her hand but she couldn't hold the snorting laughter in. From her spinsterhood to vibrators in one minute.

Her mother turned round at the noise.

'I got some of the little cakes for you,' said Connie, with an admirably straight face, and slipped into the seat beside her mother as if she hadn't been listening for the past five minutes.

'Ah, you're a great girl,' said Mrs Leonard, shaking her head ruefully. 'Tall, I'll grant you that, but all cats are grey in the dark. There's a lot to be said for the old ways, Barbara. The matchmakers had the right idea. Match them up, let them marry and they'll get on with it. There mightn't be so many unmarried girls around if the old ways still held sway.'

Barbara patted her daughter's hand.

Mrs Leonard took a couple of small cakes, and got to her feet. 'I'm off to mingle,' she informed them.

Connie put the plate down beside her mother.

'Do you think I have it all?' she asked after a moment.

'Well, you do,' her mother admitted. 'When I was your age, I had two children, not a moment to myself and there was no such thing as "me" time. That must be hard to give up.'

'Mum, I'd give all the "me" time up if I had the opportunity,' Connie said wistfully.

'But you must have opportunities, love. You must have.'

And Connie realised that her mother thought it was her own fault she was single, that she was rejecting men left, right and centre.

'If you knew how many dates I've been on, how often I've gone to a party hoping tonight would be the night. I'm fed up with it.' For a second, she thought of Gaynor discussing Connie's list and

288

how no man would ever reach its dizzy heights. 'Men don't come near me. If you know what I could do to make a difference, tell me.'

'Men like to be looked up to,' her mother began.

'I'm too tall for anyone except a basketball pro to look up to me,' Connie said.

'Don't wear heels, then!'

'I don't.'

'You never wear floaty, feminine clothes. When you're tall, you have to make an effort to look feminine,' Barbara countered.

'I can't do feminine,' Connie said. 'I look ridiculous. You need to be petite and fairy-like to wear floaty things. That suits Nicky, but I look like I'm playing dressing up.'

'Your dad and I would love to see you settled. I wonder—' Her mother's voice shook. 'I wonder if it was anything I did wrong.'

Connie felt more tears threaten. She didn't know why she'd bothered with make-up at all. 'Mum,' she said, 'it's nothing you did wrong. I'd love to settle down, but it just hasn't happened. There are lots of women living alone nowadays. That's the way life is. And I can't torture myself for the rest of my days crying over it. I have to get on with it. Don't be sad for me, Mum.'

Her mother's face wobbled.

'Really, don't be sad.' Connie pleaded. 'I'm happy, honestly I am.'

'But what will you do without Nicky?'

It was the one question Connie didn't know the answer to. Nicky had already moved into the new apartment with Freddie. In school, when asked something she didn't know, Connie was brave enough to say so. She was wise enough to realise that the best teachers were able to admit what they didn't know as well as what they did. But right now, she knew it was time to lie.

'I think it will be a whole new life for me,' she said, crossing the fingers of one hand under the snowy tablecloth. 'I've relied on Nicky and Freddie far too much. Being on my own will force me to get out more.'

'Oh, love, I do hope so,' said Barbara anxiously. 'Your father and I have been worried about you, worried what this will mean to you. You take such good care of Nicky . . .'

As if on cue, Connie's father ambled up, looking both happy and relieved.

'You're sure the speech was all right?' he asked them both, for possibly the tenth time that evening. 'The *Father of the Bride* booklet said to keep it short, and I know I went on a bit long, but I wanted them to get a picture of Nicky when she was a child, so they'd know what sort of girl she is.'

'Arthur, it was perfect.' Barbara smiled at him, a smile full of love despite her talk about how she'd never had it all.

Weddings were bittersweet, Connie realised. Full of joy for the bridal couple and anyone who was happy, and tinged with regret for everyone else.

Freddie's parents were still devastated that their huge financial losses meant they hadn't been able to give their son and his bride the deposit for a house, the way they'd always planned to. And there was Connie, watching her parents enjoy sheer happiness at seeing one daughter happily married, while with obvious awareness that the other daughter had no sign of even a date with a man on the horizon.

'Dad, what you said was wonderful. Will you bring me for a whirl on the dance floor?' Connie said.

As her father whisked her off, telling her that he was always bad at waltzing and if she wanted to lead, it was fine, Connie reflected that she was getting good at appearing stoic at weddings. First Sylvie's, now Nicky's. if she'd ever thought of a career on the stage, she was getting plenty of practice for it.

* * *

Nicky and Freddie went to the Canaries for their honeymoon. Connie went home to Golden Square and decided she'd join a walking club to help her get fit. Or perhaps she should go to the local swimming pool and do lengths a couple of times a week?

Either way, she wasn't mouldering away any more at home alone. No, sir. She was going to live her life to the fullest. Start again, as Eleanor had said. She was going to embrace life and show everyone how fulfilled she was.

And perhaps show them that a woman didn't need a man to be fulfilled. No, sir, on the double for that.

16

The Queen of Sheba

It's hard for you to imagine the hardship of those days when I was young, Eleanor. Housework wasn't as easy as it is today. You're used to me or Agnes heading to the shop for groceries or watching the coalman throw a sack of coal on the stoop, but in Kilmoney, everything we ate and everything we put on the fire we had to find ourselves.

From dawn till dusk, someone was working. If my mother wasn't making bread, she'd be out digging vegetables in the garden. We'd have been lost without that little plot of land. Wide at one end near the turf stack and the road, it narrowed down into a sliver by the house where my mother grew rocket, because she loved it, and where Agnes had a rosebush that clung to the gable wall.

'The Queen of Sheba' was what she called that rose. It was creamy white, an old rose with many layers of petals like a doll's skirts, and I've never found anything like it since. I'd know the scent at once if I ever smelled it again, but I never have, not in the garden shops or even in the florists.

I'd have loved a garden when we lived in Queens in the old clapboard house, which is funny because, when I was young, I had no time for the garden at all. Worse than gardening was the field of turnips for the cattle.

Thinning turnips was what I hated doing most. You'd have an old grain sack tied round your waist like an apron, and you'd be on your knees in a long furrow with nothing ahead of you but lines of turnips. You'd start at dawn and you had to prick out half the young growth. The cattle ate the turnips and so did we. At least with potatoes you only dug up a few at a time, letting the fresh earthy smell overwhelm you as you hauled up a plant with the pale golden potatoes clinging to the roots. Turnip thinning took hours. By evening, your knees and *your back would be in agony.*

The meitheal was the best part of the summer work, when the local men combined forces to cut everyone's hay for the winter—and woe betide us if it was a bad summer and the hay rotted in the fields.

On meitheal, the women of the house had to put on a fine feed. At lunch, myself and my mother would head to the fields with the tin flask of strong sweet tea and as many sandwiches as we could manage.

I can still smell the fresh scent of the hay when it was being stacked.

Do you know, it was simple then, now that I think of it. Today, we have all manner of geegaws to help us, but life's more complicated in other ways. Looking back, I think we knew what was important about life then.

*   *   *

For the first time ever, Rae was grateful for her mother-in-law's presence. Geraldine's hip was so well healed, she was walking around the house without wincing, and could have easily gone home to her own house. But Rae didn't want her to. Geraldine was proving a welcome distraction.

'You're so kind to my mother,' Will said every night as they lay in their double bed, sinking into the sheets after a long day. It was a time Rae normally loved, the feeling of the cool of the bed on her hot, tired body and the knowledge that Will was beside her. Now, like everything else in her life, it felt wrong. Wrong that she was lying here beside her husband with a huge lie on her conscience. Wrong that she hadn't told him about Jasmine. Wrong that she was sure the only option was to go on keeping the truth from him.

'She needs someone to look after her,' Rae said, which was a neat way of deflecting him. She didn't want to talk about how kind she was. What use was kind when she was a liar?

'She's not always easy,' Will said, and Rae loved him for saying it, even if she couldn't take comfort in it.

'She's just strong-willed, that's all. Goodness, I'm tired.'

This was code for not wanting to make love. In the three weeks that Geraldine had been there, Rae and Will had only made love once. Rae had lain in bed with Will's arms around her and she'd cried silently.

Will had stopped kissing her breasts when he'd become aware of her quiet tears.

'What's wrong, love?' he'd asked anxiously.

'It must be this getting older thing,' she'd said, shocked at how easily the lie came to her.

'We don't have to make love,' Will said, and moved so he was lying beside her, holding her. She could feel his erection against her and knew how aroused he was. But she couldn't make love. The pure honesty of the act would make her break down altogether.

'Thank you,' she mumbled into his shoulder. 'I'm just so tired.' More lies.

'You know you can talk to me about anything,' Will said, as he held her. 'Has Mum been, you know, rude to you? I know how tactless she is . . .'

Rae shook her head. His skin was so warm and he smelled familiar. The Will smell she adored. How many times had they made love over the years of their marriage? She couldn't remember and never before had she felt as if she was betraying him. It wasn't only through sex with another man that a person could betray their husband. 'Your mother's been fine.'

Which wasn't entirely true either. Bored now that she was recuperating well, Geraldine was becoming more irritable. Had Rae ever thought of sanding down the kitchen cabinets and painting them so they matched? Surely dogs weren't allowed in the square's garden off the lead? Geraldine had been looking out one day and seen a skinny girl with dreadful short hair letting two mongrel things run wild. One had done its business off the lead. Geraldine wasn't sure which was worse, the dog being allowed off the lead or that the girl had bent to pick up the poop with a bag as though it were totally normal.

'There aren't many women who'd take their mother-in-law in with grace, don't think I don't know it, Rae,' he said. 'She'll be gone soon anyway.'

'Yes,' agreed Rae, and thought how much harder

it was going to be to hide how miserable she felt when his mother wasn't there as an excuse.

* * *

On Monday, Leonora came to take Geraldine for a coffee.

'I'm still not that mobile,' Geraldine said testily as Leonora took her arm.

Rae hid a smile. Geraldine had been fine earlier and had taken a trip out to see Will in his office and to admire his work.

'Oh, Mother, it's been three weeks. If they'd taken your leg off, you'd be running around by now,' Leonora snapped.

'You've never had your hip done, so don't talk like you know anything about it,' retorted Geraldine. 'You've no idea what I'm going through. At least your brother and Rae understand the pain I've been in.'

Rae held the door open patiently and said a small prayer of thanks that she wasn't going with them. She'd been working in the tearooms all morning and was just taking a break before returning to Titania's for the afternoon shift. But there was something she needed to look for while the house was empty.

It took ages for the pair to leave. 'Hold my right arm, not my left,' said Geraldine crossly to her daughter. 'You keep forgetting I had my left hip done and you might bump into it.'

'Fine,' said Leonora in long-suffering tones.

They shuffled down the path, with Rae at the door, smiling and waiting until they'd reached the pavement. As soon as they had, Rae shut the door, ran upstairs and pulled the cord that opened the trap door to the attic. Reaching up, she pulled the folding stairs down and clicked them into place. She climbed up, flicked on the light and tried to remember where she'd left the box. The attic was a dumping ground for everything from toys to books, old clothes and Christmas decorations. Rae picked her way past Anton's old tricycle and a box with silver and red tinsel sparkling out of it. Shoved in one corner was an old brown nylon suitcase that was so battered it was entirely unsuitable for travel ever again.

She unzipped it and groped through the old sweaters and thermal underwear she'd stored there. None of it would ever be worn again, but it was a hiding place for something precious. Anton's baby clothes were in another suitcase. Rae had donated much of what he'd worn to Community Cares, but she'd kept a few things in memory of that time. Her groping fingers closed around a small, hard-framed handbag.

Rae's hands shook as she opened it and took out a baby's small pink vest. It had been old and second-hand forty-two years ago. Now, it was rough with age but her fingers stroked it as it if were the finest silk. She hadn't kept this vest in with Anton's baby clothes. Keeping it separate was deliberate. Her two children were from two different lives.

She would not betray Jasmine's memory by keeping her tiny vest with her brother's things. And Anton might have thought it odd, too, to find an old woollen vest amongst his babygros. Here alone, she could do the right thing.

After all the weeks of having Geraldine, Rae was

relieved to sit here on the attic floor alone and hold the worn old fabric to her face, trying to breathe in some scent from it. There was nothing but the musty odour of damp and age. And yet, as she held it, Rae felt the tears fall.

*   *   *

The door of the Blessed Helena Nursing Home was a sunshine yellow, as bright as a sunflower even on a misty day in May. The hostel occupied part of an old grain warehouse in Limerick and the only neighbours were a small garage and a feeding supply business. Across the road was a pub and then nothing but bare plots of land. Rae knew the existence of the hostel purely because their Civics teacher, the devout Mrs Flaherty, had dedicated many classes to explaining to the fourth years that young girls wouldn't get pregnant if there weren't spots like the hostel in the first place.

'It's calling to these unfortunate young girls, telling them that sex before marriage is allowed, when we all know that it's not!'

Shelley and Rae never paid much attention to Mrs Flaherty in Civics. It wasn't an exam subject and they were pretty sure that, even if it was, hostels for unmarried mothers was surely not on the curriculum.

'She's crazy,' said Shelley. 'Is it true the fifth years tried to get her to teach them the rhythm method of contraception and she went red in the face and screamed for the headmistress?'

Rae giggled. 'I'd love to have seen that.'

In the back of the taxi that had cruised to a halt in front of the yellow door with Blessed Helena

299

Nursing Home written on it, Rae remembered that conversation. It seemed a million years ago, when she and Shelley were friends, when she'd had a different life mapped out for herself.

'This all right for you?' the taxi driver said gruffly. He hadn't said a word during the trip. Rae almost didn't want to get out of the car, despite the nauseating air freshener. It was safe somehow, a link between the past and the future.

But there was no turning back. Whatever the baby inside her deserved, it wasn't the Hennessey household. It was enough that one of them had been destroyed by Paudge and Glory. Rae's child wouldn't be.

'This is fine,' she said in a clear strong voice. Be brave, she told herself.

She paid and began to take her bags out. Again, he let her move it all herself.

'Thanks,' Rae said, but there was no reply. He sped off and she was left with her bags outside the yellow door.

She wondered would her father be home from the pub yet. Had they noticed she'd gone?

Then she stepped forward and rang the bell.

An elderly woman with the very short hair and unmade-up face of a plainclothes nun opened it and Rae felt her blood still. The nuns of her experience had little kindness for unmarried mothers. Several girls had left the school after becoming pregnant. None had ever returned and there was no mention of them in the way the previous year's sixth years were mentioned at assembly prayers.

The woman's shrewd eyes travelled down Rae's body in her baggy school jumper and the jeans she'd pulled on before she left. The top button was undone but with the jumper over it, nobody noticed until now. Inside, Rae braced herself for the inevitable anger and disgust. If this was what she had to endure to stay here, she would, because she had nowhere else to go.

And then an astonishing thing happened. 'You're welcome, my child,' said the nun, holding out her hands and taking Rae's. 'I'm Sister Veronica.'

'I'm Rae Hennessey,' Rae said, her chin held high.

'Come in, Rae,' said Sister Veronica. 'I'll give you a hand with your things. Is there anybody with you?'

'No,' said Rae. 'I'm alone.'

'You're never alone, God is always with you,' Sister Veronica replied gently.

Rae stared at her. What a comforting thought. She hoped it was true, but she hadn't had much reason to believe in the kindness of God thus far.

Whatever the nuns in school thought about unmarried mothers, the nuns and the women who ran the Blessed Helena Nursing Home had different views. Sister Veronica was kindness itself and while she took notes of all Rae's details, there was no mention of shame or sin the way there would have been in school.

In her *old* school, Rae thought with a shock. She'd never be going back there now.

The hostel was simple yet homely. There was a large kitchen-cum-sitting room where the girls spent their time, two offices, a room where family members could come to visit, and upstairs there were two dormitory rooms along with several single rooms. There were no frills, the seats in the kitchen were old church pews covered with the multi-coloured crochet cushion covers Sister Veronica liked to make in the evening, and the single beds were made up with plain blankets and old white sheets. Despite the bareness of the place, everything was spotlessly clean.

But it was the flowers that Rae would always remember: Sister Veronica loved flowers and grew wallflowers in the tiny scrap of a garden behind the hostel. Old jam jars groaned with the weight of lilac-and-white wallflowers dotted with greenfly. Their heady garden scent filled the air better than any perfume.

There were six girls in Blessed Helena, including Rae, and she was given a bed in the second dormitory alongside Carla, a tiny red-haired girl who was near her time, and Sive, who didn't look pregnant at all and who stared silently at Rae when Sister Veronica showed her the room.

'She doesn't say anything,' Carla informed Rae. She was resting on her bed and she patted the side of it for Rae to sit with her. 'Come and visit with me and we'll talk.'

'I'll leave you to get settled,' Sister Veronica said. 'Dinner's at seven. Carla will tell you everything, won't you, Carla?'

'Can't tell her everything, Sister, or she'd walk out!'

Sister Veronica just laughed. Rae had never witnessed a nun in school behaving in such a free manner. She put her things on the floor beside her bed and went to sit on Carla's.

'Yes, I *am* huge,' Carla said as Rae stared at her belly. She wore a grey tunic that was stretched to ripping point across her swollen midriff. 'I've still got three weeks to go. The midwife says it's going to be a huge baby. Sister Fran says it's a boy because I'm carrying low. Ashling—you'll meet her later—says it can only be an elephant 'cos I'm so big. It might be two, who knows.' She gave her belly an affectionate pat. 'He's certainly wriggling around enough for two.'

Rae laughed and it was such a relief to share a joke that she couldn't stop laughing.

'It's not that funny,' Carla said with amusement.

'It is,' Rae replied. 'I haven't laughed in months.'

'How many months?' asked Carla.

'Five and a half.'

'You're small for five months,' Carla commented.

'I'm tall.' Rae shrugged. 'Made it easier to hide it. And how far along is she?' Rae didn't want to say Sive's name out loud for fear of offending her. 'She has no bump. Has she had a baby?'

'She's pregnant all right and everybody in her family knows 'cos it's her daddy's.'

Rae inhaled sharply.

'She's not eating properly. If I were her, I probably wouldn't eat either. You'd never get over that.'

Rae shook her head. She resolved not to feel so sorry for herself any more. Whatever had happened to her, at least it wasn't that.

*   *   *

For the next two weeks, Rae felt at peace for the first time in ages. There was no tension in the hostel and most of the girls shared a real sense of camaraderie. This was a safe place where nobody shouted at them for being pregnant.

Rae loved spending time with Carla. The little redhead was feisty and funny. She was seventeen and had been in the house the longest.

Sometimes they talked about boys, clothes and films, as if they hadn't bellies swollen with pregnancy. Carla loved the Beatles. She didn't like John Lennon at all.

'Hate those glasses.'

But Paul, he was gorgeous.

What nobody talked about was afterwards.

One night in bed, Rae couldn't sleep and she lay in the darkness, thinking of how she'd love to turn a light on so she could read, but she wouldn't want to wake the other girls. She shifted in her bed and then Carla whispered:

'Are you awake?'

'Yes,' Rae whispered back. 'You OK?'

'No.'

For the first time ever, Rae could hear fear in her friend's voice.

'I'm thinking about afterwards. You know, when the baby comes. What then?'

'We can worry about that later,' said Rae, which was what Sister Veronica had said to her that first day.

'That's the line Veronica uses,' Carla said, with a hint of bitterness. 'They don't want you to think too much about it because they've plans for the babies.'

'What do you mean, "plans"?'

'Adoption,' Carla said. 'We can hardly look after our kids, can we?'

'I'm going to,' said Rae with determination.

'And you're going to use what exactly as money?

Wake up, Rae. We'll have to give our babies away. It's the best for them.'

'Says who?' Rae was shocked.

'Veronica. I went into her this afternoon and she said she's got this great family in Donegal who've already adopted one baby and they'd love another. They've got a farm, the first baby is a little girl and she's nearly two. Another one, a little boy, would finish it off nicely. I wonder if it is a boy? I said, "I'm not sure about the farm, thing, Veronica." I came from a farm, and much good it did me. Getting away from it with a boy from the town is what got me in here.'

Rae got out of her own bed and crept along to Carla's. Her eyes adjusted to the darkness and she sat on Carla's bed, shifting until she got comfortable. She was six months pregnant now. Sister Veronica had a midwife who came weekly to check the girls.

'You're coming along well,' the midwife said that week. 'Into the final trimester.'

'What's that?' Rae had asked.

'Medical language,' the midwife said dismissively. 'No need to worry about it. You stay healthy, that's all, and it'll soon be over.'

Now she sat on Carla's bed, feeling the baby move inside her. He or she was always more alert at night, she didn't know why. Nobody ever talked about the actual pregnancy in the home, so her knowledge was a bit sketchy.

She reached for Carla's small hand and held it.

'I'm scared about having him,' Carla said quietly. 'It's going to hurt. I hate pain and Joely—she was gone before you came—she said the midwives here can't give us pain relief. That's only in hospital.'

'We're not having the baby in hospital?'

'Having a baby is the most natural thing in the world and you don't need to do it in hospital,' said Carla, parrot-fashion. 'Except giving it up isn't. Do you think that afterwards we'll go back to the way we were before?'

Rae bit her lip. 'How can we? It's all different now. We can't become people who haven't had babies.'

'We won't have the babies, though. Nobody will know.'

'I'll have my baby,' Rae said simply. 'And *you'll* know. You'll know you've had a baby. You're not going to forget that.'

*   *   *

Rae put away Jasmine's little vest, climbed out of the attic and slid down on to the staircase with a resounding thud.

In her bathroom, she peered at her red face and splashed water on it. She couldn't go to work looking like this. Hands shaking, she applied a layer of foundation to hide the blotchiness. That done, she went downstairs, blindly grabbed her jacket and keys, and left the house.

In Titania's, she spoke to no one, put her jacket away, and went out to work the till.

The elderly American lady was choosing a bran muffin. What her name was, Rae couldn't remember for the life of her.

'Can I get you something to drink? asked Rae, and the effort of talking made her cry again. It was as though touching Jasmine's little vest had opened the floodgates and now they couldn't be shut.

'Rae,' said a voice.

Through her tears, Rae could see the American lady's concerned face.

'You need to sit down for a minute,' the woman said in a calming voice.

'OK.' Eleanor caught the eye of one of the other members of staff who was watching Rae in shock, and she came to take Rae's place at the till.

Eleanor led Rae to a quiet booth near the back. She took Rae's hand in hers and rubbed it. Normally, she wouldn't touch a patient. But Rae wasn't a patient and this wasn't normal.

'You can talk to me,' she said softly.

Rae looked into Eleanor's warm eyes and knew that she could. 'I don't know what to do,' she said, and began to cry again.

*   *   *

There was nobody close by when Rae went into labour. She was lying on her bed in the small dormitory, trying to ease the pain in her back, when it came on. A searing pain that started in her pelvis and ripped up through her whole body.

'Carla!' she called out in her confusion, but Carla wasn't there. Her baby, a little scrap of a thing that Carla had called Paul after Paul McCartney, had gone to the sweet farming couple in Donegal. Carla had painted on make-up like war paint the day she left, although the eyeliner kept sliding down her face with the tears. 'See, I can fit into my old clothes,' she said, half crying, half smiling. She wore a leather jacket that Rae had never seen before and jeans that hugged her body. 'Back to what I was before. Stay in touch.'

Rae realised she didn't mean it. Carla never wanted to see any of them again because they would remind her of Blessed Helena and little Paul, the baby she'd kept with her for only one night before he'd been taken away by another nun, one they'd never seen before.

'Carla, I wish you were here,' Rae thought when the contraction passed and she lay panting on the narrow bed.

She staggered out to the top of the stairs to call someone, and within minutes, Sister Martin had installed her in the delivery room on the second floor. 'Can you call the midwife?' shrieked Rae as the second contraction ripped through her.

'Don't be silly,' Sister Martin said. 'You've hours to go.'

*   *   *

Six agonising hours passed before the midwife arrived.

Whipping up Rae's gown, she exclaimed: 'You're getting ready to deliver, nearly fully dilated. You should have called me earlier, Sister.'

It was still another half an hour before the baby's head crowned. Rae had never felt such pain but she knew she had to go through this for her beloved baby. She would, she could.

If only Carla were here, or Shelley . . . Rae cried through the pain. It was like being torn in half. What she wouldn't give for a friend beside her, holding her hand, helping her. Or even her mother.

'One more push, be brave now, Rae. Come on,

you can do it!'

With one huge force of effort, Rae pushed and felt the baby's body slip like a fish out of her body.

'A little girl!' said Sister Martin triumphantly. 'God bless her.'

'Let me see, let me hold her.'

'Wait a while, now,' fussed the midwife. 'We need to weigh her, check her out.'

Finally, wrapped in an old hospital blanket, the baby was passed to Rae. In wonder, she took in the tiny red face with the screwed-up eyes, the damp black curls clustering her skull, the skin as soft as silk. It was like holding a beautiful little doll, she thought in awe, touching her baby's face.

Jasmine. That was her name. For months, Rae had held it in her heart if the baby were to be a girl and now, seeing this darling, beautiful baby, she knew it was the right name. Jasmine. Kissing the soft face reverently, she murmured, 'My baby, I love you.'

The midwife had to go.

'You did well,' she said, pleased. 'She's a big girl. Nearly eight pounds. I thought we'd have to call the ambulance there for a while, but you got through it all right. I'll be back later to check you out and I'll have the tablets to dry up your milk.'

Rae didn't hear her. Her mind was full of Jasmine. It was as if there was nobody else in the room.

Rae pulled down the top of her nightgown and let Jasmine's tiny rosebud mouth close around her nipple. Instantly, as if guided by an ancient magic, the baby began to suckle. It felt like the most natural thing Rae had ever done in her life. This body wasn't for her, it was for her baby. She closed

309

her eyes and let herself sink into the peace of breastfeeding.

'Rae,' said Sister Martin sharply. 'You're not supposed to do that. We'll feed the baby formula.'

'Jasmine,' said Rae softly. 'Her name is Jasmine, and I have to feed her. She's hungry, look.'

She looked at the downy dark head nuzzled close to her and the waves of love washed over her. Jasmine, her baby.

Nobody had mentioned the pure joy of breastfeeding. Rae felt as if some part of her body was dancing on clouds. Carla had said that breastfeeding made your boobs all saggy, that's what her mother used to say. She hadn't breastfed her baby.

'It's not a good idea,' Sister Martin insisted. 'You'll get too attached.'

Rae jerked in surprise and the baby's tiny mouth came off her nipple. Jasmine began to cry but Rae didn't tend to her. Instead, she stared at the nun. 'She's my baby, I am attached to her.'

'Lord help us, Rae, will you be sensible! They'll never let you keep her,' Sister Martin said. 'The authorities don't want kids having kids. She'll be taken off you and who knows where she'll end up while they sort it all out. In a home, perhaps. Wouldn't it be better to let her have a decent life somewhere, a new start with good parents from the beginning?'

'Like the people Carla talked about?' Rae said bitterly. 'The family with the farm and the little girl? Are they all farm families with little girls or little boys, depending on the story required?'

'It's for your own good and for the child's own good,' insisted the nun.

'That's what people say when they want you to do what they want,' spat Rae. Jasmine began to cry loudly. Rae cradled her close and tried to get her to latch on to the nipple again, but it was no good. Little Jasmine sensed her mother's distress. Rae tried to calm herself but it was hard, her heart was beating so fast, threatening to leap from her chest. She would keep her baby.

'You're making a rod for your own back,' Sister Martin said. 'How much harder will it be to let her go now that you've bonded with her.'

'I won't let her go!'

The nun stared at her pityingly. 'You will. They all do.'

*   *   *

Eleanor held on to Rae until she stopped crying. It was like holding a husk of a person, someone who'd let all the pain spill away with the life force. Eleanor wanted to cry herself. She'd never felt that way before when a patient cried and perhaps that had been her problem all along. She stood stoic in the face of other people's pain. When Ralf had died, she had been unable to let go of herself and cry. For the first time since then, she wanted to sob her heart out.

They were both in the depths of grief. Rae had never been allowed to grieve for the baby she'd given up for adoption. Eleanor had been too locked into being the perfect strong woman, the psychoanalyst who knew everything, to grieve.

'Do you want to stay here?' Eleanor said. 'You could come to my apartment.'

Rae nodded. It was bad enough that she'd

311

broken down in Titania's. At least if she left now, the rest of the staff would be able to concentrate on work and not keep staring at her anxiously. She stood and went to fetch her jacket.

'Rae, are you all right?' said Phyllis, who'd worked in Titania's forever.

'Fine,' said Rae, doing her best to look semi-fine. 'Just had a shock. Eleanor's so sweet, she's talked me out of it. I think I'll go now. Don't phone me at home, though,' she added hurriedly. 'I don't want to worry Will.'

They crossed the square together, the tall dark-haired woman with the tear-ravaged face arm in arm with the equally tall silver-haired old lady who walked with the cautious steps of a frail person. Rae waited while Eleanor fiddled with her key in the lock and then followed her in. Normally she would have looked at the apartment with great interest, but today she didn't. She sank on to a couch as if she wanted to hide inside it.

'I'm sorry,' she said. 'I don't know what came over me, I'm not that sort of person, I've never told anyone, please don't tell anyone, please.'

'I won't, don't worry, Rae,' said Eleanor gently. 'There's nothing wrong with crying. I am guessing you've never had a chance to mourn Jasmine.'

Rae stared at Eleanor.

'You're the first person in my life who has ever spoken her name. The nuns didn't use it, nobody did. It was like pretending she wasn't real. But she was real, is real.'

'You might be able to meet her,' said Eleanor gently.

'How can she not hate me?' asked Rae. 'If I see her, how can Will and Anton not hate me too?'

312

'Do you hate yourself for what you did?'

Rae shook her head. 'I can't tell them, Eleanor. I can't even think about it, it's too painful.'

'Fine. I will make us tea. Earl Grey or ordinary tea? Everyone here likes their tea.'

For the first time, a hint of a smile hovered over Rae's lips. 'It's one of those clichés that turn out to be true. No matter what happens in Golden Square, someone will suggest putting the kettle on as a solution.'

'The kind gesture as comfort,' Eleanor said. 'It was the same in my mother's time. Tea and what she called "curranty cake". There was nothing that couldn't be soothed with a bit of both.'

Rae followed Eleanor into the kitchen. Watching her make tea was calming and she began to talk again.

'I think of her every day. What's she doing, who she's with. Is her hair dark like mine? Would I recognise her if I saw her? I look for people like her on the street, to see if she could be here. I would know her, wouldn't I? When Anton was small, he worried he'd get lost and I wouldn't be able to find him.

' "I'll always find you," I told him. "Mums have this radar in their hearts that takes them to their child. You can never be lost from me." He was happy with that, but in some ways it was a lie. Children go missing all the time. I had a daughter and the radar didn't work. I longed to know where she was, and I didn't. Longing with all my heart didn't help. She was gone, gone forever.'

In her great pain, the beauty had been leached from Rae's face. It was like staring at a death mask.

'Maybe the radar did work,' Eleanor told her softly. 'You were always looking for her. You kept the memory of her in your heart, and that's all you could do.'

Eleanor had rarely felt the pity she felt for Rae now. To give birth to a child and to have someone take that child away because that was the only way they could both survive? How unselfish an act was that? But oh, how painful.

'I became a mother one day and the next, my child was gone. Tears are hopeless, really. You still have the hole in your heart, a hole nothing can fill. *Nothing.*'

Rae got up and looked out of the window. 'I've made a life for myself without Jasmine, but I've never forgotten about her or forgiven myself for giving her up.'

'You were a child,' insisted Eleanor, 'and undoubtedly they took advantage of that fact. We all know that the people in charge don't always tell the truth, Rae. The girls in the Magdalen Laundries weren't told the truth. They were treated like slaves and had their babies taken away. At least you weren't kept working as a slave, but they didn't give you the chance to keep your child.'

'Times were different then, I know.' Rae said it like it was a newspaper report recited from memory. 'I've watched TV programmes about teenage pregnancy in the sixties and seventies. No young girl now would believe what it was like then. One teenager gave birth to a baby in a holy grotto and both she, the poor child, and her baby died. That was the fear and the shame involved.'

'Imagine if you had a friend this had happened

314

to all those years ago,' Eleanor said. 'Would you blame her for doing what you did, or would you understand?'

Rae looked at Eleanor sadly. 'I'd understand totally for her, but for me, I can't forgive. By not telling Will and Anton, I've been lying to them. I try never to lie. I grew up with lies. My father lied to the welfare so he could get dole money. His back, he said, was the problem. He couldn't work. I vowed not to be that sort of person—and here I am, lying, and I've been doing it all these years.'

She sounded so bitter. Eleanor noticed she was unconsciously holding her hands over her belly. The way pregnant women did.

'The question is, what can you live with? Can you live with not seeing Jasmine, if this turns out to be her? Or can you live with telling your husband the truth? There are no guarantees about how either will turn out. Your daughter may be angry you gave her up. She may not understand what it was like for you, being pregnant and sixteen in 1969. Things are different now. She may want to find her father. Think about all of this.'

Rae nodded, then said: 'Can I borrow a piece of paper and an envelope? I'm going to write back to the social worker. It'll mean facing what it does to us all, but I have to meet her. I have to meet Jasmine.'

'What about telling your husband?'

Rae shook her head. 'I'll think about all that later,' she said.

*   *   *

When Rae had gone, Eleanor looked at the small

315

travel clock that told her what time it was in New York. Noon. Naomi would be in the shop with Marcus probably. Eleanor hadn't phoned for a week. It was part of the deal she'd made with Naomi that she would check in at least once a week.

'I don't understand why you had to go away, Mom,' Naomi said almost every time.

Hearing her so upset was partly why Eleanor couldn't bear to talk to her daughter. It was impossible to explain how devastated she felt by Ralf's death, impossible to explain why coming to Ireland had been a good idea.

'I needed to be by myself,' was what she'd said every time. 'I thought coming home would help.'

'Ireland isn't your home, Mom! New York is.'

I don't know where my home is any more, Eleanor wanted to say. It was with your father and now he's gone.

But that wouldn't have helped.

She closed the curtains, switched on all the lamps and heated some soup in the microwave for dinner. She hoped Rae was doing OK. As for herself, Eleanor didn't know if she'd ever be OK again.

17

Food for the Turfcutters

Your father never carried a spare ounce on his frame, Eleanor, and it was down to the hard labour he did on the farm. The hardest of all was bringing home the turf for the fire. Here in New York, they think it's idyllic to talk about the old days and the bog. Let me tell you, there was no idyll there. It was back-breaking work.

Every home had their own piece of bog and even though there were no fences making barriers, we all knew which was our land. Bogland was passed down through the generations.

Turf was never cut until after St Patrick's Day and then, round about April or May, your father and his brothers would head for the bog. Footing the turf is what we called it and they did it with a spade with a horizontal edge to it. The best turf was a few layers down, and by the end of a week, the men would be worn out from

317

standing knee-deep in bog water.

Once the turf had dried out a bit, we'd all get on the back of the cart and head up to the bog to pile it into little reeks so it could dry out enough to be carried home and built into a proper stack to last the winter.

My mother packed a picnic for the bog. We'd have a few tin pongers or big tin cups the size of small saucepans to heat water for tea, plenty of soda bread, the home-made butter that was a deeper yellow than any butter I've ever seen since, and plenty of duck eggs.

My father would boil the eggs about noon and there was never a more welcome shout than the call to stop for a break. By evening, when your back ached from bending, little biting insects came out in force and sent us all home.

We'd all sit quiet in the cart on the way home, too tired to move, but we could always rouse ourselves later for the feast. My mother would fry great slabs of bacon with onions and sliced potatoes, and we'd gorge ourselves *until we wanted to fall asleep at the table. That was a wonderful feeling, that was.*

*   *   *

Connie didn't want to join Gaynor's book club.

'You'd enjoy it,' Gaynor said. She'd given up apologising over the Keith incident. 'I've said I'm sorry and I mean it. I said too much and it wasn't fair. You *don't* have a list of attributes that no man will ever match up to.'

Except that Connie had come to the conclusion that Gaynor had a point. What was worse: being upset by an old friend being painfully blunt, or realising that the old friend was actually right?

'Gaynor, thank you, but I'd hate to join your book club. Bet you ten euros they're all women you know fromthe school run. I would have nothing in common with them.'

'They're not—' began Gaynor crossly. 'Oh, all right, they are. But we don't talk about kids, we talk about books.'

'And husbands and what to do when Josie's French teacher is being a bitch, and should you get your eleven-year-old a phone in case he gets bullied on it via text message. Yes, Gaynor, I'll fit right in!'

'You're so grumpy in your old age,' Gaynor muttered.

'Pot, meet kettle,' said Connie.

'What are you doing to grow your social life, then, Miss Smarty Pants?'

'I was thinking of doing some charity work,' said Connie, which wasn't a total lie. She had thought

319

about it but had done nothing. She knew from talking to Rae just how hard the work was and didn't know if she was up to it. But saying she was thinking about it might get Gaynor off her back.

'Rae, the lady who lives opposite, works with Community Cares. I'm thinking of volunteering.'

'And how will that help you meet suitable men?' Gaynor demanded.

'It's not about helping me meet suitable men,' Connie said loftily. 'It's about having a life.'

When was everyone going to learn that she didn't want to devote her time to meeting a man?

*   *   *

Saturday mornings were so lonely: Connie had never realised it before. There was no Nicky to talk to, nobody to get a cup of coffee for, nobody to clatter away in the kitchen making breakfast.

And Connie kept waking early on Saturdays, even though she wanted to sleep late. Her body clock refused to obey and she woke at half seven on the dot.

It meant she was one of the first weekend customers at The Nook, when they were still stuffing glossy supplements into the papers.

'You'd need to be a weightlifter to manage all the papers, these days,' groaned an elderly man hoisting two broadsheets and a tabloid into his shopping basket.

'But it's wonderful to have so much to read,' said Connie, realising with a shock that this was the first conversation she'd had with another human being since she'd left St Matilda's yesterday afternoon.

320

Rae was behind the counter in Titania's Palace and Connie smiled at the sight of her.

'Hello, Rae, beautiful morning isn't it?'

'Beautiful,' said Rae.

Too late, Connie noticed that Rae's dark eyes were red-rimmed and she looked as if she hadn't slept soundly in a week.

'Oh, Rae, how are you?' she asked cautiously.

'Connie, please.' Rae held up a hand. 'Don't be nice to me. I couldn't stand it. I can only just cope today. Don't ask why. But if anyone is in the slightest bit nice to me, I'll collapse.'

'Righto,' said Connie. 'I'll have a latte with hazelnut syrup, and two almond pastries because I don't think the waistband on my jeans is tight enough. I can still breathe.'

She was rewarded by seeing Rae laugh a little.

'You're a panic, Connie,' said Rae lightly. 'You should be on the stage.'

'I know,' quipped Connie, 'but the back end of the horse part is already taken.'

This time, Rae didn't laugh. 'You're not allowed to say stuff like that about yourself, Connie.'

'OK, I was just trying to cheer you up.'

'Not at your own expense,' Rae said. 'You see: you've done it, you've taken my mind off myself. Don't let me hear you do that again or I'll tell Eleanor.'

'Don't you dare. I don't want to be therapied,' Connie said. 'I like being a mad spinster lady, and if Eleanor tries to sort me out, I might turn normal.'

'There's no such thing as normal,' Rae said grimly. 'We all pretend to be normal, you know. But nobody really is.'

321

The papers carried reviews of a play in the West End starring Katharine Hartnell. Connie wondered if Megan had seen them. Probably not. Megan said she never read newspapers any more.

'I'm afraid I'll see my name in them,' she said.

Connie nodded as if she understood totally. Unless she got the million cats and ended up appearing on the mad-cat-lady-who-abuses-her-animals television show, there was no way in hell *she'd* ever be in the newspapers.

She was ordinary. That was her problem, she decided miserably: being ordinary. There was nothing special about her. The only person who'd ever thought she was special was Keith, and he'd gone.

*　　　*　　　*

On Monday afternoon when she got home from school, Connie noticed the little girl from the basement flat next door sitting alone and forlorn on the steps up to the house. Since she could be only nine or ten and Connie had never seen her without her dad, she decided she'd better investigate the matter.

'Hello,' she said.

The girl looked up. Her face was small and freckled, and she had inquisitive blue eyes. 'Hi,' she said.

'Are you all right? Is your dad late or—' Connie wondered what to ask. 'Is someone coming to take care of you?'

'I walk home from school with my friend, Lilly, to her house, but today she hurt her knee and had to go to hospital and I came home myself.'

322

'Right.' Connie digested this information. 'Is your dad home soon, then?'

'He gets home at six.'

It was a quarter to five. Connie couldn't leave this child sitting out on the step for another hour and a quarter.

'You could come into my apartment and wait for him?' she suggested.

'I'm not allowed to talk to strangers or go anywhere with them.'

'That's very good advice,' Connie agreed. 'I'm a teacher and I understand that. If you know your dad's phone number, we could phone him to check what he thinks. Does he know you're on your own?'

The girl shook her head. 'I had a mean teacher once. She got cross all the time. Are you a mean teacher?'

'I only get cross once a week and I make sure I'm not in the classroom when I do it. I go into a park and get mad there. Isn't that a good plan?' Connie said. 'I'm Connie. What's your name?'

'I'm not allowed to tell strangers my name.' The girl smiled up at Connie happily.

'OK.' Connie took out her mobile phone and handed it to the girl. 'You phone your dad and tell him what's happened, and then I'll talk to him.'

'This is a boring phone. My dad's one has a screen you touch and you can play games.'

'I bet you can work a computer really well, too,' Connie said thoughtfully.

'Yes, I'm very good at it. Dad says I'm a genius.'

She dialled a number and waited patiently. 'Hi, Dad, it's me. Lilly hurt her knee and I'm on the step at home and this lady teacher who isn't mean

323

and goes into a field to be mean there says I can come to her house and play. But I said I can't talk to strangers. Her name is Connie. She's the crazy lady next door you said got angry when you parked in her place but she isn't angry now. And I told her about Miss Rochester my teacher and she has a boring phone and do you want to talk to her?'

Connie listened and bit her lip.

The voice on the other end of the phone talked urgently and the girl listened and then handed the phone to her.

'My dad,' the girl said.

'This is Steve Calman,' said the voice. 'Ella's message is a bit garbled. What exactly's going on?'

'I'm Connie O'Callaghan from the house next door and I saw her sitting on the step outside your apartment. I know I've never seen her on her own before, so I came over. I teach in St Matilda's down the road, I'm used to children. Well, older girls, it's a secondary school, but still. I think the girl she normally goes home with had an accident, and Ella came home on her own. I said she could come into my apartment until you get back. I totally understand if you don't want that. We can wait outside together till you get here.'

Connie exhaled.

'Thank you, thank you,' Steve said. 'She's never on her own. Three days a week, she gets picked up by her friend Lilly's mother, Fee—she works as a childminder and she takes Ella for me until I get home from work—and I don't know what happened, or how she came to get home on her own. It's not far, but she's not used to it—'

Connie could hear the panic in his voice.

'It's fine,' she said soothingly. 'She is absolutely

fine. She wouldn't even tell me her name because you've told her not to give it to strangers.'

Ella beamed up at her.

'Can I tell her my name now, Dad?' she roared in the direction of the phone.

'See?' said Connie. 'She's fine. She can still come to me. I have no men around my home, no strange loopers, it's just me and I was going to mark essays and have a cup of tea. She can sit and watch TV till you get home. I promise I won't be a mean teacher person, Ella,' she added.

Ella grinned her impish grin.

'Or we can wait on the step until you get here.'

'No, no. That would be fantastic, if you could bring her to your place.' He still sounded upset.

'I understand your fears totally. You can phone Matilda's and they'll tell you I'm a teacher there and—' Connie racked her brains for other proof of her trustworthiness. 'Rae in Titania's Tearooms knows me. I've lived here for eight years. I used to share with my sister, Nicky—you know, pretty blonde girl. She just got married.'

'I know her,' he said.

Connie grinned. Everyone remembered Nicky.

'I'm sorry about the whole crazy-lady-next-door thing,' he added.

'Forget it,' she said briskly. 'You have my mobile phone number now and my apartment is 2B in the house beside yours. Does Ella have a snack after school?'

'Chocolate cake and 7UP,' Ella said loudly.

'A sandwich and a glass of milk,' her father said.

Ella shook her head. 'Chocolate cake and 7UP,' she whispered.

'Slug juice and beetle buns?' Connie whispered

back.

Ella's laugh was explosive.

'You talk to your dad for a moment,' Connie said, handing the phone back.

Ella listened quietly and nodded at whatever her father said.

'Love you too,' she said and pressed the 'end' button.

She picked up her school bag and looked enquiringly at Connie. 'Do you really have slug juice?'

'Only for emergencies,' Connie said. 'It's very expensive.'

*   *   *

Ella was only a small person but she filled Connie's apartment in a way it hadn't been filled since Nicky had left. She left her coat and schoolbag on the floor by the door, took off her shoes and left them where they lay, and walked around looking at things.

She loved Connie's many candles, and her earthenware birds and the red cushions with the gingham hearts on them. She picked up ornaments, running her tiny fingers over them, then putting them back in exactly the right place.

'Oooh, I love this,' she kept saying, touching, examining, rushing from place to place. She spent ages gazing at the pictures of Nicky's wedding, taking one big group photo and looking at it steadily.

Connie watched her from behind the counter in the kitchen, making very slow work of getting a glass of milk and a sandwich. She had nothing

326

interesting to eat in her cupboards, so it would have to be the healthy snack Steve wanted her to have.

She wondered what Steve and Ella's story was. Where was her mother?

Connie only had a vague impression of Steve Calman and he was a big man, the sort of person she imagined wearing a hard hat and working on a building site, whereas Ella was a pixie with neat, skinny limbs and a tiny heart-shaped face. Ella's mother must have been a pixie person too. No wonder he'd noticed Nicky.

When Ella had finished her exploration of the living room, she looked enquiringly at Connie. 'Can I see everywhere else?' she asked politely. 'I don't get to see many houses. I've seen Lilly's and it's nice but untidy. And Petal lives in a flat, 'cos her mum's divorced. Can I see your room? Please?'

Connie grinned. 'Sure. But after your snack.'

At the table, Ella sniffed the milk cautiously. 'Is this slug juice?' she asked.

'No, I was teasing. It's plain old milk and a cheese sandwich. I'm sorry I don't have anything more interesting.' A thought occurred to her. 'I have profiteroles in the freezer.' Keeping them there was a great way to diet. That way, it took half an hour for them to defrost and normally, she couldn't wait long enough, so the desire for the sweet thing would be gone by then.

'What are proff . . . poff . . .—those things?'

'Little cakes with chocolate on the outside and cream on the inside.'

Mouth full of sandwich, Ella made a thumbs-up sign.

Connie drank her tea and wondered why it felt different to have a child in her home instead of standing in front of a classroom of them. Yet it was different. She felt responsible for this little person in a strange way. In class, she was responsible for the girls' learning and for their wellbeing in school, but that was a shared responsibility. Their parents, other teachers, a whole host of other people were involved. But now, with Ella, *she* was totally in charge.

'My dad said a shark bit someone in the sea in India,' Ella announced.

Connie considered this.

'Did that scare you?' she asked.

'A bit,' Ella admitted. 'Why do sharks eat people? Don't they like people?'

Connie believed that all children's questions should be answered seriously.

'They don't know people at all,' she said gravely. 'That's the problem. They might love us if they did, but we can't invite them in for a cup of tea, now, can we? So they're a bit scared and maybe hungry, and when a shark is scared and hungry, it bites.'

'Like the big furry dog in number 8?'

'Did he bite you?'

'No. He nearly did once.'

Connie briefly wondered what a nearly-bite was.

'The shark could be having a sad day,' she went on. 'Maybe he got up and was late to school, and the whole day didn't work out nicely, and he was so grumpy, he bit a person. Or . . .' Connie thought of the next bit. She was enjoying this. 'Maybe he had a mean teacher and that's what did it.'

'Or he had a row with another shark and they

sulked and he bumped his nose into the person and he got a fright . . .' Ella began to get into it too.

'And he wanted to say sorry, but humans don't speak shark.'

'Sharks don't know how to kiss to say sorry,' Ella said happily.

'Exactly.'

Ella performed a conversational swerve. 'Why don't you have any children?'

Connie had been a teacher long enough not to choke on her tea, but it was a close call. 'Not everyone is lucky enough,' Connie said in a voice that sounded overly pious, even to her.

'Why not?' Ella asked. 'Do you have to be very good to get children?'

'N-o. It's not about being good or bad.' This was worse than discussing licentious sixteenth-century popes with the fifth years.

But how did the pope get to have children, Miss O' Callaghan?'

And Connie wasn't used to kids Ella's age. Who knew what a ten-year-old had been taught about where babies came from.

'When mummies and daddies love each other very much, they can be lucky and have babies,' she ventured.

'You never got lucky enough with a daddy?' Ella said.

'That's it,' said Connie, relieved.

'My daddy did, but my mummy died when her car crashed into a wall,' Ella said, still chirpy.

'That must have been very sad for you,' Connie said slowly. How awful. The poor, poor child.

'I was a baby, I don't remember,' Ella said in

329

matter-of-fact tones. 'I've finished my sandwich. See? Can I see your room now?'

'Oh!' Ella's gasp was of pleasure as she stood at the door to Connie's bedroom. 'It's like a princess's room,' she breathed. She flitted around, reverently touching Connie's flower fairy lights on the dressing table, petting the pretty cushions massed on the bed. 'If I slept here, I would never go to sleep. I'd lie and look at it all,' she said softly, and suddenly Connie's heart ached for this motherless child.

Ella was keen to put on some of Connie's limited supply of make-up and Connie was equally keen that she didn't.

'Your dad mightn't like it,' she said firmly.

'He won't mind,' Ella said, dimpling up at Connie. 'I have my own lipstick. It's Hello Kitty and it's pink and sparkly and it gets on clothes and Dad puts that pink washing goo that makes stains come out on it and it works but not on his best white shirt even though he did it lots of times and I'm not allowed to put my lipstick on him any more.'

It was five to six when Steve Calman arrived and when he walked into the room, Connie felt instantly at ease with him. There wasn't any of the 'does he like me, do I like him?' anxiety she always felt when she invited in a man she was dating.

After spending the time with Ella, Connie had a clear vision of Steve Calman. He was Ella's dad and a widower and she didn't really register his looks or his suitability as a date. What she did register was his smile of delight when he picked Ella up in a great hug.

'I can't thank you enough for all of this,' he said

330

to Connie, with Ella clinging on to him like a koala.

'Lilly's mother phoned me in bits from the hospital and said she'd totally forgotten about Ella, but that when she'd phoned the school in a panic, they'd said Petal's mother had taken her. And it seems this monkey had said the same thing to the teacher and snuck out. Your teacher is going to kill you tomorrow, by the way,' he added to Ella.

'I can go home on my own now, Dad,' Ella said, affronted. 'I'm old enough.'

'No, you can't. Lilly's not in school tomorrow and I have too many meetings to come away early, but Petal's mother kindly volunteered to have you for a few days until Lilly's back at school and Fee can mind you again. I can collect you from Danielle's house if I leave work early . . .'

'I can take Ella after school.'

Even as she said it, Connie knew he'd say no. What would a single woman, who taught kids all day, want with another child around in the afternoon? He'd think she was mad. How could she explain that Ella had been like a little spark of light into her day?

'She gets into your heart, doesn't she?' Steve said.

'Yes,' said Connie instantly.

'She can be a monkey too.'

'I'm sure she can.'

Ella sat there, pretending not to listen. Whatever Steve had done, he'd made her happy and confident. How did parents do that?

'It would just be tomorrow,' Steve went on.

'Of course,' said Connie. She was too busy to

take care of Ella any other time, obviously.

'But if you're stuck anytime,' she found herself saying. 'I can babysit, you know. She can come here.'

'Dad doesn't go out,' Ella said informatively. 'People ask him. He says he gets a headache when he gets asked to boring parties and dinners and ladies smile at him.'

Connie caught Steve's eye. 'You forgot to mention the fact that I hate washing up and that I have a tattoo,' he said to Ella.

She perked up. 'Dad has a tattoo on his shoulder. It's a bit of an eagle and he said it hurt, but he got the wing done and I like it.'

Steve looked resigned. 'There are no secrets with Ella. It's easier to let her tell everyone everything.'

'Secrets are bad,' Ella recited. 'Secrets are only for your family and if anyone tells you something is a secret, you have to shout loudly until another grown-up comes along.'

'If you come tomorrow, you can tell me everything,' Connie said to Ella, casting a sideways grin at Steve. 'You can tell your dad I have fairy lights in my bedroom.'

'Really?'

'And fluffy pillows and pink things,' said Ella quickly, 'and shiny lipsticks and a picture of a man with no clothes on on the front of a book and a lady kissing him—'

'That's enough, Ella!' said Steve.

'It's a romance novel,' Connie said, her face puce. 'He's got clothes on, it's just his shirt is off—'

'Fine,' said Steve, suddenly busy getting Ella's coat.

The next day, Connie left work at four and drove

to the address Steve had given her.

Danielle was mother to Petal, a ten-year-old in Ella's class. Connie liked flower names but always wondered what happened when cute little poppets named Petal grew up and tried to get jobs as engineers or scientists.

'Dr Petal has been working on the vaccine,' sounded a bit daft.

Petal opened the door with Ella beside her. Petal was a sweet child, though not, Connie thought biasedly, as cute as Ella.

Danielle was right behind them, a slim and glamorous blonde wearing jeans, a teeny pink hoodie, and plenty of lip gloss.

Connie was in her customary navy—a long-sleeved dress and flat knee boots—and felt ninety beside this trendy creature.

'Hello, you must be Connie, I'm Danielle.'

Danielle looked at her curiously and Connie was sure that Steve was the source of much interest in his daughter's school. There probably weren't that many good-looking, unattached, single fathers around and she remembered Ella saying that Danielle was divorced. Sure enough, Danielle began a bit of idle questioning as Ella collected her school coat and bag.

'So,' Danielle said, all chatty and smiley, 'you're a friend of Steve's?'

'Yes,' said Connie, just as smiley.

'She lives next door and I go to her house sometimes,' Ella said, keen to keep secrets at a minimum.

'Yeah,' said Danielle, ignoring Ella totally. 'How long have you been—'

'—friends?' said Connie artlessly. 'Oh, not long.'

333

True.

'He parked in her space once,' Ella added.

Also true, although it sounded much more interesting than it was.

'Just once,' Connie said, nodding. She and Ella made a good double act. 'Steve really appreciates you picking Ella up. I couldn't because I was at work.'

She waited for Ella to fill in details of Connie's job, with a possible mention of fairy lights, but Ella was now keen to go.

'Come on,' she said to Connie, pulling her sleeve. 'You said we'd have more por . . . proffo . . . those cakes with the chocolate you have in the freezer.'

Connie grinned wickedly at Danielle. 'She loves profiteroles.'

'Petal's mummy thinks you're Daddy's girlfriend,' Ella announced as they got into Connie's car.

'Really?' Connie put her seatbelt on. If Danielle had a lick of sense, she'd see that this was highly unlikely. Given that Steve was surrounded by foxy mums on the prowl like Danielle, he'd hardly be dating Connie, now, would he?

'I told her he likes you a lot. More than the ladies at dinner parties who are bored. You could bring him to a dinner party.'

'But who'd take care of you?' Connie asked.

'I could sit on your bed in your fluffy pillows.'

'No you couldn't,' said Connie cheerfully. 'There are too many of them. You'd get stuck, I'd have to hang around to pull you out or else you'd get sucked into the bed and get lost in fluffy pillow land.'

'Oooh, lovely,' said Ella.

*   *   *

'I'm having fun. I don't want to go home yet,' said Ella when Steve arrived at six. 'Please can we stay?'

'Ella, we can't stay. We have to go home for dinner.'

'You could have dinner here,' Connie suggested off the top of her head. Not that she had a thing in the house suitable for dinner for three, but still. They could have takeaway. Khans was just round the corner.

'Do you eat Indian food?' she asked Ella.

Eyes wide, Ella nodded enthusiastically.

'She's never had Indian in her life,' said Steve, smiling.

'I did, too. I had a peanut butter thing in Lilly's house and it was OK.'

'Satay chicken,' Steve explained.

'Sattee chicken. I ate it all.'

'You ate half of it and said you felt sick on the way home.'

'I was in the car. I won't be in the car on the way home from Connie's, will I?'

Ella sat on the couch and folded her arms firmly. Seeing both Connie and her father begin to laugh, Ella blinked her big blue eyes, her long lashes fluttering against her cheeks.

'Did someone tell you to make puppy-dog eyes to look cute?' Connie asked.

'Yes!' Ella said. 'Daddy says I am cute when I flutter my eyes like butterflies.'

'You won't win,' Connie advised Steve.

335

He smiled at her and suddenly, she realised that Ella had inherited his eyes and long lashes. Everything else was different. He was rough-edged and big, whereas Ella was small and soft, but they both had those fabulous eyes that could light up a room.

In the end, Ella ate mainly naan bread and sweet mango pickles rather than the creamy and mild korma Connie had chosen for her.

When she was finished, she started wandering round the apartment again and ended up heading into Connie's bedroom.

'Ella, don't—' began Steve.

Connie waved a hand at him. 'It's fine,' she said. 'Ella can go anywhere she wants.'

'Thank you,' shouted Ella from the bedroom.

'You've been very kind to her, and to me,' Steve said. 'We don't have many women friends. Her grandmothers don't live nearby and I don't like bothering the other mothers too much. Fee, her friend Lilly's mum, is a childminder and we have a professional arrangement, which is great.'

'No girlfriend?' Connie asked, busying herself tidying up the plates.

'No. There's no space in my life for that,' Steve said easily. 'Who'd want to take me on? Besides, I couldn't be with someone who didn't love Ella.'

'I understand totally,' said Connie, and she did. She thought of her list with its insistence on never dating a man with children. How stupid had she been? If someone had arranged a blind date with Steve, the list would have meant she'd have said no straight up.

No to someone who'd been married before, undoubtedly a definite no to someone who was widowed, and a final no to a man who clearly put his ten-year-old daughter first.

She was in love with the idea of Ella, Connie decided: a ready-made family for her to slip into. That wasn't love and it wasn't sensible, either. Steve hadn't looked at her with any degree of romantic interest. She was his kindly neighbour. Nicky was the type of woman he'd have liked. It was Nicky he'd remembered, not her. People didn't remember her in that way.

They'd have to be friends, Connie decided. She could be happy with that.

She mentioned meeting Steve to Eleanor the next time she called in to see her. Eleanor went straight to the point.

'Do you find him attractive?' she asked.

If anyone else had said this, Connie would have retorted: 'Don't be ridiculous. We're friends, I mind his daughter for him, that's all . . .'

With Eleanor, she confessed what she had denied to herself: 'Yes, and do you know, he doesn't tick any of the boxes on my list. Except, he's handsome, for sure.'

'I could have told you that,' Eleanor interrupted.

'I know. Go on, say it, you were right to have mentioned him the first time we met.'

'I never say things like that,' Eleanor said, smiling. 'I'm glad I can still spot a good-looking man at my age.'

'I never looked at him until I met Ella,' Connie admitted. 'He's lived here for two years. Two years! To think I never spoke to him once. I know,' she held a hand up: 'let the past go.'

'I've never said that,' Eleanor said.

'It's the sort of therapy-ish thing people say,

though, isn't it? The past is the past and all that stuff. Well, the past is the past.'

'Do you think the attraction is reciprocated?'

'No.' Connie sighed. 'I don't think so. We get on well, that's all. I bet half the single mums at Ella's school have got their eye on him. Some of them are much more his type.'

'He told you this?'

'Not in so many words, no—'

'How about you don't give up on him until he does tell you in so many words?' suggested Eleanor.

'You old romantic,' teased Connie.

18

The Dairy

A good country cook had to know how to churn her own butter. Most girls learned when they were young, but I was too sickly. I spent many days watching my mother labour over the big barrel churn but I was at least fourteen before I made my own butter.

My mother had her favourite cow, a small Friesian named Baby, so called because she'd been only a heifer herself when she'd had her first calf. Baby was a great milker and produced gallons of the creamy milk you needed for good butter.

Each day after milking, my mother would pour the milk into big tin buckets and leave them to sit in the cool of the dairy. After a few hours, the cream would have risen to the top and she'd scoop that out and pour it into the separator. It was a piece of mechanical genius, except when you had to wash it, because it was made of twenty-five small steel funnels that fitted together like Russian dolls, and washing it till it was perfect took a good hour. The creamy milk went in, you turned the big handle and the milk was separated from the cream. I never cared for the cream, but I liked drinking the bluey-white skim milk. What I really loved, though, was pure buttermilk. It's not like that bitter slop you find in the shops. No, this was tangy and pure, with tiny kernels of soft butter floating in it. Once you had enough cream, it was into the churn with it and the hard work began.

There was no easy way to make butter. You had to turn that handle for hours. The moment would come when you'd start to hear a mild thump inside, and you'd lift the lid to find a small lump of butter had appeared. So you'd churn away until the lumps were bigger and then finally you could lift out great golden chunks of the stuff.

My mother would heft it into her butter basin, and begin to pat it out with the butter paddles, adding a pinch of salt until it was just right. She'd make slabs that weighed about two pounds each, and they'd be sealed in greaseproof paper and kept in the dairy until needed. When we had too much, Mam would sell some.

*   *   *

Connie was on her way back from getting milk in the shop when she saw the man in the car with the camera, without really realising what he was doing. One part of her mind registered it: man with giant lens trained in the direction of the east corner of the square. Sometimes people sat and painted in the square itself, although that was more of a summer occupation. He might be an amateur photographer, someone working on photographing architectural details, she decided. As she walked briskly past the car, Connie looked in the direction his lens was pointing. It was near the chiropodist's practice. She thought of Megan.

On cue, the door opened and Megan came out, arm stretched out with those two mad dogs pulling her along.

Connie smiled. Megan had abandoned her usual woolly hat and her hair, a bit longer now but still dark as midnight, was all over the place. She really never brushed it, and yet it looked great.

Casual chic.

Then the window of the car opened and Connie heard a great series of whirring clicks. Her mind suddenly processed what was happening.

'Megan!' she shrieked and saw her friend look in her direction, eyes widening with shock.

Connie could almost see the photographs in the newspapers: Megan's haunted eyes, her face a picture of horror.

Someone had to do something.

Connie ran in front of the camera, which gave Megan time to turn round and bundle the surprised dogs back indoors. The photographer got out of the car and swore at her, so Connie crossed the road and followed Megan inside.

Megan was hunched on the floor, shaking silently, so Connie took action.

'Nora!' she yelled.

Nora appeared from the small kitchenette, her face a question mark. Through the window, Connie noticed the photographer's car draw up outside. The car door opened.

'A photographer's outside. He's taking pictures

of Megan.'

'Merciful hour,' said Nora. 'That's all we need.' She rushed to lock the practice door.

'Let's get her out now, before a whole horde of them turns up. Out the back door,' ordered Connie. 'Quick. You can't stay here, Megan, love,' she said, helping Megan up. 'If we go out the back, we can get out the wide gate into the lane behind the gardens. We'll go that way to my house, and he won't see us if we go in the fire escape. I'll go round the front and let you in, Megan.'

'We need a different coat and a hat, Nora,' said Connie.

Kev appeared with his coat and a baseball hat.

'Perfect.'

Connie then stuck a baseball hat on Megan's head. Megan just stood unprotesting, weary.

'I'll bring a bag of her stuff round later.'

'Right.' Connie looked at them both. 'Let's go quickly.'

There was nobody watching the back of the house. The photographer must have found her on his own and come without a reporter, Connie figured. But once his photos were published, everyone would be stalking Nora's. They tramped down the long garden to the small gate at the back, and out on to the lane where some of the houses had once owned garages. Most of the garages had been sold and converted into mews houses. It was a road that only locals knew about. They hurried down the lane until they reached Connie's house. Their gate was rusted and took a lot of shaking and rattling to open.

That end of the garden was a jungle, and Nora used the hold-all to bash nettles out of the way until they reached the back of the house.

'I'll go in the front, he won't see me,' Connie said. 'Lend me the hat, just in case.'

She peered round the front of the house but couldn't see the photographer. The car was still in front of Nora's, but he wasn't in it, so perhaps he was standing outside the practice with his nose pressed to the window. Speedily, she rushed up the steps to the front door, let herself in, then raced up to her apartment. The fire escape was a modern affair that had to be let down from the kitchen window in the apartment. Connie unlocked it, let it rattle down, then watched Megan and Nora climb up.

Megan was shaking from head to foot. 'I didn't see him,' she kept saying, over and over again.

Nora was uncharacteristically mute.

'I don't know what to do,' she whispered. 'It's awful to admit it, but I don't. We don't even talk about it, and now look at her.'

Megan was in pieces. What could they do? Connie had an idea. 'Eleanor—she'll be able to manage her.'

*   *   *

In the apartment downstairs, Eleanor looked back on what she'd written.

Do what frightens you.

That sounded a little strange any way you looked a tit.

The problem with writing advice was that, unless you included details of how you came by the

343

advice, it sounded anodyne.

Do as I say and not as I do. *I never lost my heart to a stranger and fell into his bed, but I'm telling you what to do if that ever happens to you . . .*

If you fight with the people you love most in the world, running away might not be the answer . . .

No, concrete examples were required.

The knock on the door made her jump.

'Eleanor, it's Connie. It's a crisis, can you help?'

Connie's whispered explanation was quick.

'I see,' said Eleanor calmly. 'Poor Megan. Bring her in.'

'Thank you.' Connie kissed Eleanor on the cheek, and Eleanor felt a pang of loneliness at the kindness of the gesture. Nobody had kissed her cheek in so long, not since she'd left New York.

Connie came downstairs, leading poor Megan by the hand.

'Nora's going to get a number for her agent from Megan's sister. Someone needs to do something, right? And I'll close the blinds so the bloody photographer doesn't spot you in here,' Connie added, for Megan's benefit.

Eleanor smiled. 'You think of everything,' she said.

'I wish I really did,' Connie said wistfully. 'I'm great at other people's lives, it's my own I make a mess of. Bye, Megan, I'll be back later.'

When Connie had left, Eleanor went into the kitchen. 'I'm going to make us a hot drink,' she said.

From the kitchen, she watched Megan wander round the living room, staring at the paintings on the walls and picking up ornaments. There was, Eleanor observed, undoubtedly a book on what it

344

meant if a stranger caressed a female nude sculpture or put all the books on a coffee table at right angles. But she didn't need any textbook to help her. Reading people was part of what she did instinctively.

She poured boiling water on teabags, and watched the girl. She didn't visit the books on the coffee table and she bypassed the pretty little bronze nude on the sideboard. Instead, she ran a questing hand over the giant conch shell beside it, feeling the spirals as if she could see with her fingers. And she spent a while looking at the photos Eleanor had brought with her from New York.

The one she lingered over longest was of Eleanor and Gillian, taken on Gillian's eighteenth birthday.

'You look so happy,' Megan said wistfully. 'I'll never be happy again. I ran away and this is my punishment.'

It was the voice of someone in shock, who said things they mightn't normally say.

'Punishment for what, exactly?'

My sister says I want a protector and I don't care where he comes from. She thinks I stole him.'

Eleanor waited for Megan to go on. It was what she'd done all her professional life: wait for the person to continue to tell their story. And she'd waited a long time to hear Megan's.

But Megan changed the subject. 'What are you doing here? Are you running away too?'

Eleanor said uncertainly, 'No, I'm not running away. I'm where I need to be right now, there's a difference. I needed peace and quiet, and I couldn't get it back home.'

'Snap!' said Megan.

And she began to cry.

'I ruined a woman's life, totally ruined it,' she said. 'I thought he loved me, you see, and I was wrong.'

* * *

Prague was postcard pretty in the run-up to Christmas. The Hotel Sebastien was decorated with Christmas trees, dark-red velvet bows and unusual cloisonné baubles with pictures of the old city painted on them. Megan felt drunk with the atmosphere, as well as drunk from being with Rob.

They'd spent a whole day in bed, having room service sent up and making love endlessly. He was an amazing lover, patient and gentle, yet passionate.

She was still stunned that she was there with him: it wasn't easy not to gaze at the famous face when she found it on the pillow beside hers.

Megan never wanted the day and the night to end, and she thought she'd remember it forever.

She'd tried to ask him what would happen next, but Rob didn't want to talk about that.

'Let's not waste time talking,' he'd murmured and began nuzzling her breasts again.

The following morning, he was up early and on the phone to Charles in the States. Megan had heard enough about the Hollywood super agent to be impressed at the slightly cavalier way Rob talked to him.

There was none of the cautiousness that was present when she discussed things with her agent.

'Tell him to go to hell, Charles,' yelled Rob down

346

the phone. 'You should never have got me into this in the first place. I hate those commercials.'

He'd gone into the sitting room of the suite for the final part of the conversation and Megan could overhear snippets.

'Yeah, the Sebastien's still looking good . . . no, nobody else knows apart from the usual suspects—how dumb do you think I am? . . . Yes, I'll be there in two days . . .'

Megan wondered where Rob had to be in two days. He hadn't mentioned it to her, he'd mentioned nothing apart from the current moment.

She sat with her arms around her knees and wondered if she had the right to ask him about the future. Men hated that, didn't they? She could recall her mother saying so many years ago: 'Men don't like to be rushed.'

As if it were an emblem to be inscribed on every woman's heart so she wouldn't forget.

So Megan didn't ask. Instead, she obediently searched Rob's luggage for his phone charger, which he appeared to have forgotten.

'Phone Boo, he has my spare one,' Rob commanded.

Boo was one of his assistants.

'Boo thinks you're in London, doesn't he?' Megan countered.

'No,' said Rob shortly. 'He knows I'm here. He has to know.'

'Oh. What about Charles. Does he know?'

The look Rob sent her was faintly pitying. 'My love, of course he knows. Charles knows everything.'

'Does he approve, about you and me?'

347

This time, Rob didn't even favour her with a look. He busied himself with his phone, dialling another number. 'Sure.'

His legendary energy meant he didn't want to stay in the suite for another day, so despite Megan worrying about them being spotted, they both put on shades and went out shopping, Rob wearing an old cap, she a baseball hat.

His and her disguises. It reminded her of reruns of *Hart to Hart*, a TV show her mother had always loved, that featured a glamorous, rich couple who solved mysteries.

In a jewellery shop, he'd bought her a gold bracelet, a showy piece scattered with diamonds. It wasn't the sort of thing Megan liked. In fact, the thing she wanted in the window had been much simpler, an antique piece of amber the size of a gull's egg on a thin gold chain.

'No, this is how I like you,' said Rob in his deep voice, as he fastened the bracelet on her wrist.

Megan was surprised at how little he seemed to know her. She'd thought he could see into her soul, but he'd learn, wouldn't he?

Later, she realised that the extravagant gesture of buying her the diamond bracelet had let their secret out. The jeweller had known who he was as soon as he whipped his black credit card out. He'd probably phoned a newspaper pal and got paid for the tip-off.

They'd gone on to a small café and sat outside so they could smoke. Rob had his arm around her and was kissing her, telling her how much he loved the look of her new bracelet, when they heard the click of a camera.

With his lifetime experience of the press, Rob

didn't jerk up. He'd straightened his back slightly, which made him look longer and leaner in the photo.

It was Megan who'd leapt to her feet and dragged him with her back to the hotel.

'What's going to happen?' she said, frightened. 'What will Katharine think? You have to tell her what's happened. And Charles . . .'

'Relax. I'll get the photo killed.' Rob sounded so cool about the whole thing. 'It happens all the time. I'll do an exclusive interview for the newspaper, buy the snapper off. It'll be fine. Charles is good at this kind of thing.'

This kind of thing.

Megan stared at him. 'What kind of thing?' she asked, feeling a coldness flow through her body.

'Photos I don't want out there,' Rob replied. 'Come on, you know how this business works.'

'Not like this, I don't,' she stammered.

'It's simple. If you're powerful enough, you can stop the bad news leaking out.' Rob seemed to be enjoying this, this evidence of his great power. 'I'll phone Charles.'

While he phoned, Megan packed her bag, her hands shaking. She thought of phoning Carole, her agent, but didn't quite know what to say: 'Hi, I've just had an affair with Rob Hartnell and, while I thought it was love, I don't think that any more. He's changed.'

'Where are you going?' Rob demanded when he saw her with the bag.

'I don't know. Home.'

He went over to her and stroked her face, looking at her with those amazing eyes. 'You don't have to go. You're special, Megan.'

'You've done this before,' she said, knowing suddenly. 'You told me you hadn't.'

'Come on, Megan, that's what all men say.'

'I wouldn't have come here with you if I'd thought that,' she said. 'I believed what you said, that it was special, that you'd never cheated on your wife before.'

He shrugged and moved away from her. His eyes weren't so warm any more. 'We all believe what we want to believe. There's no need to go. We could have fun together.'

Megan shook her head. She desperately wanted it to go back to the way it had been before, but she knew it couldn't. There was no way of unknowing what she knew now.

She picked up her bag and walked towards the suite door. By the time she closed it gently behind her, Rob was already on the phone.

*   *   *

'Charles couldn't do his magic,' Megan told Eleanor. 'Not this time. When I got to Heathrow, the story was out. I hid in my flat for a while, and finally I came here. They're never going to stop talking about this. I'll be Mantrapper Megan forever.'

'No, you won't,' said Eleanor. 'The world does move on. This year's cause célèbre is next year's ancient history. It will all be forgotten.'

'I wish that was the case,' sighed Megan. 'I'll never forget it, anyway. Maybe I shouldn't have run away. I should have faced the music, then and there.'

Eleanor said nothing to that.

350

Megan was right. It was what Eleanor had done too.

Feeling unsettled, Eleanor stared at the girl in her apartment. She'd become so unused to company. During her stay in Golden Square, the most time she'd spent with other people had been a few hours here and there. And now Megan had burst into her life, bringing with her great drama, and her emotional pain.

Something in Eleanor recognised the pain in Megan: it was reflected in herself.

While Megan had been here, Eleanor hadn't thought of herself really, apart from the moment of recognition in realising that she, too, had run away.

Perhaps distraction was what she needed. Here was a chance to help someone else. Here was a chance to escape her own pain and perhaps heal someone else's.

The words were out of her mouth before she could edit herself.

'Megan, would you like to stay with me? You're welcome to. It would be so nice to have you here.'

The smile Megan gave her was of such sweetness that Eleanor smiled back with the sort of true smile she hadn't been capable of for a long time. It was the effect Megan must have had on many people, Eleanor thought. Her face really did light up the room.

'If you're sure, I'd love that, thank you,' Megan said.

'Wonderful,' said Eleanor briskly. 'That's settled.'

19

The Wake

There are many different traditions for a wake. A woman I met on the boat to New York told me about a whole week of a wake in the Dingle Peninsula and how the dead man's family thought it was a fitting tribute to the man himself, a musician and farmer.

It wasn't the same in Kilmoney. Two days were long enough to wake any corpse. When the children were small and there was a death in the house, the corpse would be in one bedroom and all the children would sleep in another. The people closest to the corpse would sit all night beside it, holding its hand, so to speak, and telling stories of the good times in the past.

Joe's mother would make gur cake for funerals. She'd had it in Dublin once, and she loved it, for all that it was cake made out of the leftover cake or currant bread of the day before. She was long gone, God bless her soul, by the time Joe died.

It was a mercy: she had loved him with all her heart and it would have broken that same heart if she'd had to look at him cold in the coffin.

I made gur cake for his wake. Doing it helped me somehow and I used his mother's recipe. Brew strong tea and soak the leftover bread or cake in the tea overnight, with mixed spice and chopped apple. The next day, mix in butter and egg, put the mixture between two layers of pastry, and bake.

You were so little, I know you don't remember him well. If Joe hadn't died, we'd never have left Connemara, that's for sure. Your father loved the land and the sea. It was in his soul. But with him gone, we couldn't survive.

Many people told me we should stay, that Joe would have wanted it that way.

I told them he'd have wanted us all to be happy and fed. When I said goodbye to his grave, I knew

I'd never be back. He was with me in my heart, all the same. The grave was a piece of earth with mortal remains. Joe is always with me.

*   *   *

During the week she stayed with Eleanor, Megan worked her way through the books in Eleanor's spare room. The people who owned the apartment were very into crime and there were many Agatha Christies, some Dashiell Hammett and a couple of Carl Hiaasens. There was nothing else she could do. There was only one television in the apartment, it wasn't connected to cable and Eleanor only turned it on for the news. There was also no way Megan could go outside, what with the photographers who appeared to have set up camp close to Nora's clinic since the story had broken.

What was lovely was that Eleanor had proved to be a marvellous hostess. Not in the making-meals sense, but in the leaving Megan to her own devices sense. Eleanor was very unlike Megan's aunt Nora in that she didn't organise breakfasts or dinner for them, but enquired would Megan like a bit of an omelette, perhaps?

Or what did Megan think about listening to some swing music?

It was a very relaxing way to live.

Nora had been in a few times with groceries.

'You've been so good to us,' Nora said to Eleanor each time, and Megan was greatly touched by the use of the term 'us'. It meant that, despite everything, Nora still saw Megan as family rather than as a particularly irritating black sheep.

Connie dropped in most days, often wearing mad hats as disguise—more for fun than anything else.

She kept the two women filled in on what was happening.

'Kev has been in the *Sun* twice now,' she said. 'All the photographers think he must be your new boyfriend, so they photograph him all the time. But his real girlfriend, someone he met scuba diving, marched out yesterday to tell them that *she* was his girlfriend, thank you very much, and she'd take an injunction out against them if they said otherwise again.'

'Is she a lawyer?' asked Eleanor.

'No. She does triathalons. Kev sighs romantically and says she's tough as old boots. I think it's love. I really think Kev needs a strong woman, don't you?' Connie asked Megan, in an attempt to divert her.

Megan was not diverted. 'Poor Kev,' she said. 'It's all my fault, this whole media circus.'

'Nonsense,' said Connie briskly. 'Besides, not everyone's complaining. Prudence Maguire is in her element. She spends her day talking out of the side of her mouth to the reporters, telling them about dodgy planning deals, why the council must be bent, and that the people in the top-floor flat at No. 71 are operating a drug den.'

'That nice young couple with the pug?' asked Eleanor.

'He has dreadlocks,' Connie explained. 'In Prudence's mind, it's only a hop, skip and a jump from dreadlocks to drug dealer. Any word from your agent?' she enquired gently. She'd finally tracked down Carole Baird the day the photographer had caught Megan. Finding her had involved a call to Pippa in Wales, who'd been upset at the news but had explained to Connie that there was no way she could leave her children to comfort Megan.

'Tell her I'll phone her on her mobile,' Pippa said.

'Of course,' said Connie neutrally, thinking that Megan was too upset to talk to anyone right now.

Carole had been much more matter of fact. She'd said it was inevitable someone would find Megan.

'Why won't they leave her alone?' Connie had asked.

'That's not how it works, dearie,' snapped Carole. 'The game isn't over until someone gets Megan's confession of why, what, where and how sorry she is. Plus photographs, preferably with a rescue dog or orphans in a far-flung orphanage. Sudan might be good.' Carole sounded thoughtful. 'They haven't sorted Sudan out yet, have they?'

'Should she wear combat fatigues for the pictures or would that be thoughtless in a war zone?' Connie demanded with an acidity she hadn't known she possessed.

'No, plain army green is better,' Carole said. 'More *Private Benjamin*. Is her hair still blonde? She said she'd got it dyed—it was hard to tell in the photos . . .'

Connie ignored this. 'Megan is in shock, Carole. She doesn't want to talk about it or pose with poor orphaned dogs. I need to know what she should do now. Is there a plan?'

'This is fly-by-the-seat-of-your-pants stuff,' Carole replied. 'There's no plan. She'll have to come out of hiding sometime, no matter how bruised she is. Listen, if you sign on for fame, you sign on for all that goes with it.'

'No plan, then. We can do what we like?'

'If she wants to hide, hide her. If she wants to tell the story, phone me ASAP. I know Megan. She's a fighter. She'll get bored and want some limelight soon enough. I'll call her.'

Carole had subsequently called every day.

'Your friend thinks I'm a heartless bitch,' she said. 'I could tell she didn't like my damage-limitation stories.'

Megan felt offended on Connie's behalf. 'Not everyone thinks it's OK to use other people's misfortune as a get-out-of-jail-free card,' she said.

'It's not like that,' Carole said, unconcerned. 'Everyone profits from it. The dog people profit from it and so does the star.'

'It's the African orphan idea she didn't like,' Megan said.

'Oh, that was never really a runner,' sighed Carole. 'Now that so many big Hollywood people are into the whole refugee thing, it's not easy to get your foot in the door there. No, rescue dogs are where it's at. Or inner-city drug addicts. When you're ready, Megan.'

'We've been offered half a million for my side of the story,' Megan informed Connie and Eleanor later.

'Is that good?' asked Connie.

'Carole said we shouldn't accept lower than one million.'

'Except you don't plan to sell your story,' Eleanor said quietly.

'Exactly,' said Megan, and thought that, just

months earlier, she'd treated everything Carole Baird said as if it were gospel. What Carole said went—or at least it had, before the Rob Hartnell affair. And now, after Rob and all the media reports, Megan wasn't sure if she even liked the world she'd got into.

Acting, she loved. It was all the stuff that went with it that she didn't like. Posing with rescue dogs to save her image. She hated the very idea of it. Why couldn't she simply act and not do any of the other stuff?

A little voice inside her told her why—she wouldn't be the darling 'it' girl if she didn't look for media attention and have Carole tip off photographers when she was going to the shop for a cappuccino. She'd chosen that route. There was no point being shocked about the manipulation of the media—the way Rob had planned it—when she was guilty of manipulating it herself.

Megan was leaning out the fire escape, having an after-dinner cigarette, and Connie was loading the dishwasher when Eleanor mentioned the trip to Connemara.

'I know you said you'd come with me,' she said to Megan, 'but we've never talked about it since, and I thought you'd probably forgotten about it.'

Megan coloured. She had forgotten all about it.

'I'm sorry,' she said quickly.

'No, that's fine. I never mentioned it to you again, but I actually booked a B&B, a car and a tour guide who specialises in helping people who want to find places where their families lived. I'd planned to go next month, but seeing as you're in hiding, how about we go now? If the guide is free, we could go for three days or four and, at the end of it, you might have an idea what you want to do. Your agent is right about one thing: you can't hide forever.'

'What if someone recognises me?'

'We'll get you a nice baseball hat and I'll find a couple of my oversized shirts and nobody will have a clue who you are,' said Connie. 'If they think for even one moment that you look a bit like an actress from the telly, they'll decide they must be wrong. People from the telly wouldn't be seen dead in an outfit like that.'

'After that, if you want to go to Los Angeles, you could,' added Eleanor.

Megan nodded. It had seemed like a good idea when she'd first mentioned it to Eleanor, but now she wasn't so sure.

There was somewhere she had to go first: to see her mother.

*   *   *

Later, in bed with an Agatha Christie beside her, Megan sent Pippa a text:

Hello, all ok. Going 2 West of Ireland with Eleanor 2moro. Trying 2 work out wot 2 do. Hope u + kids well, xxM

Half an hour later, she got a reply.

Glad ur well. Kim sick. Vomiting. V tired, xP

Megan sent a line of kisses back.

Give Kim my love.

Poor little darling, she thought. She'd buy Kim something nice in Connemara and send it to her, something for Toby too. And she'd visit soon. Megan smiled to herself. She'd never thought of visiting her niece and nephew before. It had always been Pippa she'd wanted to see and she'd felt a certain jealousy that the children's existence deprived her of their mother's presence. Not any more. Kim and Toby were little people, part of her family. It would all be different now. *She* was different.

*   *   *

At eleven the next morning, Nora came to Eleanor's with another packed bag for Megan.

Megan hugged her aunt but felt a certain resistance in Nora's upright form.

'You're upset,' she said with a sigh. 'I'm sorry for all this, Nora. You know what the press are like and when they happen to get wind of a story—'

Nora interrupted her furiously: 'No, I don't know and I didn't think I'd ever have to know. It's been a nightmare the past week with those people outside the gate.'

Megan was stunned. In all the time she'd spent with Nora, there had never been a moment's recrimination, and now this.

'Nothing *just happens*, Megan,' Nora went on, exasperated. 'You make it happen by doing something. Don't abdicate responsibility for six men with cameras outside my house.'

'I'm not,' said Megan, feeling ridiculously like crying. 'But you don't know what happened with me and Rob, you never asked.'

'I can read, can't I? I can see the headlines when I'm standing in the shop. I saw that poor woman's face on a magazine cover looking like she'd never get over her husband sleeping with you.'

360

'I didn't think you'd seen any of that,' Megan said, all the wind knocked out of her.

'This isn't the back of beyond,' Nora roared. 'You might think it is, but we're civilised now. We have it all: electricity, internet, the whole shebang. I heard all about it even before you got here.'

From her bedroom, Eleanor could hear the row but she didn't interrupt. It wasn't her place to do so.

Poor Megan needed to realise that people judged, even people who loved her.

'I'm sorry,' Megan said. 'I know you're hurt and I know it's my fault. I didn't mean to hurt you or Rob's wife or anyone. I was thoughtless, stupid, all those things. I apologise.'

Nora snorted but Megan could see that the anger was gone.

'Well, your mother should certainly take her share of the blame,' sniffed Nora.

Megan stared at her.

'Carrots have to grow, you know. They don't just pop out of the ground!'

'Carrots?' asked Megan, mystified.

'Your mother planted carrots from the supermarket when the seeds didn't grow. Do you remember that? They didn't grow fast enough, so she bought big fat carrots, stuck them in the earth and let you and Pippa pull them up.'

Megan suddenly remembered and the ridiculousness of it all—Marguerite planting shop-bought carrots, Nora standing by shocked—struck her. 'Poor Mum,' she said, and began to laugh. 'Poor you, Nora. I'm sorry, we're not the ideal family unit, are we? But we do our best and we love each other.'

'You're right,' sighed Nora. 'I suppose you could hardly know anything about the real world when you work in an unreal world.'

'From my mother's flight of fantasy to Hollywood in one fell swoop?' said Megan.

Nora nodded. 'Listen to Eleanor, now, will you? She's very wise. You could do with listening to a few wise people instead of flibbertygibbets like that agent of yours.'

'Carole's not a flibbertygibbet, I can tell you that,' Megan said, laughing. 'She's pretty good at what she does. It's me that's changed, not her.'

'Well, next time you're on the phone to her, you can tell her you're not going near the Sudan!' Nora insisted. 'A couple of days in Connemara will do you good.'

20

Oats

Wheat and oats were the crops of my childhood, and our staple diet had plenty of bread, oatcakes and porridge. My mother could never understand how my father's people made their porridge with sugar or honey when, in her house, they boiled it up with salt.

Salt was the way it went all my life, and winter mornings started with me putting my stockings on by the fire and then stirring the porridge—it wasn't called stir about for nothing.

Many emigrants to America went off with oatcakes in their luggage, for properly made oatcakes can last a few months. In our house, we mixed the fine oatmeal, salt, butter and a dram of hot water to make them. Work the butter and salt into the oatmeal until you have a fine crumb, add the water to make the mixture sticky, then work it with flour into a cake of bread or into smaller chunks for biscuits.

Fresh out of the oven, we'd spread them with blackberry jam or just plenty of butter.

When we were first in Brooklyn, I couldn't eat oatcakes without crying because they reminded me of home so much. Nothing else was as bad, not bacon and cabbage, not soda bread, not even potato cakes the way Agnes used to make them. Oatcakes made me think of sitting on the dry-stone wall with your father, eating and talking. We'd left him behind in the *graveyard with the wind whistling fit to skin you. But in time, I got used to them again. My mother was a great one for saying that time heals, and she's right. It does. But slowly, mind.*

*   *   *

Will Kerrigan sat in his garden office, his face turned to his computer screen. But he wasn't seeing the list of email she was working on. His mind was focused on one subject: Rae.

In all their married life, he'd never known her like this. His Rae had a warm smile for everyone, her dark eyes would light up when he made a joke, and at night, they'd lie companionably in bed and talk about their days.

But since his mother had moved in to recuperate, his Rae had vanished to be replaced by a sad-eyed woman he barely recognised.

At first, he'd thought it was his mother's presence in the house.

Rae thought he didn't notice the way his mother went on: 'This isn't the way *I'd* do it, Rae,' or 'Why don't you cut down the wisteria/change those curtains/paint the cupboards . . .'

But he did notice. And he tried to stop it.

'Mother, you're used to being mistress of your own place, so think how hard it would be for you if someone came in and criticised you.'

'What do you mean "think how hard it would be if someone criticised me"?' His mother had kicked into outrage instantly. 'I would never do such a thing.'

'But you do, you know,' Will went on stoically.

'Says who?'

'Says nobody,' Will said with a sigh. It was hard to remain patient. He'd promised his dying father he'd look after his mother. That meant not hurting her feelings if he could help it, but her feelings were unusual creatures. Sensitive as a coral reef to any personal criticism, but entirely oblivious to any hurt she inflicted on anyone else.

'You're imagining it, Will. Rae and I get on marvellously. I wish I'd had a mother-in-law to help me out when I was younger.'

'We're not younger, Mother,' Will insisted. 'Rae and I are nearly sixty. We don't need anyone to tell us that the kitchen would look nicer in taupe.'

'I'm shocked that Rae said anything—' Geraldine began, both feet on the ladder to high dudgeon by now.

'Rae said nothing. I overheard.'

'Oh, pish! Men never understand things like that. We were just talking. That's all.'

It was a lost cause.

He phoned Leonora to ask if she'd have Mother to stay for a while.

'Have you lost all your marbles?' shrieked Leonora. 'I'm not having the old dear in my house. We'd kill each other within twenty-four hours. Unless you want to be standing in court defending me for murder, don't even think about it.'

Will hung up.

To give her her due, his mother tried to be a teeny bit nicer. But it didn't help. Rae was like a wraith in the house. She got up, cooked, cleaned, went to work, and went to bed at night, all in a haze of sadness that he couldn't penetrate.

'What's wrong, love?' he'd ask, and Rae would turn those sad eyes to him and say 'Nothing, I'm just tired.' Was she ill?

He waited till she was at work one day, then phoned Dulcie in Community Cares.

'Please don't tell Rae I phoned, but, Dulcie, I'm so worried about her.'

'That's uncanny,' said Dulcie. 'I was just about to phone you to say the same thing.'

Will exhaled slowly. There was to be no joy here, either.

'Could she be sick?' Dulcie asked. 'I thought perhaps it was that, and I asked her. Well, you know me, no holding me back, but she said no, she was fit as a fiddle. Not that she looks it. She's definitely lost weight.'

'She has?'

'Lord, yes—at least half a stone. There isn't a pick on her.'

Fear gripped Will now. He hadn't really noticed the weight in the same way that he didn't really notice what Rae wore. She was simply his darling Rae and she could be fat or thin, dressed in rags or in designer clothes, and it was all immaterial. *She* was what mattered to him.

In desperation, he phoned his mother's friend, Carmel De Vere, and lied that his mother was a bit down and perhaps Carmel might take her out to see a film or a play and perhaps have a spot of supper.

'My treat,' said Will.

*   *   *

Geraldine wrapped her mink stole over her shoulders and admired herself in the hall mirror as she waited for Carmel to pick her up. It was a quarter to six and Will wanted her gone so he could talk to Rae as soon as she came home from Titania's. They never had a moment to themselves these days: perhaps that was part of the problem. At least, he hoped that's all it was. Despite what Rae had said to Dulcie, it was never off his mind now that Rae might be ill and simply didn't know how to break it to him.

'There's nothing to beat a bit of mink,' his mother said, twirling the stole.

'Your hip seems to have healed so well,' remarked Will as she twirled.

'Ah no, not really.' Geraldine reached for the injured hip instantly and sank on to the hall chair as if she'd just performed a pas de deux and was now shattered. 'I'm still weak, you know. I shouldn't stand too much.'

Carmel had to come in, kiss Will, admire the mink, and visit the cloakroom before the pair could get on their way.

'Finally,' Will said as he shut the door behind them.

He picked the post up from the wire basket hanging on the front door and walked into the kitchen with it, sorting through the envelopes. There was one for Rae with a Limerick postmark. Curious, he thought. Who did they know in Limerick?

It was nearly half past six when Rae came home.

'Where's your mother?' she asked when she saw the kitchen table set for two.

'Gone out with Carmel. I bribed them.'

'Oh, I see.'

Once, Rae would have made a funny comment, Will thought sadly. This lack of humour was just another sign everything was wrong.

'Sit,' he said, taking her coat. 'I'm going to give you a nice dinner and we're going to talk.'

Rae sat obediently. Will had put the post beside her side plate. He was just placing a glass of wine in front of her when he saw her face go white.

'What is it?'

She let him take the unopened letter from her hand. It was the one with the Limerick postmark.

'What it is? Is something wrong?'

Rae stared at him with her sad brown eyes, then she seemed to make a decision, because her chin came up and she looked like the old Rae again.

'There's no nice way to tell you this. It's a letter about my first child, a little girl I gave up for adoption when I was sixteen.'

*   *   *

The evening Jasmine was born, Sister Veronica brought Rae a tray of tea and toast, and a bottle of formula. They'd moved her into a single room so as not to upset the other girls.

'I'll take her away and feed her while you eat,' the nun said firmly.

'She's perfectly happy in the bassinet,' Rae insisted. She may have felt weak, but there was no way she was letting Jasmine out of her sight. 'I've just fed her.'

'Sister Martin is right, Rae. You're just making it harder for yourself.'

'I'm keeping her!' cried Rae.

'Can I tell you what happens to the girls who keep their babies? They come back eventually, because they have nothing and they're living in a cramped damp bedsit and the child is sick, but they've no money for the doctor and no food, and they know the baby has no future. That's what happens to them.'

'She's my child, that must count for something?'

'What counts is that you do what is right for her. Do it for her,' Sister Veronica said, her voice low and powerful. 'Do this generous thing for her. It's the most unselfish thing you'll ever do. You want to keep her for yourself, but you can't be selfish. Is that the life you want for this little scrap of a child?'

'No, but I'm her mother, I can look after her.' Rae was crying now and little Jasmine was too, soft baby moans of distress.

'You can't look after her. How can you earn money? Your family aren't there for you, you told me that. Yes, Rae, some girls do keep their babies,' Sister Veronica went on, 'but they are going home to their families. Nobody can rear a child on their own, Rae. You need some support.'

'And I have none,' said Rae bitterly.

'How would you cope? You're a beautiful girl, Rae, you'd be at the mercy of every scoundrel out there. You and that little baby of yours.'

'I can't do it.'

'You can.'

The nun sat on the bed for what felt like hours. She had stories of babies who became ill living in terrible conditions, women who went crazy with nobody to help them. Babies who grew into angry children without the love of two parents. That was

God's will, Sister Veronica went on. Two parents to raise a child.

Rae hadn't told her much about her own parents, but somehow Veronica knew. Of the hopeless couple who lived in poverty and bitterness, who'd never come to look for their daughter.

'Suppose you kept her and something happened to you,' Sister Veronica said meaningfully. 'Your little baby would go to them to raise.'

It was the one argument for which there was no answer.

'How can I let her go?' Rae asked. Her tears were flowing like a river now and dripping on to her nightgown in spite of her efforts to stem them with a tissue. She had to stay in control, had to for Jasmine's sake.

'It's what a mother's love is about,' Sister Veronica said. 'Giving her up to bring her a chance in life. You never had a chance, but she will. The other girls who've done it are happy because they knew it was the right thing to do.'

'They're happy? They're OK? How do you know?' Rae couldn't believe it. How could a person be happy if they gave up their baby?

'They're happy,' insisted the nun. 'You wouldn't believe how happy they are when they come back to see me and talk about it all. They're content, knowing they made the right choice. It's hard to see it now, but you will.'

Sister Veronica reached into the bassinet where Jasmine was lying, staring up with her great violet eyes, and picked her up. It was the first time Rae had let anyone else hold her. She looked on jealously as the nun gentled the baby, years of experience with babies showing in her movements.

'You rest and I'll get someone to bring us up some fresh tea and toast,' Sister Veronica said calmly. 'You haven't touched that.'

Rae watched her leave the room with Jasmine in her arms, knowing that the nun was showing her that Jasmine could be cared for by other people. She would not fall apart in the room on her own, as she wouldn't fall apart in another room on another day if they took Jasmine to a better future.

When the tea and toast came, Rae drank and ate. Later Sister Veronica returned with Jasmine, who was now sleeping peacefully.

'It's the best thing for her and for you,' the nun said when she left the room. 'I'll be back in the morning and we can sort it all out. Your baby's future.'

She'd never called her Jasmine, Rae noticed. Not once. As if the baby had no name, not one that Rae would give her, anyway.

That night, Rae only dozed intermittently. Each time she'd sleep, she'd wake up with a start, as if someone was already there, taking Jasmine. When she lay awake, she thought about what Veronica had said. It was all true, wasn't it? Why else would she say it? Jasmine had such a limited future with Rae. She deserved better. And there was nobody else to take care of her if something happened to Rae. She could not go to Paudge and Glory Hennessey.

Sister Veronica was back in the morning with a lady from an adoption agency.

The woman was short, kind-faced and armed with a clipboard and papers.

'What you're doing is the best thing for your

371

child,' she said in a voice like a headmistress's. 'Your baby will be happy and loved. You are a wonderful person to do this.'

She had some papers for Rae to sign and there would be more later. 'Just a formality,' she said briskly. She also had a woollen blanket and a baby basket.

'Now?' said Rae, horrified. 'I thought we'd have longer together.'

Jasmine lay content in her arms after her second feed of the morning.

'Some homes try that, but it's harder for mother and baby,' the woman said knowledgeably. 'Quicker is better. Why doesn't Sister Veronica take her while you sign the forms?'

Rae's hands shook. Carla had told her it would be quick, and she'd thought Carla wanted it that way, but perhaps they always did it like that.

'You'll want to be getting back to your old life,' the woman said when the forms were signed. 'Kiss her now. We're off. You need to rest.'

The nun held Jasmine out to Rae, Sister Martin appeared from nowhere, along with another strange woman.

Rae tried to take Jasmine but Sister Veronica held the baby tightly. 'Just a quick kiss.'

'No!' cried Rae, in wild panic at what she'd just done.

The other woman, the one she'd never met, held on to her tightly.

'No, no.'

Veronica lowered Jasmine and Rae managed to brush her lips against Jasmine's cheek but there was no real kiss.

Instantly, the nun whisked her away.

'No!' shrieked Rae.

But the door slammed and Jasmine was gone. Rae was left in the bed with a strange woman holding her down.

Jasmine had been taken away. It hurt, it hurt somewhere so deep in Rae that she couldn't find words for it.

When Sister Martin came in with a small yellow tablet and a glass of water, Rae took it numbly.

*   *   *

She didn't want to even look at Sister Veronica when she came in the next day. Rae was crying silently on the chair beside the bed, holding the little stained vest Jasmine had worn that first, that only, night.

'It's the best way, Rae my love.'

'Don't call me *love*,' hissed Rae. 'You let us all think you're caring for us and you're not. We're a baby factory.'

'Giving your baby up was for her own good, Rae. It's for your own good too.'

'Don't talk about her,' said Rae. She couldn't bear to think about Jasmine. About the softness of her skin, the baby scent of her, how her little face instinctively turned to the sound of Rae's voice. And she'd never see her again. She'd given her up for the right reasons, all the reasons Sister Veronica said now, but oh God it hurt, it hurt so much.

She fell to the floor from the chair and held on to her belly. The pain was there; where Jasmine had lain for nine long months. If only she hadn't griped about the difficult bits of pregnancy and

373

had rejoiced in them, because then Jasmine was a part of her, nobody could take her then. They were together. What she wouldn't give to have that time back.

Sister Veronica tried to help her to her feet but Rae pushed her away.

'No,' she cried, 'don't touch me.'

All she wanted was to lie in her bed with Jasmine wrapped close to her, but she'd given up on that forever. It was the right thing, wasn't it? All these people said it was the right thing for Jasmine and they must know, mustn't they?

Sister Veronica left her alone in the lonely single room. Too late Rae understood why she'd been moved there. She'd heard crying coming from there when she'd first arrived, but she hadn't thought about what it meant. She'd thought it was one of the nuns perhaps. Why hadn't she asked? If so, she might have run away from this place where they pretended to help when really they were just preaching doctrinaire Catholicism and separating single women from their babies. It messed with their morality, their sense of the world. But they were wrong with their rules and their notions of morality. Her parents had been allowed to raise her because they were married and yet they shouldn't have been allowed to raise so much as a scaldy hen. Marriage meant nothing, just that you'd followed their stupid rules. What was wrong with a woman raising a child on her own?

Rae would never play by their rules again. They'd made her lose everything.

She packed her stuff up. She was never coming back here again, never to see her family again. If they'd been any sort of family, she might have been able to keep Jasmine.

*   *   *

After she'd finished telling Will, he sat in silence for a long while.

'Do you hate me now?' Rae looked at her husband intently. She was afraid of his answer, afraid he'd say 'Yes.'

Eventually he turned to look at her and she saw the pain and shock in his eyes. Rae didn't think she'd ever seen Will look like that and she wished with all her heart that it had been different all those years ago, that she'd told him.

'I'm so sorry,' she whispered. 'I really am, my love. Please believe me.'

He studied her for a moment, then he reached out his hand and took hers. 'How could I ever hate you?' he said softly. 'I love you. I'll always love you.'

'Oh, Will,' Rae said with a sob.

She leaned against him, feeling the solidity of his body with great relief. She was almost afraid to breathe in case she upset this moment. *Keep loving me*, she willed him. *Keep forgiving me. I love you.* His hands stroked her back as she leaned against him, and she closed her eyes at the gesture. Let him not change his mind.

'Remember when Anton was sixteen,' he continued, 'and he went camping with his friends, and it rained—they got waterlogged, and they phoned us in the middle of the night to get them.'

Rae nodded.

'They were kids, weren't they, him and all his friends. They all thought they were big men, but when it rained, they got scared and they wanted their parents.' Will put his arms around her. 'You were the same age as Anton when you had a baby. I don't care how grown up you felt, you were a child.'

Rae didn't dare think he might forgive her. How could he? But he was holding her closely, he still loved her. She hugged him back.

'I should have kept her,' she breathed. 'I should have told you about her. All these years, I felt as if I was denying her by not telling you, but when I didn't tell you in the beginning, how could I tell you then? When could I do it? On our wedding day, when Anton was born—when?' She was hoarse from talking, hoarse from the emotion.

'That doesn't matter,' Will soothed.

For the first time, she pulled away from him and looked into his eyes. There was hurt there and pain, but still love.

'It does matter,' she said. 'It reached a point where I didn't know how to tell you. I loved you and I was afraid you'd stop loving me if I told you. I didn't trust your love enough, I didn't know enough about love to trust it. I am so sorry for that, Will.'

His reply was one hand stroking her face and she leaned her cheek down to his cradling hand.

'It's all right, Rae,' he said. 'Go on, open the letter.'

Her hands were shaking so much that Will had to slit the envelope with a knife and then he handed it back to Rae.

My name is Tricia O'Reilly and I think I am your daughter. I am forty-one years old, am married to a good man and am expecting my first child. I was born in the Blessed Helena Home in Limerick on 27 August 1969. I do not know what time I was born.

I am not sure what to write. I have wanted to write to you for so long and now I am doing it, I do not know what to say.

I have been trying to find you for many years to understand why. It took me a long time to find you and I have put off doing this. I can't put it off any longer.

I don't want to frighten you and I know that nobody in your life now might know about me. It's a puzzle and I need to understand it all.

Please, please answer my letter. You do not know what it would mean to me.

Tricia O'Reilly.

Rae's hands covered her mouth.

'I have a daughter named Tricia,' she said to

Will, her eyes shining. 'And a grandchild coming. Oh, Will, we have to tell Anton.'

21

Herbs

Herb lore was an important part of our family for many years, but it was lost by the time I was born, Eleanor. My great-grandmother was said to have the Sight, and she spent her whole life working as a midwife. My mother told me her grandmother, Morrigan, knew which herbs would help a woman with a difficult labour, how to help a woman who could not bear children, how to ease the pain of people dying and how to tame a dangerous fever.

It was a combination of old magic and a woman's wisdom with God's herbs, and most of it is lost. People then didn't write their wisdom down. They relied on the seanachai to tell the story aloud, and Morrigan's knowledge wasn't the sort a storyteller should know.

But I remember that my mother used to draw a circle round our house with a hazel twig once a year, and I overheard her once whisper that if a woman has difficulty carrying a child to full term, then she should eat a whole lobster, wash the shell, crush it, and wear it next to her in a small muslin bag as protection for her baby.

When I was a child, our herbs were thyme, lavender and great stalks of rosemary that grew in woody bushes outside the house. Lavender like fat lilac pillows covered the old stone wall on one side of the house. There was French lavender that Agnes had brought from the big house, and a tiny but sweeter lavender that the bees loved.

The scent of lavender and a tang of lemon thyme will always take me home.

*   *   *

Connie was exasperated because the fifth years had lost the will to work. Even grave discussions on the forthcoming exams couldn't dent their sheer joy at the long summer holidays awaiting them in two months' time.

'My cousin lives in Wales and she only gets six weeks off in the summer. Six weeks!' announced one girl.

'Cruelty to teenagers,' murmured everyone.

'About the exams . . .' said Connie, who stood at the top of the class and wondered if it was a waste of her time, or indeed a strain on her adrenal glands, to bother attempting to teach today.

'Miss O'Callaghan, the exams don't matter for us,' said one girl kindly. 'Now for the sixth years, it's different—'

Everyone sighed sympathetically. The sixth years were on the run up to the most important thing in their young lives: the Leaving Certificate. State exams on a par with the G20 Summit at least.

Connie had often wondered if the educational system was right to gear itself so totally towards one set of exams. For the girls of St Matilda's, it was as if their whole lives depended on those three weeks at the start of June. Everything was predicated towards it.

'You've got to think about your Leaving Cert . . .' was the gloomy start to many sentences.

Which was why the fifth years had happily idled away the whole year. When they were sixth years, they could panic, they told her. But for now . . . whatever.

Connie gave it one last try: 'The summer exams will determine if you can stay in honours history or pass next year,' she said loudly.

Again, nobody was too pushed. That was in September, months away. Who knew what would have happened by then. They might have been spotted by Robert Pattinson across a crowded street and been whisked away to a life of movie-star excitement . . .

'There's a fair chance that an essay question on the signing of the Declaration of Independence will come up in the exam,' Connie said. Seeing as how she'd set the exam, she should know. 'It might be worth everyone's while to sit and revise that section.'

Pay dirt. The history exam was on Wednesday. Too close for comfort. Robert Pattinson wasn't due in Dublin any time soon. The fifth years sat down and pulled out their books.

'The whole of chapter twenty-four is important,' Connie went on in a slightly cajoling tone. She sometimes wondered if she'd chosen wrongly when she plumped for being the sort of friendly-not-shouty teacher. The ones who instilled fear in the students certainly could make people sit in their seats at will, but it must be so exhausting keeping the level of tension up. No, Connie decided, she'd never be able to be one of the tough teachers. Being likeable and friendly was who she was.

Pages shuffled as everyone settled to read chapter twenty-four and peace reigned. Connie was able to sit back and think.

All she could think about were Ella and Steve. Now that the widower and his ten-year-old daughter were in her life, she couldn't get them out of her head. When she read her romances, she imagined she was the heroine and Steve was the man wrapping his muscular arms around her, saving her from pirates/highwaymen/whatever. Flicking through magazines, she kept finding articles about stepfamilies.

Normally, she'd have turned those pages at high

speed, but now she read avidly.

What to do when your children and his have to get on as one big family? Nope. Not an issue. All Ella would have to get on with were Connie's things. Still, she scanned that paragraph in case it was useful.

The only absolutely relevant article was a case history of a woman who'd married a man with two young daughters. *Don't* was her message. Connie read on glumly.

Rows, plenty of screaming fits ending with *'you're not my mother!'* and a painful break-up ensued. 'I'd never get involved with a man with children again!' said the woman.

Connie stared blankly down at the mostly silent students in front of her and tried to imagine what it must be like for a child in Ella's situation to suddenly have someone interested in her father. Up till now, apart from the predatory Daniellas of this world, Ella had had him to herself. And Steve didn't appear too interested in getting involved again.

What was she thinking of, anyway? Steve liked her purely because she was kind to Ella, that was all. He'd never once looked at her in a romantic way or brushed against her accidentally. And now she knew that she longed for him to.

*   *   *

It was five when she got home and she did her best to peer unobtrusively into Steve and Ella's basement apartment before she took the steps up to her one. It didn't look as if anyone was home.

Her own apartment felt lonely now, especially

knowing that Eleanor was away with Megan. She'd loved having Megan staying upstairs with Eleanor: it had given her a reason to pop round in the evening, bringing shopping for them or checking up to see that they were both OK.

Perhaps it was time to get that cat, Connie thought morosely as she wandered around, not able to settle at anything. She had no homework to correct: it wasn't fair to give the girls homework when they were meant to be revising. She made herself tea and somehow ended up perched by the front window with a book when Steve Calman's pick-up truck arrived. Moments later, a sky-blue sports car drew up and Danielle, Petal's mother, got out, cute as a button in purple velour this time. She seemed to have had Ella quite a lot after school recently. And didn't seem to mind bringing the girl all the way home. In the past week, Connie had seen a lot of the distinctive sky-blue sports car as Danielle dropped Ella home every evening. Danielle always looked so *perky*, Connie thought with unaccustomed venom. Petal and Ella struggled to get out of the back seat themselves. Danielle was too busy chatting with Steve to bother moving the seat for them.

Flicking her blonde ponytail at him was one thing, but not even bothering to get poor Ella out of the car: now *that* was totally unacceptable. Connie stopped thinking rationally. She stormed downstairs and out of the front door, only just grabbing her keys on the way, and marched out on to the street.

'Connie!' Ella called from the car. 'You're home! Can I come and play?'

'Of course,' said Connie, helping her out. 'Is that

OK, Steve?'

Steve looked pleased to see her but Connie noted that Danielle did not. Tough bananas, Connie thought. You can have Steve if you want, but don't be mean to Ella.

'Can I come too!' asked Petal plaintively, sliding out after Ella.

'Yes, go on,' said Danielle, not even looking.

Connie wasn't sure why she felt she'd won the lottery when she went back upstairs with the two little girls chattering with her.

'And Connie's got a bedroom like a princess and profiteroles,' Ella explained excitedly to Petal.

'My mummy says profiteroles make you fat. Cream is bad for you,' Petal informed them.

'Really?' Connie let them into her flat. She could just imagine Danielle crossly telling Petal that in a flurry of irritation after Connie had left with Ella that first day. There was no doubt about it: Danielle was mad for Steve Calman. Connie knew she couldn't compete with someone like Danielle. Connie wouldn't get one leg into Danielle's cutesy little velour track pants and even if she trained for hours in front of the mirror, she'd never be able to do that ponytail-flicking thing. She simply wasn't the seductress type.

No, she was the funny friend person. And she was a person that darling Ella loved being with. That was enough for Connie; more than enough.

*   *   *

At least half an hour went by before her doorbell rang.

'It's Steve,' he said into the intercom, sounding a

little strained. 'Danielle has to drop Petal with her gran because she has to go to pilates.'

Bet she does, Connie thought. Stomach muscles don't get that taut just from avoiding profiteroles. 'On my way down,' she called cheerily.

Neither Danielle nor Steve looked as happy as two people who'd just been afforded some privacy should. Steve's face was pale under his tan and it looked as if he'd been tugging on his tie to stop it being so close to his throat; either that, or Danielle had been pulling at it, but Connie didn't like to dwell on that. It was one thing to know Danielle was more Steve's type than she was, another entirely to think about the logistics of it all.

'Come on, Petal,' snapped Danielle. 'Oh, thank you, Connie.'

'Bye, Petal,' said Connie. 'See you, Danielle.'

The ponytail didn't twitch.

Danielle shoved the passenger seat down at high speed, this time to let her daughter in, and then drove off with a squeal of rubber.

Connie bent to give Ella a hug. 'See you soon,' she said.

'When?' demanded Ella.

Connie was lost. 'How about Saturday night?' she said. 'I can make dinner. Or if you're going out, I can babysit Ella,' she added to Steve.

'I owe you dinner after your helping us out,' he remarked. He was beginning to look more like his normal self now. Unconsciously, he reached a hand up and loosened the knot on his tie, pulling it off completely. Then he swiftly opened the top two buttons. 'That's better,' he said.

Yeah, much better, thought Connie with a gulp, looking away. Drooling always looked bad.

385

'Oh, Dad, let's go to Connie's, pleeease,' begged Ella. 'You're always cooking, it's boring eating your food. I like Connie's food. Like Indian.'

'We won't try that again,' Connie said. 'You didn't eat any of it. I'll cook,' she added rashly. Cooking and taking care of children sort of went together.

'That's too much trouble,' said Steve.

'Nonsense,' declared Connie, not looking at him. 'I love cooking! Saturday evening then, at six?'

'It's in our diary,' said Ella gravely, and both adults laughed.

Feeling as if she was floating on air, Connie went home.

*　　　*　　　*

'Gaynor, what's a simple thing to cook for a dinner party where the guests are a neighbour and his little girl?'

In the excitement of the whole event, Connie had neglected to think about the actual food until the wee small hours of Friday night.

'I'm fine thank you, Connie, and no you didn't wake me early on a Saturday morning, and how are you?' asked Gaynor.

'I don't have time for that! I'm desperate. Besides, you're always telling me you're up at the crack of dawn on Saturdays,' Connie added. 'Football, ballet, hockey . . .'

'Touché,' said Gaynor. 'When is this grand and important dinner party?'

'Tonight.'

Connie waited till Gaynor had stopped laughing hysterically. 'That's why I always phone you when

I'm in trouble,' she said. 'You're so sympathetic, so kind.'

'You can't cook.'

'And this is news? I know I can't cook, but you can and you're going to help me.'

'I can't, not today. Any other day, of course I would, but it's my niece's wedding today and we have to be out of the house by ten. Go to Marks and Spencer's and buy something to heat up. That's what everyone else does.'

'I want to cook something myself,' Connie wailed.

'*Now* she decides she wants to cook!' groaned Gaynor. 'Right, do a chicken casserole. Chicken with mushrooms and a little white wine, it never fails. You have some recipe books?'

'What would I want with recipe books? Wait till I get a pen,' said Connie.

*   *   *

At six that evening, there was a delicious smell coming from the oven, a very restaurant-y smell, in Connie's opinion. Cooking wasn't anywhere near as hard as people made out. Honestly, you just threw chicken, cream, wine, mushrooms and herbs in a pot and let it get on with itself. Simple.

She'd made two casseroles: a big one for her and Steve with wine, and a small one for Ella without wine.

'I can't put wine in hers,' Connie had said to Gaynor on the phone.

'The wine cooks off,' Gaynor explained. 'But you could do a smaller version for her with no wine. I do that all the time.'

'Oooh yummy smells,' said Ella when they arrived. She gave Connie a huge hug, dumped her cardigan on the floor and ran off to investigate what they were going to have for dessert.

'You got profiteroles!' she roared with delight when she'd scanned the fridge fully. 'And 7UP too!'

'I hope that's all right,' Connie said to Steve.

He grinned.

He was wearing the sort of fine-knit sweater that Freddie might wear, but on Freddie, a sweater always looked a bit too big, like he'd borrowed it from a larger person. On Steve, the grey knit fitted perfectly and showed off shoulders that could have graced any of the covers of Connie's romantic novels. She had a sudden vision of him ripping the sweater off and hauling her close, and she had to follow Ella into the kitchen to hide her red face in case he noticed.

'Just getting a drink of water,' Connie muttered, and had to grab a glass and fill it clumsily at the tap because Ella was watching her.

'You must be really thirsty,' Ella said innocently.

'Yes, it's been a warm day,' said Connie. She stood at the sink until she could feel her colour return to normal. She was behaving like one of the first years on Valentine's Day. She'd have to limit herself to seeing Ella without Steve.

Ella opened a couple of cupboards and peered in. 'Boring cereal,' she said dismissively. 'If I stay overnight, what would I eat?'

'You're too young for sleepovers,' said her father. 'You know that.'

'You could stay too,' Ella said hopefully.

Connie's laugh was a bit too high-pitched and

388

hysterical, even to her ears. Steve would think she'd been at the drink before he got there.

'You're so funny, Ella,' she said. 'You just live next door, you couldn't really have a sleepover here.'

'Why not?' demanded Ella. 'I do sleepovers at Granny's house and Nana's sometimes when Daddy's away. Can I play with your make-up?'

Connie looked at Steve.

'If Connie says you can,' he agreed.

'Of course,' Connie said. She turned on the lights in her bedroom. In advance of Ella's visit, she'd hidden her bodice-rippers and put a PD James beside the bed. Not that Ella was going to recognise it, but still, it might sound better if Ella's breathless report was that Connie was reading a very grown-up book instead of one with a cover of a man who had no shirt on.

'You're very kind to her,' Steve said softly when Connie returned. He was sitting on the couch and looked totally at home there. Connie felt a little flip at the sight of him there, sprawled comfortably. Dinner in the oven, Ella pootling around happily, Steve on the couch. It all felt so *right*.

'She's wonderful,' Connie said, and she was being utterly truthful. 'You're very lucky.' Oh no, *what had she said?* Steve's wife was dead. 'I mean, you're very lucky to have Ella, in spite of her mum not being around—' Blast, this was getting worse. Talk about foot in mouth disease. 'She told me her mother was dead and . . . Sorry.'

She stopped pacing anxiously and sat down beside him. 'I am putting my foot in it. I meant that Ella is a beautiful child. You're lucky with that.'

'I know,' he said gently.

'I didn't mean to say the wrong thing. I didn't know what to say. I tried to imagine what I'd feel like if I'd lost someone and the only plus would be having Ella . . .' Connie stopped, wondering if she'd said far too much.

'I know what you mean,' Steve said.

His eyes were grey, she realised. A crystalline grey that seemed to see deep into her soul.

'When Lesley died, I'd have fallen apart without Ella. I had to keep going. Ella was just seven months old.'

Connie did the maths. Ten years ago. Would a person be even slightly over that by now? No, definitely not. She'd only just begun to get over Keith, and he hadn't even died. Pity, that.

She decided she'd be a friend and not try to flirt. There was no point and she was hopeless at flirting anyway. She and Steve were friends.

'You've done an amazing job with Ella,' she said. 'You should be so proud of yourself. She's such a great little girl.'

His smile was so warm that Connie wished yet again they were more than friends.

'Thank you,' he said, 'that's a very kind thing to say, but a lot of the way Ella has turned out is down to Ella herself.'

'She is pretty special,' sighed Connie.

'Connie! You have lip gloss!' shrieked Ella.

'Don't put too much on,' said Steve.

'It's only clear gloss,' Connie pointed out. 'I hid all the stuff that turns me into a pantomime dame.'

Steve laughed. 'You're hardly pantomime dame material.'

'You should see the wart I put on for school,' Connie joked before she could stop herself. Well, what was the point in pretending she was a hot sexpot? They were friends.

Friends didn't sit on the couch gazing at each other. They talked and had dinner. Maybe they'd get to the sort of friendship where he told her about his life, girlfriends and all.

'Right,' she said briskly, 'I hope you like chicken casserole.'

'Love it,' Steve said. 'I still owe you for last week.'

'Oh, what are friends for?' Connie said cheerfully. 'There's wine on the table, as well as water, help yourself.' That sounded nice and casual, didn't it? She cast a glance at the perfectly laid table. She'd laboured over it, not wanting it to look date-like. Grabbing the stereo remote, she turned the volume up a bit.

In the kitchen, she grabbed the new red gingham oven gloves she'd bought only that day in the supermarket and took out the bubbling casserole. It smelled delicious, although the cream had split. Blast.

Gaynor had made no mention of what to do if that happened. It mightn't taste too bad, Connie thought. She stuck a spoon in, waited till it cooled and tasted. The taste was of wine, a bitter tang that did not correlate with the delicious mushroomy smell.

'How much wine do I add?' she'd asked Gaynor. 'Ella's going to be eating it too.'

Somehow, exactly how much wine to add had got lost in the discussion on making a separate casserole for Ella. Working on the theory that the more wine the better, Connie had poured in most of a bottle of white wine into the grown-up pot. Rapidly, she pulled out Ella's smaller casserole. Perfect. No bitter tang.

There was only one little breast sitting in a pool of creamy mushroom sauce. Just enough with rice for Ella, not enough to share between the three of them.

'Smells good,' Steve said.

'Yes!' she trilled.

Maybe the actual chicken might not be too bad ... But no. Immersion in nearly an entire bottle of wine had made the chicken acid-bitter and, what was more, it was overcooked. If a burglar attacked, Connie would be able to do serious damage to his head by hitting him with a piece of chicken.

'How's it doing?'

Suddenly Steve had loomed over her and was peering with interest into the dish. She watched him inhale and then flinch.

'Wine stew, anyone?' she said weakly.

'How does it taste?' he asked.

Connie shook her head. 'Don't taste it, whatever you do. I don't have fully comprehensive insurance. If you have to have half your stomach removed, my insurance company won't cover it.'

She waited for him to laugh, collect Ella and say they might head home instead.

So she was quite surprised when he smiled fondly at her and said: 'Cooking disasters can happen to anyone. Even though Ella gives out about my cooking, I'm not a bad chef.' He opened her fridge and spotted the extra chicken breasts. 'Want me to whip up something?'

Connie swallowed. Fathers of nearly ten-year-olds wouldn't appreciate double entendres. 'Yes,' she said. 'I'd love that.'

*   *   *

Ella had chicken casserole, while Steve and Connie had panfried chicken served with lemon butter.

'How did you do that and so quickly?' said Connie with her mouth half full. It was so gorgeous, she couldn't stop eating.

'You like Daddy's cooking?' said Ella. 'I like this the best.' She speared a mushroom with her fork and gobbled it up.

'Your daddy's a better cook than I am,' Connie said.

'Really?' Ella was shocked.

'Don't count yourself out just yet,' said Steve, and he glinted a smile at Connie. 'I'd say Connie has lots of talents.'

Connie smiled goofily at him and he smiled back.

'Finished!' said Ella. 'Can I have dessert now?'

'Of course,' said Connie happily. It was strange: she normally loved profiteroles but suddenly, she didn't feel hungry any more.

22

The Homestead

There was a long walk down the lane from the road to our house, but I never walked it without feeling a sense of peace. Over the years, we'd done our best to keep the place decent, and the house sort of welcomed you as soon as you set eyes on it. The few trees beside us sheltered us from the worst of the winter winds. Agnes' beloved roses clung to the gable wall, giving a spot of colour on one side. Joe used to paint the front door a lovely green and with the ivy that grew around it, and the old water barrel beside the door, our house was as pretty as a picture. When you were a small child, Eleanor, you loved that water barrel. It collected rainwater that I used for the bath and I always said that hair was never as silky as when it was rinsed with rainwater.

You loved to float leaves and sticks on it, standing up on an old stool to get at the water. I used to be frightened out of my life you'd fall in, but you never did. Your father put a bit of wire across the top of it in a criss-cross pattern to keep you safe.

If I had to go into Kilmoney for a few hours, it was so nice to walk along the lane and see you there playing with your few bits of toys outside the door. I'd see the green of the door and the trees beside the house, and I knew I was home.

*   *   *

Megan had forgotten how much she liked driving.

'I have this cute Mazda sports car,' she told Eleanor as they navigated the motorway. 'I can't believe how long it is since I drove. Pippa, my sister, hates driving, but I love it. You feel in charge when you're driving.'

'Why do you like feeling in charge?' asked Eleanor.

Megan laughed. 'Do you know that Carole has been on at me to have therapy for years. Everyone's doing it, she says. I didn't like the idea. Didn't want to look too much into my own head. But it's OK, isn't it?'

'I think so,' said Eleanor. 'But I'm hardly unbiased.'

'This is probably a good place to talk,' Megan went on. 'I've read that when you've got something hard to say to teenagers, you say it when you're in the car and nobody can actually look at anybody else.'

'That helps.'

'Here goes: I never felt in control as a kid,' Megan said, overtaking a slow driver. 'It was Marguerite's show.'

'You mean your mother.' Eleanor normally didn't operate at such high speeds in a session but there wasn't time for the measured and painful progression of true psychoanalysis here.

'She didn't like being called mother that much. That sounds bad, doesn't it? She loved us, still loves us, but she wasn't motherly material. People like Rae from Titania's Palace: she's motherly.'

Eleanor nodded and said nothing.

'My mother is more of a fun person. She liked being our friend. When I started acting, she always wanted to go along to the parties we had. I never thought that was odd. I mean, Mum looks beautiful. Guys loved her. I think I didn't like that,' Megan added thoughtfully. 'It was like, it's my turn now and yet she's interested in the guys my age. Not properly interested though. Just interested in them liking her.'

'Why do you think that was?'

Megan considered it. 'Insecurity, I suppose. She was so pretty, still is. Prettier than anyone else's mum, and that was important to her.'

'More important than anything else?' asked Connie.

'Perhaps.'

Megan's memories of the years when her father was alive were hazy. She wished she could remember more, like the house in Kent where they'd lived or the school they'd gone to until he died. But she could recall so little. Her strongest memories were from ten onwards: the time living with Nora in Golden Square, and the nomadic times with Marguerite. Their life had sounded so exciting to other children at the various schools she and Pippa went to.

'You've lived in Madrid, Martinique, Ireland?'

Foreign countries were exciting but only as a contrast. What was important was the actual home waiting for you. When slipping gaily from one foreign country to another was your whole life, it was a different story. There was no home, nothing solid to hold on to so you could enjoy the light-as-air feeling of being on holiday.

She and Pippa had gone to school most of the time. Film sets and walking into rooms on her own held no fears for a girl who'd gone to eight different schools as a child. Megan was used to being the stranger and she'd learned early on that her beauty made it easier to gain acceptance. Not friends, no. Friends were hard to come by when you were beautiful, but unlike other kids who moved schools a lot, she was never bullied.

Her mother had always been one of the most glamorous of the mothers in the various schools. Not for her a hastily assembled outfit of faded, shapeless clothes or a haircut that was past its prime. Marguerite was petite like her daughters, and no matter how little money they had, her long hair was always artfully highlighted and she had decent face creams. There was no one thing about her face that was beautiful, but she had something else, a hint of sex about her that made men stop and stare. It was nothing a person could put their finger on.

Marguerite Flynn never dressed provocatively, but on her, the simplest white camisole took on the sexuality of a negligee.

Megan was proud to have such a pretty mum and yet sometimes, although she'd never admit it to anyone, she wondered what it would be like to have one of the other mums, the ones who didn't care how they looked.

* * *

For all that Megan had been so pretty as a child, she'd had a great gift for hiding when she wanted to. It was partly so she could hang around the grown-ups, partly because she never seemed to have friends and was on the outskirts always.

Being able to blend into the background was useful. She heard things. And it was true: eavesdroppers never heard good things about themselves. Only, Megan hadn't heard bad things about herself.

It was always noisy in Gunther's house in Martinique. He liked people around, there were always guests staying from Germany and local friends dropping in for drinks. Birds squawked outside, insects hummed, music drifted from the kitchen where Yvette, Gunther's chef from New Orleans, would be concocting a delicious lunch on instinct—no cookbooks for her.

Pippa was playing with one of the visitor's daughters. Megan had left them to it, and was drifting around the house, out into the garden where a silent gardener was working, back into the terrace where the cocktails were.

'Gunther will never marry Marguerite. She thinks he will, the fool. Men never marry women like that. One day, mark my words, his mother will come along with a virginal German heiress with no looks but an impeccable pedigree, and Marguerite and the kids will be thrown out.'

Nancy was speaking. Nancy wore Dior, rattled with precious jewels and was never seen without her raven hair in a perfect up-do. Megan knew that her mother idolised Nancy.

Nancy had her own money and was a friend of Gunther's. Not Marguerite's friend. She looked at Megan's family as if she knew they wouldn't be staying very long. Chantelle, one of the maids, had told Megan and Pippa that the woman before their mother had had a son. He'd had their bedroom, which was why there were posters of cars and football teams on the walls.

Pippa took them down on her side. Megan didn't. She didn't want to stay here. She knew they wouldn't, anyhow. Gunther barely noticed her and Pippa. If he wanted to be with their mother, he'd like them too, wouldn't he?

She'd never told anyone about what she'd overheard.

Nancy was right. They'd left six months later. Few of her mother's Martinique 'friends' had said goodbye.

'We'll be fine, girls, won't we?' Marguerite had said with false bravado.

399

They'd lived with Nora for a few months, then back to London, and somehow, although Megan had forgotten how, Marguerite had fallen in love again, and they'd moved to Norfolk.

Megan and Pippa had never questioned the way they lived.

This was their mother's world and she'd learned to negotiate it as best she could. Finding a man to look after her was what she did.

*　　*　　*

'Is there somewhere to stop along the way?' Eleanor said. 'I need to use the restroom. Sorry, I know we only just had lunch.'

'Let's have a break on the outskirts of Galway,' Megan suggested. 'That's not far.'

They chatted about inconsequential things as they drank tea in a hotel beside a vast roundabout. Eleanor had been quiet for the last few miles of the journey.

'It's all so different,' she said as she stiffly got back into the car. 'Of course it's going to be different, I know that. But it's almost alien to me. Not what I expected.'

For the first time, Megan sensed that this wasn't a straightforward emigrant-returning-home trip. Up to now, she'd never questioned Eleanor's desire to visit her old home. Eleanor hadn't been to Ireland for many years, it was a pretty standard thing to want to do, right?

But now, Megan began to wonder if Eleanor's visit to Ireland was that straightforward after all.

She consulted the satellite navigation screen on the dashboard, and steered back into the traffic.

She'd have liked to have asked exactly what had brought Eleanor to Ireland, but she couldn't. Instead, she went at it indirectly.

'It must be strange to be back here,' she said. 'I felt the same when I got back to Golden Square. I hadn't lived there for years and I'd changed so much. It must feel the same for you.'

'Yes,' agreed Eleanor. 'It's so different, it's unnerving.'

Megan took a risk. 'And a bit sad?'

'Very sad, actually. Not in Golden Square. I love it there. But this—' she gestured out the window at the countryside they were driving through '—this isn't anything like the place I left.'

Megan said nothing. All she knew about therapy came from TV or Woody Allen movies—she wished he'd cast her in something—but she knew that if you said nothing, people sometimes jumped in. However, Eleanor had fallen silent. More prodding was needed.

'When we lived in Ireland, we were kids and I couldn't wait to get somewhere exciting, like New York,' Megan went on. 'Now, after everything that's happened, I love the quiet of Golden Square. Not that it's that quiet, I suppose. Stuff is always happening. I don't mean the photographers—I could do without them outside Aunt Nora's house—but other stuff.'

'It's a community and you've got friends here,' Eleanor remarked. 'That's why things are always happening. You know what's going on in people's lives.'

'That's nice, isn't it?' Megan said with enthusiasm. 'I've never had that anywhere else.'

'Community is important to people, and Nora's

401

very much a part of the local community. You've met some nice people too, like Connie, Nicky, Birdie and Rae. That's how you've become involved. It changes everything.'

Megan drove in silence for a little bit. The GPS on the car was constantly telling her where to go as she navigated a series of roundabouts, so she was concentrating.

'It's funny, we're both newcomers, really, and we've become totally involved in the place,' she said thoughtfully once they were back on a straight road again. 'Is it Golden Square, do you think?'

Eleanor shook her head. 'It's because we've both stayed on the outside for a long time. Megan. You in your starry world, your feet not touching the ground, and me in my analyst's world, watching the world and not getting involved. Suddenly we landed in Golden Square and, in spite of ourselves, we became involved.'

Megan was confused. 'You mean, you don't normally get involved with people? I thought that's what you did?'

Eleanor's laugh was soft. 'I don't,' she said. 'In spite of myself, I got involved. I was trained to stay on the outside, and it's a hard habit to break. When you meet someone in the park and they tell you their problems, you know it'll realistically take years of ripping down the barriers to get to the problem and build the person up, so you—sorry— so *I* don't say anything. Well, I never used to say anything.'

'But now you do,' Megan finished. 'Which is a positive thing. Look how much you've helped me. I hadn't told anybody all about Rob until I told you. I kept it knotted up inside me, eating away at me.

And now look at me! You've done so much for me. We're friends.'

Eleanor felt a surge of affection for the young woman beside her. It was true: for all the difference in age, she felt that Megan was her friend, as were Connie and Rae. Before Ralf died, she'd had few female friends. Her family was her world outside work. Going to Golden Square meant she'd had to open up to new support networks.

She had a twenty-six-year-old actress friend. How great was that.

Eleanor decided to do something she never did any more with other people and open up.

'Do you know, I've never been back here since my family left,' she said softly.

'Wow,' said Megan. 'That was a long time ago, wasn't it? Not that you're old or anything—'

Eleanor laughed. 'I am old,' she said. 'It's all right to say that. I know that the society constructs these days mean that women don't want to say how old they are but it's not a problem for me. I left here in nineteen thirty-seven.'

'Whoa,' said Megan. 'That's a long time.' She hesitated to do the maths but Eleanor got there before her.

'I was eleven,' she said. 'My mother, my aunt Agnes and I took the boat to New York to live with my uncle andwe never came back. It's a long time to think about a place.'

Megan wasn't sure how to respond. She did the mental calculations: Eleanor hadn't seen the place of her birth for some seventy-three years. Megan herself was only twenty-six. Imagine being alive that long, imagine having lived through so much.

'I don't think I know anybody that old,' Megan said, and Eleanor gave a rich, deep laugh.

'That's not what I meant,' Megan apologised. 'But you've seen so much. The thirties—I love the thirties, the clothes are so glamorous.'

'It wasn't very glamorous to arrive in Ellis Island in those days,' Eleanor said. 'America was in the grip of the Depression. We thought we'd jumped out of the frying pan and into the fire. When we left Kilmoney we didn't have much, but we had a roof over our heads and a garden. When we landed in New York, we had next to nothing.'

Megan's history was sketchy. The most she could remember about the Depression was a Hollywood mini-series. It had shown bleak poverty and people committing suicide due to bankruptcy.

'How did you survive?'

'My mother and Agnes worked as seamstresses. Agnes had been in service and she had training, My mother was very good with her hands. People were used to sewing in those days. At home, my mother made all our clothes.'

'Incredible. What was it like when you were a kid? Here in the West, I mean.' Megan could vaguely imagine life in New York because she'd been there. But the rural world of 1930s Ireland, *that* she couldn't imagine.

'My mother wanted me to know what it was like,' Eleanor said. 'When she died, she left me a little book about life in Connemara. Well, she called it a recipe book, but it was sort of a diary-cum-recipes-for-living-your-life book. She didn't want me to forget where I came from. It's supposed to be about food, but it's really about life.'

'I'd love to see it.'

'I'll lend it to you tonight,' Eleanor promised. She paused. 'I came back to Ireland because my husband died last December.'

There, she'd said it out loud. It was ridiculous for a psychoanalyst to have a problem saying such a thing out loud, but there it was. She felt that saying Ralf was dead made it real.

She knew it was real, it felt painfully real. But telling other people was the final act.

'I'm so sorry.' Megan took a hand off the steering wheel to touch Eleanor's hand. 'All these months, I've been telling you my problems—we've *all* been telling you our problems—and you never said a word about this.'

'It's been difficult,' Eleanor said. 'I'm not good with sharing or asking for help. Physician, heal thyself!' she joked.

'Had he been sick for a long time or was it sudden?' Megan asked.

'It was quite sudden,' Eleanor said quietly. 'We can talk about it tomorrow, perhaps? I'm so tired now . . .'

'Sure,' said Megan quickly. 'Let's drive on and get to our B&B.'

Outside Galway, the landscape began to change. Suddenly, they were on a much narrower road that sat in a bare, beautiful landscape that spread up rocky mountains to the left, and down to a jagged coast on the right. The road was set high on the land in some places, with ground falling away on each side of the road where unwary drivers might find their car stuck in a ditch if they strayed from the tarmac.

'The road is on the bog,' murmured Eleanor to herself as she gazed out the window.

The sky was big and lit with a strange, clear light. Grey rocks dotted the hillsides and wild-looking mountain sheep were scattered in groups, diminishing as the hills turned into solid, rugged mountains.

She remembered a painter her mother had loved: Paul Henry. He'd painted the expanse of Connemara and County Mayo with small thatched cottages set in lonely swathes of bog-land. She'd bought a print of one of his works: stone cottages set beneath purple mountains with brooding clouds over-head. He'd been famous for his cloud structure. When she'd seen prints of his work, she'd wondered if he'd imagined the desolate beauty of the place, but being here, she could see he hadn't.

In her memory, Connemara was smaller, tamer than this wild, beautiful country.

It was beautiful but so stark. How had her family survived here for so many years?

It was growing dark by the time they pulled into the bed and breakfast that the guide had recommended to Eleanor.

The Bay was a medium-sized Edwardian hunting lodge that had had been transformed into a B&B.

A smiling woman of about forty brought them in, showed them prettily decorated adjoining rooms, and said she could cook them scrambled eggs if they liked, or else send sandwiches up to their rooms.

'Sandwiches,' both women said at the same time.

Eleanor said goodnight to Megan, and closed the door on her room. She wasn't used to spending that much time with anyone any more and although Megan had been staying with her for a week, this was different. Both the trip and the conversations had been deeply emotional and for the first time ever, it wasn't Eleanor who'd been doing the probing: it had been someone else. She shut the curtains, glad it was dark and she didn't have to look out at Connemara any more. It was so beautiful and yet being here made her feel terribly sad. She should have been here with Ralf.

She had come to look for her past too late. Her mother and now Ralf were dead. Her daughter, Naomi, had her own life, as did her grand-daughter, Gillian. It wasn't fair to foist herself and her sadness on them now. There was nobody left who remembered her past. Nobody except herself and this lonely landscape. Perhaps it was apt that she was here now: the woman with a lonely landscape inside her visiting a lonely landscape.

She didn't really feel hungry but she made herself eat half of one of the sandwiches, drank some tea, then took a sleeping tablet. She could not bear to lie sleepless here tonight. Then she got into bed and waited for chemical oblivion.

*   *   *

Morning brought a glorious sunny day and the sounds of geese and hens at the back of the B&B. Eleanor lay in bed and listened to the noise of the birds. It had been years since she'd heard hens, probably since that time she and Ralf had gone antiquing in New England, and had stayed in a tiny country hotel adjoining a farmhouse.

She remembered how the sunny-side-up eggs at breakfast had been golden yellow from free-range hens.

407

'To hell with my cholesterol,' Ralf had chuckled, slicing his knife into one egg and letting the yolk spill out in a saffron river.

All that worry over cholesterol and checking of HDL and LDL, and he'd still died.

Eleanor could recall many patients who'd been to see her to get over the death of a loved one. The fear that they wouldn't be able to exist without the person was often the most overwhelming part of grief. And here she was, highly educated with years of experience in helping other people to get over such grief, and still totally unable to get over the grief herself.

She got up, pulled on her dressing gown and looked out one of her bedroom windows to see where the hen and geese noises were coming from. Beneath the back window she could see a small farmyard where the woman who'd let them in the previous night was out feeding geese who stretched out long necks and hissed at her.

Eleanor smiled. Geese never changed, they were always bad-tempered creatures.

Life went on, as she told her patients. Geese hissed, people survived.

Once dressed, she went outside to walk down the drive. The house was set on a curve of the road opposite a small, jagged bay. Rushes grew at the water's edge, and moss-covered rocks clustered around as if dropped haphazardly by a giant. Eleanor watched an elegant bird stand on one spindly leg and survey his empire. A heron, she thought, and wished she had a camera. Gillian would love it here. She'd taken a photography course at school and was always taking photos. Naomi would have enjoyed it too. How many times had they talked about coming 'home' and seeing where the old house had been? And then Eleanor had left them for Ireland.

She'd flattened down the guilt when she was in Golden Square. She'd had to leave New York, she was too sad after Ralf's death and getting away had been the only option. But here, in the land where she and the girls had talked of coming with Ralf, the guilt came back.

She and Megan had breakfast in a bow-windowed room looking out over the bay.

Megan had been for an early-morning walk up one of the hills. 'It's amazing,' she said enthusiastically. 'If you took away the modern houses and the telephone poles, this place probably looks like it did a hundred years ago.'

'It does, doesn't it?' agreed Eleanor.

*   *   *

The guide from Ireland of the Ancestors was a slim, middle-aged man named Phil who came equipped with a couple of historical reference books in his rucksack, binoculars, a flask of tea and a picnic blanket. He had pens and an ordnance survey map in the right top pocket of his fisherman's waistcoat, and a Swiss Army Knife in the left.

'Be prepared is my motto,' he said cheerfully. He spoke in the Connemara accent that Eleanor hadn't heard for so many years. She had a hint of it in her own voice, although a lifetime in New York had rubbed most of it out, but hearing Phil made her heart ache.

Phil installed Eleanor in the front seat and

409

Megan in the back of an old but clean Land Rover, and they set off.

'Kilmoney has almost disappeared as a town,' he explained as he drove along undulating roads. There were plenty of cars on the roads. 'April,' he said. 'Time for tourists, coarse fishermen, the whole lot. It's a great time for perch and roach. The roads go a bit mad, but we need the tourism. There haven't been so many visitors for the past years, not since 9/11. Terrible thing, that was. But the visitors are coming back. How long is it since you were at your home?' he asked Eleanor.

'Seventy years,' she said.

Phil didn't appear shocked. 'I have to warn you, it's all changed. Kilmoney was a decent-sized town if you look at the 1911 Census. Some six hundred and fifty people lived there. But, as you know, there was a lot of emigration after that. There was a slowing down of emigration during the American Depression, but of course, many people from Connemara took the Mail Boat to Britain. They'd work for a few years and come home. Then off again when the work here dried up.'

Megan was silent in the back of the car. It sounded so grim, so frightening. Work meant food in those days. Having a job was the difference between living and dying. She looked out at the stunning countryside around her and shivered at the thought of how different it must have looked to people with nothing to live on.

'There was seasonal employment for people in the big houses when the aristocracy came to their country estates in summer and autumn, but that began to die off too. The young men and women left the village, they wanted something else for

410

their futures. Four of the big houses went empty during the Emergency—World War Two,' he explained to Megan.

'A fellow by the name of McGeraghty opened a small distillery a few miles from Kilmoney in 1953, and that kept the town alive a little longer, but the fire in 1958 destroyed the church and the local school, and it was all over then. It's a bit of a ghost town now, just a main street with a couple of houses and a very nice little hotel named The Sheep's Head. Run by a Kiwi couple. They do good business bringing walking tours up the mountains, and sending fishermen off in the right direction. You can even bring your dogs with you.'

Eleanor laughed. 'We'll have to stop there,' she said. 'I like the sound of these people.'

'They're a decent pair of skins,' Phil went on. 'I'd hate to see you upset, Mrs Levine, when you see the place. The old stone cottages are in rack and ruin. The tourists love it, picking their way through the ruins and imagining it all fifty years ago, but it might be upsetting for you.'

Eleanor smiled bravely. 'Let's just see it all. Have you worked out where my home was?'

'More or less,' Phil replied. 'It's a ruin, I have to tell you. But you were expecting that, weren't you?'

'Do you know, I'm not sure what I'm expecting,' Eleanor said.

*   *   *

The lonely main street was a bit of a shock to Eleanor. To visitors, it probably looked pretty with a few cottages and a couple of bungalows on either

411

side of the road, along with a small petrol station, and at the end, The Sheep's Head, painted white with black timber on the walls and colourful window boxes. Behind a small monument were black gates to a very old cemetery with nothing but a bare patch of ground where the church used to be.

To someone who could remember a public bar, the post office with the grocery attached, and the big grey church set back from the road with a hill graveyard beside it, Kilmoney looked almost deserted. As if someone had described the village badly to a artist, who'd then drawn only half of it in.

Eleanor found her hand covering her mouth as she looked around, trying to recall landmarks and wondering if her memories of the place were accurate at all. People romanticised places, she knew that. Had she?

'It's cute,' said Megan from the back seat, watching Eleanor carefully. 'But very different?'

'Very,' breathed Eleanor.

'The O'Neill homestead was out on the Clifden Road,' Phil went on, driving straight through. 'We can stop later for tea. Let's see the house first.'

It had been nearly three miles from the church to Eleanor's home. Three miles the family had walked many, many times. On Sundays, holy days, for christenings, marriages and burials.

She looked in vain for something she remembered as they drove out of the town and along a barren stretch of road with rushes on either side, and boggy, heather-strewn land that led to a couple of small ponds. Did she recognise those trees? Was that hump-backed bridge the one

412

she remembered, or was her memory tricking her?

She felt a surge of sadness at how different it all seemed. Where was the comforting sense of homecoming?

And then the Land Rover turned right down another long road and then left in what was once a gateway. Two stone gateposts marked the entrance and a stone track with grass in the middle led to the ruins of a stone house in a small glade of trees.

Home. At that instant, Eleanor remembered. She could see her childish self skipping down the lane after school, rushing to see her mother and father, and Granny. She could remember holding on to her mother's arm as they walked down after Christmas morning Mass, frost covering the lane with diamond brightness, towards the small house with turf smoke rising out of the chimney.

She no longer wanted to cry, she wanted to run down the lane the way she used to.

'Can we stop here so I can walk down?' she said to Phil.

'No bother.' He parked quickly. Megan and Eleanor got out, and Phil diplomatically stayed with the car.

Megan's hand slipped into Eleanor's, for which she was grateful.

'Is it familiar?' asked Megan softly.

'Yes.' Eleanor knew that even her voice was light now. 'I used to run down this lane like a thing possessed. I was so close to my mother that I'd run home from school to see her. I'd sometimes get a lift on a cart from the village, and I'd be home quicker than usual. I'd run to find her and I'd be so happy that I was early. I could spend more of the day with her. The ducks used to come round here

413

to that bit of boggy ground and look for snails,' she said, pointing to a spot just before the trees. 'My mother preferred them to stay round the back of the house, but it was useless trying to stop them. The water barrel was here. It was very soft water. Mother used to wash my hair in it rather than the water from the spring at the back of the house.'

They were at the house now.

Megan saw a ruined stone cottage with an assortment of small outhouses all in states of disrepair.

Eleanor saw what had been the home she loved. She touched the remains of the lintel of the doorway, closed her eyes and said a small prayer.

'Keep them all safe, Our Lady,' she whispered.

The rooms seemed so small now.

'This was the kitchen,' she told Megan animatedly. 'The range was here. A big black thing, it ate turf like a monster, but the heat out of it was amazing. We had to blacken it every week because the top went white from the heat. It killed my mother to leave it when we went to America. She loved that range, it was so much easier to cook on than the fire. Her chair was here and she'd sit and sew at night, by lamplight. My grandmother, my father's mother, would sit on the other side of the range and make knitted lace.'

She pointed out the bedrooms, and the outhouse they used as the dairy. 'I'll let you borrow my mother's book, Brigid's Recipe Book,' she told Megan joyfully. 'Wait till you read all about making butter. It was such hard work. I can barely remember a lot of that stuff, but it's all in the book.'

'I'm sorry your husband's not here to share this

414

with you,' Megan said. 'Nora has great faith. She believes the dead are with us, watching over us. Maybe your husband's here with all the rest of your family, smiling at us standing here.'

Eleanor stared at her in astonishment. 'That's exactly what I was just thinking. This great sense of peace has just come over me. I haven't felt like that in a long time, not since Ralf died.'

'Tell me about him. Did you have children?' Megan linked arms with Eleanor again.

'He was an optician. Levine and Sons, established 1925 by his father,' Eleanor said, eyes shining. 'Except that, from us, there were no sons. We have a daughter, Naomi, and she married a wonderful man named Marcus Filan. They have a daughter, my grand-daughter Gillian, who's nineteen—well, twenty now. She's wonderful.' Eleanor's face softened with pride.'

'What do they think about you being away from New York for so long?'

Eleanor sat down on a bit of broken wall.

'They hate it. I needed to get away from everything. I couldn't stand being in my apartment without Ralf. He had a mild stroke and then, a month later, a massive, fatal one. We thought he was fine, he was on all the meds, but it still hit him. I thought—' Eleanor broke off and looked at the ruined house all around her. 'I thought that coming to Ireland might ground me, remind me of something precious. I was feeling so lost and alone and I didn't want to be a burden on Naomi or Gillian. I ran away.'

'Sounds like the sort of thing I might do myself,' said Megan softly, crouching down at Eleanor's feet. She laid her hands on the older woman's arm,

415

comforting.

'The problem with running away is that the problem runs with you,' Eleanor sighed. She kept looking round the room, as if scared that the sense of peace would vanish when her eyes stopped brimming over. But no, it was still there.

*   *   *

The second stroke had happened so quickly, in spite of all the drugs Ralf was on. She'd been there this time, sitting beside him with the television on. That's what they did now: sat in front of the television watching documentaries on subjects that might have once interested him. War ones, science ones, archaeology ones that Eleanor might have watched too. Anything. She didn't see the screen really, and she was quite sure he didn't either. His eyes, dark eyes that had loved her with fierce passion, gazed blankly at the television, no longer burning with that inner fire.

Ralf was gone. She could feel him slipping away from her with each passing day, no matter that she clung to his frail body and wished him better. His speech seemed to be worse. He could barely move his left hand at all, and when she spoke to him, she could see a total lack of comprehension in his eyes. He should have stayed longer in the nursing home, but she'd insisted he come home. She could pay a nurse to come in. She needed him here. Except, he wasn't really here.

Eleanor had often thought she'd die before him and she hadn't wanted to. Men withered and died when their wives died, she knew that. Women were stronger. Hadn't her mother survived all those

416

years in New York without her father?

But the reality was crushing and different. Eleanor watched Ralf disappear and she wanted to go with him too.

When the second stroke had come, there had been one moment when she'd held him tightly and thought—hoped—the old Ralf had been there for one second. Then he'd gone for good.

'Mr Levine,' said the nurse, coming back from the kitchen where she'd been getting Ralf's lunch.

'He's gone,' Eleanor sobbed. It was over, she was over.

Naomi and Gillian insisted she stay with them for the week after the memorial service. Years earlier, Ralf had made it clear that he wanted cremation.

'More ecologically sound,' he'd said.

If he'd wanted a rocket to the moon, Eleanor would have done her best to organise it. But now that he was gone, there was nothing for her to organise.

Naomi had taken time off from the business to care for her mother.

'Mom, you must eat. A little chicken soup, something?'

'Thanks, honey, I'm not hungry.'

'Just sit with us for lunch?' Naomi had begged.

Eleanor shook her head. She was too broken to sit with Gillian and Naomi and attempt to chat. It was beyond her, even though it would have comforted them to know she was recovering in some way. For the first time ever, she couldn't comfort them. It was as if her transformation from nurturing mother person to old woman was complete. Everything had been leached from her

417

with Ralf's death. Her very being had changed.

Eleanor felt stiff and old. In December it was chilly in New York, even in Naomi and Marcus's warm apartment with its views of the river. Eleanor sat on the white ottoman and looked out at the Hudson and the grey skies.

Gillian wanted to remember her grandfather. Rejoice in his life.

'Gran, can I put on Gramp's favourite CD, the Chet Baker one?'

Ralf had gifted his love of music to his granddaughter and her iPod boasted an eclectic mix of old and new.

Eleanor nodded. She didn't really care. Nothing touched her.

But when the mellow strains of Chet Baker reached her, she gasped. The music speared into her. It was unbearable.

'Naomi, I need to go home,' Eleanor said. 'I'll be better there, honestly.'

She'd let Gillian pack for her, while Naomi fussed and said why didn't she stay.

'I'll be better at home,' Eleanor insisted. She didn't know why, but she needed to be away from people.

In the apartment, she knew that she couldn't stay there either. Every shred of furniture reminded her of Ralf and the life they'd had. Every cup was one he'd drunk from, every painting one he'd bought or hung on the wall.

There was no peace in either home.

And it was then the thought came to her: her true home, where she'd been happy when she was young. She and Ralf had talked of going there so often. She might find some peace in a place where

418

he'd never been. And if she didn't find peace, she had options.

It had taken only days to arrange.

Naomi had been horrified.

'Mom, don't do this, please,' she'd said, sitting on the bed in her parents' apartment while Eleanor slowly packed things in her two suitcases. 'You're too upset to go alone. Wait, and I'll come with you after Christmas.'

'No.' Eleanor knew how to be firm and to sound as if she was coping, even when she wasn't. Even if it meant lying to get away, she would do it. 'You stay here. I need to be on my own, Naomi. I'm not senile or stupid. Being eighty-four doesn't make a person incapable of travelling on their own.'

In the end, there had been nothing Naomi could do about it. Eleanor had promised to phone every week.

'I'll be fine,' she insisted. 'I don't need to be taken care of, Naomi. I'm not at that stage yet.' And never would be, she added in her mind.

*   *   *

Sitting in the remains of her old home in Kilmoney, she felt that sense of peace flooding through her. It was like drinking cool water after being parched. The relief flooded through her again. The burden in her chest seemed to be genuinely lifting. Something or someone was taking the pain away.

Ralf, are you here? she asked silently.

She hoped he was. If only she had the gift of faith and could believe in the hereafter. She'd never longed for faith until Ralf had died, and

419

then she'd lain awake at night, praying to the God she'd learned about in school for help. 'Please help me to believe.'

But here, in this wild spot with wind and rocks all around her, there was something else, something spiritual and deeply healing.

What if it didn't last, though? What if she left this place and the pain was back?

I'll come to you, she told Ralf. I'm ready. I'm not much good to anyone here, am I?

It was the final terrible thought she'd carried round with her: that she could save up her pills—the doctor had given her plenty of sleeping tablets, assuming that the very old wouldn't dream of hastening their end—and take them all at once. She didn't know if that was a good way to die or not, but with luck, she'd be so deeply drugged she wouldn't feel the pain. It had seemed like the only way. A crazy, unhinged way, she knew. But the only way that made sense.

Here, she asked whatever spirits or memories were in this place if she should do it.

'They must miss you so much,' Megan said suddenly. 'If you were my mother or grandmother, I'd miss you. Will you go home once you've seen all of this?'

Eleanor felt a little more of the pain lift. If there were such things as signs, surely that was a sign?

She moved further out of the mental fog and into the now. Megan was staring up at her and again, Megan's face reminded her of Gillian.

What would it do to Gillian if she killed herself? It would be the most destructive thing ever. Eleanor thought of all the lessons she'd learned from her mother and grandmother, via the little recipe book. Imagine if that book had been ripped in two by suicide.

Was that what Ralf would have wanted, or her mother, or even Aunt Agnes?

She could feel them all with her. Their wisdom communicating itself to her now. Or was it her wisdom, learned from all of them, reflecting back into her heart?

No, she couldn't do that to Gillian or her darling Naomi. She would go back to them. She could. Back home.

'Thank you.' Her fingers found Megan's. 'You're right. I should go home.'

'I'm so glad,' Megan said. 'That just seems like the right thing to do, doesn't it? Do you know, I was just thinking the weirdest things—that I suddenly feel better about Rob.' A month ago, Megan might have burst into tears at the mere thought of his name. Not any more.

She felt stronger now. He was a stupid, vain man and she'd been silly not to have seen through him. She hadn't been bad or deliberately cruel. Just stupid and innocent.

'The person I hated most in all of this was me,' she went on. 'But I don't hate me any more. Is that odd?'

'Not odd at all.'

Eleanor could barely speak. She felt so weak, but it was a lovely weakness. The weakness of being happy.

'It's this place,' Megan added, looking around. 'All those beautiful trees. What are they?'

'Mainly ash,' said Eleanor, closing her eyes and sighing. The peace, it was wonderful.

'And that little one beside us, the silvery one?'

Eleanor opened her eyes and looked at the small silver birch.

She recalled an old silver birch beside the door when she was a child. Her mother had told her that it was one of the most important trees in Celtic mythology.

'It's about birth and new beginnings,' Brigid had said.

But birch trees didn't live for that long, perhaps eighty years. There were no other birches around, just this one. Somehow, it had grown out of the remains of the old one. Rebirth.

Eleanor smiled at the small tree with its heart-shaped leaves and the silvery bark.

'Cattle won't eat young birch trees,' she said to Megan. 'They let it grow. It's about new beginnings and rebirth.'

'How fascinating,' said Megan. 'And just right. I'm starting again.'

'Me too,' said Eleanor.

'Ladies, how are the pair of you getting on?' called Phil from the car.

'I think we might repair to The Sheep's Head for some tea,' said Eleanor brightly. 'We deserve it.'

*   *   *

That night in her big bed in the B&B overlooking the bay, Eleanor took out her mother's recipe book. Tucked away at the back in a small folder were some of the final pages of the book. She'd read them when she was much younger, after her mother had died.

These weren't recipes for life but a letter written to Eleanor about her father's death. He'd died when she had just turned eleven. Three months later, Brigid, Agnes and Eleanor had taken the boat to New York. It was in the tenement house in the Bronx that Brigid had written this letter.

For Death was written on the outside of the little folder. Eleanor had thought it might be her mother's will, so she'd opened it. The letter made her cry so much, she had to stop. Her mother's body was barely cold, and Eleanor was reading of the pain Brigid went through when her husband, Joe, had died.

If only I'd known how hard his death was for you, Eleanor had thought. But it was too late.

Like all children, she'd assumed nobody but she understood love. Here was proof of that true love and the pain that came when it was gone.

Over fifty years had gone by since she'd read the letter. Brigid hadn't had long enough to enjoy the new life in New York.

She and Agnes had worked so hard to make a new life for them all. Uncle Dennis had married and their families had grown up together, but Brigid had died of pneumonia in 1967, robbing her of the chance to retire and properly enjoy life. Her chest had never quite recovered from the illnesses of her youth.

Even at the end, she'd been brave.

'I love you, remember that. Knowing you're happy is what lets me leave you, Eleanor.'

Eleanor rubbed her eyes with the sleeve of her nightdress and read:

My dearest Eleanor, I thought of not writing this. I thought I'd cheat death by not telling you about it. A mother's foolishness, is all you could call it. I've told you about food and life. Part of the circle of life is death. You were too young when your father died. Thank the Lord you were spared the pain of it. We fought the pain, Agnes and I. We pushed it away from you and took it ourselves. You'll know what I mean when you have a child of your own. You will fight to spare them pain.

I'd lie in bed at night and cry, but only when you slept. Daddy was happy, we told you. He's with God and the angels, and his own Mammy and Daddy, and the baby his mammy had that died.

But I missed him, Eleanor. Without Joe, there was no sunlight in my day.

I would remember all his kindnesses, how he used to make me laugh, the breadth of his shoulders beside me in the bed. When he was gone, nobody would ever do any of that for me again.

But I survived. I survived, you survived and Agnes survived. We made it across the Atlantic on the boat, we got through Ellis Island, we survived a first year with your Uncle Dennis when I was sure we'd starve or freeze or both. Life will find a way, as your grandfather used to say. Don't forget that. Life will find a way.

Eleanor laid down the book calmly. In the morning, she'd lend it to Megan. She'd read enough herself for the moment. Tomorrow, she'd phone New York to speak to Naomi. It was time she went home.

424

23

Family reunions

In Kilmoney, the only reunions we were used to were ones in the big house, when the Captain and Mrs Fitzmaurice had guests to stay from the Captain's time in India. Agnes would be plain exhausted from the preparations and she said Mrs Fitzmaurice wasn't much better.

There were many servants in India, it seemed, and no matter how many there were in the house in Kilmoney, it wouldn't impress the old India hands who weren't used to so much as moving an inch to pick up their own teacup.

The weather was a problem too. The house was always too cold for those used to the Indian sun, and Agnes would have to air every blanket in the premises to keep them all warm at night.

In New York, we had reunions too but they were different, I can tell you. After the first year we spent in the boarding house on Lennox Avenue, we'd made good friends of the O'Dohertys, the Koufonicolas and the McCloskeys. When we moved down the street to the apartment with the fire escape above Dimarco's Restaurant, we kept in touch with the other families. Every year, we'd meet up on Easter Sunday for a party and in the early years, oh my, did we party.

Mr Dimarco would say it was like St Patrick's Day all over again, but there was no drunkenness at our reunions.

'My sister and I keep a sober house, Mr Dimarco,' Agnes would tell him primly.

We'd laugh when she got upstairs because Agnes liked the odd tipple herself, but just the one. We didn't need whiskey to celebrate. I'd cook something Greek with Vania Koufonicola, like Avgolemono. It's a chicken soup with lemon and eggs. You make a stock from poaching a whole chicken with onion, celery, carrots, parsley and peppercorns. When the meat is falling off the bones, remove the chicken, strain the poaching liquid and cook this with several cups of rice. At the end, whisk up *the eggs, add the juice of one or two lemons, and slowly add your poaching liquid so the eggs don't scramble. Finally heat it all up, add some shredded chicken and eat. Anna McCloskey would bring proper shortbread biscuits, the way her mother used to make them.*

By the end of the day, we'd sit on the fire escape and drink to our homelands. There might be a few tears, but not many. We were happy in those years.

*   *   *

Geraldine's moving back home was on a par with a European principality moving court.

It all had to be done on a certain day, in a certain way, and the furniture in Geraldine's bedroom in her house in Howth had to be rearranged to her satisfaction.

Rae thought that if only there were ladies in waiting and a few minstrels in the wings, it would be perfect.

'I like having the bed with the sunlight coming in from the side,' Geraldine told Will with a certain petulance. 'It's so gorgeous in your house in Golden Square, the sun coming in on top of you in the morning, I'd like it like that all the time.'

It was five in the afternoon when the move finally took place, and Will shifted the furniture while Geraldine sat on a chair in duchess mode and directed operations. Downstairs, Rae organised flowers: 'I must have flowers,' Geraldine insisted. 'The house will seem so lonely now I'm back on my own.'

*   *   *

Rae had dutifully bought armfuls of flowers that morning at the Smithfield market and was now shoving them pell-mell into Geraldine's precious Waterford crystal vases. She simply wanted to be out of there because Anton was coming home for the weekend.

'We have to tell him,' Will had said, and Rae loved the way he said '*we*'. It was no longer her secret: it was his too.

'He'll be fine with it,' he said reassuringly. 'You know Anton. He takes everything in his stride, love.'

Still, Rae worried. Taking everything in his stride was one thing when it came to dodgy apartments, difficult college assignments, or low pay in his first job. It was another thing entirely when it came to the words: 'You have a sister—well, a half-sister, if you want to be pedantic. I had a baby when I was sixteen and I gave her up for adoption.'

All through his childhood, Will and Rae had drummed into their son the concept that telling the truth was important, even if it meant you got into trouble.

What she had to tell him would negate the effect of all of that. Would he hate her for it?

Upstairs, Geraldine wasn't happy with the arrangement of her bedroom.

428

'Rae, can you look at this and tell me what you think?' she roared.

Rae stomped upstairs. She wanted to get home quickly and tell Anton. She didn't want to be here. But when she saw Geraldine sitting on her chair, looking strangely frail and lonely in the room, Rae felt a pang of pity. There was pain in all lives. Geraldine had lived her glory days in her youth when she was the daughter of the big house, with plenty of suitors and lots of hunt balls to go to. That life had vanished long ago and then she'd lost her husband. With both her children grown up, she'd been lost. Plus, her daughter Leonora was hardly a model daughter, given as she was to her own tantrums.

It was a small price for Rae to pay to listen to Geraldine's talk of the past and her mild delusions of grandeur.

'Hold on a minute, Geraldine,' she called and ran back downstairs. She found the vase with the long-stemmed cream roses. They'd have cost several body parts in a florists but in the market, she'd got twenty blooms for half the price. Quickly arranging them more elegantly, she added some greenery, then brought the vase upstairs along with a candle from the hallway.

Will had his long-suffering face on when she arrived, so Rae showed the flowers to her mother-in-law. 'These will add the final touch,' she said. 'You can light the candle tonight to get you settled. It's lavender.'

'Thank you, Rae.' Geraldine's stern features softened. 'You're very kind to me.'

Rae smiled back. No, it wouldn't cost her anything to be kind to Geraldine.

With the flowers installed on the dressing table and the candle lit, Geraldine liked the arrangement more.

When Rae and Will left, Geraldine did something she'd never done before: she hugged her daughter-in-law. It was a formal hug, but it was more than the cool cheek that Geraldine had offered for kissing for all the years Rae had known her.

'You've been so kind to me,' Geraldine said shortly, 'better than my own daughter. Thank you, Rae.'

'We'll pick you up tomorrow for dinner with Anton,' Rae reminded her. 'He says it's his treat because work is going so well.'

If he's still talking to me, she added silently.

*   *   *

Anton's presence filled the house on Golden Square as it always had. Somehow slender Rae and lean Will had produced this giant of a young man who topped six foot four and had to buy XL sweatshirts to fit his shoulders. The sports teams at school had always looked longingly at him, but Anton had never been a rugby or GAA man. He'd loved the chess club and fewer of the jocks had poked fun at the speccy-wearing chess nerds when Anton Kerrigan was on the team. Not that Anton had ever hit anyone, but only the foolish ever tried to find out what would happen if he did.

'Mum!' He grabbed her in a bear hug and whirled her around. 'You've sent Granny home, have you? Has she got you drinking Earl Grey yet?'

430

Will laughed. Nobody could take offence at Anton with his gentle teasing. Even Geraldine adored him.

'Lapsang souchong,' joked his father. 'And lemon, of course.'

They went to the kitchen where Rae busied herself with dinner while Anton and Will sat at the kitchen table and talked. Anton filled them in on his life, how the world of political writing was, and how he'd met this very nice girl whose father was half-Irish and owned a couple of horses in Millstreet.

'Horses? Have you found yourself a moneyed girlfriend?' joked his father. 'They don't have stables full of Arabian thoroughbreds and a hotline to the Gulf States, do they?'

'No,' said Anton. 'Or at least, I don't think so.'

'I was reading a very interesting thing about new breeding techniques,' began Will and they were off talking about that while Rae reheated the boeuf bourguignon and took the dauphinois potatoes out of the oven.

'My favourites,' said Anton appreciatively as he picked up his knife and fork.

Rae found that she couldn't eat. Her stomach felt acid with anxiety and she pushed the food around her plate. The glass of red wine Will had poured her went untouched too. Even the very idea of eating made her feel ill. She had no idea how to broach this subject.

Finally, Will did it for her when he'd finished his meal.

'We've got news for you,' he said, pushing his cutlery together and leaning over to pour Anton another glass of red.

Anton looked at his parents cautiously, his gaze going from one to the other.

'Mum,' he said finally, 'what's wrong?'

Her mouth worked but nothing came out at first. 'I have a daughter,' she said finally. Bluntly; perhaps that was the only way after all.

Anton didn't fall off his chair or scream. 'A daughter,' he said evenly. He hadn't been a chess player for nothing. 'You had her before you met Dad?'

She nodded. 'A long time before. I was sixteen.'

Her son winced and one long arm stretched across the table to her hand.

'What happened?'

She could tell he knew what had happened. She'd always been able to read Anton like a book. He understood itall in an instant. 'She was adopted and she's contacted me.'

'Did Dad know?' he asked.

Rae shook her head. 'I kept it from both of you. When I met your Dad, there was never the right time to tell him, and then it was too late to tell him.'

'Is that why you were estranged from your parents?' Anton asked shrewdly.

This startled Rae. 'No,' she began, and then stopped. She'd never told Anton that much about her upbringing. She was afraid her bitterness over her parents would seep into him and she wanted to exorcise them from her new life. They were the past; he and Will were the future. 'Probably that was part of it,' she admitted. 'I was ashamed. Not of getting pregnant, but of giving her up.'

'So tell me everything you know about her,' said Anton. 'A sister,' he added with a hint of boyish excitement. 'I've got a sister.'

* * *

Rae sat on the edge of the seat in the hotel reception. She was so nervous and her bladder was playing up. But she daren't leave to rush to the loo, in case Tricia turned up and Rae wasn't there to meet her.

Tricia might think that Rae had changed her mind.

It had been a week since she'd opened the letter from her daughter.

Rae had wanted to phone Tricia instantly, but Will said she ought to sleep on it.

'Not so you'll change your mind,' he said, holding her. 'Simply so you can get your mind around this. It's emotionally shocking stuff.'

'You're so wise and so good,' Rae murmured. She leaned against his shoulder. 'I'm really sorry I didn't tell you.'

'I wish you had. I hate thinking you couldn't trust me—' There was a faint note of reproach in his voice.

'I'm sorry,' Rae said again. Saying sorry felt so useless: if only there was something she could do to show him how sorry she was, but there was nothing. She could only explain what it had been like, how frightened she'd felt, how much pressure had been put on her to give Jasmine up. Even then, it was almost impossible to explain.

'You've always been mysterious about your past,' he went on. 'I never quite knew if it was because Mother was so insistent about trying to ferret out details of your family and connections—'

At this, Rae laughed. Her secret was out in the open. Will hadn't packed his bags with the news. Somehow, telling him had been the worst. She felt hopeful that Anton would take it the same way.

'Telling you about my parents would have been impossible because they were so linked in my head with having to give up Jasmine—Tricia,' she corrected herself.

Her daughter had been Jasmine for so many years, and it was hard to get used to another name.

'If they'd been normal or in any way supportive, I'd never have given her up. But then, I'd never have left home so early, gone to college and met you, would I?'

'No.'

After dinner, they'd gone upstairs and laid on their bed talking. Geraldine and Carmel wouldn't be back for hours, and Will said he'd wait up for his mother.

'She'd take one look at your face and want to know what's wrong,' he said.

Rae nodded. 'In the early days, I wanted to tell you about Jasmine and my family,' she said. 'But when I went to your house for the first time and met your parents . . .'

She thought back to the early weeks of their courtship.

'I had a baby when I was sixteen' wasn't something you could say on the first date. 'It's a defining part of me. I called her Jasmine.'

By the tenth date, she knew she had to say it. Will was special, kind. He would understand and attach no blame, even though Rae blamed herself.

And then he'd taken her home to meet his parents.

The Kerrigan family home was as far from Rae's childhood home as it was possible to be. It was a detached house in Raheny, with a huge garden mowed in perfect stripes. Rae stared at the stripes as she and Will walked up the drive, and wondered how you achieved such a thing. Or why you would bother.

Will's father was like his son, tall and genial.

In his presence, Rae managed not to feel like the cleaner's daughter who'd come round the front door by mistake. She stilled her breath and allowed herself to admire the paintings on the wall, the flowers on the occasional tables, the bronze statue on a vast round table. And then Geraldine had come down the stairs, like a duchess bestowing her presence on her loyal followers, and Rae had realised she'd never be able to tell this woman's son about her past.

'I was too young and scared, to be honest with you,' she told Will. 'I was a bit over-awed by your home and your mother.'

'She liked people being over-awed,' Will said grimly.

'Perhaps.' Rae could be magnanimous now. 'She did grow up in a big house with staff, stables and a chauffeur. She can't have been happy to see her son turn up with a girl with none of what she liked to call "background". I had a background, all right, but it wasn't one she'd care for. So I said nothing. I made out my parents didn't travel and there was no question of you going to see them.'

Over the years, Rae had told her husband a little about her upbringing, but never the whole unvarnished truth. He'd seen the Hennesseys a few times on neutral territory, like the time they met

435

up at a classy hotel in Limerick when Anton was little. Paudge and Glory were on their best behaviour because Rae had bluntly told them she'd cut them out of her life completely if they turned up drunk.

'They're not that bad,' Will said.

'Oh, they are,' Rae interrupted darkly. 'I heard someone say recently that forgiveness means realising that the past is never going to improve. Your past is your past and it's a waste of time to think "what if . . . ?" I'm still not at that stage yet. I can't forgive them for what they did to me and Jasmine.'

'Maybe meeting Tricia will help,' Will pointed out.

That had been a week ago. The following day, Rae had phoned the mobile number on Tricia's letter. Will sat beside her in their bedroom—the only place where Geraldine wouldn't interrupt.

'Hello,' said a bright voice.

Rae's hand began to shake. 'Is that Tricia O'Reilly?' she said.

'Yes, who's this?'

Rae couldn't speak. She might hang up, anything to avoid the anger Tricia would have for her. How could she not be angry? Rae had abandoned her forty-one years ago.

'I'm hanging up,' said the voice. 'If this is a crank call—'

'It's not,' whispered Rae. 'It's Rae Kerrigan, née Hennessey. I'm your birth mother.'

There was a power in words, after all, she thought suddenly. *I'm your birth mother.* She'd been waiting a lifetime to say that.

'Oh my God,' gasped the other voice. 'It's you.'

'Yes.' Rae breathed out. 'I had a baby in the Blessed Helena Home on the date you were born. She was a little girl with dark brown hair. I'm tall, have dark hair, dark eyebrows and brown eyes.'

'Do people say you look like that actress Ali MacGraw, the one who was in *Love Story*?'

Rae nodded tearfully and then realised that nods couldn't be heard.

'Yes,' she said.

'I can't believe this,' the woman said. 'I'm Tricia.'

'I know. I'm Rae. I was Rae Hennessey when you were born and I'm Kerrigan now.'

'Have you other children?' Tricia asked hesitantly.

Rae knew the answer would hurt. She had a son whom she hadn't given up for adoption. But she'd been pregnant with Tricia in a different time, a different world.

'I have a son who's twenty-nine,' she said. 'I was pregnant with you when I was sixteen. I had no support. That's why . . .' She couldn't finish the sentence, even though she wanted to explain it all instantly.

'You know, I've waited years to find out all of this, but it's a bit much in one go,' Tricia said. 'Can I call you back another time? Or would you not like that? Does anyone know about me?'

It was the most heartbreaking question Rae could imagine anyone having to ask. *Was I remembered in your life?*

'My husband knows and you can phone me on my mobile number when you feel up to it,' Rae said calmly. She must be strong for her daughter's sake. 'Giving you up broke my heart. I thought about you every day of my life. Every single

437

birthday, I cried. I wondered where you were, were your new family good to you, what was your life like? Giving you away was the biggest tragedy of my life, Tricia. I just want you to know that.'

There was silence on the other end of the phone.

'Have you got a pen?' Rae added.

She listed her phone number slowly.

'Please call me,' she said.

'Yes,' Tricia whispered and hung up.

Tricia had sent a text message two days later.

Can you meet me near my home? I live in Mullingar and I can't travel much right now.

With shaking hands, Rae had replied. Tell me when and I'll be there.

Will drove her to the hotel in Mullingar and said he'd sit in the bar and wait while she sat in reception, as agreed.

'I won't come out unless you want me to,' he said. 'Now, Rae, she might not turn up. You've got to be ready for that. These reunions don't always work out the way you want them to.'

Rae smiled at him. He'd been researching it all on the Internet and was terrified in case Rae was hurt by this long-lost daughter.

'I don't think she can hurt me any more than I've hurt myself over the years,' Rae said simply. 'It's been torture. She has a right to be angry with me.'

Will stared at her for a while. 'I can understand why you didn't tell me,' he said, 'but it still hurts to think of you keeping it to yourself for so long.'

Rae knew it would take a long time, if ever, before Will could understand, but she simply couldn't think about that now. This moment was about her daughter and forty-one missing years.

As she sat waiting, Rae took out the letter Tricia

had sent her and traced the signature.

Tricia. She had to stop thinking her daughter was called Jasmine.

Rae hoped she'd be able to make Tricia understand that, no matter how phoney it sounded, she *had* thought of her daughter every day for forty-one years.

In the early days, she'd thought of Jasmine with enormous pain and sorrow. And as the years had gone by, she'd wondered what her daughter was doing. The summer Jasmine would be doing exams, on her eighteenth birthday, at New Year. What did Jasmine look like now? Where was she? And, the worst fear of all, was she happy? Had she been adopted by people who'd love her and take care of her properly, the way sixteen-year-old Rae wouldn't have been able to?

Rae had been staring down at her letter, but something made her look up just as a tall, pregnant woman with dark hair and dark eyebrows walked into the reception area. It was like looking into a mirror from twenty years ago. Rae stood up as the woman's eyes found her.

'I can't believe it's you,' said Tricia, coming face to face with her mother.

Rae knew all the right things to do. Will had been telling her them in the car on the drive here. Don't crowd her, don't hug her. She might not want that level of intimacy yet.

But despite all this knowledge, she put her arms around her daughter.

Then they were both crying, dark heads beside each other, making the same husky noises as they cried.

'We even sound the same,' Rae sobbed. 'You

439

should sit, you're pregnant.'

They sat and she wanted to go on touching Tricia, to run her fingers over her hair, her face, even the swelling belly inside which her grandchild was growing. But she forced herself to hold back a little. It had to be done at Tricia's pace.

Tricia settled herself on an armchair beside Rae's. As if regretting her earlier intimacy, she sat back in the chair a little, creating space between them.

'Are you happy? Were you happy?' Rae blurted out. 'It's all I ever wondered.'

'Very happy,' Tricia said. 'My parents had only two children, me and my older brother, and they adored us. Ruined us, my mother used to tease us.'

Rae felt a twinge of pain at the way Tricia said 'my mother' with such affection. Of course, Rae hadn't been her mother. The mother who'd reared her was the real mother. Rae knew that, but it still hurt.

'Does she mind that you wanted to find me?' she asked.

Tricia shook her head. 'Quite the contrary. She wanted me to find you years ago and I refused. I thought it would be like telling her that she and my dad hadn't done a good enough job. She passed away last year.'

Rae saw Tricia's eyes brim up.

'I wanted to find you then, but I couldn't do that to her memory, if that makes sense. And then—' She touched her belly. 'Stephen and I got pregnant. We've been trying a long time; we'd had fertility treatment, but it never worked. We'd given up hope, actually. And one day, bingo—I'm pregnant. I knew then that I had to see you to understand why.'

Rae nodded calmly but inside she was shaking. She knew that adopted women suffered huge sorrow when they themselves became mothers and realised what an enormous act giving up a baby was. *How could you give me away?* was what any mother or would-be mother would ask.

She said none of this. Instead, she smiled her warmest smile at Tricia and said: 'That's so wonderful.'

She couldn't come out with the clichés like 'It's the most special time of your life'. After the alleged most special time of her own life, she'd handed her baby daughter over to a stranger.

Tricia beamed. It was like looking into a mirror, Rae thought with a pang. Her daughter had the same smile, the same dark brows that winged out at the sides, the same wide mouth.

Anton didn't look like her at all. He was the image of his father. God, this all *hurt*.

'How far along are you?'

'Eight weeks. We found out early and, once I knew I was pregnant, I started searching for you. I didn't think it would all happen so quickly, to be honest.'

There was a pause in the conversation. The noise of the hotel reception went on around them: phones ringing, people carrying bags to and from the reception desk.

Rae had to say something. 'I can't imagine how hard all this has been for you,' she began, 'especially after losing your mother. But I have thought about you every day of my life, Tricia.'

Tricia was looking down at her lap, studying her fingers intently.

'I'd like to explain it all to you so you understand why I gave you away, but you may never understand because it was a different time, a different Ireland. Most of all I want you to understand that I loved you.'

There, she'd said it.

'Mum always told me that whoever my birth mother was must have loved me to have given me up.'

At that moment, Rae felt a passionate affection for the woman who'd reared her daughter.

'She was right. The nuns told me I couldn't care for you and that the only kind thing was to give you up,' Rae said, forcing herself to be calm and not cry. 'I wanted to keep you, you see. When they took you, they pulled you out of my arms.'

Tricia's head was to one side as she listened, almost detached. It was probably easier that way, Rae knew: to remove oneself from this difficult information.

'I'd love to tell you everything,' Rae went on. 'Would you like to hear?'

'Yes,' said Tricia.

Rae nodded. She'd been through this so many times in her head: explaining to her daughter why she'd given her up for adoption. The dream-like explanations had been simpler. Now that she was sitting opposite this bright-eyed, intelligent woman, she felt as if all the imaginary conversations had been geared towards a child and not a grown-up.

'It's almost impossible to explain what it was like forty-two years ago, finding out I was pregnant. They were different times,' Rae started off. 'Having a child as an unmarried teenager then was just about the worst thing you could do. It's almost unbelievable to think of how shocking it was then. If you admitted you'd killed someone, I think people would have been less shocked. Women who had babies outside marriage were shunned. The nuns didn't talk about it in school,' she said thoughtfully. 'Not even to say, "Don't do this." It was that unthinkable. They didn't talk about sex at all, but we knew to be afraid of getting pregnant.'

'But you did,' said Tricia.

Rae watched her daughter's face and wondered if Tricia's expression was a little cold? Perhaps she was imagining it. How to explain that she hadn't been recklessly and joyfully having sex with everyone, that it hadn't been like that. She suddenly could see her mother's cold face saying, 'You're up the pole, aren't you?' and she shuddered at the memory.

'I did get pregnant,' Rae said finally. 'I didn't tell the boy I was pregnant. I'm sure it became known in the area that I'd gone into an unmarried mother's home. His name was Davie Sullivan.' It felt odd saying his name after all these years, but if Tricia wanted to know, she'd want to know it all. Poor Davie. Rae wondered where he was now— flirting with jail like so many of the Sullivans, or still there in their hometown, not knowing he had a daughter of forty-one? Ten minutes in his uncle's shop had changed her and Tricia's lives forever. It had changed Tricia's adoptive parents' lives too. But Davie's? Had his life changed?

'I never saw him again. My family weren't . . .' she struggled for the right word '. . . supportive. They weren't the sort of people who could cope with my pregnancy.'

'They were religious?' asked Tricia.

Rae wanted to laugh at the notion, but she wouldn't. Tricia would not be touched by Paudge and Glory Hennessey any more than need be. She didn't have to know what sort of people they were. Even if she'd been raised at a distance from them, she shouldn't have to feel the touch of their bitterness and dysfunction. Rae could protect her from them like any mother would. 'No, they weren't religious. They weren't the right people to be parents, Tricia. Some people aren't. They're both dead a few years.'

Perhaps one day she could tell Tricia the truth, but not yet. Perhaps there would never be a 'some day'.

'I went by myself to the home and stayed there till you were born.' It was Rae's turn to look down at her hands. She wasn't seeing them: she was seeing the small room in the home where Jasmine had been born, and the room where they'd taken her away from Rae. 'I said I was going to raise you myself, but the nuns kept at me, convincing me I couldn't. I had no support. I'd be on my own with you and no money. If anything happened to me, you'd go back to my parents.' Sister Veronica's face was in her mind now. Those honeyed words with their powerful message. *You don't want your daughter to end up like you, do you? Unloved and alone.*

The cool softness of her daughter's hand on hers brought her out of the past. Tricia's fingers were long and elegant, like Rae's own hands.

'Mum told me what it was like in those days,' Tricia said softly. 'She told me that it wasn't easy then. They were so grateful for having us, my

444

brother and I. They told me how much they thanked you and my brother's mother. Thanks to you, we had a family.'

Rae nodded and took the tissue Tricia offered.

'Let's go into the bar and have tea or something,' Tricia said.

'My husband, Will, is in there,' said Rae.

Tricia laughed. 'My husband, Stephen, is in there too.'

*　　　*　　　*

Stephen and Will were sitting almost opposite each other, separated by the pathway through the lounge.

Both men stood up when Tricia and Rae entered. Both hesitated for a moment, clearly having been told not to intrude.

And then they came over to be introduced.

Stephen was as tall as Tricia, and nearly as dark, with a beard and blue eyes. He looked younger than forty, but then, so did Tricia. Rae held her hand out formally, then couldn't stop herself hugging him. She was so emotional.

'It's so wonderful to meet you,' she said, wiping the tears away. 'I'm so glad about the pregnancy.'

He beamed but shot a careful look at Tricia. She gave him one back that said, *I'm OK*.

Deciphering it, Rae felt a surge of relief. It was going to be all right.

Will was more formal with Tricia and shook her hand gently.

'It's an honour to meet you at last,' he said.

Rae gazed at him with love. With those words, he'd implied that Tricia had been a part of his life because Rae had talked about her. It wasn't a lie as such. Only Will understood her enough to know the depth of Rae's feelings about things. He might not have known about her daughter, but he knew now that when Rae said she thought of Tricia every day, she had.

*   *   *

Introductions over, the two women sat apart again and ordered tea and scones.

'You need lots of little snacks,' said Rae, then worried she'd been too motherly. It wasn't her place.

But it appeared that Tricia hadn't noticed.

'They always told me I was adopted,' explained Tricia. 'I had an older brother, Leo. He was four years older and because he knew he was adopted, I did too. Mum wanted it to be open so there would be no awful secret coming out years later.'

'She sounds wonderful and wise,' Rae commented. 'I wish I'd been able to meet her.'

Tricia dabbed her eyes with a tissue. 'I wish you had too. I wish she was still here. I don't know how to be a mother. I was the career girl. She was the one who'd have been able to tell me how to do it.'

Rae made herself stifle the shameful envy of Tricia's adoptive mother. She'd brought Tricia up.

Then it occurred to her that she didn't even know the woman's name. 'What are your parents' names?'

'Josephine and Tom Noonan.'

'Josephine and Tom,' whispered Rae. How many years had she wondered where her daughter was, and it turned out she'd been living in Galway,

446

beloved daughter to Josephine and Tom, sister to Leo.

Tricia went back to her story. 'I thought people had a choice when it came to babies. You could have them yourselves or have one that someone else couldn't take care of.'

Rae nodded.

'We were happy. I wanted to adopt babies when I grew up because I thought that's what people did. I work in banking.' She grimaced. 'Not the most popular job in the world now, but I travelled a lot in my thirties. Stephen and I got married and we didn't start trying to have a baby until I was thirty-six. I thought we had lots of time, and we didn't. I couldn't get pregnant. We tried it all, acupuncture, healthy diets, everything. Then we went to a fertility clinic.' Her eyes gazed over towards where her husband was sitting. 'Three years and six cycles of IVF, including two frozen embryo transfers. We'd almost given up. I thought I didn't deserve it, you know the way you do.'

Rae knew. She'd felt that way about her pregnancy with Anton. Huge guilt over being pregnant again when she'd given away her first child. But now wasn't the time to mention it.

'Mum had bowel cancer. By the time we knew, she only had months left to live. It was so fast. And I got pregnant. After all that healthy living and doses of fertility-controlling drugs, and I get pregnant when my mother's about to die.'

'New life comes in all the time,' Rae said. 'It's the endless cycle. We die and our children live on.'

They talked of inconsequential things for a while. The conversation had been so intense for ages, and it was nice to slip into idle chat about work and friends. Tricia talked about the smart two-bedroom apartment she and Stephen shared in Mullingar.

'We turned the second bedroom into a study,' she said ruefully. 'We'll have to make it a nursery now.'

Rae told Tricia that she ran Titania's Palace and described it so, that Tricia clapped her hands together and said: 'I'd love to see it.'

'I'd love you to, too.'

An hour passed before Tricia got up to leave.

Rae knew a bridge had been crossed. She was lucky: her daughter had been adopted by an open-minded couple who'd been determined to raise their adoptive children to think warmly of their birth parents.

'Would you like to meet your brother?' she asked.

Tricia's beaming smile turned on again, like a Klieg light illuminating the whole bar. Suddenly Rae could see Tricia as she'd been as a child: eager and warm-hearted.

'I'd love that. Anton, I love that name. He has another brother too, if he wants. My brother, Leo.'

'Leo hasn't searched for his birth parents?' Rae asked.

Tricia shook her head. 'He's a contented sort of guy. Very laid back.'

'He and Anton will get on like a house on fire, then,' Rae commented. 'He's like his father, he's very calm and gentle.'

'I'm glad you're happy,' Tricia said. 'I used to wonder, too, when I was old enough to know the difference, what your life was like. I'm glad it's happy.'

Geraldine had a new cleaner.

Zareen. Zareen now worked for Carmel, who declared her the best thing since sliced bread.

'She's so quick and efficient. Doesn't talk much. You'll love her.'

'Yes, but where is she *from*?' Geraldine couldn't identify the name. *Zareen*. What language was it?

'I don't know,' whispered Carmel. 'She's a lovely colour. Very pretty too and her English is impeccable, like someone taught her really well.'

Zareen was a statuesque dark-skinned young woman who wore skinny jeans, a pink T-shirt and had a mane of glossy straight hair. She listened in silence as Geraldine listed her duties, and repeated a few of them on the grounds that Zareen hadn't replied and perhaps she was one of those girls who didn't understand.

'How long have you been here?' Geraldine asked kindly at the end. A bit of politeness always put the girls at their ease.

'Since I was born,' Zareen said crisply. 'I'm from Artane. I'm doing a Fine Arts course at night and this work is to tide me over. Did you think I was foreign?'

Geraldine blinked rapidly.

'Goodness no.'

'She's very good,' whispered Geraldine as she tried to usher Will and Rae into the small living room, while Zareen steered the vacuum around skilfully. 'She's going to university.'

'Nice to meet you, Zareen,' said Rae, and held out her hand. 'I'm Rae. My mother-in-law says

449

you're at university. What are you studying?'

'Fine Arts,' said Zareen.

'How wonderful,' said Rae. 'I'd have loved that.'

Geraldine waited patiently while her daughter-in-law talked to her cleaner. Things were changing so quickly in the world. It wasn't as easy to place people any more. Zareen talked about art as if she'd grown up surrounded by Picassos. It was all very confusing.

Finally, Rae moved on to the drawing room with Will by her side.

'We've something to tell you, Mother,' said Will.

Geraldine's legs went weak and she had to sit on her beige velour pouffe.

'You're getting a divorce,' she said.

Rae actually laughed.

How callous, thought Geraldine.

'No, Mother,' said Will, 'we're not.'

'We've actually got an even bigger family now, which is sort of the reverse of that.'

'You're not pregnant! I think those fertility doctors should stay away from anyone over the age of forty-five,' shrieked Geraldine.

Rae sat beside her mother-in-law. 'I'm not pregnant, Geraldine. I had a daughter when I was sixteen and I gave her up for adoption. She contacted me and we've just met up.'

'A daughter. Before you met Will?'

'A long time before I met Will, yes. I was sixteen, I gave her up for adoption and I've regretted it every day since,' Rae said calmly.

The truth, the whole truth and nothing but the truth was the only way forward here.

'Goodness gracious,' Geraldine said.

'I know you're a bit shocked,' Rae went on.

'She's a beautiful woman of forty-one and, incidentally, she is pregnant for the first time.'

'Really?'

Geraldine thought of Carmel's daughter-in-law, the one with the tummy tuck scar and the new breasts. Compared to her, Rae was a plaster saint. And it wasn't as if Geraldine didn't know other people who'd been born the wrong side of the blanket.

Geraldine tried to think of the most forgiving question she could ask. 'What does she do?'

'She's works in banking,' Rae said.

Geraldine's face lifted. 'How handy. Someone to explain where all the money's gone. When am I meeting her?'

24

Weddings

When your father and I got married, my mother made a porter cake and her mother iced it. Porter cake is still made here in Brooklyn, but it's not the same, as Agnes likes to say. The stout isn't as good as it is back home. The trick is in soaking the dried fruit long enough in the porter till it's dark and soft as treacle.

It's not the easiest cake to ice,

but Agnes got plenty of experience at the big house and she could whip an icing up on anything.

We ate roast stuffed pork for the meal because it was September, just after we killed the pig, so the house was jammed to the rafters with pork.

Joe wore his Sunday best and I had a dress with a linen underdress and an overdress purely of the whitest knitted lace you can imagine.

It's old now, yellow with time, but I still take it out sometimes to look at it and feel the finery of it.

It was one of the happiest days of my life, the one you were born being the other. I wasn't travelling anywhere—Joe moved into the house with us because it was only my mother, Agnes and me, and it was easier than joining the house of men above where he lived, but still, it was like we were coming home to a whole new family.

*   *   *

The heat hit Megan with a hazy punch as soon as she left the airport in Ibiza. The little gold-framed glasses she was wearing as part of her disguise darkened with the sun. At passport control, when she'd had to take them off, she felt vulnerable. Strange how a centimetre of glass could make her feel safer. But nobody had recognised her.

Holidaymakers thronged the pavement heading to tour buses and taxis, joyful holiday mood bursting out of everyone. She joined the taxi queue and was soon in the back of a white cab on her way to Villa Aphrodite.

The name sounded stupid to her. Why did people give houses such ridiculous names? Only a palace would suit being called after a goddess.

Away from the airport and the serried apartment blocks, the island was quietly beautiful. Megan had been there once before and hadn't noticed the tranquillity. The taxi finally deposited her on a road with many high walls in shades of white and pale pink behind which villas shimmered in the heat.

Suddenly anxious about her mother being there at all, Megan left her bags in the car and asked the driver to wait.

There was no chink in the vast wooden gate to see in. Megan rang the intercom at a matching wooden side gate and waited.

'Si?' said a female voice. Not her mother.

'Señora Flynn?' said Megan.

The only reply was a metallic clunk and the whirr of the wooden gate swinging open.

Megan got back into the taxi and he drove her through the gates into a small circular driveway. Villa Aphrodite was certainly pretty, though no longer an immaculately kept place. Like an ageing beauty queen, she was still glamorous but paint had chipped off the stone columns at the porch and the glazed blue-and-white tiles on the ground were broken in places. Yet the overall effect was of beauty: a classic Spanish seaside house with climbing flowers clinging to the walls, a tiled roof in rich terracotta, and cast-iron railings on balcony windows. Her mother had been living here for the past year with Vincente, a man Megan had never met.

Megan paid the driver, took her bags and waited.

At first, the only noises were the insects and the hum of heat. Then she heard the faint staccato of high heels on tiled floors, followed by a door slamming and then the front door was opened.

Her mother appeared. And all of a sudden, it was as if the sun had come out.

'Megan, sweetheart!' Smiling broadly, as if this was a wonderful surprise instead of something which had been planned, Marguerite Flynn held out her slender, tanned arms.

Megan hugged her mother tightly, smelling the familiar scents of Shalimar, sinking into the embrace. She hadn't realised until she got here how much she'd wanted to be held by her mother.

'You look wonderful, Mum,' she said, finally, as they walked, arms linked, into the house.

Her mother looked years younger than her fifty-five years. She could pass for forties, easily. Her long fair hair tipped the edges of her eyebrows, hanging in casual ripples around her shoulders. She was still very slender, but it didn't show badly on her face, which looked remarkably dewy. Her make-up was different around the eyes. The rock-chick heavy eyeliner had been replaced by a more sedate application of kohl.

'You look very different, darling,' Marguerite said. She put her head to one side, admiring Megan's cropped dark hair. She'd had Patsy cut it again and put more dye in. It was inkier than ever, a sharper, tougher version of the old Megan. 'I like the hair. Makes you stand out. Always important to stand out.'

Megan murmured yes. She didn't want to talk about how she looked: it was how she felt that mattered right now.

'I've missed you, Mum,' she said.

'Me too,' Marguerite said lightly.

They'd reached an airy, marble-floored room that led on to the garden. It was clearly a room made for parties, with lots of couches and day beds, huge Spanish paintings on the walls, and many pots of orchids and exotic plants dotted around. On the verandah, a tiled table had been set with coffee and Marguerite led her daughter out there. In front of them, the Mediterranean glittered.

'I thought we could sit here,' Marguerite said, as if she were entertaining any other guest. 'I like having my coffee here and looking out at the sea.' She turned and shouted in the direction of the house: 'Anna-Marina!'

A middle-aged woman appeared and Marguerite spoke to her in Spanish.

Megan sat down and breathed in the heady smell of the garden. Jasmine, she thought, with something else, a woody smell that reminded her of other houses she'd lived in with her mother.

'It's very peaceful,' she said, taking in the view.

455

'We love it,' her mother said contentedly. 'I don't know why you haven't come before.'

Megan said nothing. She'd phoned her mother when the affair with Rob had made the newspapers and her mother had said it wasn't a good time for Megan to visit. Marguerite had made it sound like a mild crisis with rooms. Vincente's son and his family were staying, the house was full.

'Next month?' Marguerite had said vaguely.

And Megan had gone to Nora's house in Golden Square instead.

'Cigarette?' Her mother proferred a packet.

Megan nodded. Even though she'd cut down so much lately, smoking was the perfect thing to do in this strange, in-between moment when they were together for the first time after so long. This was her mother, after all, but the time and distance between them made her feel strangely numb. She'd longed for a sense of homecoming, but there was none. She'd felt so much more peace with Eleanor at the ruined stone cottage in Connemara.

That had been truly beautiful. She'd felt healed there and she'd known then that she had to see her mother before she'd feel she'd done it all. Well, most of it.

Here, with her mother, there was only the faintest tide of sadness in her because *she*'d made the trip to visit Marguerite. Her mother hadn't come to her. It wasn't her mother's fault, Megan realised now.

She watched her mother take two cigarettes from her pack, light one delicately, then pass it to her daughter. It was one of Marguerite's little trademarks: lighting cigarettes for other people,

456

usually men.

Megan used to think it sophisticated, but now she found it a little sad, a forced gesture to please men. This realisation jolted her.

'It's great to be here,' Megan lied, determined to quash the feelings of anger and irritation. So her mother hadn't come to Golden Square to comfort her. Big deal. Marguerite wasn't the comforting sort of mother.

'I'm so thrilled you're here too!' Marguerite's face glowed with pleasure.

She'd had surgery on her eyes, Megan realised. It was subtle, but suddenly Megan could see it. Or rather she could see what was no longer there. The faint hooding over Marguerite's eyes was now gone, leaving her looking girlish with high, arched eyebrows. That was why she looked so good. It shouldn't have been surprising that her mother would have cosmetic surgery, and yet Megan was surprised. She'd always thought of her mother as ageless, forever youthful.

'Vincente can't wait to meet you. Nor can my pals. I've organised a little drinks party tonight in the club—you'll love it. Smart casual, but you can wear anything, darling. After all, you're the guest of honour. I've got lots of dresses if you didn't bring anything suitable. I want to show my beautiful daughter off!'

After their coffee, they walked around the downstairs of the villa, with Marguerite showing her daughter photos of her friends, the huge jade elephants she and Vincente had bought in Bangkok, the diamond ring she'd got in Brunei. Vincente dabbled in many things: property management, leisure club management, the car

457

business. Of course, money was tighter these days. Once, Marguerite said, he'd been very wealthy. Still, he was generous, kind, so wise.

'We both love to travel,' Marguerite said. 'We were so lucky to find each other.'

In the many silver-framed photographs of the couple with friends, Marguerite looked like a movie star and Vincent, who was a short, full-figured man with a Roman nose and no hair, looked proud of his gorgeous girlfriend.

'I'm glad you're happy,' Megan said.

Marguerite beamed at her. 'You're going to love him,' she said, as if this trip was about nothing more than Megan meeting her mother's latest man. There was no mention of Megan's happiness or what had happened with Rob Hartnell.

*　　　*　　　*

Megan's bedroom was a pretty blue-and-white room with a snowy bed dominated by broderie anglaise pillows and cushions. The sight of it made Megan tired, even though it was only late afternoon. But she longed to lie down and let her eyes close, not have to go out tonight and be the old Megan, the charming movie-star version people would want to meet.

She thought about phoning Nora to say hello, but in the sultry heat of Villa Aphrodite, Golden Square seemed a long way away. Nora would want to know how her mother was and would hope that Megan was happy to be able to spend time with her. Saying that Marguerite had organised an impromptu party for their first night together would result in a pause on the other end of the phone.

Nora's way of nurturing Megan on their first night had been to insulate her with animal programmes, two dogs and love. Marguerite's was to go out and party. There would be no chance of a heart-to heart about everything Megan had been through when they were in a noisy club.

Instead, Megan sent a text message.

At Mum's house, all fine. Talk soon, love, Megan.

She wondered briefly how all her Golden Square friends were. Would Connie be out with the hunky Steve and cute little Ella? Megan certainly hoped so.

Nicky might be going to that cosmetic surgery book launch. She'd said it was this week and the surgeon had said nobody would turn up because he had no clients.

'Officially, he has no clients,' Nicky said. 'Nobody will admit to knowing him. The people who go to him pay cash in case their husbands find out. The reality is, he has zillions of clients!'

Megan didn't know what Rae might be doing. And Eleanor—suddenly, Megan longed to be sitting with Eleanor right now, just talking.

I came here to see her and it's like there's a screen between us. She knows it and I know it but we don't talk about it. We don't talk about anything. You'd think she'd want to know how I am, and how awful it all was, but she hasn't asked a single thing. Is that normal?

In her mind, she could hear more of Eleanor's advice and that low voice gently saying that she couldn't change other people's behaviour. She could only change her own, could only find her

459

own truth.

*　　　*　　　*

Megan must have fallen asleep on the bed.

'Darling, wake up! We're going out soon. Vincente is home and I can't wait for you two to meet!'

Marguerite was made up and wearing an ankle-length silvery dress with spaghetti straps. A heavy silver and pearl necklace was coiled around her neck. She'd obviously reapplied the Shalimar with a heavy hand as its scent was very strong.

'You look great, Mum,' said Megan sleepily. Her mother had turned the lights on in Megan's bedroom and in the warm evening glow, with the familiar perfume filling her senses, it was like being a child again, waiting for her mother to go out. She and Pippa loved watching Marguerite put on her face: the careful anointing of her skin with cosmetics and how time seemed to stand still as Marguerite admired herself critically, checking, dusting on face powder, putting on her lips.

'It takes more work these days,' Marguerite said now, and for the first time since Megan had arrived, she hadn't spoken in her bright shiny voice. She sounded tired, serious even.

'You still look great,' Megan said, surprising herself with the need to cheer her mother up.

Marguerite's real laugh rang out. The low, throaty one and not the light, girlish one she used when she was with men. 'The old girl's still got it,' she said. 'But believe me, it takes longer to get the magic going. Now, sweetie, Vincente wants to go out for dinner. We're going in ten minutes. Do you

460

want one of my dresses or not?'

Vincente's photographs didn't do him justice. He was shorter in real life, and rounder, but no photo could catch the warmth of his smile or the genuine welcome in his tiny black eyes.

'I've heard so much about you,' he said, holding her hands in welcome as he kissed her on both cheeks. Aramis fought valiantly to overpower her mother's Shalimar. 'It is an honour to meet you at last. You look different in real life.'

'It's a disguise,' Megan said, grinning at him.

Vincente's black eyes twinkled back. 'A clever idea,' he said. 'Everyone deserves privacy. You will find it here. Many famous people come to Ibiza and we do not like people to take photographs of them. This is an island for being private. You are with me and your mother, you will be safe.'

*   *   *

The club wasn't the sort of throbbing Ibizan hotspot she'd been to when she'd been here before. Her mother's club was a large restaurant-cum-bar called Victor's, and was the hang-out of all sorts of expatriates who liked somewhere they could get their own brand of vodka and talk to people who remembered Berlin/London/ Washington in the old days.

'I haven't a clue why, but everyone calls it the club,' Marguerite said as she took Megan on a whistle-stop tour of the place. 'They like the sound of it, I suppose. Whatever makes them happy, isn't that the motto?'

Megan hadn't expected to enjoy the night, but she did. She wasn't the prodigal daughter on show:

461

she was Marguerite's little girl, and if there was an added factor in her being an actress who'd recently featured in all the gossip columns, then nobody seemed too bothered. Marguerite and Vincente's crowd were an international gang who didn't read gossip columns. Their stars were the people in their lives or the people back home. Why had Bobo and Sammy sold their house? Was it true that the widow of a Swiss millionaire was having tax problems?

Who had bought the restaurant beside the club?

Megan wasn't the youngest person there. There were daughters, sons, grandkids, all eating and drinking, chatting or watching sport on the huge television in the bar area. There was no blasting techno beat: Julio and Enrique Iglesias CDs were on a loop all night, playing just loud enough to be heard over the sound of forks clattering and people eating tapas. Nobody wanted Megan's life story or details about Rob, even if she spotted recognition in some of their eyes.

'I did not know Marguerite had such a beautiful daughter,' said one older man, with the profile and the manners of a Spanish duke. He kissed her hand in greeting instead of shaking it.

Megan loved it. She'd forgotten how nice it was to be flirted with, even if he was just being polite.

'I bet you say that to all the girls,' she replied.

'Tonight I mean it,' he said, without relinquishing her hand.

'Antonio, what would Erica say if she saw you holding on to this young lady so tightly?' Vincente joked.

'But she will not see!' said Antonio triumphantly. 'She is sitting down over there, look. I am not in her vision.' He beamed.

After so much enforced staying in, Megan found the evening wonderfully relaxing.

'Your mother is wonderful,' Vincente informed her when Antonio had gone.

Megan knew he meant it. She'd been watching him and saw how often his eyes followed her mother, whether she was giggling up at the bar with one of her girlfriends, or chattering with one of their husbands. 'She brings light into the world.'

'I know. She seems very happy with you,' Megan said. She'd never spoken to one of her mother's men before with such frankness. Then, she wondered if she'd ever spoken to anyone with such frankness. It was hanging around with Connie and Eleanor. They'd created a filter in her head so that all words sounded fake unless they were coming straight from the heart.

'I wish I was good at saying the sort of things people want to hear,' Connie had said to her once. 'You know, artless, girlish talk. I just can't do it. What I think comes out instead and people don't really want to hear what you think.'

They might not want to hear it, Megan thought in a wave of self-realisation, but it's fantastic to be able to say it. Speaking the truth felt fantastic. She tried it again.

'Are you going to get married?'

Vincente didn't have a heart attack at this question. He considered it.

'I have thought of asking her, but you know your mother. She is not interested in being tied down. In that, she is unusual, the most unusual woman I know. She is a free spirit, you cannot tie her down.'

Someone interrupted them at that moment, and

the chance to reply was gone but Megan kept thinking about it. Her mother as a free spirit. Certainly that was how she liked to be seen by everyone and by the men she'd lived with over the years.

Keep it light, never let them know how you feel,' she'd told Megan and Pippa.

But that didn't always work out. Sometimes you had to let people know how you felt.

Keeping it light, concealing your true feelings, meant nobody knew you. You were a mystery, and being a mystery was all well and good, but it was a lonely way to live.

As they drove home to the Villa Aphrodite, Megan sat in the back of the car and listened to her mother chattering away to Vincente, discussing the evening and their friends. It was happy gossip from a couple who were comfortable with each other. So different from all the other men Megan could remember. Then, there had been so much effort on her mother's part. Megan could remember no sense of ease. It was all hard work.

The car stopped outside the villa as the wooden gates opened slowly.

'Tonight was fun, darling, wasn't it?' Marguerite said, turning back in her seat to smile at her daughter. The same hopeful look on her face, Megan realised, as she'd had all those years ago when she talked to Gunther.

Her mother had desperately wanted Gunther to marry her. She'd craved it. Not the ring so much as the security. There was no fun being the woman who raced around the world with her two little girls. She'd been prepared to put up with anything for the security and it had never come.

464

Even now, she pretended to be happy and carefree because that's what she thought Vincente wanted.

Never let them know how you feel.

Marguerite had been trying to find peace all along, she just hadn't known how to go about it. Just because her mother had lived her life that way, didn't mean Megan had to copy her.

Her mother went upstairs to change her high heels and Megan went out on to the verandah where Vincente stood smoking a cigar.

'Vincente,' she said urgently, 'do you want to get married to my mother?'

Of course,' he said.

'Ask her to marry you, then. She would love it.'

'But she says we are happy like this, she is a free agent—'

'Vincente, trust me on this: what a woman says and what she means are sometimes different things. If you ask her, I guarantee that she will say yes.'

'You think?'

'Yes,' Megan said, 'I think.'

'What makes you tell me this?' Vincente asked curiously.

'Mum won't tell you how she truly feels because she's afraid of rejection,' Megan said. 'She doesn't say what she thinks. Not that she lies,' she added, 'it's not that at all. It's just that she thinks it's easier not to say what you really think instead of telling the truth.'

'And you?'

'I do the same. I'm a chameleon, I can change to fit the mood. But not any more,' Megan added. 'Nowadays, I tell the truth.'

465

She went upstairs to bed, thinking of what she'd left unsaid. That she was going to live the truth from now on too. Never again was she going to fall for a man like Rob Hartnell. Never again would she be that silly, naïve girl who believed in fairytale endings with the handsome, protective prince. She'd be her own prince, not wait for someone to rescue her. Megan would rescue herself.

*　　　*　　　*

Carole Baird was staring at the wall in her central London office, eyes on the photos of her famous clients, mind elsewhere. There were so many client photos, the wall itself was barely visible. She knew of one Los Angeles agent who kept photos on his desk. His assistants were charged with changing the photo library depending on which client was coming into the office.

She was so lost in contemplation that she barely noticed her private phone was ringing. When she didn't answer her office line, it went back to her assistant after four rings. But this wasn't the office line: it was the private line, for which very few clients knew the number.

She snatched it up. 'Hello,' she said briskly.

'Carole, it's Megan.'

Carole smothered a sigh. Megan made her feel simultaneously guilty and annoyed. Guilty because she wondered if she and Zara should have put Megan up for the role in *Warrior Queen* in the first place; annoyance, because Megan's fall from grace had made their agency look unprofessional. No matter what the talent did, the agency were supposed to be on top of it. By not having a clue that Megan Bouchier was having a fling with Rob Hartnell, they'd looked like idiots.

'How are you, Megan?'

'Great,' was the entirely unexpected reply.

Carole sat up a little straighter in her black leather Arne Jacobson chair.

'I've made a decision. I'm going to come out of hiding and tell the truth.'

'The truth?' Carole thought the truth was over-rated.

'Not the truth as in stand on a pillar and proclaim what happened, but I'm going back to work. Theatre, if you can get it for me. I think I'll stay away from film for a while. And hiding is a mistake. This will never go away, I have to face it. I'm not doing a spill-the-beans interview. I'll deal with questions whenever I'm promoting my next job.'

'They'll skewer you,' Carole said.

'I know.' Megan's voice didn't falter.

'Fine by me. It's a good decision, brave but good.'

'I was thinking that I'd try theatre in New York. Something off-Broadway, low-key but good training,' Megan went on. This new life would have to be totally different from the old one if it were to work. She was saying goodbye to the crazy 'it' girl life and saying hello to proper training at her craft. She missed acting so much. It was time to get back to it properly.

'One more thing. I want to talk to one person first.'

'OK, shoot. Who?' Carole was taking notes now.

'Katharine Hartnell.'

Now Carole was surprised. Beyond surprised.

467

'You want to talk to Katharine?'

She could understand Megan wanting to talk to Rob. It could be the 'You scumbag, why did you disappear on me?' conversation or the 'I love you, let's try again, we could be a Hollywood power couple' conversation. But Carole couldn't envision any discussion between Megan and Katharine Hartnell that Megan would want to have.

'Yes, I need to talk to her, if possible, as soon as possible.'

'You're sure about this?'

'Absolutely,' Megan replied. 'Sometimes a girl's gotta do what a girl's gotta do, right?'

*   *   *

Katharine Hartnell woke to the sound of pigeons squabbling under the eaves near her bedroom window. The noise hadn't woken her up. Now, she woke before six every morning, pigeons or no pigeons.

Once, she'd bought a daylight alarm clock so that soothing natural light would wake her up on dark winter mornings when she had to get up for an early call.

The simulated daylight was meant to help the body clock adjust to morning better, although she'd never noticed the slightest difference. If only the makers had known about the shocking affect on the system of your husband betraying you, Katharine thought.

The Pain Stimulation Alarm clock might sell billions. And you woke up instantly: no fuzzy confusion about where you were. No, you knew it all straight away. Your husband had humiliated

468

you in front of millions and you were in your super kingsize bed on your own.

At least she didn't feel so shattered when she woke up any more.

She'd had seven months to recover from Rob's betrayal. Seven months was too long to lie in bed all day and cry. She'd moved on to the next stage of grief: doing what she wanted, instead of what people expected.

She clicked on her bedside lamp, reached for the television control and lay back on her pillows, searching for something to watch. She'd watched a lot of television since Rob left. Soaps, movies, cooking shows. She loved the cooking shows most of all.

There was something faintly hypnotic about watching someone cooking in front of you. Even the ingredients were soothing. Crushed garlic, giant lumps of butter tossed to fizzle in a hot frying pan. Why had nobody come up with smell-o-vision yet?

Not that Katharine cooked or even ate much. She was an actress. Thin was where it was at.

It was too early for cooking shows. She watched a couple of bronzed girls with toned bodies try to sell a sit-up machine, but the sight of their taut abdomens was too much. Her own abdomen needed more than a contraption to help her do sit-ups. She'd made a movie once where she'd had an ex-Israeli army guy train her. The workouts were agonising. She'd been in the best physical shape of her life for that film, but of course, it wasn't sustainable for a normal human being. Within six months, the tone was gone.

Irritated, she got out of bed and went down three

flights of stairs into the basement to make a cup of tea.

Once she'd made it, she climbed back into bed and began to plan her day.

That itself was a major improvement. When Rob had left, she hadn't been able to so much as speak, never mind plan a day which involved rehearsals for a play and dinner with the director.

It was too early to phone her assistant, Tiggy. She'd have been lost without Tiggy for the past six months.

It was she who'd been there the day the news broke. They'd been going through Katharine's diary at the time. She had charity functions to attend, fittings to set up for a children's movie where she was playing an eccentric aunt and the opening night of a small production of *Lear* where an old pal from RADA was playing Regan.

'There's almost no money in it, but at least I'm working,' the old friend, Anne, had said on the phone to Katharine. 'You'll come for moral support, please? And bring Rob, if he's around.'

Bring Rob. Code for: *It will do my standing no end of good if I can get Rob Hartnell to my opening night.*

'Yes,' Katharine said automatically. 'If he's around.'

Rob wouldn't be around, as it turned out. He was still filming in Romania. Katharine sat with Tiggy and wished she was the sort of person who could make up an excuse and not go to the opening night. She wasn't the person Anne really wanted there. She wanted Rob, exuding glamour and Hollywood movie money.

'About the costume fitting,' said Tiggy, running a

French-manicured nail down her list. Tiggy was not the beguiling Home Counties girl her name suggested. She was chic, wore little grey suits she sourced in Paris, and kept her glossy dark hair in a swinging bob. She was efficient and polite but never scary like some of the assistants Katharine knew. Many stars liked a scary assistant as the contrast was so favourable and the assistant made a useful fall guy.

'It's not me being difficult, it's my people' was the standard line for any outrageous demands.

Katharine never made outrageous demands. The very notion of such a thing offended her.

'What about next Thursday? We have that photo on Tuesday, so you can rest on Wednesday, and the costume fitting won't be too bad. You said you wanted to pop into Armani to pick up some things. We can fit that in too. I'll phone to tell them you're coming.'

A date for the fitting for the movie was set up. Katharine liked working with designers and wardrobe people. Clothes helped her fit into a role. They didn't for Rob. He just transformed himself into it, like a speeded-up caterpillar becoming a butterfly in five seconds. She'd seen him walk on to a set as Rob Hartnell, and become another person in the steps it took to reach his mark.

'It does sound like fun,' Tiggy said, reading the email from the costume designer about the director's vision: ' "Aunt Astrid is a colourful woman with a velvet coat with a fur collar that's actually her pet, a real live mink." Oh, it says here: "We'll be using computer generated images and live action—you won't be acting with the real mink." Pity,' Tiggy said, grinning, 'it might be fun to act with a mink.'

'Cute but slow,' said Katharine, who'd once worked on a film with several dogs. 'Every time you get it right, the animal gets it wrong. It takes hours. I knitted an entire sweater on that doggie movie.'

'I didn't know you could knit,' Tiggy had said with interest.

Katharine suddenly felt very old. Tiggy was a marvellous assistant and had been working with her for two years, but she was so young. Twenty-nine. Compared to Alice, solid dependable Alice who'd been Katharine's assistant for the previous fifteen years and had seen her through all her successes and failures, Tiggy was a child. Doubtless, she'd do another year with Katharine before running off to become head of a major studio or something, but still, she was a child now.

Alice had seen Katharine knit, do tapestry, paint watercolours and practice Tai Chi.

'I preferred the tapestry,' Alice had remarked wryly when Katharine had taken up knitting. 'You are the most awful knitter.'

'That's not the point.' Katharine had laughed loudly. 'I'm not asking anyone to wear any of these things.' She held up a scarf. 'It's therapeutic.'

Why did Alice have to retire?

'I can't stay attached to your side forever, Katharine,' she'd said.

And Katharine had had Rob by her side then. *Had.*

She and Tiggy had still been in the study that day when Tiggy's BlackBerry rang.

Tiggy answered, listened and went pale.

'It's Rob, isn't it?' Katharine had stayed in her chair but it felt as if all the blood in her body had drained into the floor. She felt cold with fear. 'He's had an accident—'

'No,' Tiggy interrupted. 'It's David Shultz, the producer. Rob has been photographed in Prague with his co-star, Megan Bouchier.'

For a moment, Katharine thought she might laugh. *Megan Bouchier,* she wanted to say. *That girl? Who next? The papers all want gossip and what's better than pretending that a pair of actors onset are actually doing for real what they're being paid to do on film.*

Tiggy was back on the phone, listening carefully. 'OK,' she said at intervals. 'OK.'

She took the phone away from her ear. 'Do you want to talk to him?' she asked.

The confidence began to slide away from Katharine. There had been pictures over the years and none of them had meant a thing. Rob had never cheated on her. But she'd never received a phone call from one of her husband's producers before. David Shultz was one of the good ones. A successful, charming man. A busy man who didn't have time to be the one phoning her assistant to mention that some tabloid had photos of Rob and his co-star.

'David, hello,' she said cautiously.

'Katharine,' he said, and his voice was full of the regret of a man who has awful news to deliver. 'There are these photos—'

'There have been lots of photos, David,' she said, still managing to sound calm. 'Why are you phoning over these ones?'

'Because this time, it looks as if it's—' He halted,

473

then took the plunge: 'As if these aren't set-up pictures. They're real. Megan's phoned her agent in distress. They were in a hotel in Prague. I can't get hold of Rob. He's not answering his phone.'

'But you're filming in Prague,' Katharine said, confused.

'No, we're not. Rob and Megan had the weekend off.'

Katharine breathed out slowly. Rob had lied to her. He'd said they were shooting night scenes and he mightn't phone in case he woke her up.

'No night scenes, then?' she asked, and was instantly sorry she'd spoken. The lied-to wife.

'No, no night scenes.'

'When did this happen?'

'I got the call this morning.'

'Does Charles know?'

Charles LeBoyer was Rob's agent, a Hollywood super agent who only slept when his two personal assistants were handling his calls.

'He does,' said David formally.

There was nothing more for him to say. Katharine had worked it all out. Charles knew everything. Rob used to say that when one of Charles's clients sneezed in Ulan Bator, Charles knew about it in Los Angeles. It was why he was such a good agent. He missed nothing.

She realised that Charles must have known about this all along. He wasn't shocked at Rob being photographed with Megan Bouchier. And he was in Rob's camp, obviously, rather than in Katharine's.

Katharine was the wife of a client, not one herself. Which was like being the third violin in an orchestra. If Rob had moved on, Charles would be four steps ahead of him.

'Thank you for calling, David,' she said. 'I appreciate your kindness.'

'For my money, he's crazy,' David replied quickly. 'Really crazy.'

Katharine felt a tear slip down her cheek.

'Thank you,' she said, and hung up.

Prague had been one of her favourite places in the world. The cupolas with their candied almond colours and the sense that the whole city was a magical film set waiting for the child catcher in *Chitty Chitty Bang Bang*.

She'd said she might come to Romania for the end of filming.

'Not a good idea, darling,' Rob had said. His voice was part Welsh gravel, part molten steel. Instantly recognisable. When he phoned restaurants asking for a reservation, the person on the other end of the line always hesitated. As if the voice that had graced so many films couldn't actually do anything so mundane as book a table.

Not that he'd phoned anywhere himself for years. He had an assistant to do that for him. Or Katharine.

There was always one person in a famous couple who deferred to the other. On the outside, they were the Hartnells, dually famous and successful. But in reality, Rob was the one who got the mega-budget Hollywood movies, while Katharine got quirkier, character parts in thoughtful films. She did theatre while American Express asked Rob to do commercials.

She had a line of BAFTAs, but Rob had the power. He wasn't the sort of man who could come second to anyone. Katharine had understood that.

Now she got out of bed and went into her huge dressing room to prepare for her busy day.

A wardrobe expert had set it all up for her. With money, one could pay people to do absolutely everything. From organising what to wear to what to eat. And yet it wasn't possible to pay a person to live your life. You still had to do that yourself, and when it went wrong, nobody but you felt the pain.

'Pain helps us grow,' insisted Anders Frolichsen. 'You must embrace pain, Katharine, my love. Pain is what we are about. Pain and love.'

'Anders, you say the most wonderfully crazy things, darling,' she used to say affectionately. 'Wait till you're older. You won't say that. You'll say, "No more pain, bring me vodka and happiness!"'

Anders was the young playwright who'd written a play specially for her. A dark drama about an older woman's affair with her son's best friend, it was beautifully written and a joy for any actress. A passionate Swede, he was twenty years her junior and she was having a marvellous time with him.

She didn't love him, not the way she'd loved Rob. She might never love anyone like that again, with that naked, pure love that laid a person open to being hurt.

But she adored being with Anders. He was funny, warm, kind and mad about her. It didn't hurt that he had the body of an athlete and a definite resemblance to Viggo Mortensen.

She'd grinned when the first photos of her and Anders appeared in the tabloids.

Katharine gets over grief with younger man screamed the headlines.

The pictures were a thrill after the horrific

photos of her after Rob had vanished.

Her CV had been reduced to one hideous photo of her leaving her house with no make-up. The picture of tragedy.

The shots with Anders rather made up for that. She hoped Rob had seen them too.

He'd contacted her only once: a drunken phone call on a crackly line from somewhere in the Caribbean. LeBoyer's tentacles stretched wide. There would be plenty of wealthy people with nice private islands willing to let Rob Hartnell stay for a few months. Imagine the cocktail-party gossip among the super-rich: 'I got a super yacht.' 'I bought a football club.' 'I let Rob Hartnell have the house on the island for two months. We're close friends, you know.'

Katharine had been watching *Sunset Boulevard* for the nth time one evening when she picked up the call. Normally, she let the answering machine handle it after six rings, but tonight, she didn't think and picked it up. Nobody spoke. She knew it was him, though. She could sense his breathing, even that was memorable.

'I'm sorry. I can't tell you how sorry I am, Katharine.'

He'd been drinking: it was obvious in his voice. Not to many people, but obvious to her. The clipped RADA-esque syllables, although he'd never been to RADA and was bitter about it, were slurred just a fraction.

'Is that what you phoned to tell me?' she said, unable to hide the bitterness in her own voice. This wasn't how she'd intended to play it. She'd planned to be coolly magnanimous, not the shrewish woman scorned. But in her mental fantasies, she'd always had time to prepare. Now, late in the evening and unprepared, she was raw and bitter. The real Katharine.

'Yes, I had to say sorry,' he said. He was using his humble voice.

'Why?' she asked.

More silence.

'I don't know.' He wasn't being Rob the actor any more, he was being Rob the man. 'I don't know.'

'You've broken what we had,' she said. 'It's over. There's no going back. But you know that,' she added, 'else you wouldn't have run away.'

'Charles said I should disappear.'

'Thank you, Charles,' she said acidly. 'Is he listening in?'

Charles listened in on many of Rob's calls, especially the potentially difficult ones.

'He's not here.'

'Is *she* with you?'

Katharine didn't want to say Megan Bouchier's name. Naming her gave her a dignity.

'No, it ended there and then. She's disappeared.'

'Waiting to appear naked in *Playboy* and tell all, I daresay,' Katharine snapped, and then was sorry. She'd sounded so bitter. 'That was beneath me,' she said. 'I better go, Rob. I've got company.'

'Your young Swedish lover, no doubt?'

He was the one who sounded bitter now.

Katharine allowed herself a small smile. 'Perhaps,' she said and gently put the phone down.

*   *   *

Today, Rob was not on her mind as she sat in the

478

back of the chauffeured car on her way to the theatre for rehearsals. The play was opening within a week. The producer was so excited that he was now talking Broadway.

'With an actress of your calibre, it can't fail,' he said.

'Don't count your chickens,' said Katharine. She'd never have said that before. Before Rob left her. She'd have pretended that her excitement matched his, because that's what the money men wanted, wasn't it? Enthusiasm. But the new Katharine said what she thought. It was a very freeing thing to do. 'Let's find out whether people want to see it in London before we get excited about New York.'

The car slid to a halt outside the stage door, and Katharine was ready to run in when a woman appeared and blocked her way. A small, dark-haired girl with huge eyes and –

Katharine drew back instinctively.

'I'm sorry,' said Megan Bouchier. 'It was the only way I knew to talk to you.'

Katharine stared. 'You? What are you doing here?'

'I came to say that I should never have gone to bed with your husband, that I can only say sorry. It sounds lame, but I had to do it, come to see you face to face.'

Katharine had recovered somewhat. She looked Megan up and down. The girl was stunning in the flesh. No lines furrowing her brow, no grooves of experience turning her young face into an old woman's mask: she was young and beautiful. She could have *anyone*. Why Rob?

For a brief moment, Katharine wanted to reach

out and hit Megan Bouchier so hard, she'd fall over.

This woman had been responsible for the destruction of Katharine's life.

But no. She'd been partly responsible herself. She looked around quickly. No photographers, thank heavens. She said to Megan, 'I was just going into the theatre. You should come into my dressing room. This should not be done on the street.'

Megan nodded.

'You're brave, I'll give you that,' she said to Megan and strode through the stage door and on to her dressing room.

Katharine could destroy this young woman forever, brand her a whore, a publicity-grabber. She would never recover professionally. The risk was that neither would Katharine. They'd both be tarred with the same brush: Rob Hartnell's roadkill.

No, that shouldn't happen.

'And I am sorry,' Megan said humbly.

They'd reached the sanctity of Katharine's dressing room now. Nobody had looked askance at the two women walking in, they'd clearly assumed Katharine had brought somebody with her that day.

Nobody would guess that this girl was Megan Bouchier.

Katharine shut the door and stared at Megan critically. Why Megan had turned up was beyond her, yet she could tell that this woman wasn't the enemy. She wasn't the weapon of destruction in Katharine's life. Rob had been that. Those other pictures before Megan, they'd been affairs too, except he'd managed to lie his way out of them. Shame on Katharine for not knowing.

Besides, life happened. People changed, men grew tired of what they'd insisted they always wanted and, one day, they reached out to a different woman simply because she was there.

No reason, just the opportunity had been there.

'Why did you come?'

'To say sorry. I hurt you and I am sorry. I wanted to say that I thought he loved me. I didn't fall into bed with him as an on-location thrill. I'm not that sort of person, although,' Megan admitted, 'you probably think I am. But I'm not. I was seduced by what he said to me and . . .' This was the hardest to admit: '. . . what I thought he meant to me. I wanted to be protected and loved. I thought Rob was the man to do it. I never thought about you, and I'm sorry. I think about you all the time now.'

Katharine roared with laughter. She was sexy when she laughed, Megan realised. This award-winning actress was a real-life woman away from the cool image of the BAFTA-winning professional.

'I have thought about you too,' she said. 'Not kindly.'

Megan flushed. 'I can understand that. But I had to see you face to face and apologise. He wasn't in love with me, you see. You could have had your marriage back if we hadn't been caught . . .'

'Oh no, little girl,' said Katharine, shaking her head. 'We couldn't. You see, I am not one of those women who let their man stray, hoping he will come back eventually. I believed him when he said he loved me. I never knew there were other women. I trusted him implicitly. Now I'm pretty sure that all those other times he was seen with women and he told me it was purely innocent, it was anything but. Did you think we had a deal going where I turned a blind eye? Not me, Megan.'

It was the first time she'd said Megan's name and although Megan knew that Katharine could make any word sound any way she liked, her name did not sound like a curse coming out of Katharine's mouth.

'I loved him too. He betrayed both of us, although it's not such a betrayal when you are young and the man is not your husband.'

'I was stupid. I didn't see through him and I hurt you. I hurt me, too, but I know that's immaterial. My mistake, my punishment.' Megan shrugged. 'But if it's any consolation, I've learned a lot. I've learned that if you don't have absolute truth in your own heart, you can't expect it from anyone else.'

She needed to say all this to Katharine, even if the other woman didn't want to listen. Hurriedly, she rushed on: 'I've learned about true friends and about moving on from silly notions I'd carried through from being a child. I grew up.'

'That's good,' said Katharine, amazing herself with how calm she was being right now.

She poked around in this mental forgiveness. Very strange. It wasn't what she'd expected. She'd played the wronged wife a few times on stage and screen, and this wasn't the usual response.

'I've wondered a lot about Rob and you,' she said. 'I like to think it must have happened because he's getting older. It's hard for him. Ageing hurts men, too. Plus, the business is changing. The fans want the same, but different and better. That's a hard act to follow. They remember a film like a moment in time. They see something like *Storm Cloud* and they remember themselves then, the world then, and they want every one of Rob's films to recreate that magic, but it can't. *They're* no longer the same person. But they don't understand that. They say "Why is Rob Hartnell losing it?" when, really, they have changed too much for them ever to see him the same way again.'

Megan sensed that Katharine was voicing, perhaps for the first time, the thoughts that had filled her mind for the last seven months as she tried to make sense of Rob's betrayal. 'Why are you being nice to me?' she asked.

Katharine was taken aback by the question. I'm not particularly being nice to you, she thought. I'm being nice to myself. If it's all your fault, it means he chose you over me because you're younger and he ignored all our history, all the love we had. That way, it's my fault because I couldn't hold him. That's not what happened. This is about Rob and what he chose to do. Many women, I think before you. Lots of lies to me. No, it's not you, you were just there. And it's not me, I just wasn't there.

'When it's over, it's over,' was what she said out loud. 'I didn't think it was over with Rob, but clearly he had other ideas. Anders, the man I'm seeing, is right: you did me a favour. I would have preferred if the favour had been done quietly, without the whole world knowing and watching, but Rob and I have lived in public view for a long time. I know the score. You're young, so he can look foolish and middle-aged. If you were my age, it would be worse. This way, he rejected a woman who became older. His loss.'

'Thank you and, for the last time, I am sorry,' Megan said.

The door to the dressing room opened.

'Katharine—'

The words died on the lips of the tall, blond man at the door. Anders loomed over the pair of them, in tattered jeans and a snowy-white dress shirt. He hadn't shaved that morning and blond stubble covered his broad, chiselled chin.

He recognised Megan instantly, despite her new hair.

'What's happening?' he growled, standing protectively by Katharine's side. He expected a catfight, Katharine thought, amused. Wasn't that what men thought women did: claw each other's eyes out with nails, pull hair. The real female fights were much worse—women ripped into each other with scorn and then continued the verbal hatchet job forever afterwards.

Anders grabbed Katharine's shoulders and held her so tightly, it hurt. He glared down at her.

'If she has come to gloat, don't say anything. Don't do this to yourself. He is not worth it.'

'She came to say sorry,' said Katharine.

His grip relaxed. He looked from Megan to Katharine and continued in a softer voice: 'That took courage. It is the sort of thing you'd do.' He looked at her proudly and proprietarily. 'You're brave and strong. I don't understand why you stayed with *him*.'

Anders had never, as far as Katharine could recall, ever said Rob's name out loud. said it was always *your husband* or *him*.

'He's a coward, runs away rather than facing the music. She did you a favour, I told you already. Wouldn't you rather know you were married to a coward?'

'You're a romantic, Anders,' Katharine said in wonderment. 'I never realised.'

'The soul of a poet, my mother says,' he murmured.

'I should leave,' Megan said. Just once more, she stared into Katharine's eyes. 'I wish you only happiness,' she said, and walked out of the dressing room.

As she made her back through the theatre and on to the street, her whole body was shaking with nerves. She'd promised herself she'd do this, and she had. The truth was hard to stand up to but once you started, you had to keep doing it. Apologising to Katharine was one of the first steps in her new life. Talking to Rob didn't register. She didn't need to see him ever again. She could get on with the rest of her life now.

25

Beltane

We talked about the old festivals when we lived in New York. Strange that we didn't talk about them so much at home. The canon didn't like talk about the old ways, and people didn't like to upset him for fear the bishop would be round.

I loved Beltane. It's a pagan festival of fires and the potency of the earth, when the earth gods and goddesses joined together in a wild dance. The church isn't so keen on that type of carry on. My mother liked to sleep outside on Beltane, but we had to promise not to tell anyone.

She never allowed me to do it because of my bad chest, but I said I would, someday.

I never did, you know. I never danced and hopped over the fire the way some people told me they did in their hometowns. I missed all that. If I had my time again, I'd do it all, Eleanor.

486

*   *   *

Connie's fortieth birthday arrived with midsummer. As a teenager, she'd hated having her birthday during the summer because there was nobody around to have a party with.

'What will we do for your birthday?' asked Nicky on a Saturday afternoon in June as the sisters sat in Titania's and worked their way through two beautiful pastries.

'Dunno,' said Connie, with her mouth full. School had broken up for the summer holidays and the big exams had gone well, she thought, although nobody would know for sure until the results came in August. But she'd made no plans and given little thought to how she'd fill the time. 'I could go on one of those "holidays" where you have a facelift and, when you come home, everyone says you look great and you say: "It's the sun!"'

'You don't need that,' said Nicky dismissively.

'Yes, I do,' sighed Connie. 'Nobody ever asks me if I've had Botox, do they?' She wrinkled her brows until she looked as if she was in pain. 'See? The new young assistant in Patsy's was washing my hair the other day and she told me I looked like I think a lot.'

Nicky giggled. 'She'd better not let Patsy hear her say that, or she'll be fired. Most of Patsy's customers look like they must spend all their time thinking.'

'You're being ageist,' said Connie.

'I'm not. You're being paranoid. Forty is the new thirty, haven't you heard?'

'Forty is only the new thirty if you have a personal trainer, Botox and a hot man to come home to,' insisted Connie. 'When you live alone, hate the gym and don't have Botox, forty is the new seventy-five.'

'Oh, Connie, don't be like that. You don't really feel that way, do you?' said Nicky, worried. 'You're fabulous and everyone loves you. Why did we end up discussing plastic surgery anyway?'

'I think Danielle has had work done,' Connie said in a low voice.

'Danielle? You mean the woman from Ella's schoolwho fancies the rocks off Steve?' Nicky didn't lower her voice.

'Speak up, why don't you?' said Connie. 'There are a few people down the back who didn't hear you.'

'OK. That Danielle?' whispered Nicky.

'Yes, perky Danielle with the velour tracksuit bottoms. I tried a pair on once,' Connie revealed. 'The changing room had one of those mirrors where you can see your behind—I looked like a cinema seat. A Pullman cinema seat. That's one of the double ones, for those of you under forty who have never seen one.'

'Danielle isn't going out with Steve, is she?'

'Keep your voice down!' hissed Connie. 'I'm not going out with Steve, either.'

'Oh.' Crestfallen, Nicky finished her pastry. 'I thought it was all going so well.'

'It is, we're friends,' said Connie. 'But that's it. Just friends. If he asks Danielle to marry him, he'll probably ask me to be his best man.'

'No, you're wrong,' said Nicky. 'I've seen the way he looks at you—'

'He looks at me like an old friend, or the way people look at Labrador retrievers. If you've ever seen the way he looks at bloody Danielle . . .'

'Have you offered to babysit while he goes out with Danielle?'

'I'm not that stupid,' said Connie.

Nicky stared at her sister blankly. 'I'm saying nothing.'

*　　　*　　　*

Sylvie, who'd recently left the school and moved to Belfast, was pregnant.

'Am I not the size of the house?' she demanded when she met Connie off the Dublin to Belfast train. Her hands encompassed a small bump lovingly showcased in a maternity wrap dress that Connie was sure was some designer or other. It was still probably a smaller size than Connie's own dress.

'A hotel,' said Connie, kissing her friend French-style on both cheeks. 'You're the size of a hotel. A very chic hotel.'

'Pah!'

Sylvie's house was every bit as elegant as Connie had anticipated. The spare bedroom boasted wall-to-wall wardrobes and a small single bed.

Thrilled to show off her home, Sylvie was keen to explain where she'd sourced each bit of furniture and what she personally had done to make it better.

'This needed more distressing,' she said, gesturing to the kitchen table, a slab of pale wood with giant carved legs. 'I am very good with the sandpaper now.'

'It's all so pretty that I'm very distressed,' teased Connie.

She was staying for one night and, in honour of her visit, Sylvie had cooked classic French onion soup and a peasanty beef dish with crusty bread. It was all delicious and Connie made a complete pig of herself.

Sylvie's husband, Isaac, was a charming man with exquisite manners and was happy to let the two women gossip about the staff in Matilda's.

What Connie wasn't that interested in talking about, and what Sylvie was determined to cover, was Connie's love life.

'This man, this Steve, he sounds perfect!'

He was, Connie thought wistfully. Sad that he'd been under her nose for so long and she'd only really taken notice of him just when Danielle had got her claws into him. But that was life.

'What are you doing about him?' Sylvie demanded.

'Nothing,' retorted Connie. 'He's seeing someone else, the mother of a kid from his daughter's class.'

Sylvie didn't like the sound of this one bit.

'But he likes you?'

'He does, but more as a friend.'

'Pah. Men don't like women as friends. Do they, Isaac?' she entreated her husband.

'Leave me out of it, my love,' he said in his deep purring voice.

'Isaac! Help me out!

'Fine, men don't like women as friends. Not often. If we like you, then we like you.'

'See?' Sylvie smiled like a cat licking cream off its whiskers. 'He likes you. Do not let this other

490

woman get him. You are handier, you live beside him and you have no children. Men like convenience.'

'Never mind, Isaac,' said Connie, patting his arm. 'You'll get used to it.'

'Do not let this one get away!' ordered Sylvie.

'It's too late,' said Connie. 'We're only friends. We've had dinner in my house several times, dinner in his house, and a pizza out. If he hasn't made a move yet, he wants to be friends.'

Sylvie got up to bring in the cheese. 'Have I taught you nothing? You make the first move, stupid.'

*　　　*　　　*

The following Monday, Ella rang Connie's doorbell. Her grandmother was taking care of her in Steve's house and Elisabeth had already met Connie and been told that Ella liked dropping in from time to time. The rule was that Ella had to phone first, with Elisabeth's permission, and then drop round.

'Come on up,' said Connie happily.

Ella bounced in the door and immediately made for the fridge.

'No 7UP,' she said miserably, after a millisecond's reconnaissance.

'Your father will kill me if I give you fizzy drinks,' Connie said.

'Danielle lets me have them,' said Ella.

Connie's brow furrowed. The girl in Patsy's would assume she'd been thinking an awful lot if they met again.

'Danielle's not me,' she said. 'You can have one

profiterole, though.'

'Super dooper!' whooped Ella.

They sat on the steps up to the front door and ate their profiteroles.

Ella chatted about holidays and how she and her father were going to France for a week camping.

It was all Connie could do not to ask: Will Petal and her mum be going too?

Ella moved on to talking about the tennis camp she was going to the following week and how she liked tennis, but she'd never done it before.

'Is it hard? I don't think so. Not for me,' Ella said excitedly.

Connie's mind wandered off.

She'd start working for Community Cares, she decided. It would be good for her soul to stop moping and worrying about herself. Look how many other people were suffering in the economic downturn. She'd met Mrs Mills in the square the other day and despite all the poor dear had to contend with she kept saying how cheered up she and Terence had been by their trip to Lourdes.

'I know Rae put in a good word for me,' Mrs Mills said, as they walked slowly round the gardens with Terence. 'I couldn't have afforded it without CC's help. Eleanor gave me a little gift for spending money when we went away, too. Said she'd love to think of myself and Terence having a few nice meals over there. She's a gorgeous woman, so kind. And look at Terence, can't you see how improved he is?'

Connie couldn't see any improvement, but she thought how nice it would be to help people like Mrs Mills.

Rae said it wasn't always easy, and Connie knew

492

that, but still . . .

'Dulcie and I will train you, if you get accepted,' Rae said. 'There are police checks—not that you'll have a problem with that, but we all need them these days. It's tough work, though. There are a lot of people we deal with now who would have been the ones donating money to CC a few years ago. It's hard, going into houses where the people are devastated and aren't sure if they're going to lose their homes or not.'

Rae was thinking, though she didn't say it to Connie, of Shona, the woman with the huge house who'd stood to lose it all. Her husband had found another job abroad, so they'd left Ireland and were renting out their old house for about a quarter of what they'd have got for it pre-crash. Rae hoped Shona was finding it easier abroad than she'd found it at home.

'Are you sure you're able for it? We'd love to have you, Connie. We need all the help we can get.'

'I'm sure,' Connie had said.

She put her arms around Ella and gave her a hug as they sat on the steps in the sun. Ella mightn't have time for her soon, when she got older and spent more time with Danielle. After all, a child only needed one mother substitute.

*   *   *

Gaynor was surprised to see Nicky at her front door on a Saturday afternoon.

'Is something wrong with Connie?' she asked.

'Yes,' said Nicky, stepping into the hall. 'She's making a complete mess of her life. We're going to have to do something or that nice Steve will go off thinking she doesn't like him.'

'But she's crazy about him.'

'I know that, you know that, but does Steve know that?' demanded Nicky.

'Has she told him about Keith?' Gaynor asked suddenly.

'Yes,' said Nicky. 'When he talks about his dead wife, she talks about Keith. She thinks it helps him to talk. I think he assumes that Keith is the great love of her life and she'll never want another man.'

'For a clever woman, she's an absolute idiot when it comes to men.'

'She thinks someone like Steve could never be interested in her,' Nicky said.

'I know,' sighed Gaynor.

'But,' smiled Nicky, 'I have a plan.'

*   *   *

It wasn't a surprise fortieth birthday, but there would be a surprise element, Nicky told Connie.

'What does that mean, exactly?' said Connie.

'You'll love it,' Nicky assured her. 'There will be a big gang of us and it'll be a blast.'

'What do you mean by "a blast"?' Connie was still suspicious. 'If a man appears dressed like a fireman and starts to rip off his clothes, I'm going home.'

'Blimey,' said Nicky, stunned. 'Turning forty has had a bad effect on you! Once upon a time, you'd have loved that.'

'I've changed,' said Connie. 'I put my name forward to work with Community Cares this afternoon. Rae says they'd love to have me. It'll be

494

great to have a purpose in my life.'

Nicky nodded. 'Yeah, purpose, great. Come on, we don't want to be late.'

Freddie and Nicky escorted Connie to the restaurant in their car.

'Do I look all right?' Connie said, pulling out a compact to check her lipstick again. She'd got her hair blowdried in Patsy's so that it fell in dark waves around her shoulders. Nicky had done her make-up, although she'd gone very heavy with the eyeliner and the dark shadow.

'You need to look sexy,' she said.

'Why?' demanded Connie.

'It's a rule,' insisted Nicky. 'Women need to look sexy on their fortieth birthdays.'

'If you say so,' sighed Connie, although she had to admit that she did look rather good in the mirror. She never bothered with that much make-up normally, and it was nice. Definitely sexy. Perhaps if she'd shown Steve this look instead of her normal schoolteacher-in-plain-navy look, then he'd have fancied her.

'You look fabulous,' Freddie said. Nicky had primed him.

'Freddie, thank you,' said Connie in surprise.

Nicky had given her a beautiful pink-and-purple silk shift dress as a present and she was wearing it.

'You're giving me too much,' said Connie when she opened the wrapping. 'A surprise party and a present. You're so good, I love you.'

Connie adored the dress. It wasn't the sort of thing she'd buy for herself, but it was gorgeous. It skimmed her hips and made her legs look endless. Plus there was no waistband to stick into her middle, no matter how much she ate. The perfect

495

dress, really.

'Oh, I know where we're going!' said Connie delightedly when they pulled up beside an elegant restaurant with two fruit trees outside the door.

'The Lemon Tree. I've read about this. It's supposed to be gorgeous but a bit romantic.' She looked at Freddie and Nicky in alarm. 'This isn't the sort of place for a big gang of people.'

'Yes, it is,' said Nicky, getting out of the car.

The three of them walked to the door, with Connie vainly trying to see in through the darkened windows to see which of her friends were already there. Sylvie had promised to come from Belfast, Rae was to come with Will, Eleanor was coming too, but she might be a bit late, she said.

The maître d' greeted them.

'The O'Callaghan table,' said Nicky, pushing Connie forward.

'This way, madam,' he said, and led the way.

Connie followed, tugging the bottom of her shift dress down. She looked for a big table but there were none so far, just lots of tables for two or four. And then, round a corner by a window on to a pretty garden, she saw a long table set for twenty. There were subtle cream roses in small vases and nightlights, and sitting there were all her friends. Gaynor and Pete, Sylvie and Isaac, some of the teachers from school, Rae and Will, three of her college friends, and even Eleanor. Megan had wanted to come too, but she was spending some time with her sister. And there sitting in the banquette with an empty place beside him, was Steve. Connie's heart skipped a beat just looking at him. He was here, at her party. She looked about but there was no sign of Danielle.

496

'Surprise!' they all said.

They ordered pink champagne and Connie went round and kissed all her guests before sliding into the empty seat beside Steve.

He looked particularly gorgeous tonight and Connie wondered, as she always did when she saw him, how she'd lived beside him for two years without ever really noticing him.

'Happy birthday,' he murmured.

'Thank you!' she said, still a little shell-shocked.

She didn't kiss him. Not because she hadn't thought of it but because she *had.* She wasn't quite sure what bright red colour her face and chest would go if she did kiss him. But he had no such compunction.

'Don't I get a kiss?' he said quietly.

' 'Course,' she answered in her bright voice and gave him a peck on the cheek.

'Is that the best you can do?' he asked.

Around them, everyone was chattering and leaning forward for their glasses to be filled with champagne. Connie let herself assimilate the fact that these people were here for her, that Steve appeared to be here for her, that she looked better than she'd ever looked in her life. Then she gave herself a little shake. No, don't be silly. Steve is just being nice . . .

She almost jumped when one large hand cradled her cheek and gently turned her face to his. It was no peck on the cheek: it was a proper kiss on the lips.

In shock at the feel of Steve's mouth on hers, Connie gave a little squawk and opened her mouth, whereupon Steve moaned.

He moaned! Connie pulled back an inch, aware

497

that everyone at the table was watching but pretending not to. 'Why are you kissing me?'

'Did you not want me to?'

Connie didn't know how to describe the melting feeling in her insides. The girl in *The Bride's Ransom* would. *She* melted and went hot inside, and reached great peaks of tension and excitement. But Connie O'Callaghan just felt pure happiness rush though her.

Experimentally, she reached up and touched his face. He smiled at her. A hot, sexy smile. Not a you're-my-neighbour smile.

'That wasn't a neighbourly kiss?' she said, just to be sure.

'Not neighbourly at all.'

'OK,' she said. 'Just checking. Where's Ella tonight?'

'Oh, she's staying with my mother.' His eyes didn't leave her face.

'Cheers! Happy birthday, Connie!' roared Freddie, who had no sense of timing.

They went though five courses, all gorgeous, all filled with fun, and Connie sat there in absolute bliss with Steve sitting beside her, his knee sometimes touching hers. Other times, he sat back with his arm around her shoulders. As if they'd been doing this for months, Connie leaned against him. It felt so right, but she couldn't quite believe it.

Before dessert, she escaped to the loo with Nicky.

'Do you think . . . ?' she began, before Nicky cut her off.

'Of course I think. He fancies the pants off you and you're the only person who didn't realise it.

This is our present to you. I set it all up and it wouldn't have worked if Steve didn't want it too. By the way, he never was interested in Danielle. "Superficial" was the exact word he used.'

'You didn't ask him?' Connie was scandalised.

'Connie, we don't have time to waste waiting for the moon to enter the seventh house of the sun or whatever crap you're hoping for. Steve is crazy about you—and you're the only person who doesn't see it, because you think you're too old and you think he fancies Danielle.'

'But she makes it so obvious . . .'

'Danielle fancies him, which is different.'

'But how did you get him here?'

'I said we were having a party for you and he said he'd love to come. Then he asked me if you were still in love with Keith. You talked to him a lot about Keith?'

Connie grimaced. 'I figured he needed to talk to a friend about Ella's mum, so to help him along, I talked to him about Keith. You know, you bond by sharing personal stories.'

'Not personal stories about your ex who lies about his age on networking sites,' Nicky went on. Connie had told her about that and Nicky thought it was hilarious. Sad, too. 'Now you've got a chance, Sis, off you go and have fun.'

By half twelve, the restaurant was clearing out and the birthday party was slowly departing. Taxis were hailed and it made sense for the Golden Square people to go together.

'Eleanor can come with us,' said Rae decisively at the taxi rank, before whisking Eleanor and Will into a cab and making the driver speed away.

'Oh,' said Connie.

'Guess it's just you and me then,' said Steve.

They sat beside each other in the taxi, but now they were alone he didn't touch her, and Connie felt the weight of so many years of unfulfilled dates upon her. She had no idea what to do.

She'd screw it up, she was sure of it.

When the taxi pulled up in Golden Square, they got out and Steve insisted on paying.

'Right,' said Connie, as he straightened up. She felt a terrible panic. This was it. He'd go into his house and she'd go into hers and the moment would be gone.

'I don't suppose I can come up for a coffee?' Steve asked.

'Oh yes,' said Connie joyfully.

In her apartment, she fluttered around turning on table lamps to make the lighting more flattering, while Steve stood and watched. She plumped up a couple of cushions too and then said: 'I'll put on the kettle?'

Steve shook his head. He moved closer to her. She could smell his cologne, something with musk and a woody smell that she'd tried to identify in a perfume hall recently. She'd sniffed lots of bottles trying to work out what it was, or perhaps it was just Steve.

'I don't want coffee. Do you?'

'No,' squeaked Connie.

His hands went up to caress her glossy hair, then paused. 'If you want, I can go,' he said.

'No,' she said. 'Don't go.'

'You're sure?'

It was Connie's turn to put her hands up to his shoulders, feeling the strength of him. She was tall and he was taller, just like the romantic heroes she

500

read about, except the romantic heroes were fantasy and Steve was better than fantasy. He was real.

'Nicky didn't have to twist your arm to get you to my party?' she said.

'I've been chasing you for months,' Steve said, stroking her face. 'I did wonder if you were totally obsessed with Keith, but then Nicky came along to ask me to your party. And she explained a few things.'

'Did she?' Connie and Steve were so close that their bodies were almost touching. Connie's breasts in her silk dress were centimetres away from his chest. If she leaned forward, they'd be touching him and perhaps she'd slide her hands up around his neck to pull him close, and his hand would move on to her lower back to haul her in to him.

Steve moved closer. Connie breathed heavily and put her hands around his neck. He pulled her tightly to him and his mouth lowered on hers, kissing her hard.

She could hear someone moaning in ecstasy and realised it was her.

'You sure?' he murmured, his mouth on hers.

'I'm sure,' she gasped, as he began to kiss her neck. 'I'm warning you, I have twinkly fairy lights in my bedroom.'

'Ella told me,' he said, holding her face and smiling. 'I've been looking forward to seeing them for a very long time.' And then he picked her up and carried her into the bedroom, and for once, Connie didn't worry about pushing all the cushions off the bed. The last thing she was thinking about was cushions.

Epilogue

Megan booked herself into business class for the flight to New York. Once, she'd have hoped for an upgrade for an economy flight. Airlines liked famous people sitting up the front of the plane. It made the people who'd actually paid full whack for their big seat feel like they were getting something extra. A movie star beside them was better than a double helping of vintage champagne at take-off.

Those days were gone, Megan had decided.

A code of ethics started with the simple things. She didn't want free flights, free handbags or free bottles of Krug in posh clubs. Everything had a price at the end of the day, and people who wanted free stuff all the time slipped very easily into saying things like: *Don't you know who I am?*

Megan had finally found out who she really was. She was a woman with standards and values, both for herself and for other people.

She took orange juice from the steward and took out the small book on mindfulness that Rae had given her.

'I like this, I thought you might enjoy it too,' she'd said when they'd hugged goodbye.

They had been in Titania's the previous Saturday morning where Connie, Rae and Nicky had arranged to meet Megan to wish her farewell. The others hadn't arrived yet, which gave Megan some time with Rae, who looked as if she might burst with happiness. Her face glowed with an innerlight that had nothing to do with beauty creams. It was pure joy.

'Tricia only has two more weeks to go,' Rae said. 'She says she's enormous, although I can't imagine it. I saw her last month and her bump was very neat. She's tall, though, and you can carry it better when you're tall.'

For a moment, Rae's eyes brimmed and Megan, who knew most of the story but not all of it, figured she was thinking back to being a pregnant teenager.

'Tricia's so lucky to have you,' Megan said warmly. 'When Eleanor and I did the trip to Connemara, I said that you were such a naturally maternal person. That's a great gift,' she added, seeing that Rae's tears were beginning to fall, 'even though circumstances at the time meant you couldn't raise Tricia. You have each other now, and you will be such an amazing grandmother.'

'I hope so,' said Rae, hugging Megan. 'Thank you for that.'

Connie had rushed in at that point, with Nicky and Ella in tow.

'Swimming,' gasped Connie. 'Ella's like a dolphin now.'

'I'm too good for the Little Fishes class at half nine on Saturdays,' said Ella proudly. 'I'm a Starfish now.'

'I bet you're brilliant at being a starfish,' said Megan. She was better talking to children now, since she'd gone with Pippa, Kim and Toby to a French campsite in the summer.

'I am almost the best,' Ella agreed.

'She is,' said Connie adoringly, and everyone laughed.

*　　　*　　　*

504

In her 1930s three-bedroom apartment on the Lower East Side, Eleanor watched as her granddaughter Gillian finished making the bed in the yellow guest room. Megan would be arriving the following day for a week-long stay. Gillian was home from college for the holidays and volunteered to help her gran get the apartment sorted out.

Gillian had arranged the white Christmas roses Eleanor bought from Lansky's, and she'd just put fresh linen on the bed. It was such a pretty room with yellow toile de jouy wallpaper, oak floors like the rest of the apartment, and elegant cream furniture of the kind Gillian described as Disney fairytale meets Louis XIV.

'I'll buy some magazines for her night stand,' Gillian said as she smoothed the cream brocade coverlet. '*InStyle* and the *New Yorker*, that sort of thing?'

Gillian repositioned a throw pillow embroidered with yellow-tipped ranunculus. Then she straightened up, swept her auburn hair out of her eyes and nodded. The year and a half in college had made her seem more grown-up in so many ways, Eleanor thought.

Gillian was still the gorgeous girl she'd always been, but she had a quiet confidence now. There was nothing like moving away from home for making a person mature.

Perhaps one day she'd pass on the diary she'd written for Gillian when she was living in Golden Square. She'd never finished it. It had been so painful to write lessons she'd wanted to pass on when the reason she had to write them was her possible suicide. It hadn't felt right doing that, which was why it had been so hard. Now she could pass on her wisdom to Gillian face-to-face, which was the right way to do it. In time, when Eleanor was gone, she could keep the diary and her great grandmother's recipe book, and hopefully they'd comfort her as they'd comforted Eleanor.

'You don't mind having someone who isn't part of the family here for the holidays?' Eleanor asked.

It had been her idea to invite Megan because it would make this a very different sort of Christmas. Last Christmas, Eleanor had been in Ireland, cooped up in luxury in a cool hotel room, lost and alone. This would be the first family Christmas that she'd spend with her family since Ralf had died.

'It'll be great,' said Gillian enthusiastically.

'Did your mum ever tell you about your great-grandmother's recipe book?' Eleanor asked as Gillian cast a critical eye over her efforts.

'Yes, she did. She said you'd let me read it sometime. I'd love to, can I?'

Eleanor smiled. 'Of course. I've added a little and I want to give it to you. It's about life and love and cooking.'

'I'd love that! Can I see it now?'

Eleanor nodded. It was time to pass the book on. She'd got everything she needed out of it. People survived somehow. She'd see Ralf again one day, just not yet. She hadn't finished.

APL		CCS	
Cen		Ear	
Mob		Cou	
ALL		Jub	
WH		CHE	
Ald		Bel	
Fin		Fol	
Can		STO	
Til		HCL	